KEEPING
SECRETS

FIONA BRAND

RUNAWAY
TEMPTATION

MAUREEN CHILD

MIX
Paper from
responsible sources
FSC
FSC C007454

This book is produced from independently certified FSC™
paper to ensure responsible forest management.

For more information visit: www.harpercollins.co.uk/green

Printed and bound in Spain
by CPI, Barcelona

MILLS & BOON

First Published in Great Britain 2018
by Mills & Boon, an imprint of HarperCollinsPublishers,
1 London Bridge Street, London, SE1 9GF

Keeping Secrets © 2018 Fiona Gillibrand
Runaway Temptation © 2018 Harlequin Books S.A.

Special thanks and acknowledgement are given to Maureen Child for her contribution to the Texas Cattleman's Club: Bachelor Auction series.

ISBN: 978-0-263-93617-9

0918

Fiona Brand lives in the sunny Bay of Islands, New Zealand. Aside from writing books and gardening, Fiona hosts international students. After a life-changing time in which she met Christ, Fiona has undertaken study for a bachelor of theology, is active in Christ's healing ministry and has become an ordained priest in the Anglican Church.

Maureen Child writes for the Mills & Boon Desire line and can't imagine a better job. A seven-time finalist for a prestigious Romance Writers of America RITA® Award, Maureen is an author of more than one hundred romance novels. Her books regularly appear on bestseller lists and have won several awards, including a Prism Award, a National Readers' Choice Award, a Colorado Romance Writers Award of Excellence and a Golden Quill Award. She is a native Californian but has recently moved to the mountains of Utah.

KEEPING
SECRETS

FIONA BRAND

To the Lord, who says, "Come to me, all you who are weary and burdened, and I will give you rest...for I am gentle and humble in heart, and you will find rest for your souls."

–Matthew 11:28–29

Many thanks to Stacy Boyd and Charles Griemsman.

One

The discreet vibration of his cell interrupted Damon Smith's stride as he jogged the hard-packed sand of his private island in New Zealand's Hauraki Gulf.

The conversation was to the point. His younger brother, Ben, was quitting. He would not be in the office tomorrow, or in the foreseeable future.

Reason? He had run off with Damon's pretty blonde personal assistant.

Jaw locked, Damon turned his back on the glare of the setting sun. An icy breeze cooled his overheated skin and flattened his damp T-shirt against the tense muscles of his back, but he barely noticed. For an odd moment sensory perception seemed to fall away and Damon was spun back in time. Almost a year to the day, when another PA, Zara Westlake, had run out on *him*, leaving her job *and his bed*.

Zara. Damon frowned at the image that instantly surfaced. Dark hair, direct blue eyes, finely molded cheekbones made more intriguing by a scattering of freckles. A faintly tip-tilted nose and a firm jaw, all softened by a quirky, generous mouth, which added a fascinating, mercurial depth to a face that was somehow infinitely more riveting than conventional prettiness.

The wind gusted more strongly, the chill registering, as an old wound in his shoulder and another at his hip—both courtesy of his time in the military—stiffened and began to ache. Grimly, Damon dismissed the memories of Zara, annoyed that they still had the power to stop him in his tracks, despite his attempts to put the brief fling in its proper perspective.

After all, their involvement had lasted barely a month. On a scale of one to ten, given that he had once been married for seven years, it shouldn't have registered. Especially since Zara herself, with her usual trademark efficiency, had made it crystal clear she had only ever been interested in a short, very private affair.

"We're in love," Ben helpfully supplied now.

The words *in love* made Damon's jaw tighten. They echoed through a childhood he preferred to forget, one Ben had no knowledge of because he had been lucky enough to be born after the untimely death of their father. Ben had never been around to experience Guy Smith's infidelities or his corrosive temper, the long nights when Damon and his mother had borne the brunt of that temper, and the scars.

"In love." He tried to keep the distaste out of his voice, and failed.

The words dredged up memories of the beautiful women who had hung at the edges of his father's life, expensive women who had demanded diamonds, exotic holidays and credit cards with dizzying limits that had eaten away at the family fortune. Guy Smith had claimed to be "in love" a number of times despite his marriage. When the money had finally run out, his latest mistress had left him. He had ended up in a bar, drunk enough to make the mistake of picking a fight with someone who could hit back. He had been found unconscious on the street the next morning, and had died of a fractured skull on the way to hospital.

When Adeline Smith had gotten the news of her husband's death, she had broken down and cried, but the tears had been ones of relief. Damon, at ten years old, nursing two cracked ribs and a broken jaw courtesy of his attempt to protect his mother from Guy's red-faced fury when he'd discovered they were broke, hadn't shed so much as a tear. Life had been gray and drained of hope. In the instant he heard his father had died, it had felt like stepping out of the shadows into blazing light. Six months later, Ben had been born.

Now, as Ben's only close family, Damon had to tread carefully. His brother hadn't endured the experiences that had shaped Damon. Ben didn't understand how destructive out-of-control emotions could be, and he carelessly fell in and out of love on a regular basis. In a way, Ben's cavalier approach to relationships was an uncomfortable reminder of their father. Although, thankfully, Ben had none of their father's meanness.

Flexing his stiffening shoulder, Damon paced the hard-packed sand of the curving bay, which was punctuated by dark drifts of rock at each end. He forced himself to concentrate on his brother's latest crisis, which this time impacted Damon directly.

For the past eighteen months he had been training Ben to help run their family's sprawling security empire. The one his mother, with the help of her brother, Tyler McCall—Damon's uncle—had pulled from the financial fires of near bankruptcy. Unfortunately, *like their father*, Ben had proven to be spectacularly disinterested in Magnum Security. It was a fact that Damon would have gotten a great deal more done if Ben had not been in the office. His assistant, Emily, however, had been smart, intuitive and almost as efficient as Zara.

With effort, he shook off a further raft of memories and refocused on the problem at hand: saving Ben from himself and retrieving Damon's assistant. Emily was significantly involved in a crucial deal he was working on. At this juncture, it would be nearly impossible to replace her.

"Walk me through this. I didn't think you even liked Emily."

"How would you know? You've had your head buried in the McCall takeover for weeks."

Damon could feel his blood pressure rising. "So has Emily. If you will recall she's my PA."

Although, to put a fine point on it, he had never appointed her to the position. Emily was a temp, the third temp he had employed over the past year while continuing to interview numerous candidates, both male and female, some with impressive degrees. Unfortunately, not one of them had possessed the exacting qualities required for the position. Qualities that had been oddly defined in Zara and which he had not realized he needed until she left him.

"Uh, not any longer. Check your email and you'll find Emily's resignation."

A boarding call echoed through the phone, informing Damon that Ben and Emily were already at the airport.

Damon kept a lid on his frustration. He could live with the inconvenience of losing Emily. What really worried him was what was happening to Ben. The partying and dating aside, he was becoming immersed in the darker, undisciplined passions that had overtaken their father. Passions that had even extended to Tyler McCall, who had become the CEO of Magnum Security and the boys' guardian following Adeline's death from cancer when Damon was fourteen and Ben just four. As stable as Tyler, an ex-SEAL and intelligence expert had seemed, in his late forties he had fallen for a spectacularly beautiful model, then died along with her in a car accident on the romantic Mediterranean island of Medinos.

Damon's chest tightened at the memory of the loss that, four years ago, had hit him hard. Tyler had been the father Guy Smith should have been. He had been a safe haven for both Damon and Ben until he had been ensnared by Petra Hunt, an aging model turned A-list party girl.

To lose Tyler, whose watchwords had been *reliability* and *common sense*, to the kind of liaison that had gone hand in glove with Damon's father's degenerate lifestyle… It had, to put it mildly, shaken Damon.

Damned if he'd let Ben fall into the same trap.

Damon's fingers tightened on the phone. Technically, Ben had not run off with Emily yet; they were both still at the airport. There was a chance to nip the relationship in the bud if Damon kept his cool. "Don't board the flight. I can be at the airport in an hour—we can talk this through."

"There's nothing to talk about," Ben said curtly. "Emily and I have been seeing each other for the past month. Long enough to decide that this is something special."

"You're only twenty—"

"Old enough to make my own decisions. Last I heard,

I could go to war at eighteen if I wanted. You were younger when you married Lily."

Damon's brows jerked together at the mention of his ex-wife. "The two situations don't equate."

"Why? Because Lily left you?"

For a vibrating moment Damon was confronted by a past he took great pains to avoid thinking about, because it highlighted the singular difficulty he had with relationships. There hadn't been one thing wrong with Lily. She had been beautiful, intelligent and sweet-natured and he had *liked* her, all good reasons to choose her as his wife. Unfortunately, he had never been able to give Lily the two things she had decided she wanted from him *after* the wedding. First, that he would fall in love with her. Second, that he would give her the children she had decided were now a deal breaker.

There was a loaded pause. "Or is it because you slept with your assistant last year," Ben asked softly, "and you've suddenly decided *that's* a forbidden sin?"

Damon stopped dead in his tracks. Flashes of the stark, heated passion Zara had unlocked in him, and which he had constantly failed to control, rushed back at him, making his chest tighten. "How could you know about that?"

Zara had insisted they keep the liaison secret. She had made it clear she couldn't work for him if people knew they were involved. Damon had complied even though he hadn't liked the condition. It had smacked of his father's illicit affairs. Emotion might be a no-go area, but Damon preferred to keep his sexual relationships straightforward and aboveboard.

Ben's tone was impatient. "Zara is Emily's agent. Emily put two and two together."

Damon's stomach tensed as more memories of Zara

surfaced. In every way, Zara was his ex-wife's polar opposite. Exactly the kind of woman he usually took care to avoid, because of the subtle, locked-down sensuality that was just a little too interesting. Zara had been dark and curvaceous, where Lily had been blonde, athletic and slender. The differences hadn't stopped at physical appearance. From the first moment, Zara had been a vivid, fascinating mixture of efficiency, quirky humor and unexpected passion.

Their connection had blindsided them both.

"The two situations are not the same."

"Right on to that. What Emily and I share is more than just convenient sex."

An image of Zara lying in bed, dark satiny hair spread over the pillow, blue eyes veiled with mysteries and secrets, assaulted him. Convenient sex? There had been nothing convenient about it. The words that sprang to mind were more along the lines of *hot, reckless.*

Addictive.

The same brand of intense, unruly passion that had ruined his father and Tyler and which had kept Damon awake nights because he had vowed it would never control him.

A clarifying thought that made sense of Ben and Emily's elopement suddenly occurred to Damon. He could kick himself for not thinking of it before. "Emily's pregnant."

Ben made a sound of disbelief. "Emily's not the one who got pregnant."

Not the one who got pregnant.

The words seemed to hang in the air. Suddenly, like a piece of a puzzle falling neatly into place, Zara's abrupt exit from Damon's life, her disappearance for months, made perfect sense.

She had left because she had been pregnant. With *his* child.

Damon sucked in a deep breath and tried to think, tried to orient himself. He felt like he'd been kicked in the chest.

If Zara had had a baby—and by now, over a year on, the baby would be four months old—why hadn't she told him?

Admittedly, they hadn't known each other long, six weeks in total.

Long enough to get messily involved and for Damon to break a whole list of personal rules.

Long enough that he'd had trouble forgetting her. That he'd broken his last intact rule, a rule that should have been inviolable. Instead of letting Zara go and regaining his equilibrium, *his distance*, when she left town, he had gone after her.

He had tracked her to a small cottage in the South Island city of Dunedin. On the verge of knocking on her front door, he had abruptly come to his senses. He had known that if he walked through that door they would be in bed within minutes. Added to that, if he continued an affair that had become dangerously irresistible, he risked becoming engaged to and marrying a woman who was the exact opposite of the kind of wife he needed. A passionate, addictive, unpredictable lover who had made it clear she had no interest in a committed relationship.

Disgusted with the obsession that had clearly gotten an unhealthy grip on him, he had walked away. The only problem was, he had not been able to stay away. Months later, when he had discovered Zara had opened her own employment agency in town, instead of steering clear, he had requested that his office manager ditch the large, established firm that usually fulfilled their employment needs and start using Zara's agency.

His fingers tightened on the cell. "How long have you known that Zara had a baby?"

Ben made an exasperated sound. "Right at this moment I'm not sure if you're burying your head in the sand out on that fortress island of yours or if you really didn't know. If Emily was expecting my child, *I* wouldn't be afraid of fatherhood."

Fatherhood.

Damon stared bleakly at the misty line where sky met sea. Unwittingly, Ben had gone straight for the jugular, exposing a truth Damon had no wish to confront. The whole issue of fatherhood was something he usually avoided, because it entailed facing a past he had gone to a great deal of trouble to bury and forget. It meant coming to grips with another relationship for which he was not ready or equipped.

Lily's words when she had stormed out of their apartment came back to haunt him. *I must have been out of my mind thinking I could live with a man who approaches marriage as if it's some kind of business contract and who doesn't want kids, ever!*

He took another deep breath but, even so, when he spoke his voice was raspy. "The baby's…all right?"

Ben said something short and flat. "You really didn't know. Well, that takes the cake. You're a security guru. You wrote the book on surveillance techniques and you produce software for half a dozen governments, and you don't know when your ex-girlfriend has your child? I thought you didn't want to know, because you don't want kids. Lily said enough about the sub—"

"Don't bring Lily into this." The response was automatic, because every thought was blasted away by the fact that Zara had given birth to his child.

The one outcome he had taken care to avoid, *except on one notable occasion*, had happened.

He was a father.

A final boarding call echoed down the phone.

"I've gotta go," Ben muttered. "Look, I'm sorry about breaking the news about Zara and the baby like this. The fact was, I thought you did know but were… you know, *avoiding* the whole issue." There was a rustling sound as if Ben was holding the phone awkwardly jammed to his ear as he surrendered his boarding pass. "Emily was fairly sure you didn't know. She seemed to think it was more that you lack emotional intelligence… whatever that means."

There was a feminine yelp in the background along with a further rustling noise as if Ben had jammed the phone against his chest to muffle the sound for a few seconds.

Ben's voice came back, loud and clear. "Anyway, I think we both know that trying to turn me into an executive wasn't working. I told you right from the start that the kind of locked-down life you lead isn't for me. I want to travel and do something with my fine arts degree. Anything but add up soulless numbers all day and stare at computer code, which, by the way, I will never understand. Don't try to find us. I'll send a postcard…eventually."

A click signaled the call had been terminated.

Damon slipped the phone back into the pocket of his sweatpants. There was no point in running after Ben now. The boarding calls meant that whatever flight Ben and Emily had booked, they would be airborne before he could pull the strings needed to either detain them or delay the flight. That was no doubt the reason Ben had rung just before the flight left. Damon guessed he was lucky that Ben, who had been kicking against Damon's authority for the past year, had called at all.

Feeling like an automaton, Damon went back over the conversation. Ben's crack about his lack of emotional intelligence grated. Apparently, he had missed two major cues in his life, Ben's utter lack of interest in Magnum Security and the fact that Damon had fathered a child, *despite Zara assuring him there was no chance of a pregnancy.*

He tried to remember the exact words Zara had used immediately after they'd had crazy, passionate, unprotected sex. She had dragged on a robe and escaped to the bathroom, pausing to send him an irritatingly neutral smile, before assuring him that he had no need to worry.

He had taken that to mean Zara had taken care of contraception. But now he knew it could also have meant that his assistant, in her usual brisk, efficient way, had been stating her intention to take full responsibility if there was a pregnancy.

Cold water splashed his ankles and Damon became aware that the tide had advanced and water was now surging around his shoes. Still absorbed with his thoughts, he strolled up the beach and headed for his house. Perched on a headland, the large multilevel house seemed to grow from the dark cliffs, stark and spare and a little forbidding. Built of stone, it reminded him of the medieval fortress Tyler had owned on the Mediterranean island of Medinos and which Damon had spent his adolescence exploring.

Fatherhood. The realization sank in a little deeper.

Damon turned to stare across the water in the direction of Auckland's cityscape, the first glimmer of evening lights visible in the distance. Somewhere across the water existed a child who, in a profound, unassailable way, belonged to him.

Just beyond the breaking waves a sleek gannet arrowed into the water, then surfaced with a silvery fish in its beak. Damon drew in a lungful of cold air as he struggled with imperatives that were as opposite as black and white. He had long ago decided that fatherhood was not for him, but fate had intervened and he was caught and held as fast as the small, flapping fish. He could not turn his back on his child.

The sun was sinking fast, the last burnished glow infusing the clear winter air with rose and gold. The sea breeze had dropped, leaving the water glassily smooth.

He did not understand why Zara had chosen to cut him out of his child's life, but that would soon change. In the methodical way of his mind, Damon began to formulate a plan to meet with Zara and discover what he could about the child. Although the practical to-do list seemed cold and antiseptic when he considered exactly what it meant—confronting his ex-lover about the child they had made together. And he knew exactly when that had happened—the first time they had made love.

As Damon climbed the steep cliff path to his house, memories flickered, vivid and irresistible.

Torrential rain pounding down as he held his jacket over Zara's head to shelter her as he dropped her home after a late business dinner. He shook out the wet jacket in the dimness of her porch. She laughed as she swept soaked hair back from her forehead. With her dark hair gleaming with moisture, her cheeks flushed, suddenly she was quite startlingly beautiful.

There was a moment when he bent his head, a split second before their mouths touched, when she could have stepped away and didn't. Instead, her breath hitched, her fingers closed on the lapels of his jacket and she lifted up on her toes for his kiss.

He caught the scent of her skin and desire closed around him like heated manacles. Sensation shuddered through him in waves as they kissed for long, spellbinding minutes. They made it to her bedroom, just.

He used a condom the first and even the second time, but in the hour before dawn, waking to Zara making slow, exquisite love to him, and caught in that strange halfway state between dream and reality, he did not.

The unprotected lovemaking had happened with blinding speed, over almost before he realized it, but that did not negate his responsibility. Zara's pregnancy had been his fault.

Damon climbed the steps to his house and paused in the shelter of the heavy stone portico, which protected the entryway from the wind. Peeling out of his wet shoes, he pushed open the heavy, ancient door made of thick oak and bands of iron that he had imported from Medinos and headed for his shower. After drying off, he pulled on soft, faded jeans with the fluid economy of movement he had learned during his years with the military in Afghanistan and the Middle East.

Not bothering with a shirt, Damon padded into his cavernous bedroom, found his laptop and keyed in the GPS program his firm used as a security measure for the company's top executives. He typed in his brother's phone number. Instantly a map materialized along with a tracking icon, which indicated that Ben was over the Pacific Ocean, just northeast of Auckland. It was somehow typical that Ben, with his utter disinterest in all things to do with Magnum Security, had been careless enough to forget that his phone could be tracked.

Damon checked the time then rang Walter, his head of security and one of his most trusted employees. Minutes later, Ben's flight details were confirmed. He was headed for the island of Medinos, and would, no doubt, be staying in the clifftop fortress Tyler had left to him and Ben jointly.

Retrieving his cell, he found the only number for Zara that he had, her employment agency. After a moment of hesitation, he dialed. In the past two months, ever since he had discovered that Zara had opened her own agency, apart from picking up his initial call, he had invariably found himself shunted through to her answering service. His jaw compressed when, as usual, the call went straight through to voice mail. He left a terse message and set the phone down on his bedside table.

Stepping out onto his balcony, he studied the gray clouds building overhead, blotting out the first scattering of stars. Ben had been right in pointing out the irony that Damon specialized in designing hardware and software to collect, unlock and decode information, and yet he could not unlock the mystery of the woman who had shared his bed and then attempted to disappear with all the skill of a master spy.

Cold droplets spattered Damon's broad shoulders as he turned from the darkening view, strolled through to the kitchen and lifted the lid on the casserole Walter's wife, Margot, had left for him. Not for the first time, he was keenly aware of the utter emptiness of his house.

For years he had been living in a kind of deep freeze. Just over a year ago, when Zara had strolled into his office in a beige jacket and skirt that on most women would have looked shapeless and boring, but on her had somehow looked sexy, the thaw had been instant and profound.

He had wanted her. If he was ruthlessly honest, that was also the reason he had reconnected with Zara again when he found out she had opened her own employment agency. To date, he had resisted what he'd come to view as a fatal attraction, but that was about to change. The knowledge that Zara had had his child had kicked away some invisible barrier. They were linked in the most primal, intimate way a man and woman could be linked and he was no longer prepared to tolerate the distance she seemed to prefer.

From now on, they were playing by his rules.

He had not forgotten Ben. As Ben's only close relative and the trustee of Ben's inheritance, Damon's course of action was clear. He needed to retrieve his brother before Ben did something completely irresponsible, like get married to a woman he had only known for a few weeks.

The retrieval of Ben, as luck would have it, dovetailed with Damon's need to gain access to his child. Zara Westlake stood at the center of both issues, which meant that, whether she liked it or not, she would have to meet with him face-to-face.

Out of the murk of the first two objectives, a third emerged. Despite Zara's betrayal, despite the grip the past still had on his life, he needed one more thing.

Zara Westlake back in his bed.

Two

A soft chime, indicating that a much-needed client had just opened the door of Zara's fledgling employment agency, diverted her attention from her four-month-old baby, Rosie. Thankfully, after a marathon effort to get Rosie to nap, her tiny daughter had finally drifted into a restless slumber.

Anxious to snag her client before he or she lost interest and decided to take their very valuable business elsewhere, Zara tiptoed out of the smallest interview room, which today doubled as Rosie's makeshift nursery. Makeshift, because normally, when Zara was working, Rosie was in day care. But, because Rosie had been a little off-color, the center hadn't wanted to take her, so Zara had planned to work from home while she kept an eye on her daughter. However, that arrangement had crashed and burned when her assistant, Molly, had called in sick at the last minute, meaning that Zara had been forced to bring Rosie to the office.

It wasn't until she had gently closed the door behind her that Zara realized she had left her high heels, which she had slipped out of while she had fed and changed Rosie, behind her desk. Added to that, her hair, once smoothed into an immaculate French pleat, was now disheveled from the playful grip of Rosie's fingers.

Pinning a smoothly professional smile on her face, she turned to her client. In that instant, the room seemed to whirl, reminding her of the last month of pregnancy when bouts of dizziness would hit out of the blue.

Disbelief froze her in place as Zara's gaze traveled from the rock-solid shape of a masculine jaw, with the hint of a five o'clock shadow, to the scar that sliced across one cheekbone, a fascinating counterpart to the damaged line of a once-aquiline nose. Her own jaw taut, she braced herself for the impact of the magnetic silvery gaze, which had always put her in mind of that of a very large, very focused wolf.

Her heart slammed against the wall of her chest. A complicated mix of panic, edged with another purely feminine reaction she refused to acknowledge.

He had found her.

Damon Smith.

Six foot two inches of scarred, muscular, reclusive billionaire standing in her tiny office, taking all the air, his sleek shoulders broad enough that they stretched the dark fabric of a very expensive black coat.

A stomach-churning anxiety kicked in as she wondered why he was here. Damon Smith had the kind of wealth and power that meant he did not have to leave his private island or his penthouse office unless he chose to do so. There was a small army of devoted, ex-military employees who had been with him for years and who were ready and willing to do his slightest bidding.

Damon turning up in her office was significant.

Cold air gusted, shaking the windows. Predictably, her door, which had a malfunctioning catch, flung open. Damon caught the door before it could bang against the wall, his dark coat swirling like a mantle as he did so, cloaking its owner in the shadows and secrets that permeated his life. Public secrets due to his work. Private secrets, which she was privy to and wished she wasn't, because they also scored *her* life.

He closed the door and tested it to make sure the catch had engaged. His gaze, now distinctly irritable, pinned her again. "You need to get that fixed."

"It's on my list."

Along with fixing the leaky tap in the tiny bathroom and replacing some of the light fittings, which looked like they had been salvaged from a Second World War junk sale. Knowing her landlord, they probably had.

Keeping a neutral smile fixed firmly in place, Zara girded herself to hold Damon's gaze with the equanimity she had learned in an elite finishing school in Switzerland, all paid for by her gorgeous, restless, jet-setting supermodel mother, Petra Atrides, who had been known in the fashion and media worlds as Petra Hunt. A practiced composure, which had been put to the test by the paparazzi when Petra had plunged to her death along with her new fiancé—Damon's uncle Tyler McCall.

Not that Damon knew any of that, which was the way she wanted to keep it. There was no way Damon would believe she had not known who he was when she accepted the job as his personal assistant and then practically flung herself into his bed. Not when he discovered she was Petra Hunt's daughter *and* had given birth to his child.

The wind buffeted the front door again, the force of it actually making the lights flicker, but this time the door held.

Damon took in her small office in one sweeping glance. "So this is where you've been hiding out."

"What do you mean, 'hiding out'?"

Although the fact that she *had* been in hiding for the past thirteen months, hiding a pregnancy and now a baby, put an annoying blush on her cheeks.

Damon's expression was deceptively mild. "You haven't been answering your phone or returning calls, and the address you gave me over the phone a couple of months ago is incorrect. I've spent the past half hour walking the streets and questioning shop owners who had never heard of you. It wasn't until I went online and checked your social media site that I managed to get your real address."

Zara struggled to control another surge of heat to her cheeks. Weeks ago, when Damon had contacted her out of the blue, she hadn't meant to give him incorrect information. In a moment of panic, thinking that he had somehow found out about Rosie, the transposed figures had just tumbled out of her. But neither should he, a CEO, have been even remotely interested in the whereabouts of her office. When she had agreed to take on Magnum Security as a client, she had only done so because she had desperately needed the money and on the condition that all of her dealings were with Damon's dry-as-dust business manager, Howard Prosser. In theory she should never have had to deal with Damon, period.

She stiffened at the image of the extraordinarily

wealthy and private Damon Smith walking the streets
and questioning shop owners.

Hunting her.

A sharp little thrill shot down her spine. Instantly,
her jaw firmed. That was the kind of feminine reaction
toward Damon that she had never been able to afford,
because he was, literally, the one man she should not
want and could not have in her life.

Aside from being a link to a past she was determined
to leave behind, she had found out that Damon was
also the trustee of his uncle's estate. He had requested,
through his lawyers, that she, as Angel Atrides—her
name before she had legally changed it to Zara Westlake—sign a legal document relinquishing any claim
on Tyler's estate in exchange for a one-off, extremely
offensive cash offer.

Raw with grief, insulted and *hurt*, Zara had refused
the offer and had refused to sign the horrible legal
agreement. She had been sickened by the tactics of a
family who had obviously bought into the media hype
around her mother as a model who was past her prime
and who had inveigled her way into Tyler's über-rich,
normally sensible life. No doubt Damon believed that
Angel Atrides was just as trashy and opportunistic, and
that a chunk of cash and a legal agreement was a necessary insurance against her ever darkening his door-
step or, horror of horrors, trying to make a claim on
Tyler's fortune.

Once again, the calculated risk of accepting Magnum as a client made her heart pound. Her chest seized
on a sudden thought. Could Damon know about Rosie?

Last night he had left a message on her answering
service, a terse command to call him back. It was something she had deliberately left for Molly to attend to.

Summoning a smooth smile, and trying to control her racing pulse, Zara made it to the safe haven of her desk. "I'm sorry you had trouble finding me."

Feeling pinned by his gaze, she opened a drawer on the pretext that she wanted to check the address on her business cards. Although, she knew there was nothing wrong with her cards. Her mother might have been a creative, artistic personality who resisted being organized and hated dealing with numbers, but Zara was her polar opposite. A perfectionist and a details person, she preferred to lead, not follow, and she liked to get things right.

The flush on her cheeks seemed to grow more heated as she jerkily closed the drawer on her stack of perfectly aligned, perfectly correct business cards. "I'm sorry you somehow ended up with the wrong address."

Grim amusement flickered at the corners of Damon's mouth. "The number was reversed. But something tells me you already knew that."

Her chin jerked up. "What are you insinuating?"

Damon shrugged. "Thirteen months ago, you quit your job and disappeared. For the past couple of months, ever since I discovered you had opened up your own employment agency, apart from picking up my first call, you've consistently failed to return my calls—"

"You know I prefer to work via email. Besides, all the correspondence and contracts go through Howard."

He glanced around her office again, his gaze briefly settling on the door of the interview room where Rosie was sleeping. "Maybe the address you gave me was a genuine mistake."

But his tone told her he didn't believe that.

His gaze shifted thoughtfully back to the door of the

interview room and a sharp jolt of adrenaline made her
heart pound.

She was suddenly certain that he *knew*.

A little feverishly, she straightened piles of paper
that did not need straightening. The only way Damon
could have found out about Rosie was through Emily,
although her contact with Emily had been minimal, two
interviews and a couple of phone updates. She was not
even sure Emily was aware that Zara had a baby. Of
course, there were other ways he could have pried into
her life. Given that he was in the security and surveillance business and had once been some kind of Special
Forces agent in the military, she was certain he could
find out whatever he wanted.

Damon's gaze skimmed her neatly arranged office
and Zara did her best to conceal her relief that he was no
longer concentrated on the door to the interview room
in which Rosie was sleeping. When it came to Damon,
usually, she erred on the side of fighting, but today
running was at the top of the list—with Rosie tucked
invisibly under one arm so he would not uncover that
particular guilty secret.

Shockingly, his gaze touched on hers before shifting and she realized he had noticed her hair. She took a
calming breath and willed her heart rate to slow. There
was nothing wrong with messy hair. It was a windy
day. Her hair could have gotten disheveled when she'd
gone out for coffee.

A weird part of her acknowledged that she had always known this could happen, that one day her most
lucrative client, who also happened to be the father of
her child, would walk into her office and she would
have to deal with him face-to-face. But, not now, not

today, when she was struggling from lack of sleep and with Rosie just feet away in the next room.

The last thing either of them needed was to be inescapably linked by Rosie. A small shudder went through Zara at the thought of the media attention that would erupt once it was found out that Petra Hunt's daughter, using a new identity, had had a child with Tyler McCall's nephew. They would come after her; they would come after Rosie. And Damon, apart from making it crystal clear that Zara was not welcome in his life, would hate that she had fooled him.

On cue, a small, snuffling sound came from the interview room. Zara's heart sped up. Lately, Rosie, who was usually a very good sleeper, was waking up after just a few minutes of restless slumber. A little desperately, she reached for a random file and slapped it down on the desk, trying to make enough noise that Damon would not hear Rosie. "So, now that you've found me, what can I do for you? Is there a problem with one of the employees I sent to you? Troy? Or Harold?"

Troy was young, just eighteen, with tattoos and a brow piercing, but he was bright and earnest. Zara had thought he would be perfect for Damon's IT team. Harold had been an older public servant who had failed to find a job through other employment agencies, owing to a rather unfortunate skin condition, and in desperation had come to Zara. She had found a place for him in Damon's accounts department.

Damon frowned slightly, as if he didn't know who either Troy or Harold were, then his face cleared. "They're fine, as far as I know. *This* is the problem."

He dropped the tabloid newspaper, which he had been carrying under one arm, on her desk. It was folded open at a tacky gossip columnist's page.

She drew a calming breath and forced herself to study a grainy black-and-white photo of Damon's younger brother, Ben, who had his arm flung around Emily's slim waist. The blaring caption, Magnum Security Heir's Hot Affair with Blonde Temp, practically leaped off the page.

Snatching up the paper, she skimmed the story—which was the stuff of her nightmares—with growing horror. Thankfully, the detail was minimal. To her relief, the name of her employment agency had not been mentioned...yet.

She took a closer look at the photograph. Details she had not noticed first off finally registered. Emily's hair seemed longer and curlier. Gone were the subtle makeup and low-key suits, the crisp blouses that had seemed to summarize Zara's star temp as sensible, trustworthy and professional. Emily looked younger and a touch bohemian. She certainly no longer looked like the poster girl for Westlake Employment Agency.

Zara quickly read the sketchy article. Of course, the journalist had painted Emily as a fortune-hunting employee and Ben as the kind of high-powered playboy businessman who was only interested in a quick fling and who would not be easily caught by a mere office girl.

Compassion for Emily mixed with a surge of outrage and a fierce desire to protect her protégé. Just because Emily had fallen for Ben and decided to make the best of herself did not make her a cheap, trashy opportunist. Zara had lost count of the times the papers had portrayed her mother as cheap and on the make, when the truth was that her mother had been so gorgeous she had literally had to fend off men. And yes, some of those men had been breathtakingly rich.

When Petra died, the behavior of the tabloids and women's magazines had worsened. They had smeared her reputation even more before turning their malicious spotlight on Zara. Although, luckily, Petra had always made sure Zara was hidden from the media, so their store of background information had been meager. Most of the photos they'd had were blurred shots of Zara as a child or as a plump teenager taken through telephoto lenses.

Horrified and frightened by the relentless pursuit of the media, Zara had ditched her degree and disappeared. Angel Atrides, the fictional spoiled party girl the media seemed intent on creating, had become the ordinary, invisible person she longed to be—Zara Westlake. Zara had been her paternal grandmother's name, Westlake her maternal grandmother's maiden name.

Her mother's cousin Phoebe Westlake, a sharp-edged accountant who was ill with leukemia, had provided the hideout Zara needed in the South Island city of Dunedin while she had painstakingly reinvented her life. Which had made it all the more frustrating when, almost three years later, with a new name and a degree in business management—in effect a new life—Phoebe's last act before she had died had been to secure Zara a job interview with the nephew of Tyler McCall.

Not that Zara had made *that* connection until after she had taken the job, because Damon's surname, Smith, was so neutral and ordinary that she hadn't suspected the link. To further muddy the waters, Damon was reclusive by nature, avoiding the media. It hadn't been until two weeks into her job and *after* she had made the mistake of sleeping with Damon, that he had handed her a takeover bid for Tyler McCall's electric company.

She had finally understood exactly who Damon was.

As much as she needed to sit down now, Zara remained standing. Once again, the desire to run was uppermost, but she instantly dismissed that option. In setting up her business after Rosie was born she had made a stand. She was over running.

She was tired of giving up things that were important, like home and friendships and career choices, and having to start fresh somewhere else. Having to *be* someone else. If she ran now, she would have to give up her cozy rented cottage, which was just a twenty-minute commute from her office. She would have to abandon her business, which she loved with passion, because, finally, all of her study and hard work had paid off and she had something of substance that was *hers*. Plus, if she walked away now she would be deeply in debt, with no way to repay it.

The thought of defaulting on her business loan made her stomach tighten. It was a sharp reminder of exactly why she had buckled and taken on Damon as a client in the first place. It had been a huge risk, but if she hadn't, she would have gone under. Damon, against all odds, was her most lucrative client and had taken on a staggering number of personnel, most of them temps, which meant she continued to accrue fees.

Her jaw firmed. Right now, she could not cope with another debt. It had taken her years to pay off her mother's funeral expenses. However, not running meant she might have to face the press, and probably sooner rather than later.

The way she saw it, her only viable option was damage control. Luckily, due to her current line of work, she had become quite skilled at it. Refolding the paper so she no longer had to look at the damaging article or the gleeful smile of the gossip columnist, and utterly relieved that the situation with Ben and Emily was Damon's reason for seeking her out, she directed a brisk glance at him. "When did they leave?"

"Last night, on a scheduled flight. Which is why the tabloids got hold of the story."

If it had been the firm's private jet, the press wouldn't have gotten a look in, but Damon would have been notified. Damon had been caught by surprise, which meant Ben had kept his plans secret. That being the case, it was entirely possible, given that Zara hadn't known about the relationship, that Damon had not, either.

Light glimmered at the end of a very long, very dark tunnel. Damon had clearly bought into the tabloid story, but there were other constructions that could apply to Ben and Emily leaving the country together—constructions that did not place the blame on either Emily or Westlake Employment.

Mind working quickly, Zara examined and discarded a number of options, finally settling on attack as the best form of defense. "It's highly irregular that Ben has taken Emily out of the country." She lifted her chin, but even so, in her bare feet, her gaze was only just level with Damon's throat. She tried not to be fascinated by a very interesting pulse along the side of his jaw. "When might I expect my temp to be returned?"

Damon's brows jerked together. "Emily was not kidnapped."

Surreptitiously, Zara felt around with her toes for her shoes. "I didn't say *kidnapped*, exactly."

Damon crossed his arms over his chest, which only served to make him seem even larger and more ticked off. "You're implying that she has been coerced in some way. Since Emily, at twenty-six, is older than Ben by a good six years, I doubt any coercion was involved."

The age twenty-six hit an unexpected nerve. It was the same age she had been when she'd had the wild, silly affair with Damon. Heat surged into her cheeks. It was hard to believe it had been little more than a year ago. So much had happened it felt like centuries had passed. "You're right, at twenty-six, she should have known better."

Zara only wished she had.

Damon's gaze clashed with hers. Zara dragged her gaze free, but not before her fiery irritation was replaced by other, more disturbing sensations coiling low in the pit of her stomach.

Upset and annoyed at the intense, too-familiar awareness that had hit her out of left field, as if they were still connected—*still lovers*—in desperation, Zara recommenced the search for her shoes. She finally located them in the shadowed recesses beneath her desk. Relieved to have a distraction, she bent down and snatched them up. Unlike her suit, which was black and neatly tailored, the shoes were a tad subversive, a gorgeous sea blue that unashamedly matched her eyes.

On the subject of eyes, she thought grimly, *note to self, never look into Damon's eyes for too long.* Apparently, despite dismissing him from her life and putting a great deal of effort into forgetting about him completely, even one second was too long.

With an effort of will, Zara smoothed out her expression, but there was another tiny issue that was bugging her. "And Emily being older than Ben by several years would, of course, make her the predatory one." She could not forget that the paparazzi had nicknamed Petra, who had been several years older than Tyler, "the Huntress." As if Petra had been cold and calculating, and had deliberately set out to ensnare a rich lover, when Zara knew that it had been Tyler who had pursued Petra.

Damon frowned. "I wasn't trying to imply that Emily was predatory because she's older—"

"Good, because we both know Ben is something of a party animal."

Damon seemed briefly riveted by the shoes, and she realized she was brandishing them in front of her like a weapon. Taking a deep breath, she placed the shoes on the floor and methodically slipped them on. The heels gave her an extra inch and half, which wasn't nearly enough.

Damon's gaze clashed with hers again, the hard edge tempered by something she had never seen before, something new, an intent curiosity, as if he was logging the changes in her and taking stock in a completely masculine way.

She suppressed her automatic panic that Damon would somehow equate her extra curves with motherhood. She had to keep reminding herself that Damon's focus was on rescuing Ben from Emily; he didn't know Zara had had his child. In any case, the obvious explanation for her more rounded shape was a whole lot simpler, that she had just put on a little weight.

Damon's expression shuttered. "You know very well that I meant Ben couldn't take a woman like Emily anywhere she didn't want to go."

In the midst of what was for Zara a stressful encounter, Damon's flat statement informed her that he knew exactly what she was trying to achieve with her line of reasoning. It was also a reminder of just why she had fallen for him in the first place. Most people, quite rightly, viewed him as cold and formidable, even dangerous. But that had not been Zara's experience. As an employer she had found him to be demanding but utterly straightforward. Far from being intimidated, she had found that, on a purely feminine level, she had liked his air of command and the knowledge that, in a company full of alpha males, Damon was the scariest, most alpha of them all.

Grudgingly, she conceded Damon's point that Emily was not the type to be coerced. "Even so, this is out of character for her. If she had wanted to take time off, she would have emailed me or left a message."

Although the instant Zara said the words she remembered that she had seen an email from Emily but hadn't opened it because she'd been so busy with Rosie and walk-in clients.

Damon extracted his cell from his pocket, flicked the screen with his thumb, then placed the phone down on her desk so she could see Emily's email. "Her resignation is there in black and white."

Shocked, Zara flipped her laptop open and scrolled down her inbox to confirm that she had received almost exactly the same message. Hers, however, was peppered with apologies and assurances that Emily would ring once they got to Medinos.

Medinos. Zara tensed even further.

The island was exotic and beautiful and was popularly styled as the Mediterranean isle of romance. It had also been Zara's home as a child while her father, Angelo Atrides, the last *conte* of the once-aristocratic but now-impoverished Atrides line, had been alive. But in Zara's experience, since Angelo's death when she was barely seven years old, the only thing that had come out of Medinos was trouble. "I don't know why Emily would run off with Ben. They're total opposites."

Ben, though ridiculously handsome, was too young

for Emily and a little spoiled. He hadn't been born with a silver spoon in his mouth; it had been platinum.

While Zara had been reading, Damon had been pacing around her office, examining her walls with their job-notice boards and career displays, reminding her of nothing so much as a large wolf on the prowl. "It would seem Emily's decided to take a break from work with Ben—"

"You think this is just a holiday?" Damon's tone was laced with disbelief.

Still upset at the physicality of her reaction to Damon, a reaction that should have been as dead as a doornail by now, Zara snatched up the newspaper and stared at the grainy photo. "What else could you call it? I don't see an engagement ring, so they're not eloping—"

Damon's gaze pinned her. "Damn right. Ben will not be marrying Emily."

The flat denial, which somehow implied that Emily was not good enough to marry Ben, flicked Zara on the raw. "Ben should be so lucky. Emily is smart and mature. Apart from this…*error* of judgment, she's an exemplary personal assistant."

"If there's been an error of judgment, then that also applies to Ben."

Zara slapped the newspaper back down on the desk. "Why does it always come back to that? You know, people can simply fall in love. When my father died, it took my mother years to find—" She stopped, appalled by what she had almost given away.

There was a moment of vibrating silence. "What do you mean by 'Why does it always come back to that?'"

Relieved that Damon had bypassed her comment about her mother, Zara blurted out her thoughts. "Isn't that what rich men automatically think? That women are attracted by their wealth?"

She cringed the moment the words were out, because she didn't actually believe that about all wealthy men.

Damon's gaze pinned her. "Is that what you believed about me?"

Three

The soft, flat question made her chest go tight and her heart pound. Damon zeroing in on their short, secretive fling was disorienting when a moment ago they had been firmly focused on Ben and Emily.

Zara found herself once more staring at the pulse throbbing along the side of Damon's jaw as she desperately tried to find a neutral way out of a conversation that had careered out of control.

She took a deep breath and decided on the truth. After all, what did it matter now? "Yes."

A curious satisfaction registered in Damon's gaze. "So that's why you didn't want a relationship. You thought I would think you were after my money."

It was only part of the truth.

The whole of it was that if Damon ever found out her real identity, he wouldn't just think she was after his money, he would be certain of it. Although, the irony was that, from the first moment she had met him, she couldn't have cared less about his wealth.

When she had walked into the interview with Damon, his remote gaze had connected with hers and for a split second she'd had a weird premonition that everything was about to change. She could not explain exactly what the phenomenon was, just that for her, at least, it had been instant, visceral and electric. Like a piece of flotsam caught in a powerful current, she had allowed herself to be swept along and had accepted the job. Two weeks later, she had ended up in Damon's bed.

Determined to redirect the conversation back to the situation with Emily and Ben, and hustle Damon out of the door before Rosie woke up, Zara briskly stepped around her desk and busied herself tidying piles of pamphlets that did not need tidying. "I'm sorry for the inconvenience of Emily taking an unplanned leave of absence—"

"Along with my little brother," Damon said drily.

With effort, Zara controlled her temper. She tended to see things from another angle entirely. It was a matter of record that the men in Damon's family were extremely good at seduction. Damon's uncle Tyler had swept Zara's mother off her feet; Damon had gotten Zara into bed in a matter of days. And now it seemed clear that Ben—who had routinely shambled into work around ten o'clock, taken long lunches and drifted away by four—had seduced poor Emily!

Zara moved on to another shelf of pamphlets, which was much nearer the front door, hoping Damon would take the hint. "As far as I'm concerned, Emily is outstandingly qualified and my best temp, and Ben has enticed her away. If anyone needs protection, it's Emily."

Damon gave Zara an incredulous look.

She checked her watch as if she was in a hurry to be somewhere. She had gotten seriously distracted by the Emily/Ben situation, but now she needed to wrap up the issue and get Damon out of her office before Rosie woke up. "I investigated Emily thoroughly before placing her on the books—she's perfectly trustworthy."

"Emily Harris is, but Emily Woodhouse-Harris isn't."

Zara froze as Damon slipped a folded sheet of paper out of his coat pocket and handed it to her. She stared at what was obviously a photocopy of a newspaper cutting depicting a more youthful Emily, the daughter of a disgraced financier who had lost all of his money, and that of the pension fund he had founded, in a financial crash. In the shot, Emily was dressed for the beach in a bikini and filmy sarong, and she was clinging to the arm of a prominent playboy businessman. One who, from the caption, had apparently dumped her in favor of marrying a socialite with her fortune intact.

Zara's jaw tightened. Her motto for Westlake Employment Agency was Reliable, High Quality, Vetted Office Staff, Privacy and Discretion Guaranteed. In this case, the reliability part of the motto hadn't held. Neither had the privacy or the discretion.

However, the tacky little article, far from making Zara feel disappointed in Emily, only made her feel even more fiercely protective of an employee who reminded her an awful lot of herself. *Even down to the way Emily had lost everything and had been forced to invent a new life.* She knew exactly how Emily was going to feel when she saw the piece.

She set the incriminating article down on her desk. "You had Emily *investigated.*"

Damon's expression grew impatient. "I waited for you to call back. When you didn't, I made some calls of my own. As it turns out, I should have done it a whole lot earlier."

"Choosing to use one half of a double-barreled surname, and a previous relationship do not make Emily a bad risk!"

"Maybe not, but before Vitalis, Emily was involved with another wealthy businessman."

Now that she knew Emily's full name, the whole embarrassing scandal was coming back to her, which made her feel even sorrier for Emily. "From memory, the Woodhouse-Harrises moved in wealthy circles, so, of course, Emily would meet wealthy men."

"The relationships wouldn't be such a problem if Emily hadn't tried to conceal her past."

"Maybe she had good reasons for doing so."

Damon crossed his arms over his chest. "Such as?"

Zara's chin came up. She felt she was fighting on two fronts, for Emily and for herself. "For a start, it can't have been much fun having the media hounding her."

"Granted."

The curtness of his reply seemed to emphasize that the bottom line for Damon was Emily's so-called deception. "Emily happens to be very good at her job."

"I'm not disputing that, just her motives in seeking employment with wealthy men."

That touched a nerve, guiltily reminding Zara that if Damon found out her true identity, he would ascribe the same kind of gold-digging motivation to her. She doubted he would believe that it had been Zara's well-connected aunt who had set up the job interview and set her up by placing her back in Damon's orbit in the hope that she might score another cash offer. Or that

Zara had zero interest in that money! "So you still think all Emily wanted was a wealthy husband?"

His expression cooled. "Or a lover. It's not exactly an uncommon motive."

His flat statement once again dredged up the stark memory of the legal letter she had received from Damon's lawyers. They'd offered to pay her off so she would not go to the press, attempt to contact his family or get her sticky fingers on the family inheritance. *As if.*

Zara could feel her blood pressure shooting through the roof. Before that moment, she had been able to separate Damon from the contents of that insulting letter, even though she knew he was the one who had authorized it. But now she realized how naive she had been. Damon's contempt for her and Petra was not so different from his ruthless assessment of Emily.

"There are women who don't give a hoot about your family's money, and Emily is one of them. She is not predatory."

A faint rustling sound from the interview room, as if Rosie was struggling out of her cozy blanket, sent a fresh surge of adrenaline shooting through Zara's veins. Damon's cool gaze fixed on the door, reminding her that not only did he possess exceptional eyesight, but that his hearing was no doubt excellent, as well. Attributes that, along with an uncanny sixth sense had, apparently, made him some kind of superspy during his time in the Special Forces. She needed to get Damon out of her office, now.

She forced a professional smile and apologized, which was more difficult than she expected. Bleakly, she realized she was still surprisingly angry with Damon. Although, she didn't know quite why that should be, since she was the one who had left Damon and not the other way around. Plus, she was *over* him, and had been for months.

She directed another breezy smile in Damon's general direction. As much as she thought Ben was at fault, it was clear the responsibility for the employment part of this disaster belonged with her. Damon's firm paid her to supply Magnum with the temping services they required, so it was up to her to fulfill the contract. She needed to find someone else to fill Emily's position, and fast, before Magnum took their business elsewhere.

"As luck would have it, I've got a temp on the books who might do to replace Emily. She's a little older, but extremely efficient—"

"No."

Zara blinked and plowed on. "Harriet has a long work record and an extremely good skill set—"

"I don't want Harriet," he said in a flat, cool voice. "I want you."

A pang of heat shot clear to Zara's toes, despite the fact that she knew Damon could only be referring to his need for an assistant. Even so, memories flickered, vivid and earthy, drawing every muscle of her body tight. She swallowed against a coiling tension that should not exist and desperately willed her body to return to normal. "Why?"

Damon's darkened gaze locked with hers for a piercing moment, and the reason she'd succumbed to a wild, irresponsible fling with him when she had known it was a huge mistake to sleep with the boss was suddenly crystal clear: chemistry. It shimmered in the air and ran through her veins like liquid fire, the pressure of it banding her chest, making it hard to breathe. For some unknown reason Damon had wanted her and, against all common sense, she had wanted him too.

Damon frowned and dragged lean fingers through his hair and she received the indelible impression that for a long, stretched-out moment he had actually forgotten what he was going to say. "Uh, the McCall takeover. Before you disappeared, you did a lot of the groundwork—"

She stiffened at the mention of the McCall takeover. McCall Electrical being the company that had belonged to Tyler McCall. If there was ever a project she did not want to work on, it would be that one!

"I didn't disappear—I resigned without notice." *Then* she had disappeared. She'd had to get out of town quickly, because she had known that if she had tried to have a normal, aboveboard relationship with Damon, the press would have become interested in her. Even though they had no clue what Angel Atrides looked like, it would only have been a matter of time before her true identity was uncovered, then all the careful work she had done to invent a normal life and career would have been for nothing.

"Resignation?" he muttered in a low growl. "You sent a text."

Warmth rose in her cheeks. "But I did resign."

She knew she shouldn't belabor the point, but a combination of her anxiety over Damon walking into her office and her extreme physical response to him were having a bad effect on her. She couldn't seem to stop arguing with him, which was counterproductive. She needed to concentrate on getting rid of him before Rosie woke up.

Swallowing the exhilarating desire to argue some more, she reached for calm. "I agree that texting was not the ideal way to finish." It had just been necessary at the time, because she had not wanted Damon to have her private email address. Email addresses opened too many online doors, some of which led back to her old life, and she knew how adept Damon was at utilizing those sorts of opportunities.

Damon's thoughtful gaze seemed to burn right through her. "Whatever. Before you *left* without any notice or forwarding address, you did the groundwork for the McCall takeover. Despite a hitch in the proceedings, I'm now on the point of closing the deal, so I would prefer to have someone who knows their way around the issues."

Zara had the sudden, suffocating sense of being entangled in a sticky web from which she could not escape. "I had thought you would have completed that months ago."

"There's been an unexpected complication, a missing block of voters' shares that could jeopardize the takeover. And I've had…other things that have needed attention."

A picture of the gorgeous blonde he'd been dating lately, heiress to a media empire, Caroline Grant, flashed into Zara's mind. That image was instantly followed by a snapshot of the reed-slim redhead he had started seeing on a regular basis not long after Zara had left. Another hot dart of anger unsettled her further.

She did not want to admit that the anger could be linked with the fact that Damon had started dating less than a month after she left his bed. Wining and dining beautiful women while she had been hiding out in her aunt's country cottage, feeling exhausted and nauseous in the first trimester of her pregnancy. Because, if she was angry, that meant Damon was still important to her, or worse, that she was jealous.

Another small sound drew Damon's attention back to the door of the interview room. Zara's heart rate increased another notch. Rosie was definitely awake.

The vibration of a cell, thankfully, distracted Damon. Despite her clear need to get rid of Damon fast, a sudden intense curiosity manifested itself as he extracted the phone from his coat pocket and checked the screen.

Jaw taut, she watched as he slipped the phone back into his pocket. She wondered if the call had been from Caroline Grant, and suddenly her mind was made up.

"No. Working for you is out of the question, I have—"

"I realize you have a business to run," Damon cut in smoothly. "But I only need you for three weeks, four at most, until the negotiations are completed. And you do have a part-time assistant who could fill in for you."

Damon offered a fee that was so generous it would cover her agency costs for the next year. More, she would finally be able to afford to fly to Medinos to check out a mysterious safe-deposit box she had recently discovered her mother had obtained not long before she died.

But, as tempting as the money was, as much as she needed it, she could not risk being that close to Damon. As it was, she was kicking herself that she had allowed financial desperation to hold sway when she had accepted him as a client.

"I'm sorry. I can't work for you."

Walking briskly to her front door, she yanked it open. She had to get Damon out of her office before he discovered Rosie. He would take one look at her coal-black hair and eyes that were changing by the day to look eerily like his and would instantly know she was his daughter.

Cold, damp air flowed in, making Zara shiver, but instead of taking the hint and walking through the door, Damon paused and she made the fatal mistake of looking into his eyes.

Long, tense seconds later, Damon's gaze dropped to her mouth and the heady tension she had so far failed to control tightened another notch.

"Damn," he muttered, "I promised myself I wasn't going to do this."

Zara froze as he cupped her jaw, unwillingly riveted by the tingling heat that radiated out from that one point of contact, the unbearably familiar masculine scents of soap and skin. Despite the cold air, she could feel herself growing warmer by the second. Damon's touch was featherlight; all she needed to do was step away, so why couldn't she do that one simple thing?

It was a bad time to discover that, despite everything that had happened, the heady excitement that had been her downfall a year ago was still just as potent, just as seductive.

It shouldn't be, she thought a little desperately. She had changed; she had moved on. When she did decide to allow a man back into her life it would not be because of an off-the-register sexual attraction. This time she would choose carefully. She needed steady and reliable, not—

Damon's mouth slanted across hers and any idea that the day was cold was blasted away by a torrent of heat. Her heart pounded so hard she found it difficult to breathe and her legs suddenly felt as limp as noodles.

This was why she had made "the mistake," she thought dimly. Her palms slid up over Damon's chest; her fingers convulsively gripped the lapels of his coat, as a familiar, guilty pleasure flooded her. Damon's hands settled at her waist, molding her more firmly against him and she found herself responding with an automatic, mindless pleasure, lifting up on her toes as she pressed into the kiss, clutching at his shoulders as if she couldn't get enough of him.

It was moth-to-the-flame stuff, irresistible and utterly dangerous, because it was abruptly clear to her that Damon was nothing short of an intoxicating addiction. When he was in the room she couldn't think; worse, she didn't want to think. As emancipated and independent as she was, as determined as she was to run her life in a practical, logical way, she had never been able to resist him.

Long, drugging seconds later Damon lifted his head. "Before I go, I have one more question."

A thin, high cry pierced the air. Zara's stomach sank. With a convulsive movement, she released her grip on Damon's coat.

Damon's gaze turned wintry. "Question answered."

With a sense of fatalism, undergirded by the sudden wrenching suspicion that Damon had known all along that there was a baby, Zara watched as he reached the door to the interview room in two gliding strides and pushed the door open wide.

Four

Damon stared at the baby in the bassinet.

He thought he had been prepared for this moment, but the reality of the tiny baby literally flipped his world upside down in the space of a moment.

The first thing he noticed about the child, *his child*, was the color of her sleep suit. Pink.

The tension banding his chest increased exponentially. Not only did he have a baby, he had a daughter.

"What's her name?" His voice came out more roughly than he cared for, but then it wasn't every day he discovered he was a father.

Emotion, painful and inchoate, seemed to burst through some interior barrier. With it came a torrent of memories. Memories that should have faded, but hadn't: his father's voice late at night, the muffled sounds that meant his mother was being hit and was trying to stay quiet so he wouldn't know. Later, when he was older, the breathless pain of broken ribs, the harsh chemical scents of the hospital emergency room.

Once, a memory of reckless fury bursting through him when his father had attacked Damon's mother, who had been pregnant with Ben at the time. Ten years old, but big for his age, Damon had hit out and caught Guy Smith by surprise. He could still remember the rage behind that punch, the hot rush of satisfaction that had poured through him when his father had gone down.

Fatherhood, he thought bleakly. It was something he had consciously avoided, just as he avoided emotional relationships in general. As a child he had learned that the kind of intense out-of-control love most people seemed to wish for was neither a practical nor a safe basis for any relationship. Although, looking at the tiny baby whose gaze had latched onto his with single-minded intensity as she sucked on one small fist, he registered that you could not prove that by him. The first night he had spent with Zara had been characterized by a distinct lack of control.

He noted the fact that Zara was hovering at the door. "She's mine."

"Yes."

"And you didn't tell me, because…?"

Her gaze met his squarely before falling away. "It's… complicated." Her gaze homed in on his again, brows jerked together in a frown. "How did you find out? Let me guess… Emily?"

"Ben. When he phoned from the airport, he let it slip." Damon's jaw tightened. "He thought I already knew—"

"But if you'd known, we would have had this conversation a long time ago."

Damon tensed against the waft of a familiar flowery perfume as Zara brushed by him and slung a piece of muslin over one shoulder, presumably in case of spills. Picking the baby up with unconsciously graceful movements, she cuddled the infant close, Zara's expression softening in a way that briefly riveted him and, out of nowhere, desire kicked. Jaw tight, he registered the stubborn, visceral need to reclaim Zara, which should have evaporated in the instant he had uncovered the baby and her deception, and yet it hadn't.

In a moment of self-knowledge, he noted that it was tied to the fact that Zara was now the mother of his child and therefore qualified for his protection and support. As strong and independent as Zara seemed, he could no more abandon her and the baby than he had been able to step away from his own mother when she had been the victim of his father's abusive nature.

Added to that, as much as he had tried to intellectualize the process, the fact that Zara had given birth to his child had tipped some internal balance. He had felt the change in the instant that Ben had told him there was a baby. The primitive, testosterone-fueled desire that had gripped him to claim not just his child, but Zara too.

He watched as Zara rubbed the baby's back and he waited for more unwelcome memories of his childhood to surface and douse a need he didn't want. The memories didn't come. Probably, he thought bleakly, because his only memories of a baby in the family were of Ben. And by the time Ben was born their father had been dead and buried.

Damon began noticing other things in the room. A desk, which held what looked like Zara's handbag and, beside it, a newspaper and a small pile of mail. There were also a couple of chairs, and a large bag in one corner that seemed jam-packed full of baby things. Feeling suddenly overwarm, he shrugged out of his coat and dropped it over the back of a chair.

"Were you ever going to tell me?"

Her gaze flashed to his as, one-handed, she rummaged through the baby bag and extracted an insulated container holding a bottle of what he guessed was baby formula. "I didn't think, given that I was just an employee and that we'd had an office affair, that you would want to be tied to me by a chil—"

"It wasn't an affair."

"It was temporary."

Damon frowned at her clipped reply. He was still processing the fact that there really was a baby, but he was clear on one point. "Temporary or not doesn't change a thing. She's my child. I had a right to know."

And in the saying of it, he felt a further internal shift, the forging of a link that was irrevocable. It quietly but absolutely changed everything.

Zara's expression was taut as she settled the baby in her lap and coaxed her to accept the bottle. "You don't want children—you made no secret about that. I came across a magazine article where your wife claimed the reason your marriage broke up was that you didn't want children. She wasn't exactly reticent about the subject."

Damon frowned, irritated, despite the fact that for once the media was accurate. "That was true enough. Lily and I had an…arrangement—"

"As I remember it, so did we. A short-term liaison, no strings." She sent him the kind of crisp, business-like glance that assured him everything was settled.

Unfortunately, the slick managerial technique—

straight out of Business Troubleshooting 101—only increased the fascination that had gripped Damon from the very first time he had met Zara. Over the years he had become used to being pursued by beautiful, successful women. With Zara, the opposite had proven to be true. And despite the clear evidence that she wanted him, she still seemed intent on avoiding him.

He should have been pleased. It was permission to step back, to keep his emotional involvement to a minimum, to simply be a biological father with legal access. No messy emotion or fallout when it all came apart.

The problem was, he thought grimly, that just minutes ago, Zara hadn't just let him kiss her, she had kissed him back. Despite walking out on him a year ago, she still wanted him. The mix of attraction and avoidance had an interesting but frustrating effect, fueling his need to have her back.

With every minute that passed, the desire to understand why Zara had run when she still clearly wanted him intensified. She had said she didn't want him to think she was after his money, and that she knew he didn't want children. Both were valid reasons, *if* their physical attraction had cooled off. But clearly it hadn't, which left him with a question mark.

"What's her name?"

The front door chime sounded.

Distracted, Zara peered past him into the office. "Rosamund, Rosie for short." She looked briefly torn. "Will you hold her while she finishes her bottle?"

A split second later, Zara was close enough that he could smell the flowery scent of her hair and other scents: the sourness of the milk spill on the muslin over her shoulder, the soft sweetness of baby powder.

"Hold her so her head is supported on your arm."

Damon froze as he found himself awkwardly cradling his daughter.

Zara handed him the bottle of formula, her expression both anxious and imperious. "Don't hold her so loosely. Closer, like this…"

She readjusted his hold so Rosie was cradled closer against his chest, her head resting comfortably in the crook of his arm. "And tilt the bottle—like this—so she doesn't gulp air."

Seconds later, Zara stepped out into the main office, closing the door firmly behind her.

Fumbling with the soft, warm bundle that wriggled and moved, Damon took the chair Zara had vacated and touched the nipple of the bottle to Rosie's lips. His anxiety that he was doing it all wrong evaporated almost instantly as Rosie's small hands clamped either side of the bottle and she began to drain what was left of the milk. After a minute or so the nipple popped out of her mouth, signaling that she was done. She stared at him unblinkingly, then put her fist into her mouth.

Gently, he attempted to lift her fist away and succeeded long enough that he caught a pearly flash against the redness of her gum before she was once again sucking on her fist. Feeling out of his depth, Damon let her have her way. If it was her fist that made her happy, who was he to argue?

Setting the bottle down on the desk, he eased himself into a more comfortable position and simply looked at the tiny warm creature in his arms. Something about Rosie informed him that even if she hadn't been wearing pink, he would have known she was a girl. It wasn't just that her skin was like porcelain and her features delicate—he guessed all babies shared those in common. And it wasn't the shock of silky dark hair that already showed a trace of curl, just like her mother's. Rather it was an indefinable, faintly imperious quality that announced her femininity, a quality her mother had in spades.

He dragged at his tie, loosening it. Rosie's gaze followed his action before she once more returned to a study of his face as if she was intent on imprinting his features. Caught in the net of his daughter's gaze, a profound sense of recognition riveted Damon. If there had been any doubt that he was Rosie's father, those doubts would have been nixed in that moment. Zara's eyes were a deep sapphire blue; Rosie's were already lightening to the unusual silvery gray that had run in his family for generations.

She had his eyes.

Something weird happened in the region of Damon's chest. He reached out a lean finger to touch a silky wisp of hair. Petal-soft fingers closed around his finger with surprising strength.

Rosie stared into his eyes, her gaze direct and fearless and, suddenly, she was her mother's daughter. Pale, delicate skin flushed and for a moment he thought she would cry. Instead her mouth curved in a gummy smile and he logged the moment that he fell utterly and completely under his daughter's spell.

"This complicates things," he muttered. "I'm not fit to be anyone's dad."

Rosie made a cute cooing sound. He tried to free his finger from her fierce grip, then was completely fascinated when she refused to let go.

"Babies have surprising strength." Zara's quiet voice broke his intense focus on his daughter.

He watched as she picked up the length of muslin,

which had fallen to the floor, and briskly tucked it away in the baby bag, the movement jerky. "What's wrong?"

"Nothing! At least I hope it's nothing. But that was not the normal type of client that strolls in off the street. She was too well dressed, too pushy and she seemed more interested in the fact that you were seen walking in here than in applying for a job. I'm pretty sure she was a reporter of some kind."

Damon frowned. Normally the press didn't bother him too much. But that was because he usually made damn sure he wasn't in the public eye. For the past few months, however, he'd had an uncomfortable amount of exposure, because his current date, Caroline, championed a number of charities and had insisted on dragging him along to some high-profile events. As a result, he'd had one reporter in particular dogging his footsteps, trying to snag some kind of exclusive on his personal life.

"Was she blonde, thin, with red-rimmed glasses?"

Zara looked up from jamming the empty bottle into the baby bag, her expression arrested. "You *know* her?"

"Not exactly. She's a friend of Caroline's. She usually covers charity events."

"Caroline?" Zara zipped the bag closed with unnecessary force. "That would be your current girlfriend, which would make Red Glasses what? A gossip columnist?"

Now distinctly irritated, Damon rose to his feet. The motion seemed to distract Rosie, because she finally let go of his finger. "If we're talking about the same person, then her name's Vanessa Gardiner. She freelances for the tabloids and a couple of women's magazines."

He knew that because he had seen her parked outside his apartment a couple of times and just last week she had followed him to an exclusive restaurant where he'd had a client lunch. The intrusion had ticked him off to the point that he had tasked Walter, his head of security, with calling her off. Apparently, the tactic hadn't worked.

"So, she followed you here, to *my* employment agency? Why on earth would she want to do that?"

Damon worked to release the sudden tension in his jaw. Lately, it felt like he'd landed in the middle of a soap opera. At times like this, he missed the simplicity of the life in the military he had been forced to relinquish when he took over the family business. Chain of command was clear-cut and logical, unlike personal relationships.

"A few days ago, at an awards dinner, Caroline accused me of seeing someone else. Unfortunately, Gardiner must have been close enough to pick up on the conversation."

Zara straightened, her eyes shooting blue fire. "And are you seeing someone else?"

Damon got the sudden, arresting notion that if he'd said yes to Zara's snapped-out question she would have done something interestingly violent, like throw something at him. An odd, warm glow spread through him. "I'm not exactly in the habit of dating two women at the same time. Besides, you know my work schedule."

She blinked as if she was still having trouble controlling her emotions. "So this reporter is stalking you, trying to find evidence that there's another woman and she ends up in *my* office, where there's not only another woman, but a baby, as well!" Zara drew a deep breath. "Just what I need in my life right now."

Dragging a trailing tendril of hair behind one ear, she began to pace, even though there was very little room for pacing. "You should have called me before showing up—"

"I did. You didn't return my call."

Zara stared at him, frustrated. "What I don't get is why you want to be involved with Rosie or with me! From all accounts, it didn't take you long to get over me. Within a month you were dating that redhead. What was her name? Janet, Jessica—"

"Jemima."

She glared at him. "Whatever. Now you're dating Caroline and her little reporter friend is following you."

The silence in the small room stretched out, fraught and intense. Somewhere in the distance a car horn honked. The gusting wind was now laced by rain, which pattered on a barred window. It was an odd moment to discover one salient fact that somehow changed everything: Zara had been jealous of Jemima. And if Damon didn't miss his guess, she was jealous of Caroline.

Out of nowhere, his pulse rate lifted. Dealing with Zara was like trying to get information from a sphinx on lockdown. In normal conversation she was guarded and controlled. The only chink in her armor was that she hadn't yet learned to control her emotions or her body language.

Just minutes ago, she had kissed him. The memory of it still made every muscle in his body tighten. Now her eyes were shooting fire and she was making no bones about the fact that she didn't like it that he dated other women. Against all the odds, Zara's unguarded response settled something in him, a question that had remained unanswered for the past year. He didn't know why she had left him, but he was now certain it had not been because she didn't want him.

Feeling oddly buoyed, he cradled a now-sleepy Rosie

a little closer and walked the few paces to the window, which looked out over a service lane. The rain had gotten heavier and the temperature in the room had dropped a couple of degrees. He made a mental note to ensure Zara and Rosie had adequate heating. "So, when did you discover you were pregnant?"

"A few days before I left."

That explained a few things: Zara had had a sick day when she had not seemed to be ill; her suddenly crammed schedule when, from the time they had started sleeping together, they had seldom spent a night apart.

His jaw tightened as memories he thought he had jettisoned came crowding back. He had to keep reminding himself that their relationship, such as it was, had lasted barely four weeks.

"I thought something had happened to you."

Until he had gone to her apartment and discovered that Zara had systematically packed up and left town. A quick word with the manager of the building had supplied the information that Zara had given notice some days before, which indicated the move had been carefully planned. "You could have talked to me. We could have worked something out."

Zara sent him a cool glance, left the room and returned almost immediately with the newspaper he had brought. She held it so that Ben and Emily's picture and the insulting headline were clearly visible. "Like this?"

"I'm not Ben."

"No, you're way more newsworthy. The media would have cut me to shreds. They would have made my life a misery." She tossed the newspaper into the trash can to one side of the desk.

Damon's gaze narrowed at the extremity of her reaction to the kind of publicity that was literally a five-minute wonder. He adjusted his hold on Rosie. "I could have arranged financial support."

Zara's head came up. "Money. Why did I know that it would come back to that? Do you always use money to solve your 'problems'?" She sketched quotation marks in the air.

He frowned at her reaction. "Not always. Sometimes a conversation works."

The phone ringing out in the office broke a tension that was suddenly thick enough to cut. There was an audible click as the call went through to the answering service.

"News flash," she said curtly. "With regard to your money, I don't want it. That's why I'm in business—I like to earn my own way."

Her glance was laced with defiance. With the flush on her cheeks and glossy tendrils of hair curling around her cheekbones, he couldn't help thinking that despite the buttoned-down suit and the attempt to tame her hair, Zara looked exotic and tempestuous.

Her flat statement underlined the certainty that had grown in him as he had cradled Rosie. He had thought that if there really was a child he would be able to control what he felt, that he could preserve his distance, but that idea had crashed and burned the second Rosie smiled at him.

One gummy smile and suddenly he had a whole new priority list.

He still intended to retrieve Ben ASAP, but, for the moment, Rosie and the attraction that was still very much alive between him and Zara had taken precedence over Ben and Emily's departure.

The implications were dizzying. After years of managing all his relationships, he was faced with two relationships that were distinctly out of his control. He should be drawing back, looking for ways to lessen his involvement and neutralize his dangerous emotions. The only trouble was, this time he didn't want to pull back. After years of being out in the cold, he couldn't seem to resist the warmth.

Damon glanced down at Rosie, who had dropped off to sleep in his arms with a relaxed abandon that was mesmerizing. Her cheeks were delicately flushed, her lashes dark, silky crescents against her skin. For a moment, he was transfixed by the phenomenon, which had at its heart the absolute trust a child gave to a parent. The kind of trust he had never thought would be given to him, but which now seemed vital.

He felt the moment of decision, a quiet settling into place of a plan that, less than an hour ago, would have been out of the question. A plan that would include both Rosie and Zara in his life.

The risk of attempting such a thing registered, but the concept of that risk was almost instantly swamped by a surge of possessiveness.

There was no reason he couldn't successfully incorporate Zara and Rosie into his life. But he had to be careful. Zara had walked away from him once before, disappearing almost without trace; he could not afford for that to happen again. This time he would move more slowly and the way forward seemed clear.

"Okay, let's talk business. Now that Emily's gone, I need a PA."

The wariness disappeared from Zara's expression with fascinating speed as she shifted into business mode. "I have a couple more possibilities on the books," she said smoothly. "A retired accountant who is looking for part-time work—although I'm sure he'd be happy to fill in for Emily for a couple of weeks. And a researcher who will probably be perfect—"

"Like I said before," Damon said flatly. "I don't want the temps on your books. We're out of time and you've worked on the takeover. I want you."

Shock reverberated through Zara at the flat demand of the last three words.

Even though Damon had couched the barely concealed demand in business terms, for a sharp, visceral moment Zara still registered that he wanted *her.* Not good.

She took a deep breath, which she suddenly desperately needed. The chemistry thing was happening again. Her heart was beating too fast and her skin felt oddly sensitive, her breasts taut. In certain places there was a distressing, tingling heat that was all too familiar...

She crossed her arms over her chest and tried to get a grip on herself. Because this was the same craziness that had gotten her into trouble in the first place. "I'm not available."

"If you're worried about this office, I'll compensate you for the cost of increasing Molly's hours, or even employing someone to replace you while you work for me. I'm also happy to pay for childcare. In fact, *all* of Rosie's childcare."

He glanced around the small room, which normally Zara barely registered, but she was noticing it now. Aside from Rosie's clutter, there was just the cheap desk and two chairs. Even the carpet, which was gray and threadbare in places, highlighted the fact that she had run out of money when it came to this room. The small decor budget she'd allowed herself had all been expended on the front office, because first impressions counted.

Damon's gaze pinned her. "This isn't charity—it's a business proposition."

Zara drew a swift breath. Damon's offer shouldn't have flicked her on the raw, but it did, since the last time Damon had offered her money it had been so she would go away for good. Not that he knew that!

"Like I said before, I really don't want your money."

"But you need it."

Shock jerked through her at the flat certainty in his voice, as if he knew just how financially stretched she was. Panic gripped her, making it hard to breathe. "You've been investigating me."

She didn't know why she hadn't thought of that before. Damon was in the surveillance business after all and she had read enough about Magnum to know that the company included a range of complementary businesses, one of them an actual detective agency.

Damon's gaze narrowed. "Believe it or not, I don't make a practice of investigating the women I sleep with. I like to think I can step away from the paranoia of the security business and have something approaching a normal life outside work hours. The reason I know you need the money is that you agreed to take Magnum Security on as a client. Given your reluctance to even take a phone call from me, it was fairly easy to conclude that you needed the money."

Zara drew a deep breath and tried to calm down. She had always known that if Damon decided to put her life under a microscope, he would unravel her secrets fairly quickly. Logically, the fact that he hadn't turned up at her door until now meant that he hadn't. Even so...

"It's still got to be no when it comes to money," she said stiffly. "I can manage."

Damon frowned. "Whether you want my money or not, the second I declare my paternity and apply to pay child support, you'll receive it, anyway."

The words *declare paternity* and *child support* stopped Zara in her tracks. Damon declaring his paternity was a legal process, which would inevitably result in Rosie's birth certificate being updated to include his name. Then that document would be supplied to Damon. When Damon looked at the birth certificate he would see Zara's name change and that her mother had been Petra Atrides, aka Petra Hunt.

If that wasn't bad enough, when the tax agency assessed his income and began making her mandatory child support payments from his bank account, he would hate her even more. Originally, he had tried to get rid of Zara, aka Angel, with one cash payment; now he would be stuck with years of payments. And because Damon earned a great deal, those payments would be substantial.

Zara tried to think, but she felt like she was caught in a whirlwind. Now that he had discovered Rosie, those legal processes would happen. There was nothing she could do to stop them. The only thing she could do was angle for time while she tried to figure out how to tell Damon the truth about herself without forever damaging his relationship with Rosie. And how to make the money problem go away.

Suddenly the interview room seemed claustrophobically small. In need of air and a few seconds' respite so she could *think*, Zara opened the door and peered out into her office. It was empty, and thanks to the rain, the street outside was fairly deserted.

The reporter seemed to have disappeared. Although, Zara didn't think she had seen the last of Vanessa Gardiner. She had stared at Zara as if she was a hound dog on the scent. Zara had gotten the distinct impression that Vanessa knew Zara used to work for Damon and now she was busily putting two and two together. That meant Vanessa would be back, and if she saw Zara with Rosie, the game would be up.

Zara tried to shake the horribly familiar hunted feeling—the same feeling she'd experienced when the press had tracked her after Petra's death—but it wouldn't go away. Whether she was right or wrong, her instincts told her she needed to be absent from Westlake Employment for a while.

Right now, her only option seemed to be to work for Damon. It felt a little like jumping out of the frying pan into the fire, but it was a fact that Damon worked in a hermetically sealed, high-security environment, fourteen stories up. Even the underground parking area was private and secure. To all intents and purposes, unless Gardiner found out where Zara lived, she would have seemed to have disappeared off the face of the planet.

Turning back, she met Damon's gaze squarely. "I could work for you, but on the condition that I'll need to bring Rosie with me. If that reporter tracked you here and thinks we might be involved, then there's no way I'm risking having her find out about Rosie or tracking her to her day care center."

"Not a problem. If you want an alternative center, I have a friend who owns a childcare franchise."

He mentioned the name of an exclusive franchise that was way out of her price range. The only problem was, she didn't think any center was safe, at least for the moment. And the way the tabloids had jumped on the story about Ben and Emily was just a dress rehearsal for the way they would behave when they discovered Zara had given birth to Damon's child.

"I just don't want to risk the press finding out Rosie is yours until we've had time to…settle things."

Suddenly, needing to have her daughter close, Zara held out her arms and was inordinately relieved when Damon instantly handed Rosie over. Unfortunately, in the process, Zara had to get closer to Damon than she liked. His arms brushed hers and his breath washed over one cheek. The intimacy of the contact sent another one of those sharp little pangs through her.

Damon shrugged out of his jacket, which had a small milky spill on it and picked up a container of baby wipes that resided on the desk. "Can I use one of these?"

She nodded and tried not to watch as Damon perched on the edge of the desk and dabbed at the stain. Suddenly, he seemed too large and too male for the tiny office, with the breadth of his shoulders stretching the cut of his jacket and the bronze color of his skin glowing through the white cotton of his shirt.

Feeling edgy and unsettled and still whirling from the decisions she'd had to make, Zara placed Rosie on one shoulder and gently rubbed her back, encouraging her daughter to stay asleep. Anything but dwell on the relaxed intimacy of Damon cleaning the stain from his jacket with Rosie's wipes—the kind of small, fascinating action that went with couplehood, or families.

He looked up, catching her off guard. "Rosie's teething, by the way. When she put her fist in her mouth her gums were red and I saw a glimpse of white."

Instantly distracted, Zara lowered Rosie into the bassinet. Gently, she examined her mouth and was stunned to see a tiny glimmer of white edging through Rosie's gum.

Three months was very early for teething, although Zara had learned from another young mother whose baby had been born with tiny "milk teeth" that anything could happen. "You're right, it must have just come through. No wonder she's had trouble sleeping." She shot Damon a faintly chagrined look. "How did you know?"

"My ex-wife's sister had twins. They both teethed early."

Zara could feel herself stiffening at his easy mention of his ex-wife, Lily. Shortly after Zara had discovered who Damon really was, two weeks into her tempestuous six weeks with him, she had searched online for snippets about his gorgeous, blonde and seemingly perfect ex-wife. Lily had since married again to an extremely wealthy banker.

Lily and Damon had seemed to have a poster-perfect marriage, which had ended in a quick and quiet divorce a few years ago. Logically, Zara knew that all the talk about perfection had to be untrue, since Lily and Damon had divorced, but Zara's mood had plummeted, anyway. It had underlined her decision to leave without telling Damon she was pregnant. If Damon had not been satisfied with Lily, how on earth could he ever contemplate a real relationship with Zara?

Damon shrugged back into his jacket. Zara was caught and held by the way his shirt briefly stretched across his muscled chest, and the flood of intimate memories that sight evoked, most of which had to do with breathless heat and naked skin. Predictably, his gaze caught hers in that moment, but this time she managed to quickly look away, although she couldn't do a thing about the warmth that seared her cheeks.

A split second later, he closed the distance between

them as he came to look down at Rosie. Zara was caught and held by the softness of his expression. It was a softness she had only ever seen in flashes, usually for the elderly or the very young.

"I'll let Howard know you're taking the job."

Her heart jolted at the singular clarity of Damon's gaze, the silvery irises with their dark striations, the thick, silky fringe of lashes. For a long, breathless moment her mind went completely blank. "Just so we're clear, I'll work for you for the time it takes to complete the McCall takeover, on the condition that your relationship to Rosie is kept secret until after the deal is completed."

Damon's incisive, wintry gaze settled on hers for an uncomfortable period of time, reminding her that when it came to deception she was a desperate amateur, while he had a formidable skill set. In terms of her deception she was suddenly profoundly aware that the clock was ticking.

He shot the cuff of his jacket and checked his watch, as if he needed to be somewhere. "Agreed. I've no more wish that the press get wind of this than you. I won't let on that Rosie is mine until the takeover is completed, and until after we've settled the custody arrangements."

Custody. Another crazy jolt to her heart. Implications she hadn't thought of flooded her, such as the fact that Rosie now had two parents instead of one. Rosie was no longer solely Zara's. She was so used to having her soft, sweet daughter all to herself, of being a cozy, self-sufficient family of two, that it was hard to consider the changes that were coming.

She was quite sure Damon would never try to take Rosie from her. She was equally certain that he would be entirely reasonable in terms of custody. Even so, the notion of sharing Rosie shook Zara, underlining that her cut-and-dried, controllable life had just swung wildly off course.

Added to that, with the inescapable link of Rosie binding Zara to Damon, she no longer had the option of running and hiding. She would once more have to face the world as Petra Hunt's daughter.

The last woman in the world Damon would wish to be the mother of his child.

Five

Damon strolled down the windswept road in the direction of his Jeep Cherokee. His phone vibrated again. He ignored it, just like he'd ignored the last call, then grimaced as he saw his security chief camped out by Damon's Jeep, phone to his ear.

Walter, a retired assault specialist in the Special Forces, terminated his call. "You could have answered. I was worried. The whole office is in an uproar—"

"Can't see why." Damon found his car keys and unlocked the Jeep. "I was only gone for a couple of hours."

Walter tapped his watch. "Four hours. You missed two appointments, but don't worry, Howard rescheduled. He's more of a blunt instrument than a personal assistant, but he managed to quiet old man Sanderson down. Didn't have much success with Caroline though. Think you've got a bit of work to do there."

Damon went still. "You let Howard talk to Caroline?" Howard Prosser was another ex-army employee—an accountant and steely-eyed auditor who had routinely struck fear into entire military bases. Conversation was an art form that Howard had never mastered. Normally, he happily remained locked in his office and preferred communicating via email.

"It was more a succession of grunts than actual speech." Walter looked reflective. "I think he likes her."

Damon could feel a familiar frustration kicking in. Caroline Grant, the daughter of a real estate magnate, was elegant, beautiful and intelligent. She epitomized the qualities of the kind of woman he wanted to be attracted to, but unfortunately, that was where it ended. There was a vital component missing. Ever since his marriage to Lily had quietly imploded, Damon had become acutely aware of what that component was. As perfect as she was, he did not truly want Caroline.

The situation reminded him of his marriage. On the surface everything looked perfect, but there was a lack of spontaneity, of *warmth* that ruled out real intimacy. The problem was that Caroline, and almost every other woman he had dated aside from Zara, was just a little too much like him, more interested in a cool, carefully negotiated partnership than in flinging caution to the wind and plunging into a fiery, risky liaison.

He tensed as a vivid image of Zara, wrapping her arms around his neck and lifting up on her toes to kiss him, momentarily blanked his mind and made every cell in his body tighten. The honking of a car as it braked behind a delivery truck dragged him back to the chilly gray present and the conversation with Walter.

"Uh, what did Caroline say?"

Walter reached into his pocket. "She left you a note."

Damon took and opened the note. A ticket fluttered to the pavement. He skimmed the neat, slanted writing, which was heavily indented into the page, as if Caroline had pressed quite hard with the pen as she wrote. The message was succinct. Since he had missed their discussion about his promise of support for her latest charity over lunch last week and canceled their lunch date today, she had taken the liberty of signing him up for the gala evening she had arranged that evening. He could pick her up at six, sharp.

Walter scooped up the ticket and handed it to him. "A ticket to a gala ball. You hate gala balls."

With passion. Damon slipped the ticket into his wallet.

Walter's brows jerked together. "I hope you're not getting maneuvered into anything serious here."

A grim smile quirked one corner of Damon's mouth. Walter had been around for his marriage breakup and was somewhat protective. "Don't worry. I've got a feeling Caroline and I are strictly short-term."

Caroline needed an escort for tonight, but from the brevity of the note and the depth of the indentations, even piercing the page on the final period, whatever it was they had shared was over.

"All I can say," Walter muttered, "is that this city lifestyle is a far cry from Afghanistan."

"You hated Afghanistan."

"Margot hated Afghanistan," Walter corrected. "If I wanted to save my marriage, something had to go. Turns out it was the job. By the way, pretty sure I saw Vanessa Gardiner driving away just as I got here."

Damon's gaze narrowed as he automatically skimmed the flow of traffic. "She tried to fool Zara into thinking she needed a job."

Walter's eyebrows shot up. "I'll bet that went well."

Damon climbed behind the wheel and nosed into

traffic. He hadn't told Zara, but he was pretty sure it was Caroline who had manipulated the reporter into doing a little digging. She had become increasingly suspicious that there was another woman. For him, the suspicion spelled the end to a relationship that had grown increasingly irritating.

He was aware of Walter following close behind. Walter and Margot were longtime friends. There was nothing flashy or luxe about them. They had three kids, all grown now, and they lived a comfortable but low-key life. However, ordinary or not, they possessed something that had eluded Damon—a relationship that had lasted through thick and thin, characterized by warmth, loyalty and family values.

The fact that he was a father hit him anew.

He braked as traffic ahead slowed. He was still struggling to come to grips with the surge of possessiveness that had hit him out of left field for Rosie *and* Zara, and which was now driving a whole bunch of decisions that, twenty-four hours ago, would not have been viable.

Zara was making no bones about wanting to preserve her distance, which should have pleased him. After all, her reaction dovetailed with his own preference for avoiding emotional entanglements. Instead, contrarily, Zara's determination to remain independent had only served to aggravate and annoy him even more for one salient reason: he still wanted her.

His tactics in forcing Zara to work for him had been blunt and crude, but the situation was nonnegotiable. He was a father and that changed everything. He didn't just want to be a weekend visitor; he wanted Rosie in his life.

And, against all the odds, that was the way he was beginning to think about Zara too.

The lights changed. He accelerated into the inner city and took the ramp down into the parking garage beneath the gleaming office block that contained his offices and a penthouse apartment.

Damon held the private elevator for Walter, who had driven in directly behind him.

Walter grunted his thanks. As the elevator shot upward, Walter stared blandly at the floor numbers as they flashed. "What are you going to do about the baby?"

With a sense of resignation, Damon met Walter's gaze. He tried to tell himself that if his head of security couldn't find out that kind of information he would have been disappointed. "You've spoken to Ben."

"First thing when he landed. He's worried about you."

The elevator doors glided open. Damon checked his watch as he stepped into the foyer of Magnum Security. By his calculation, Ben and Emily would have landed a couple of hours ago, right about when Damon had been walking the streets, looking for Zara's office.

Walter waited until they were in the privacy of his office before he fired his next question. "Don't tell me you're going to marry her."

Damon shrugged out of his coat and hung it on the hook behind the door. "With a child in the mix, maybe it's the logical solution."

Walter gave him the kind of polite stare that said he wasn't buying that for an instant. "There are other solutions."

Damon had thought of them all. He could simply arrange access, offer financial assistance and step out of the picture, job done.

The problem was, he thought broodingly, that Zara

had kissed him. And it hadn't been just a kiss. There had been a fierceness to it that had riveted him.

"The baby changes things."

Walter frowned. "I don't see why you would even consider marriage. Zara's not exactly your usual type."

Damon's brows jerked together. "My usual type?"

Walter looked uncomfortable. "Classy, thin, *blonde*—"

"Instead of brunette, curvy, in charge." Despite the raft of problems involved with even attempting to have a relationship with Zara, Damon found himself grinning. "Favorite word, *no*."

There was a heavy silence. "So there's nothing I can say?"

"Relax, I'm not proposing a normal marriage." *With its inherent emotional instability.* "I'm talking about a marriage of convenience."

Walter's expression turned dour. "Seems to me I've heard those words before."

Right before Damon had married Lily. And there was his dilemma.

If a marriage of convenience hadn't worked with someone as sweet and straightforward as Lily, he was going to have his work cut out convincing a complicated career woman like Zara that it was the ideal solution.

On the plus side, he thought grimly, there would be no issues about whether or not to have children, because there was already a baby. Then there was the sex.

The thought of having Zara back in his bed made every muscle in his body lock up. He was abruptly aware of just how sexy and gorgeous Zara was, and that he had left her alone for over a year. In that time, he had to assume the only reason she hadn't gotten involved with another man had been because she was pregnant, then dealing with a new baby.

Damon stared out his window, barely noticing the bustling marina below or the grey, scudding clouds. He felt like a sleeper waking up. Just over a year ago, he had convinced himself he needed to walk away from Zara, but in doing so he had left her alone and available. Now he was acutely aware that if he didn't lay claim to Zara ASAP, it was only a matter of time before some other man did.

And that was happening over his dead body.

Zara opened the door of her tiny rented house in Mount Eden, which had become her haven in the last few months, and carried Rosie, who was sleeping peacefully after the car ride, through to her room. Frowning a little at the damp chill of the house, Zara laid Rosie down in her cot and tucked a warm quilt around her before turning on the wall heater and tiptoeing out.

She walked back out to the garage, shivering in the chill of the evening as she retrieved her handbag from the car. Hooking the strap over one shoulder, she hefted the bulging baby bag, which was now mostly filled with dirty things that needed laundering and bottles that needed to be washed out. Locking the car, she walked back into the house, awkwardly flicking on lights as she went.

The comforting scent of the chicken casserole she had put into the slow cooker that morning made her mouth water and her stomach rumble. After Damon's disruptive visit, she'd been too unsettled to eat more than a few bites of the sandwich she had packed. Until that moment, she hadn't realized just how hungry she was.

With a sigh of relief, she dropped the bags onto a couch. As she straightened, she caught a disorienting flash of her reflection in the mirror over an antique drinks cabinet that had once belonged to her aunt. Apart from her hair wisping around her face and the color in her cheeks, she didn't look a lot different from that morning. The problem was she *felt* different, off balance and distinctly unsettled, as if a low-grade electric current was shimmering through her veins, making her heart beat faster and putting her subtly on edge.

And she knew exactly why that was. In the space of a few hours, everything had changed. Emily had run off with Ben; Damon had discovered Rosie; Zara was back working for Damon; that darned reporter had found her…and Zara had kissed Damon.

A sharp pang of awareness zapped through her at the memory of the heated, out-of-control kiss. She had tried to convince herself that it had been an experiment, that in kissing Damon she could somehow exorcise the craziness of their past attraction and put him firmly in his place: in the past. But the truth was, aside from acknowledging her own unwilling attraction to Damon, she had been blindsided by the fierceness of her own need and utterly seduced by the fact that *he* still wanted her.

Frowning at her instant and unwanted reaction just to the memory, Zara turned on the heater in the sitting room, then walked through to the kitchen. She lifted the lid on the slow cooker. The rich fragrance of the chicken filled her tiny kitchen. She switched the cooker off so that by the time she was ready to eat, the food would have cooled a little. She put water in the kettle, and when it boiled and the tea was made, she wrapped her fingers around the mug and sipped, enjoying the comfort and the warmth and the automatic cue to wind down and relax.

Her cell chimed. She carried the tea out to the sitting room, set it down on the coffee table and fished her phone out of her bag. She picked up the call, then stiffened as she registered an unfamiliar number.

The low timbre of Damon's voice made her clench her stomach.

"How did you get this number?"

"I needed to access some of Emily's email correspondence. I found your number listed in her contacts."

Zara's stomach sank. She should have seen this coming. Since Emily had actually resigned, of course Damon would have to retrieve correspondence and files from her computer, along with contact information.

"I'm sending a car for you and Rosie in the morning—"

"I don't need you to send a car. I have a car."

"That's hardly practical since you'll have to find parking and carry Rosie and all of her baby gear through the streets."

Zara stiffened. The fact that Damon now had a legitimate stake in Rosie's life was suddenly real and she couldn't help feeling a certain resistance to the idea. "It's not a problem—I can put Rosie in a front pack. She's light, and the bag isn't much heavier than—"

"This is purely a practical solution, designed to make things easier for you."

She tensed at the low, curt timbre of his voice. When she had first gone to work for Damon, before she had known exactly who he was, he had made a lot of things easier and much more enjoyable for her. Gorgeous working lunches, a car and driver for office errands or when she'd had to work late. There had even been a clothing allowance, which, of course, she had not spent on clothes but had put aside for a deposit on a house. And the problem was, that generosity hadn't been just for

her. He had been generous to everyone, no matter their
position in the firm. Working for Damon, and falling
for him, had been heaven—until she had discovered he
was Tyler McCall's nephew.

Zara forced herself to loosen her grip on the phone.
She could not allow herself to dwell on the past or become emotional about things she could not change.
It had been a stressful day; tomorrow would be even
worse.

All she knew was that she had to lay down some
ground rules, fast. She could not afford to be seduced
by Damon's openhanded generosity. Especially since,
once he knew who she was, he would regret ever employing her. He would regret sleeping with her.

"Thanks, but no thanks. I don't need you, or anyone,
to make things easier for me."

There was a small silence. "I thought you wanted
to keep Rosie under wraps. If you park somewhere in
town and walk to the building, that won't be possible."

Her stomach sank. "I hadn't thought about that." She
stared bleakly into space and tried to think. She hated
to admit it, but Damon was right. Entering Damon's
office building lugging a baby bag and carrying Rosie
was too big a risk. "Okay."

There was a brief silence. "The car will be outside
your house at eight thirty."

"I suppose you also know where I live?"

"Don't make it sound creepy. Emily didn't have that
information, but there was mail on the desk in the interview room where Rosie was sleeping. Since the street
address was different to your agency address, it didn't
take a genius to figure out that was where you lived."

Her fingers tightened on the phone. In the panic of
Damon discovering Rosie, she had completely forgot-

ten that she had left some personal mail on the desk. At the time it had seemed an innocuous thing to do, because she hadn't imagined anyone but herself entering that particular interview room. And, somehow, over the past year she had forgotten what Damon had done for a living, that beneath the designer suit and white linen shirt were the kinds of scars that did not come from a tame city existence. That, as effective as he was in the boardroom, he had another far more formidable skill set.

A feminine voice, somewhere in the background, shattered the last illusory remnants of intimacy. Damon coolly requested that Zara give him a minute.

Zara knew she shouldn't continue to listen, that she should allow Damon a measure of privacy, but she couldn't help straining to pick up snatches of the muffled conversation and the name *Caroline*.

Zara jerked the phone from her ear. That would be Damon's beautiful, wealthy, current girlfriend.

The kind of woman who moved in Damon's circles and who the tabloids and magazines and social media forums uniformly pronounced had the perfect profile to be the next Mrs. Smith.

Zara's cheeks burned with a sudden bone-deep embarrassment as she remembered the way she had kissed Damon that morning. She had completely forgotten that he was dating Caroline.

Out of nowhere, gloom settled over her, which was annoying. She should be happy that Damon had moved on so quickly. It put the fling they had shared in perspective.

Suddenly done with the conversation and just a little panicked by her own response to Damon, she terminated the call. Her behavior was abrupt and rude, cutting Damon off midspeech, but she didn't care. Setting the phone down on the coffee table, Zara paced to the window and stared out at the cold, rain-spattered night. She felt horribly off balance, one minute vibrating with anger at Damon, the next with anger at herself for responding to him. The loss of control was worrying. She couldn't help thinking that the last time she'd lost control of her emotions, she had gotten pregnant.

Her stomach churned hollowly, reminding her that she still hadn't eaten, which was probably why she felt so emotional and vulnerable. She was suffering from a blood sugar low.

Walking to the kitchen, she ladled some of the casserole into a bowl, grabbed a fork, returned to the sitting room and curled up on the sofa. After saying grace, she turned on her small TV and ate the chicken. Despite her hunger, she barely tasted it. She even had trouble concentrating on her favorite show, which was all about couples buying their dream homes. It had an irresistible appeal for Zara, because ever since she and Petra had lost their pretty villa on Medinos, she'd longed for a home, something that wasn't possible with Petra's jet-setting lifestyle.

For most of the year, she had been away at boarding school. During vacations, Petra would fly Zara to some exotic location, often someone else's house, or a holiday villa Petra had rented for the summer.

Very occasionally, Zara had stayed with her aunt Phoebe, which she had actually adored because Phoebe's house had become the closest thing she'd had to a home. She had loved the "sameness" of Phoebe's old Victorian villa, even if it had involved heavy furniture and walls of dusty books. She had loved having the same room every time, and the same narrow single bed with the squeaky spring. Even the scents of the garden and the fragrant meadow beyond had somehow spelled home.

The show came to an end. Still tense and unsettled, Zara switched the TV off and sat for long minutes just enjoying the sound of rain pattering on the roof and the cozy ticking of the heater. Sounds that should have relaxed her, but which barely registered. Because beneath the anger and the nervy tension was a thread of awareness, a feminine response to Damon, that shouldn't have been there.

Thoroughly annoyed with herself, she carried her bowl and fork back to the kitchen and rinsed them. If she was going to get through these next few weeks, she needed to get her head straight. It was a chance to sort out the future in a way that was acceptable to them both. A chance to earn money that would help her achieve the dream of her own home. A chance to afford the trip to Medinos to retrieve her mother's safe-deposit box.

Zara stopped, a damp tea towel in her hand, as the possibility of a future with some measure of financial security opened up. She did not want to be all about money, but with Rosie in the picture, she had to be.

The safe-deposit box could change everything for her and Rosie.

Zara had discovered that there was a safe-deposit box when her cousin Lena had given her a packet of letters that had been stored in Aunt Phoebe's house. Phoebe had died several months ago, but it hadn't been until recently that Lena, who lived in Australia, had been able to clean out the house and put it up for sale. When she'd cleaned out her mother's desk, she'd found the letters Zara's mother had sent to Phoebe over the years.

One evening, a couple of weeks ago, Zara had fi-

nally read through them. The hairs at the back of her
neck had stood on end when she had read the final letter her mother had written, which mentioned that she
had decided to get a safe-deposit box after a string of
burglaries near the apartment she had rented. When
Phoebe received the letter, she had been hospitalized,
so, understandably, she had never mentioned the possibility to Zara.

After learning of the box, Zara had searched through
her mother's effects, which she had stored in her spare
room. She had finally found a small tagged key with
the address of her mother's bank on Medinos.

Her knees wobbly, Zara had sat on the edge of her
bed, staring at the key, a tingle electrifying her spine.
Petra had always said she would look after Zara, that
she had an investment plan. Zara had taken that to mean
that her mother had invested with some financial insti-
tution or had deposits at her bank, but nothing of the
sort had ever come to light.

Petra had, at times, made a great deal of money and
she had also possessed some expensive pieces of jewelry
that had vanished. Petra could have sold the jewelry to
supplement her income as her career tailed off. However, a safe-deposit box suggested otherwise.

With any luck, there might be items of sufficient
value to put a deposit down on a house. It was also possible that Zara's Atrides grandmother's jewelry, which
had been missing from Petra's personal things, might
also be in the box.

Zara did not know if the Atrides jewelry was valuable or not. The important thing was that pieces had
been handed down the family line. They were her last
tangible link to her father's family, aside from the name
itself and a defunct title, both of which she did not use.

The safe-deposit box could be an Aladdin's cave of jewelry that would restore her grandmother's pieces to her, with the addition of enough soulless diamonds to fund a house. Then again, it could contain a disappointing array of trinkets that would not cover the cost of the airfare.

When she completed this temping job with Damon, she would finally be in a position to find out.

She finished drying the dishes, then divided up the remaining casserole, which was enough to make several meals, into containers. Once they were labeled and dated, she stacked them in her small freezer, then moved on to sorting through Rosie's bag, disposing of rubbish and putting soiled things into the laundry. Zara finished by washing Rosie's bottles and repacking the bag with formula, fresh diapers and the one hundred other things a baby seemed to need.

Feeling much calmer and more in control, Zara quickly showered and changed into leggings and a soft T-shirt. Shivering at the chill in her bedroom, she also pulled on a thick sweater.

Combing her hair out and leaving it to dry naturally, she padded back to the kitchen. She caught a glimpse of her reflection in the window over the bench. Not for the first time she was confronted by the fact that, with her dark hair and curvy figure, she was starkly different from the elegant blondes Damon seemed attracted to.

Caroline was a case in point. She was classically beautiful and stylish, a virtual carbon copy of Damon's ex-wife, Lily. The similarities reaffirmed that Zara was the exact opposite of the kind of woman he clearly preferred.

Which begged the question, why had he slept with her in the first place?

Feeling annoyed with herself for falling into the trap of comparing herself with other women who had nothing whatsoever to do with her life—unless one of them became Rosie's stepmother, and she didn't want to think about that—Zara found her laptop. Sitting down on the couch, she flipped it open. Usually she checked in with a few friends on social media or read a downloaded book until she felt sleepy, but on impulse, she typed Caroline's name into a popular search engine.

A huge selection of hits appeared. At the top of the list was a video feed of a charity dinner that had been posted less than thirty minutes before.

Stomach tight, knowing she shouldn't do it but unable to resist, she hit the play button. Her screen filled with an image of Caroline in a sexy pale peach gown with a plunging neckline and a slit that revealed one slender, perfectly tanned leg. According to the commentary, normally, Caroline preferred her blonde hair up, but tonight she had opted for a more natural look, and had styled her hair smooth and straight so that it flowed silkily around her shoulders. The reason? Her soon-to-be fiancé, Damon Smith.

Zara stabbed the pause button, but she was too late. The screen froze on a shot of Caroline, one arm coiled around a dark sleeve as Damon, looking broodingly masculine in a tux, half turned to end up center shot.

Her chest tight and burning with an emotion she did not want to label, Zara wondered if she was actually going to be sick.

Suddenly, the dilemma of accepting a lift to work, even with the risk of a nosy reporter, was decided. She would rather die than get into one of Damon's fabulous, glossy company cars. If Damon's driver was parked outside her house at eight thirty, then he would have a wasted trip, because she would be gone by eight.

She dragged in one breath, then another. Dimly, she registered a piece of knowledge that she had avoided for some time through the simple tactic of refusing to think about it, period.

She was jealous of Caroline. And there was nothing either gentle or half-hearted about the emotion, which pulsed through Zara in fiery waves. She had been jealous for months, ever since she had read on a social media site that Damon had started dating the blonde.

Jumping to her feet, Zara began to pace. Just seconds ago, she had felt tired, maybe even a little depressed. Now restless energy hummed through her.

Damon was going to marry Caroline.

How could he? When he had just found out he had fathered a child? *Their* child.

Clearly, Rosie did not mean as much to him as he had implied today. Although, unpalatably, it wasn't Damon's relationship with his daughter that was upsetting her so badly. It was his utter lack of a relationship with *her*.

The reason she was jealous of Caroline was blazingly simple. It had been staring her in the face for weeks, but she had been too intent on burying her head, and her emotions, in the sand.

She still wanted Damon.

Six

Zara ended up at one end of her tiny sitting room, staring at the rain streaming down her window. Feeling like an automaton, she jerked the curtains together, closing out the night.

Blankly, she forced herself to face the fact that Damon and Caroline were soon to be engaged. And why not? They had been dating for months. It should not have come as a shock.

But it had, she thought grimly, especially after the kiss they'd shared.

Numbly, she moved to the small set of French doors that opened out onto a drenched patio and yanked a second set of curtains closed. The fact was, the kiss had stirred up feelings she had thought she had suppressed, making her feel intimately, possessively connected with Damon, as if he was still her lover. And now Caroline had taken him.

The reality was that Damon had never been hers.

Neither of them had ever committed to anything more than a brief, secretive fling, and that fling had been more than a year ago.

But they had a baby together. That meant something.

Surely Damon could have taken some time to reassess. She took a deep breath and let it out slowly as she tried to rationalize the emotions that kept hitting her out of left field. Maybe she felt so shocked because, for the past year, even though she had left Damon, in a sense he had still been hers because, until Caroline, he had only dated sporadically.

Jemima had only lasted three weeks. Zara knew, because she had checked.

As she sat down, her knee brushed the mouse pad of her laptop, jolting it. The screen saver dissolved and she found herself once more looking at the happy couple.

If Damon was getting married, that meant Caroline would become Rosie's stepmother. Somehow that thought made her feel even more miserable.

If she was brutally honest, it was the knowledge that while Damon had been happy to sleep with her on the quiet, he clearly wanted marriage with the kind of woman who moved in his own social circle. Just seeing Caroline and Damon together ignited the same kind of deep, tender hurt Zara had experienced when she had left him and realized that, as formidably equipped as he was to find her, he had not cared enough to do so.

An unpleasant thought struck her. If Damon was planning on remarrying, it made all the sense in the world to clean out any skeletons in the cupboard. She and Rosie were a substantial skeleton.

Zara found herself back on her feet and pacing. Just seconds ago, she had felt chilled and more than a little sorry for herself. Now heat flamed through her, flushing her cheeks and making her heart pound.

It was no wonder Damon had left his sealed penthouse office and prowled the streets to find her. No wonder he was suddenly so keen to keep her close, even down to offering her a job and dangling a huge fee! Locked in his high-security office with all his ex-army cronies there to help him keep an eye on her—that was the definition of keeping her and Rosie, his two shady secrets, under wraps.

Zara tried to calm down. She had been feeling guilty about keeping Rosie a secret. She had even been feeling guilty about *who* she was, Petra's daughter, as if she had to apologize for her very existence.

But she wasn't the only one with secrets. She did not imagine that Caroline would be very happy to find out Damon had recently become a father.

Burning with indignation at Damon's double-dealing sneakiness and suddenly sick to death of living in the shadows and trying to be invisible—of feeling that she had committed some terrible crime just because she had slept with Damon a few times—she snatched up her phone. Unlocking it, she hit Redial on Damon's number. The second Damon picked up, Zara froze, caught in the kind of panicked state that usually had no part in her carefully organized life.

"Zara?" Damon's deep, curt voice sent adrenaline zinging through her veins.

Her throat seized up. A fraught second later, she disconnected the call.

Horrified that she'd lost control to the point that she had actually called Damon to find out whether he really was marrying Caroline—as if she had a right to ask that question—Zara placed the cell on the coffee table. She needed to pull herself together, to get back to the crisp, businesslike state of mind that had been her go-to with all things Damon over the past few weeks.

The phone chimed, almost stopping her heart. Damon's number glowed on the screen.

She stared at the cell as if it was a bomb about to explode, then kicked herself for not answering when a message popped up, informing her she had a new voice mail. With a sense of inevitability, she picked up the phone. Damon's message was edged with impatience. He wanted to know if Rosie was okay. He finished with the command that she call him.

When hell freezes over.

She should never have called him in the first place. With a jerky movement she did what she should have done just minutes ago—she turned the phone off altogether.

Still feeling crazily on edge, she looked in on Rosie, who had finally fallen into a deep sleep. Softly closing the door, Zara padded to the laundry and put on a load of clothes to wash, then did her last job of the night, which was preparing a bottle for Rosie's night feeding. As she tightened the screw lid on the bottle, the chime of her doorbell made her hand jerk.

Her first thought was that it was Damon, but she dismissed that possibility, because he was at the charity ball with the love of his life, Caroline. She glanced at the oven clock, disoriented to see that it was only nine thirty. It felt a whole lot later, probably because it had gotten dark so early.

Frowning, she put the bottle in the fridge and walked through the hall. Her front security light was on, illuminating the porch. Through the frosted glass side panels of the door she could make out a tall masculine figure, wearing a dark suit.

Adrenaline pumped. It *was* Damon.

Keeping the chain on, she opened the door a few inches.

Damon's gaze pinned hers. "You didn't call me back. What's wrong?"

The cool directness of his gaze paired with the five o'clock shadow decorating his jaw gave Damon a remote edge that made her spine tighten. "Nothing's wrong." She tried for a neutral smile. "It was a mistake."

His cool gaze seemed to laser right through her. "Is it Rosie? I thought she might be sick."

"Rosie's fine. She's asleep." Despite knowing she shouldn't, but too furious not to, Zara took the chain off the hook and opened the door wide enough that she could look past Damon to where his car was parked. She wanted to know if Caroline was with him. Frustratingly, because the windows of his car were tinted, she couldn't see a thing. He could have half a dozen women in the car for all she knew.

A little impatiently, Damon's gaze recaptured hers. "Now that I'm here, we should talk. I think we need to get clear on a couple of things."

Such as his impending marriage to a woman who was perfect for him, and the fact that Zara and Rosie had the potential to ruin those plans.

Zara gave the sleek black car at her gate a last probing glare. "It's late. Can't we do this some other time?"

Damon gave her a look of disbelief. "It's only just past nine thirty."

Zara stared at Damon's jaw. Now that she was aware of the scary chinks in her armor when it came to him, she was determined to avoid eye contact where possible. The last thing she needed was for him to know how much he affected her. "I usually go to bed early, because I have to get up for Rosie in the night."

He leaned one shoulder against her porch wall and crossed his arms over her chest. "Okay, let's talk here."

"Can't we discuss whatever it is you want to talk about at work?"

"We could, but I thought you were concerned about keeping our relationship and Rosie under wraps."

Her gaze snapped to his, which was a problem because then she had trouble ripping it away. "We don't have a relationship."

His expression was infuriatingly calm. "But we do have a daughter."

And suddenly the gloves were off. "And I guess, at this point, keeping *our relationship* and Rosie under wraps suits you just fine, doesn't it?"

His brows jerked together. "Would you care to explain that?"

Bright light, intense enough to make her wince, washed across Zara's front lawn and lit up her porch. Her next-door neighbor's security lights had just come on. That meant that Edna Cross, who lived alone and seemed to be unusually inquisitive about every move Zara made, had no doubt logged that she had a visitor. Edna was the secretary of the local neighborhood watch group, and so was also likely now to be out with her flashlight and possibly even a digital camera. Any conversation on Zara's porch could no longer be considered private.

Damon stared in the direction of the high-powered light. His gaze narrowed. "There's someone standing on the other side of your hedge."

"My neighbor Edna Cross. She's head of the local neighborhood watch."

"That would explain the military-grade spotlights."

Ignoring the dryness of his voice and feeling embattled, Zara opened the door a little wider. She didn't want Damon in her house, but he clearly wasn't going to leave anytime soon and what she had to say needed to be said in private. "You had better come in."

With a last glance in the direction of Edna's silhouette, Damon stepped into Zara's hall, dwarfing it and making the space feel distinctly claustrophobic. Zara closed the door and, out of sheer habit, locked it, although the second she did so, it occurred to her that the one person she didn't want in her house was already inside.

As she turned, she realized Damon was waiting for her. She noticed that his tie was dragged loose, the top button of his white shirt was undone and his hair was disheveled as if he'd run his fingers through it repeatedly. All of it made him look even more sexily gorgeous. A pang of heat shot through her, making her clench her stomach. She could not believe she was turned-on, even in a marginal way when she was still so angry. Grimly, she reminded herself that it was far more likely that it was Caroline who had run her fingers through his hair.

Suddenly self-conscious about her leggings, the old sweater that dragged past her thighs and the fact that beneath all the soft layers she wasn't wearing a bra, Zara led the way to her sitting room.

Damon padded straight to the window that looked over Edna's property, pulled back the curtain and looked out. He lifted a hand. Seconds later, the glaring security lights flicked off. Amazing. Usually, if Edna felt impelled to investigate at night, the place was lit up like a landing strip for a good hour. In his blunt, masculine way, Damon had dealt with Edna by summarily checking her out and dismissing her.

He closed the curtains. "She's persistent."

Amusement invested his tone with an intimacy that spun Zara back to evenings spent together in his apartment watching movies and eating gourmet takeout. As he turned from the window, the easy humor was replaced by a flicker of masculine awareness that informed her that if she thought he hadn't noticed she wasn't wearing a bra, she was wrong.

Folding her arms across her chest, Zara indicated that Damon should have a seat. Unfortunately, he chose the seat she had been sitting in and her laptop was still sitting on the coffee table.

Panic gripped her. She couldn't remember whether she'd closed the video clip about Damon and Caroline, or not. In her rush to grab the laptop, all while avoiding getting too close to Damon, she brushed the mouse pad again and the screen saver dissolved.

Damon's gaze settled on the screen a split second before she snapped the laptop closed.

His expression answered the question. No, she had not closed down the video.

Cheeks burning, she found her briefcase, which was on a sideboard, and stowed the offending laptop away. When she turned, Damon was no longer seated, but prowling her small sitting room. He came to a stop in front of a small oil of a Medinian ancestor, one of the few family pieces left from her Atrides past. As he studied the gloomy picture, she felt a crazy sense of relief that, in keeping with her new identity and her new life, she had made it a rule not to have any family photos on show. Those were all kept in albums in a drawer in her room.

Plastering a bright smile on her face, she decided to grab the bull by the horns.

"I hear congratulations are in order."

Damon seemed to go very still. "What for, exactly?"

"Your engagement to Caroline Grant." Despite every effort at control, she couldn't quite keep the husky note from her voice. "No mystery now as to why you were so keen that I should come and work for you *and* bring Rosie along."

There was an odd moment of silence. "I'm guessing that would be because you think I don't want Caro to find out that you've given birth to my child."

Caro. A red mist seemed to form in front of her eyes. Zara could feel her precarious hold on her temper slipping. "I don't think—I know. I can see why we never had a chance, quite apart from the fact that Caroline's *blonde.*"

Two steps and Damon had covered the distance between them. "As I recall, you were the one who laid down the ground rules for the time we spent together."

Zara flushed guiltily at the reminder that she'd had very good reasons for limiting their involvement. "Ground rules that suited you."

His brows jerked together. "Why, exactly, did they suit me?"

Zara met his gaze squarely. "Because I'm not your type."

"Which is…?"

"Blonde. Your wife was blonde. Caroline is blonde."

Damon pinched his nose, which made her even more furious, so she listed another three blonde socialites from the past. Even the names made her feel slightly crazy: Jenna, Hayley, *Tiffany.* They were all pretty, flirty names, nothing like Zara, which sounded somehow heftier. "It's all over the media that you like blondes. And not just blondes. You like a certain type of blonde. Basically, slim, elegant and rich. I'm not any of those—"

"Therefore, I couldn't possibly want you."

She drew a rapid breath and tried to calm down, but she couldn't seem to stop hemorrhaging the disappointment and anger she'd bottled up for over a year. At some point she must have taken a half step closer to Damon, close enough to feel the heat radiating off his body, smell the faint, enticing scents of soap and cologne.

She jabbed a finger at his chest. "Couldn't have said it better myself. Maybe if I had dyed my hair blonde or bought a wig, we would have had a chance at a real relationship." She delivered the kicker. "I don't even know why you slept with me in the first place."

His fingers closed around her upper arms. "That would be because I wanted you," he growled.

Shock reverberated through her at the statement. Both palms were flattened on his chest. She could feel the steady pound of his heart, feel the heat blasting off him. She could have pulled back, stepped free, because his hold was loose but, crazily, it was the last thing she wanted to do.

Something had happened to her in the last hour or so; it was as if all the emotions she had suppressed had burst free and, like a Pandora's box, she couldn't put them back in. And if that wasn't enough, being held close to Damon, having his complete, undivided attention even though they were arguing, filled her with an intoxicating elation.

She glared at him. "Wanted, as in past tense."

In answer, he fitted her close enough against him that she could feel his clear arousal. "Does this feel like past tense?"

She drew an impeded breath and tried to think, which was difficult when tingling heat was pouring through her and all she wanted to do was drown in the intense sensations. Damon bent his head and bit down gently on the sensitive lobe of one ear. A white-hot pang of heat lanced through her.

His jaw brushed her cheek, sending a sensual shiver through her. With a breathless effort, she resisted the urge to sag against him, even though her bones had turned to water. "You can't kiss me. You're engaged."

Irritation registered in Damon's gaze. "There's no engagement. As a matter of fact, Caroline and I are finished."

"Because of Rosie?"

"Rosie is part of it."

Damon lifted his head before she could ask if the rest of the reason was that he thought he now had some kind of responsibility toward them both. Afraid that she was pushing him away with her questioning, Zara's fingers gripped the lapels of his jacket, keeping him close. Minutes ago, she had been furious with Damon and determined to keep him at a distance but, in the space of a few seconds, somehow everything had changed. She took a deep breath, then finally asked the question that had tormented her ever since she had found Damon on her porch. "So… Caroline's not in your car?"

Damon gave her a look of disbelief. "Why would she be in my car?"

Relief and pleasure cascaded through Zara. He really wasn't going to marry Caroline, after all. The media had made up the story, and didn't Zara know how that went?

In some distant corner of her mind she knew she should be reacting differently; she shouldn't feel so happy and so relieved that Caroline was out of the picture.

Damon's expression was curiously intent. "What would you have done if Caroline had been in the car?"

Emotion surged through Zara. A list of scenarios

flashed through her mind, all of which involved getting Caroline *out* of the car.

Damon grinned. "Thought so." He dropped his hands to her hips and pulled her closer still but, frustratingly, he didn't kiss her. Zara finally realized that he was waiting for her to make the next move.

Her mouth dry, her heart pounding—the memory of the kiss they'd shared that morning emboldening her—she lifted up on her toes, looped her arms around his neck and kissed him A split second later his arms came around her, locking her tight against him, as if he had missed her, as if he wanted her just as badly as she wanted him, as if he truly needed her close.

Ridiculous tears burned beneath her lids as she gave in to the simple pleasure of soaking up the heat and comfort of being back in Damon's arms. A comfort that she had tried to forget but which, against the odds, she still desperately needed.

He released his hold for the moment it took to shrug out of his jacket and toss it over the back of a chair. Another slow, drugging kiss, then she found herself slowly, irresistibly propelled backward into the narrow hall, which led to the bedrooms.

Damon lifted his head. In the deep shadows of the hall the narrow band of light that flowed out from the sitting room glanced across mouthwatering cheekbones and the rock-solid line of his jaw, turning his gray gaze molten. "This room?"

Dimly, Zara logged another opportunity to call a halt, to throw cold water on a passionate interlude she should already be regretting. Somehow, they had gone from zero to out-of-control passion in the space of minutes. The problem was, she had been so upset at the thought that Damon was engaged, then so relieved when he wasn't, that her rules for dealing with him had dissolved. She had become someone she barely recognized—fiercely possessive and determined to reclaim him, even if only for one night.

By pure luck Damon had chosen her room. She caught a glimpse of her bed with its rich red coverlet and pretty cushions, the deep blue drapes and the jewel-bright Medinian rug at the foot of her bed. The lush riot of color was very different from the restrained image she was so careful to project through the rest of the house, and in the way she dressed. She was suddenly unbearably conscious of her vulnerability in inviting Damon into a room that was an intimate and unashamed expression of herself.

But for the first time in years she didn't feel like apologizing for loving the flamboyant colors and rich fabrics of her childhood, for being Angel Atrides. With him, right now, she felt bold and passionate, and she knew exactly what she wanted.

"Yes."

Lifting up on her toes, she kissed Damon on the mouth, tangled her fingers with his and drew him into the room. Three steps and she felt the soft quilt of her bed brush the backs of her legs. Another kiss and she had managed to undo most of the buttons on Damon's shirt.

With an impatient movement, Damon completed the job and shrugged out of the shirt, revealing tanned and sleekly powerful shoulders, a broad chest and washboard abs.

She caught the quick gleam of his teeth. "Time this went."

His hands settled on her waist then swept upward, peeling her sweater and T-shirt up and over her head.

The chill of the air was instantly replaced by the hot shock of skin-on-skin as he pulled her close.

Feeling a little vulnerable, because it had been more than a year since they had made love, Zara buried her face in the curve of Damon's throat and allowed herself to be swamped by his masculine heat and scent. It occurred to her that being held in Damon's arms made her feel oddly like she had come home. She stiffened at the thought.

"What's wrong?"

With relief, she decided that the familiar timbre of Damon's voice provided the explanation for what she was really feeling. Not homecoming, but familiarity.

"Nothing. Absolutely nothing."

This time the hungry pressure of the kiss made her head swim.

Long seconds later, Damon cupped her breasts then bent and took one nipple into his mouth. Her breath came in as sensation coiled and burned for long aching moments then, with shocking abruptness, splintered.

Damon said something short and flat. A split second later she found herself lifted and deposited onto the bed. The cool softness of the quilt beneath her overheated skin was subtly shocking, but not as much as the disorienting fact that Damon had barely touched her and she had climaxed.

When he began peeling her leggings and panties down her legs, she automatically lifted her hips then felt hopelessly shy because her body wasn't as toned and sleek as it had been before she'd had Rosie. The chill of the air made her shiver, which was a convenient excuse to wriggle under the coverlet, dragging it high as Damon stripped off his pants.

When he straightened, she caught her breath at how

beautiful he was with the murky half light turning his skin to bronze and making the trace of scars that crisscrossed his chest seem beautiful in a completely masculine way.

Damon retrieved something from his pants pocket, a condom. She watched as he sheathed himself and the blunt awareness of what they were about to do hit home. Somehow, in the space of one day, they had gone from cool, businesslike distance to passionate lovemaking. The knowledge should have made her feel disoriented and angsty, instead, for the first time in a year, she felt oddly settled and, for want of a better word, happy.

She wasn't yet ready to examine exactly what it was she still felt for Damon. For now, all she wanted was to forget the heartache and loneliness of the past year and simply *feel*. For this one night it was enough that Damon was hers.

Damon joined her in the bed, flipping the coverlet aside as he did so. Zara surreptitiously attempted to drag the sheet over her breasts, but he stymied her plan by pulling her close so that she was half-sprawled against his chest.

Pleasure cascaded through her at the blazing heat of his body, the clean, faintly musky scent of his skin and the automatic, sensual way they fitted together, almost as if more than a year hadn't passed since they had last made love.

"Don't cover yourself," he said quietly. "You're beautiful."

She cupped his jaw, enjoying the faintly abrasive feel of his five o'clock shadow. "It's been a while."

He stopped in the process of trailing his fingers from the small of her back to the curve of her bottom. "No one else?"

She tried to muster up some indignation, but with the slow, enticing stroke of his hands it was hard to concentrate. "Why would there be anyone else? I was pregnant, then having a baby. There was barely time to breathe."

An entirely masculine brand of satisfaction registered in his gaze. "My baby."

He rolled, taking her beneath him. The fiery, seductive heat of Damon's weight pressing her down into the bed made it incredibly difficult to marshal her thoughts. And why would she want to think?

As much as she might deny it, this was what she had missed so much and still craved. The plain fact was that she had never gotten over the attraction that had hit her the very first time she had walked into his office. It was the reason she had slept with Damon in the first place, the reason she had let him back into her life. It was probably also the reason why there had been no other man in her life.

Zara went still inside as a thought she had resolutely suppressed over the last year once again surfaced.

Could she be in love with Damon?

She desperately dismissed the sudden tension that gripped her, because loving Damon was a worst-case scenario...*unless he fell in love with her.*

Suddenly, intensely curious about how he felt, she cupped his face. "Would it have mattered if there was someone else?"

"You were pregnant with my child."

The answer was flat and unequivocal, and sent a sharp thrill through her. Despite being a modern woman, she couldn't help but adore that Damon was possessive of her, even if it was only because she had borne his child. And his response was proof that he felt something genuine, even if only sexual desire.

Although, in her heart of hearts, she didn't want just the desire, she thought fiercely.

She was very much afraid that she *was* falling for Damon, despite all the reasons they should never be in the same room together, let alone in the same bed.

But perhaps making love could create a bond that would hold. And maybe, just maybe, that bond would be strong enough to survive the revelation of her past.

Dipping his head, Damon kissed her. Feeling suddenly acutely vulnerable, Zara gripped his shoulders, arching against the blunt pressure of penetration as he slowly, carefully entered her. When they were fully joined, Damon stopped, his darkened gaze locking with hers.

"Are you sure this is all right? It's not so long since the birth."

With the aching heat of him deep inside her, it was difficult to think. "It's been four months." And before that, nine months. In total it had been thirteen long months since they had last made love. She inhaled at the sensations that gripped her, some familiar, some even more intense than she remembered.

"I'll take it easy."

In answer, she pressed closer still. An agonizing second later, Damon began to move. The heated, stirring pleasure that, lately, had only been a part of her dreams, wound tight, pressing all the air from her lungs until it finally peaked, splintering into the night.

Seven

Damon stirred, awakened by the heavy drumming of rain on the roof and the first stirrings of arousal as Zara trailed her hand down his abdomen. The silky curtain of her hair brushed across his chest as she bent and kissed him slowly and deliberately on the mouth. Her hand slid lower, found him and gently squeezed.

He held on to his control, just. "The last time this happened, I seem to remember we got pregnant."

She waved the foil packet of a condom at him.

"Resourceful."

Long minutes later, Zara collapsed on his chest and he rolled, taking her with him so that they lay sprawled together. The rain had stopped and the wind had dropped, making the night seem almost unnaturally still and quiet.

After long minutes, she readjusted her position, so that her head was snuggled into the curve of his shoulder and neck. One hand trailed over his jaw.

"Do you know why we made love?" she murmured sleepily.

Damon stiffened at the question. "Why?"

Zara yawned. "Can't resist you. It's fate, kismet. Last thing either of us need."

There was a curious, vibrating silence following the slightly slurred pronouncement. But the tension, Damon realized after a few seconds, was his and his alone. Zara didn't require an answer because she had fallen asleep.

She couldn't resist him.

Unbidden, warmth and forbidden delight unfolded in Damon. That was a first, he thought ruefully. But then there had never been anything calculated or pragmatic about making love with Zara. It had always been spontaneous. This time they had actually made it to a bed.

He didn't know about either fate or kismet. He preferred to operate with cool, hard facts. If Zara couldn't resist him, then that dovetailed nicely with his plans for the future…and the undeniable fact that he was having a whole lot of trouble resisting her too.

The next time Damon awoke it was to a small, unfamiliar sound.

Rosie was awake.

He noted the time on the digital clock on the bedside table: three thirty. If he didn't miss his guess, because Rosie was so young, she needed feeding in the night. Carefully disentangling himself from Zara, he found his pants and quickly pulled them on. As he did so, he found himself automatically mulling over Zara's declaration that she couldn't resist him.

Fierce satisfaction filled him at that fact, even though desire itself was uncomfortably akin to the kind of dangerous, unstable emotions he was careful to avoid. If they were going to continue—and now that he had gotten Zara back in his bed, he fully intended they would— he needed to find a way to control the relationship.

Grimly, he noted that the hot, out-of-control sex could have been because he hadn't made love in a year, ever since Zara had left his bed. That fact, in itself, was disturbing.

He had dated a number of beautiful, interesting women. Caroline was a case in point. Any man with red blood cells in his veins would have wanted her, and yet he had not even been vaguely interested in taking her to bed.

Because he had not been able to stop thinking about Zara.

And there was his problem, the same kind of obsessive behavior that had dogged his father, his uncle Tyler and now Ben. The kind of behavior Damon had sworn off all of his adult life and which experience had taught him he could not afford.

Not bothering with a shirt, he stepped out into the hall. It wasn't difficult to find where Rosie slept, since there was only one other bedroom in the cottage.

When he opened the door, it squeaked. Cursing beneath his breath, he checked on Zara, who still seemed to be sleeping deeply, before going to Rosie. The baby waved her arms at him so he picked her up and propped her on one bare shoulder, figuring that was the easiest and most stable way to hold her if he was going to attempt to feed her.

Grabbing a small shawl that was folded over the end of her cot, he draped that across her back in case she got cold, and made his way to the small kitchen. He closed the door, which also squeaked, before switching on the light. Absently, he noted that was two doors that needed oil on their hinges.

He immediately saw that the baby bag sat on the bench. Although he figured that Zara probably had a bottle already prepared in the fridge since she must do regular night feeds.

He opened the door and saw it straight off. Guessing it needed to be warmed, he ran the bottle under hot water for a minute or two. When it was done, he checked the temperature of the milk. He seemed to remember, after visiting friends who had a baby, that the milk needed to be lukewarm, so he tested it by shaking a little onto the back of his hand.

"Seems good to go."

Rosie, who had half twisted around on his shoulder to check what he was doing, made a cooing sound, patted him on the jaw and smiled, flashing the clean edge of one pearly tooth.

Damon was momentarily transfixed by the sight of his daughter's first tooth, his chest swelling with a raw hit of emotion. If he had planned on being distant and disconnected from his daughter, that idea had just crashed and burned.

Opening the kitchen door just enough to allow a sliver of light to flow into the sitting room, he sat in an armchair and attempted to resettle Rosie in the crook of his arm, all while juggling the bottle. But if he had thought Rosie would allow herself to be carefully repositioned while there was a full bottle of milk tantalizingly within reach, he was wrong. She wriggled and squirmed, her gaze zeroing in on the bottle. The instant it got close enough, strong small hands wrapped around the neck and almost wrenched the formula from his grasp.

She drained the milk in sixty seconds flat, spat out the nipple, then with imperiousness attempted to fling the empty bottle away. Damon found himself grinning as he fielded the bottle, placed it on the coffee table and rose to his feet with his daughter in his arms. When he had noticed Rosie's eyes the previous day, he had seen himself, but right now she was *definitely* her mother's daughter.

In that moment he understood how people became so centered on their children that they married when they'd sworn off marriage, and made career U-turns that were detrimental to success. The answer was simple: their priorities changed because they were besotted by the baby.

Rosie's face screwed up, her pale skin flushing. For a heart-stopping moment he thought she was going to cry. He seemed to remember that after Rosie had been fed the previous day, Zara had put her over her shoulder to burp her, so he figured he should do that next.

After circling the small room a couple of times and carefully rubbing her small back, Rosie made a hiccuping sound and spit up on his shoulder. Feeling ridiculously proud that Rosie had burped right on cue, he headed back to the kitchen, found a paper towel and cleaned around her mouth, before blotting the milk from his shoulder.

After disposing of the paper towel in the trash can he found beneath the counter, he carried his daughter back to the sitting room.

"So, what do we do now?"

Rosie patted his jaw again, as if she was fascinated by the roughness of his five o'clock shadow and, at that point, Damon noted a certain sogginess at her rear end.

"Problem solved. We change your diaper."

Rosie made a small crowing sound, as if that was a hilarious idea, so he returned to the kitchen and did a brief search through the baby bag, finding disposable diapers and baby wipes. Walking through to the sitting room, he carefully laid Rosie down on the carpet. Five minutes later, he had the dirty diaper off and the clean diaper fitted. Feeling a sense of achievement, he bagged up the dirty diaper and soiled wipes and placed them in the trash. After washing his hands, he collected a now-sleepy Rosie and carried her back to her room and tucked her into her crib.

After watching her for long minutes to make sure she really had fallen asleep, he walked back to the bedroom. It was four thirty; an hour had passed while he'd fed and changed Rosie. In that time, Zara hadn't moved and still seemed soundly asleep. With effort, he curbed the instinct to get back into bed with her. If he did that, he wouldn't be able to resist making love to her again, which would be counterproductive, given that his first priority had to be control.

Collecting his shirt and shoes, he walked back to the sitting room and finished dressing. He shrugged into his jacket and checked that he had his cell before he let himself out of the house. As he walked down the steps, the next-door neighbor's obnoxiously bright security lights came on.

Damon frowned. If Zara and Rosie were going to stay in the cottage, he would ensure that the motion sensors for those security lights were repositioned so they would no longer be triggered by movement on Zara's property. But, now that he knew Zara was the mother of his child, *now that Zara was back in his bed*, he did not intend for her and Rosie to remain in a suburban cottage with minimal security.

The solution he had arrived at the previous day settled in more firmly.

It was logical, practical and would cut through a whole lot of red tape. It also had the added advantage of nixing dangerously unstable emotions and dampening any media hype.

A marriage of convenience.

Zara's alarm pulled her out of sleep at six thirty.

She groped for the clock. The low buzz ceased and she stared at the numbers that glowed in the pitch dark of early dawn, amazed at the time. By some miracle, Rosie had slept through the night.

Bracing herself, she switched on the bedside lamp. Gold light flooded her room, making her blink and pushing home the reality that she was alone in the bed. Although she had known Damon was gone the second she had reached across the cold expanse of the bed to get to the alarm.

Heated memories cascaded through her, making her blush. Jackknifing, she sat up. Cold air raised gooseflesh on her skin. Shivering, she dragged the quilt up around her chin, because, of course, she was naked, having spent the night making love to Damon. Claiming him physically.

Another memory took center stage. In the moments before she had fallen asleep, she had blurted out something about not being able to resist Damon.

Another wave of embarrassed heat burned through her. She could vaguely remember the silence after she had made her pronouncement, the stiffening of his shoulder beneath her head—probably because he didn't find her irresistible—then nothing more because she had dropped into a deep, dreamless sleep.

Feeling mortified at the way she had exposed a very private weakness, she pushed the thick feather duvet aside and scrambled out of bed. The icy chill of the marble-smooth, polished wood floor struck through her bare feet as she toed on her slippers and quickly wrapped herself in the thick fluffy robe that was hooked on the back of her door.

She shouldn't feel embarrassed, she thought a little desperately. But it was hard to blot out the fact that Damon hadn't responded to her declaration.

Opening her bedroom door, she glanced down the hall and through the sitting room to the kitchen. She tensed when she realized she was looking for Damon on the off chance he was sitting on the couch doing business on his phone or in the kitchen making breakfast.

Of course, Damon wasn't here. His side of the bed had been stone cold; he had been gone for hours. Her mood plummeted even further. He had probably left at a run not long after she had gone to sleep.

She opened Rosie's door. Rosie was still fast asleep. Gently, so as not to wake her, she checked her diaper, which seemed inordinately dry. Frowning, Zara walked through to the kitchen and saw the night feed bottle, which had been rinsed and was sitting on the kitchen counter. A quick check of the trash can confirmed there was also a diaper wrapped in a plastic bag sitting on top.

Clearly, Damon had not left as quickly as she had thought. She closed the cupboard door. The last thing she would have expected was for Damon to feed and change Rosie, but that was exactly what had happened.

Moving on automatic, she put hot water on to boil for tea. She made herself a piece of toast, smeared it with butter and the fig-and-ginger jam she'd made with fruit from the fig tree in the backyard, then prepared a morning feeding for Rosie.

She took a half-hearted bite of the toast, barely tasting it. She guessed she should be happy that Damon was interested in forming a relationship with Rosie, since it was less than a day since he had found out he was a father. But she couldn't help thinking that Damon's interest in her, Zara, was depressingly linked with his focus on his daughter and that any idea that she and Damon could remain lovers was majorly flawed.

First, Damon had shown up at her house not for her, but because he had thought Rosie was ill. Second, yes, he had made love to Zara, but that had probably happened because she had literally thrown herself at him.

Another even more horrifying thought froze her in place. Damon was probably under the impression that since she'd had his baby, and now had managed to get him back into her bed, that she was angling for marriage.

She groaned inwardly and ate some more toast. It was no wonder he had left in the night without waking her. He had come for Rosie's sake and Zara had not only seduced him, but made the silly mistake of revealing how much she wanted him.

Given that Damon had never once said he wanted to be in a committed relationship with her, even when they were first sleeping together, the odds that he did now were bleak. Damon's true motivation in showing up at her house was his caring for Rosie.

Wiping crumbs from her fingers, she carried her plate to the sink and washed and dried it. As she was putting the plate away a brief flash of the kiss they'd shared in her office stopped her in her tracks. She did not know if Damon had known about Rosie at that point, but she had been clear on the fact that he had wanted her.

Closing the cupboard door, she straightened. It was also a fact that Damon had walked back into her life weeks *before* he had known about Rosie. And he hadn't just walked back in, he had pushed his way back into her life, insistently forging a business link and employing people she knew for a fact he did not need. That all pointed to the fact that Damon's desire for her was genuine and persistent.

Feeling suddenly cheered, she wrapped chilled fingers around her gently steaming mug of tea and sipped. There was hope. She just had to hold her nerve and look for the right opportunity to tell him who she was, in such a way that he wouldn't despise her.

Feeling buoyed, she checked on Rosie, who was still sleeping soundly. Zara quickly showered, dried off and wrapped herself in the robe while she searched out something to wear.

Dressing wasn't normally a problem, but today she felt the feminine need to dress for attractiveness as well as for business. Unfortunately, most of her suits were quite plain and, owing to the fact that she had lost a little weight, were becoming a little loose and shapeless.

Happy that her figure had improved, but annoyed at the wardrobe dilemma, she flicked through the closet. Her fingers lingered on an outfit she had worn before she had gotten pregnant.

She pulled out the blue dress and the fitted black jacket that went with it. It was a deceptively simple but gorgeous outfit she hadn't been able to fit into since her pregnancy.

The dress was also soft and warm and extremely comfortable, but would it fit? She held the blue dress against her and stared into the full-length mirror, which was hung on the inside of her closet door. The sapphire blue did great things for her skin, giving it a honey glow and making her eyes look brighter and her hair more lustrous. The dress also had a V neckline, which showed the merest shadow of cleavage, but wasn't too blatant.

After slipping into clean underwear, she pulled on the dress, which—happily—was made of a stretchy, bouclé material. Her figure was still more rounded than it had once been, and her waist wasn't as narrow, but the dress was unexpectedly forgiving. To her surprise the jacket also fitted, cinching in neatly at her waist.

She studied her reflection, her breath momentarily suspended. With her hair still knotted on top of her head from her shower, and dark tendrils clinging to her neck, she looked businesslike, but subtly, classily sexy.

With quick movements, she brushed out her hair and coiled it up into a loose knot, then applied smoky makeup to her eyes and a layer of pink gloss to her mouth.

She had just fitted blue-and-silver earrings to her lobes when Rosie woke up and began crowing happily to herself. Checking her watch and groaning because she was fast running out of time if she wanted to leave early, Zara hurried into Rosie's room.

Rosie stopped crying the instant she spotted her mother, held out her small arms and smiled her wide, gummy smile, which now contained one tiny, gleaming half tooth.

Warmth and a fierce, tender love suffused Zara as she lifted her daughter out of her crib and cuddled her close. Rosie's soft, sweet baby scent rose to Zara's nostrils and the anxious fears around being in a relationship with Damon, if that was even possible, drifted away.

In moments like these, *everything* was worth it—
the months of worry and uncertainty, the solitary birth
without anyone to support her except her midwife. The
effort and frustration of learning all the things a mother
needed to know without her own mother to show her.

Half an hour later, after feeding and changing Rosie
and dressing her in a cute pink playsuit, Zara finally
got Rosie back to sleep in her fleece-lined car seat.
She draped a warm fluffy blanket around her daughter and settled a cute pink beanie on her head so she
would stay cozily asleep. Then Zara carried the car seat
out to the hall.

After propping Rosie's portable crib beside the car
seat, Zara rinsed out the used bottle and put it into the
dishwasher. She checked her watch. Shock reverberated
through her when she saw that it was eight o'clock. If
she wanted to avoid Damon's driver and keep her independence, she needed to leave, *now.*

Moving quickly, she found a pair of black boots that
would go perfectly with the dress and slipped them on.
She zipped the baby bag closed and set it in the hallway, then found her handbag and cell. As she looped
the strap of her handbag over one shoulder, the sound
of a car made her stiffen. She peered through the narrow glass panes of her front door just in time to see a
gleaming black car glide to a halt outside her front gate.

Her heart thumped once, hard. She was too late;
Damon had second-guessed her and sent the car early.

Eight

Feeling distinctly outmaneuvered, Zara tried to check out the driver, but the windows of the car were too darkly tinted.

Another pump of adrenaline made her stomach churn as she noted the kind of car Damon had sent. She had hoped for a taxi, and had been resigned to a company car, but the glossy curves of a long, low sports car did not bode well. It looked like the car Damon had been driving last night. A split second later, Damon climbed out from behind the wheel.

Feeling suddenly vulnerable, she opened the door a split second before Damon could knock and tried not to notice how broodingly masculine he looked in a dark suit teamed with a black V-neck T-shirt. A pair of dark glasses added a remote edge that seemed to negate the intimate things they had done in bed just hours ago.

Movement off to the right caught her eye. Her heart sank when she saw Edna, who, if Zara wasn't mistaken, was in the process of noting Damon's license plate and the make and model of his car.

"I thought you were sending a driver."

"I'm the driver." Damon's glittering gaze swept over her, making her feel acutely conscious of how sexy the blue dress was and the fact that, from his height, he could probably see more than just the hint of cleavage she had noted in the mirror. "I thought we should spend some time together before we go into the office."

Desperate to control the sudden warmth in her cheeks, Zara switched her attention back to Edna, who was now taking down details about Damon himself. No doubt height, weight, hair color and any other distinguishing features.

Although she wouldn't find any of those unless she managed to get Damon naked.

"What do you mean, 'spend some time together'?"

"There's a little café along the waterfront. It's quiet. The coffee's good, and we could walk on the beach, if you want."

In public? A small shudder went through her at the thought that they could get snapped together by a reporter. If that happened, her quiet life of anonymity, and the chance she needed to tell Damon who she was before the media spoiled everything, would be gone. "I don't think that's a good idea."

"We need to talk about Rosie and I'd prefer a more private setting than the office."

Zara noticed a bright blue hatchback driving slowly down the street, as if the driver was searching for an address. The hatchback glided past. Maybe she was being paranoid, but after what had happened yesterday, she could not help the crawling suspicion that the driver was a reporter, in which case, the sooner they left the better.

"A walk on the beach is not a good idea right now," she said hurriedly. "Rosie's sleeping." And if that had been a reporter, they could be followed to the beach. "We should go straight to the office."

Damon lifted a brow. "The sooner you start working, the sooner you can finish up and leave?"

Zara picked up the baby bag and portable crib and handed them to Damon, before collecting Rosie, who was still sound asleep in the car seat. Zara set the car seat down on the step and locked the front door. By the time she'd returned the key to her bag, Damon was back and had picked up the car seat.

Zara hurried after Damon, stepped outside her front gate and stopped dead. Last night when she had seen Damon's car, it had been dark, but now, in the full light of day she realized Damon was driving the same car he'd had when they had been dating.

The very last time they had made love, before she had disappeared, had been in *that* car. Memories she had ruthlessly suppressed unfolded. Her acute emotionalism at being pregnant with Damon's child coupled with her need to be with him just one last time, to store up memories. The awful feeling of emptiness when she had thought she would never see him again.

The car flashed and beeped as Damon unlocked it. "What's wrong?"

Zara quickly smoothed out her expression. Note to self, she thought grimly, if she wanted to conceal her emotions, she needed to get a pair of dark glasses herself.

"Nothing," she said brightly.

She slipped into the front passenger seat while Damon strapped Rosie into the rear. As Damon slid behind the wheel of the Audi, Zara fastened her seat belt, then turned to check on the baby. She noticed a second safety seat, which Damon had installed in the back. A much nicer, more expensive seat than the basic model she had bought.

Suddenly, any notion that Rosie could be just a novelty for Damon evaporated. He must have gone shopping for the seat the previous afternoon. If he had gone to the trouble of buying a car seat, then that meant he was serious about fatherhood.

As Damon pulled away from the curb, Zara sank back into the luxurious seat. "I don't mind accepting a lift today, but in the future, I would prefer to take my own car to work."

Damon braked for a traffic light before accelerating through an intersection and joining the flow of cars heading for the central city. "If you want to drive your car to work, you can have Ben's parking space."

She glared at Damon. "You could have let me use that today!"

His gaze, still frustratingly masked by the dark glasses, connected with hers. "I didn't want to risk you not turning up for work."

"I agreed to work for you. I honor my agreements."

Damon stopped for another light, this one in the busy hub of downtown. "You walked out on me a year ago."

She dragged her gaze from the taut cut of Damon's cheekbones, the clean line of his jaw. Her heart was pounding again, but this time for an entirely different reason. It suddenly occurred to her that no employer manipulated and then personally drove an employee to work because they couldn't risk them not showing up. Certainly not a billionaire like Damon.

And he had refused to accept just any assistant;

Damon had wanted *her*. He wanted her in his bed *and* at his work.

She was abruptly certain that whatever Damon was feeling, it wasn't just sexual attraction.

Her mood soared. Suddenly, Damon wanting her *as a person*, maybe even falling for her, seemed... possible.

Minutes later, using a key card to gain entrance, dim shadow swamped the car as Damon took the ramp down into the underground garage of his building. Zara's stomach did a nervous flip at the sheer familiarity of the garage as Damon removed his sunglasses, killed the engine and exited the Audi.

Before he could walk around the front of the car and help her out, Zara hurriedly unfastened her seat belt, collected her handbag and swung the door of the sleek, low car wide.

As she exited the car and straightened, she found herself close enough to Damon that when she inhaled she caught the clean scent of his skin, the utterly familiar tang of his cologne. In the dimness of the garage the impact of his gaze made her breath catch in her throat. Yesterday she would have kept her manner neutral and breezed past him, but today was a new world.

Hooking the strap of her bag over her shoulder, she allowed Damon to close the door with a *thunk*. Before she could lose her nerve, she met his gaze. "Thanks for being so understanding about Rosie. The last thing I wanted was for you to feel trapped into fatherhood." And trapped into a relationship with her.

Balancing herself by resting one palm on his shoulder, she lifted up on her toes to kiss him on the cheek.

Damon cupped her neck, stopping her from stepping back. The heat of his palm burned into her skin as, slowly and deliberately, he bent his head and kissed her on the mouth.

Long seconds later, her legs feeling as limp as noodles, she stumbled back a half step. It occurred to her that while the garage was a secure one, it did still service a number of clients.

"Maybe we shouldn't kiss in public," she said a little breathlessly. As soon as she said the words she realized that Damon would pick up on the clear implication that he could continue to kiss her in private.

Surprise and a glint of masculine satisfaction registered in his gaze as he caught her close and kissed her again. The kind of kiss shared by couples who were not just lovers, but who were in a real relationship. Couples who liked one another. The very nature of it filled Zara with hope because she was certain that in the past few minutes they had turned some kind of corner.

As he released her, Zara noticed a blue-suited janitor and froze. As quiet as their conversation had been, in the cavernous garage it had echoed. From his frozen posture, the janitor had heard every word.

Zara's breath froze in her throat as he disappeared from sight behind a large concrete pillar. For a split second she tried to buy into the fantasy that maybe the janitor hadn't heard. And if he had, who would he tell, anyway?

Potentially everyone.

Now thoroughly rattled, the warm sense of togetherness with Damon splintered, Zara freed Rosie from her car seat and lifted her out. As she straightened, in her hurry, the back of her head caught the frame of the Audi's door, which was lower than that of her own car. She winced and straightened. As she did so, her bag, which she'd hooked over her shoulder, flopped to the ground, sending items scattering.

Damon steadied her. "Babe, are you all right?"

Muttering that she was fine, Zara clutched Rosie's warm, soft little body securely against her own and rubbed at the sore patch.

Babe. The surprise of the endearment was so distracting that Zara forgot she'd dropped her handbag and stepped back. Something crunched beneath her heel.

Her mood plummeted even further. That would be her phone. A little awkwardly, she retrieved it. A cracked screen, and the insides were undoubtedly mashed too. It would be a miracle if it ever worked again.

Before she could pick up any other items, Damon collected the keys and compact that had scattered, dropped them into her bag and handed the bag to her. Seconds later, he collected Rosie's things, locked the car and indicated the elevator. "If you're worried about the phone, don't be. I was giving you a company phone in any case."

Zara walked into the familiar private elevator. As Damon joined her, the feeling of disorientation that she was actually returning to work for Damon intensified.

The first person Zara saw as she stepped into the foyer was Howard Prosser, Damon's office manager. Howard's look of surprise that Zara was holding a baby informed her that Damon had been true to his word. If he hadn't confided the fact that Rosie was his child to Howard, then he hadn't told anyone.

Zara adjusted her grip on Rosie, who was becoming restless, and tried to look as if her relationship with Damon was as casual and incidental as Howard clearly thought it to be.

Damon glanced at a file Howard handed him. "Zara's just filling in for a few days, until the McCall takeover is complete."

Howard looked distinctly grumpy. "That's not likely to happen unless you track down whoever has that block of missing voting shares."

Damon's palm briefly cupped her elbow as he urged her toward the door to her old office. The small, proprietorial touch sent a small thrill of awareness through her.

"A rival firm's been buying shares," he explained as he set the baby bag and portable crib down behind the desk. "That wouldn't be a problem except that ten percent of the voting shares are held by an anonymous shareholder, something that should never have happened. The net result is we've been having difficulty securing a majority of the stock."

Zara set her handbag down beside the desk. "Why shouldn't the shares be held by an anonymous shareholder? Surely that happens all the time."

"Not with voting shares. And these were Tyler's personal shares. By rights they should have remained in the family, since they guaranteed the majority vote. At some point, and for some reason I can't fathom, he must have sold them. We'd buy them back but, unfortunately, there's no record of the transaction."

Zara shifted Rosie from one arm to another and became immediately aware that the baby needed a diaper change. As she rummaged in the baby bag for a changing pad and a diaper, Rosie wriggled and craned around and sent Damon a smile that was literally blinding. She held out her arms as if she had already recognized that Damon was her daddy.

Damon lifted a brow. "May I?"

"She needs a diaper change."

"If that's supposed to frighten me, you're failing."

"Because you're already an old hand at it, having changed her diaper last night."

Damon's gaze caught hers. "I figured you could use the sleep."

Zara's cheeks burned as she considered exactly why she had needed the sleep and, with an odd reluctance, because up until now Rosie had been solely hers, she allowed Damon to take his daughter. As he balanced Rosie against one broad shoulder, his hand cradling her head, Zara experienced a curious sinking feeling in the pit of her stomach. She should look away, she thought a little desperately, except that she couldn't. There was something about Damon cradling Rosie that was utterly mesmerizing.

With effort, she dragged her gaze from the too-fascinating juxtaposition of Rosie's cute pink beanie and the tough line of Damon's jaw and concentrated on laying the changing pad out on the desk. While Damon was dealing with the dirty diaper, she found baby wipes, ointment and a plastic bag.

When Rosie was freshly changed, Damon picked her up as if she was a fragile piece of porcelain, hugged her close for a few seconds, then handed her back to Zara. "By the way, I've received confirmation that Ben and Emily are on Medinos, staying at a house we own there. I've arranged to fly out in the company jet and talk to Ben."

Sudden crashing disappointment hit Zara. A trip to Medinos and back meant Damon would be away for the best part of four days. When she didn't know how much time they had before the media discovered Damon had a daughter, four days was an eternity.

"Can't you just talk to Ben on the phone?"

"He would have to answer his phone for that to happen." Damon walked to the windows and stared out at the view as if he was mulling something over. When he turned, the morning light threw his face into shadow. "Since it'll be a working trip," he said quietly, "I want you and Rosie to come with me."

As shocking as the idea of flying overseas anywhere with Damon was, the idea of going to Medinos irresistibly appealed. For one thing, because she'd been absent for so long it wasn't likely that she'd be recognized. And the trip could prove a lifeline because it would buy her more time with Damon away from the Auckland reporters. It would also allow her to check out her mother's safe-deposit box. Added to that, traveling in the Magnum company jet would cost her nothing.

A cautious sense of relief gripped her. Could it be, after so much had gone wrong with her life, that her luck had finally turned? "Okay."

Damon didn't try to hide his disbelief. "You agree?"

"Either way I'll still be working, and at least it'll stop that nosy reporter from sniffing around." Zara struggled to keep her expression bland when what she really wanted to do was give in to the relief and either grin or cry. She checked her watch and saw it was time for Rosie's feeding. She grabbed at the excuse to do something, anything, that would distract her from revealing to Damon just how important it was for her to get to Medinos.

Frowning, Damon perched on one corner of the desk as she made a production of finding the insulated container that held Rosie's bottle.

"There's just one glitch—we'll need to get Rosie a passport. Walter can probably pull some strings and get one in a day or—"

"Rosie already has a passport." Zara could feel her cheeks burning as she directed what she hoped was a matter-of-fact smile in Damon's direction. As if it wasn't at all unusual for a four-month-old baby to have a passport. As if they hadn't been planning to go to Medinos all along. "When do we leave?"

There was a small silence during which the sounds of the office registered: a phone ringing, the low burr of Howard's voice, the tapping of a keyboard.

Damon checked his watch, his expression oddly grim. "The only holdup would have been getting Rosie a passport. Since you've taken care of that already, I'll call the flight crew. We leave this afternoon."

Nine

An hour later Damon gave up on his efforts to call Ben, who had clearly turned his phone off, or more probably thrown it into the deep blue Mediterranean Sea.

He paced to the enormous glass doors that stretched the length of one entire wall in his office. The heavy cloud from last night had gone and the day was clear and dry, the sun sparkling on the harbor and gleaming off the glossy, expensive yachts tied up in the viaduct. But the view, spectacular as it was, barely impinged on his thoughts. At this point, even Ben was the least of his problems.

Zara had gotten Rosie a passport.

There was no point doing that unless Zara had intended to leave the country with Rosie. Disappearing from sight again as she had tried to do just over a year ago.

Broodingly, he considered that maybe Zara had only

wanted to take a vacation? The problem with that scenario was that he knew Zara didn't have that kind of money. Walter had made a few discreet inquiries, so Damon knew that in financial terms, Zara was struggling to keep her head above water. The fact was, *he* had been propping up her finances for months, by hiring people he didn't need.

If Zara couldn't afford a holiday there was only one scenario left, she had been planning on leaving the country with Rosie and, in the process, *leaving him*.

But why start a new business if she was planning on emigrating? None of it made sense.

With sudden decision, he walked through to Walter's office. "I need you to run a security check on Zara."

Walter looked up from a thick legal pad on which he was making notes. "Didn't we do that last year?"

"Not in depth." Since Zara was fresh out of college, he had just asked for a standard check, which was relatively superficial, establishing whether or not there were any criminal convictions or debt issues that might compromise business loyalties, checking that qualifications and references were authentic. Since Zara had just graduated with an honors degree, and had been referred by a business acquaintance, an in-depth check had seemed like overkill.

"What exactly are you worried about?" Walter's gaze narrowed. "The baby's not yours."

"Rosie's mine."

Walter gave him a bland look. "Knew it as soon as I saw her."

Despite his irritation, Damon had to stop himself from grinning. "That obvious?"

"'Fraid so." Walter shook his head. "At least the baby

explains why Zara left. Although it still doesn't really add up."

Damon's brows jerked together. "Explain."

"Disclosure. It's big with women."

Damon waited for more; when it didn't come he kept a grip on his irritation. "Walter, you're going to have to use more words."

Walter sat back in his chair. "Margot made me join this group for men who have difficulty communicating—"

"I thought Margot liked the strong, silent type."

Walter gave him a stony look. "Do you want to hear this or not? According to the group facilitator, women actually like to talk about their emotional lives. It's called disclosure. Darned irritating and a waste of time if you ask me, but Margot has got some bee in her bonnet because, *apparently*, I don't discl—"

"Let's take it back to Zara."

Walter blinked as if he'd just returned from a dark place. "Okay. Simple equation. Zara was in love with you, so, being a woman, she should have told you about the pregnancy."

Damon's chest locked up. He felt like he'd just been kicked by a mule. "What makes you think Zara was in love with me?"

Walter gave him an "are you serious?" look. "Zara has all the raw materials of a sergeant major or a general. She could organize a war. So, it figures, why else would she let down her guard and sleep with you if she wasn't, you know, *in love*?"

Damon's jaw tightened on a complex surge of emotions—heat, raw possessiveness, unaccountable relief. An hour ago, any idea that Zara was in love with him would have had him warily backing off. But that was before she had calmly admitted that she already had a passport for Rosie. The passport was a game changer because it signaled that Zara and Rosie were leaving, and he did not want that to happen.

"So why do you think, if Zara was in love with me, that she didn't 'disclose' the pregnancy?"

Walter looked reflective. "Zara's a decisive woman. Maybe she just got tired of you." He nodded his head. "Yep, that's a pretty clear-cut reason for leaving."

Damon restrained his irritation with difficulty. He could see why Margot had sent Walter to counseling. "She didn't get tired of me."

Walter drummed his fingers on the desk. "I guess, since she's back."

Damon's jaw tightened. *And* she still wanted him.

"Which is why I need that security check. ASAP."

Given Walter's summation of Zara's character, which was startlingly accurate, Zara's contention that she had left him because she didn't think he would want her in his wealthy, successful life now seemed both wimpy and implausible.

There had to be another reason.

That meant she was hiding something. Something important.

Several frantic hours later, Zara boarded Damon's private jet, carrying Rosie. A uniformed steward followed, carrying the baby bag and all of Zara's and Rosie's luggage.

Since Zara had only ever worked for Damon for a few weeks, she had never seen the jet, which was unashamedly luxurious, with spacious cabin seating and a well-appointed bathroom and sleeping cabin at the rear.

Damon stepped into the cabin, instantly dwarfing the

compact space. His cool gaze briefly connected with hers, leaving her feeling oddly confused, because the warmth of that morning seemed to have disappeared. He tossed his jacket over the back of a leather seat and chatted with the steward, whose name was Mark.

Predictably, Mark was an older man with a lean, muscled physique and a somewhat grizzled face marred by what looked like a serious burn scar on one side. She had no doubt whatsoever that this was another of Damon's ex-soldiers.

As Zara tried to settle Rosie, enough that she could put the baby down to sleep in the portable crib Damon had sent ahead, the door to the flight deck popped open. Zara expected another ex-army type would have the job of pilot. Instead, a stunning blonde wearing a crisp flight uniform stepped into the cabin.

Zara continued to rock Rosie on her shoulder as the blonde introduced herself as Buffy McNamara, the pilot. Buffy lifted a hand at Damon, her polite smile transforming into a sparkling grin. Her casual "Hey, Damon" made Zara tense up inside.

Rosie chose that moment to spit up on Zara's shoulder. Feeling distracted and out of sorts, Zara searched for some baby wipes.

When Damon didn't end the conversation with Buffy, but showed every evidence of enjoying the exchange, even down to calling her Mac—the first part of her surname, and obviously some kind of extra special pet name—Zara's tension coalesced into annoyance. She was busy trying to untie Rosie's bib. What she really wanted to do was frog-march *Mac* back to the flight deck and tell her to stay there.

Jaw taut, Zara located a laundry bag and jammed the soiled bib inside it. She knew what the problem was.

She was jealous, horribly jealous, although she could not afford to let Damon know that.

Damon took the seat next to her and dragged at his tie. "Is there something wrong?"

Zara found herself snared in the net of his gaze. Adrenaline zinged through her and her heart sped up. She took a deep breath and attempted a smile. "Rosie's just a little unsettled, that's all."

At that moment Buffy strolled by on her way back to the flight deck. She paused by Damon's seat and beamed at Rosie. "Cute baby. If you need help settling her, Mark can give you a hand. In fact, you could think about moving her into the bedroom at the rear—it's quieter there and she might sleep better."

And no doubt with Rosie tidily out of sight and out of Damon's sleek, high-powered executive space, the flight would go more smoothly for the boss.

Zara fought another unreasoning spurt of annoyance. Buffy couldn't know that Rosie was Damon's daughter because they'd agreed to keep that a secret for now. "Thanks, that's a good idea, but I think Rosie will be happier here in the cabin with me."

When Buffy strode through the door of the flight deck Zara glimpsed the copilot, who *was* an older military type, just before the door closed.

Damon, his gaze tinged with amusement, offered to take Rosie. Feeling embattled, Zara handed over the baby and Rosie settled like a lamb on his shoulder.

Mark, who was busy stowing bags, looked bemused. "Hidden talents, Damon?"

"Looks like." Damon patted Rosie on the back, but he scarcely needed to because she had already fallen asleep.

Minutes later, Damon lowered Rosie into the crib and

tucked a cotton blanket around her. Zara busied herself zipping the baby bag closed before stowing it beneath the seat closest to the crib. She searched through her handbag and found her phone so she could check and see if Molly, who had agreed to work full-time in the agency until Zara got back, had sent her any last-minute texts. There were none, which was a relief—

"You should come and sit down."

The low timbre of Damon's voice made her tense. She took a deep breath and tried to calm down, but despite the good talking-to she had given herself, she was still terminally annoyed at the way he had flirted with Buffy. The kind of conversation that underlined the fact that despite Rosie, despite them sleeping together *again*, she had absolutely no claim on Damon at all.

Slipping her phone back into her handbag, she took her seat and snapped open the magazine she had bought for the flight and found herself staring at a page filled with photographs of women dressed for glamorous occasions. Caroline Grant was center stage, wearing the exact same dress she had worn to the charity gala she had attended with Damon.

Zara stuffed the magazine into her bag.

"You don't have to be jealous of Mac," Damon said quietly.

Zara fastened her seat belt with a crisp click. "I'm not jealous," she muttered, keeping her voice equally low, so that Mark, who was seated at the rear of the cabin, couldn't hear. "Although I guess Buffy *is* blonde, and you do seem to have this thing for blondes."

"You're not blonde."

The jet picked up speed before leaving the ground.

Zara's stomach tightened automatically as they gained height.

"And neither am I your date." She made the mistake of turning her head and was instantly ensnared by the molten silver of Damon's gaze.

"You were last night."

Heat flooded her along with a raft of memories she had been working hard to suppress and which now, literally, welded her to the seat.

"Mac is the wife of a friend. She was in the air force, part of the crew attached to our Special Forces group. She married one of the team, Brendan McNamara, which is why she goes by the nickname Mac."

Relief surged through Zara, making her feel a little shaky and ridiculously happy. Happy that Buffy/Mac was just a friend, but even happier that Damon had been considerate enough to reassure Zara. It seemed to signal another positive turn in their relationship.

"I wasn't going to do this right now," Damon murmured with an odd flatness to his voice, "but now that we're in the air and you can't walk out on me, I have a proposition for you."

Zara tensed. "A proposition?"

"As in marriage. We have a daughter. We're good together. It won't be a marriage in the usual sense, but I think what we have is workable."

Not a marriage in the usual sense... Workable.

Zara wondered if she'd just time warped back to the nineteenth century. "Let me get this right. You're proposing a marriage—with sex—on the basis that we have a child?"

She drew a deep breath. The conditions he was offering were businesslike but more than a little hurtful. In a blinding moment of clarity she understood why. It

was because a 'workable' marriage of convenience was
the absolute opposite of what she wanted.

*Because somehow, despite everything, she had fallen
in love with Damon.*

For a split second her heart seemed to stop in her
chest. When it started up again, it pounded so hard she
could barely breathe.

"I think you know by now that I'd like to, but I...
need some time."

Because there was no way she could agree to an engagement, no matter how much she longed to. Not until
he knew who she really was.

And once he knew that, he probably wouldn't want
to marry her.

Ten

When Zara exited Damon's private jet, it was night. She didn't think she would be recognizable as Petra Hunt's daughter on Medinos, since it had been years since she was last here, but even so, she took precautions.

As she stepped onto the tarmac outside the terminal, she fished in her handbag and pulled out the white ball cap she had bought before boarding the flight. She had bought it expressly because it matched her white linen shirt and she could pull the bill of the cap down low over her forehead so the upper half of her face was shaded.

They stepped into the terminal and waited to clear customs. Zara relaxed a little when she noticed groups of tired tourists, a couple of people with high-visibility vests and uniformed officials, but no one resembling either a journalist or photographer.

She sent Damon a brilliant smile and tried not to notice how gorgeous and natural he looked with Rosie over his shoulder. She glanced anxiously around for their luggage. "Mark's taking a long time with the suitcases."

Damon gave her an odd look. "It's only been fifteen minutes."

Just then Mark appeared, trundling some kind of prehistoric cart with all the luggage from the flight, including that of the flight crew, who would be staying on the island until Damon and Zara were ready to fly back.

Despite the fact that it was night, it seemed to have gotten even steamier. She wiggled her toes in her white sneakers, which had been perfectly comfortable on the flight, but which were now hot and sticky.

Damon glanced at her hat as they collected their luggage. "Aren't you hot in that cap?"

Beneath the cap she was pretty sure her hair was already wet and plastered to her scalp. That was the second reason she wasn't taking it off. "It's not that hot."

"It's got to be over ninety degrees."

"I like the cap."

Damon lifted a hand to his mouth. It could have been an innocent gesture, but as Zara wheeled her case to the customs line she was pretty sure Damon had the nerve to think something about her cap was amusing. She sucked in a lungful of damp, warm air, feeling irritated because she longed to fling the blasted thing off. Her hair was already thick; the cap just added an extra sweltering layer. She caught Damon's gaze on her again as he joined her and this time she was sure he was laughing.

"I guess Rosie's going to be just like this."

"Just like *what*?"

"Frustrating. Cute."

There was a moment of vibrating silence during

which Zara found it increasingly difficult to breathe. The moment was broken as the line moved forward to the customs desk. Zara dragged the hat off and quickly tried to finger comb her hair, which did feel horribly flattened and damp. The cooling relief was only momentary because a pair of dark, vaguely familiar eyes met hers. She froze like a deer caught in the headlights. Jorge—the son of her mother's gardener, Aldo—who now clearly worked for airport customs, was looking at her as if he had seen a ghost.

Before he could open his mouth and say the only name he had ever known her by—*Angel*—she shook her head. His eyes widened perceptibly, but he seemed to get the message, because his gaze swiveled to Damon.

Groaning, she kept her head down, and Jorge whisked her through customs so quickly she barely had time to look around and log the changes. The last time she had been on Medinos, the airport had been on the small side and lacking in amenities. Now it was considerably larger and more complicated, with a sophisticated set of duty-free shops attached.

Half an hour later, they arrived at the hotel, an old but sumptuous building that looked like it had once been a palace of some sort, with gorgeous tiled floors, jewel-like water features and lavish displays of white roses and trailing star jasmine.

The suite Damon had booked was on the sixth floor. It was was breathtakingly luxurious, with three bedrooms, two reception rooms, a study and a fully equipped kitchen.

Feeling a little off balance that Damon had booked a multiroomed suite rather than two separate suites, as if they were already a family, Zara stowed Rosie's things in one of the rooms. When the bellhop had gone, and

Rosie was tucked into bed, Damon opened the French doors that led out onto a stone balcony. He threaded his fingers with hers, sending a sharp pulse of awareness through her as he pulled her outside.

As distracted as she was by Damon standing beside her, muscular and relaxed in a white T-shirt and jeans, as problematic as being on Medinos was, Zara couldn't help but drink in the view.

The stars were out, along with a silver half-moon. Whitewashed buildings, bleached by moonlight, with their dark, terra-cotta tiled roofs, tumbled down to the bay below. In the distance, she could make out the promontory, with its cluster of villas that used to be home.

Out of nowhere, her throat closed up. She hadn't realized how much she had missed Medinos, missed having a place to truly call home. Added to that, since her mother had died, she hadn't been able to afford to come back. This would be her first opportunity to visit Petra's grave.

"It's...beautiful."

Damon plucked the cap from her head and tossed it over the balcony.

Utterly surprised, Zara yelped. She had no time to grab for the cap; all she could do was watch as it sailed down to the gardens below.

Damon tugged at her fingers, coaxing her in close. "That's better." His fingers tangled in her hair. "Your hair is too gorgeous to hide. Never wear that cap again."

Terminally annoyed, because she *needed* that cap, Zara's palms landed on his chest. Although, as annoyed as she was, a renegade part of her loved that he had pulled her close and didn't want to push him away. "That hat was *mine*."

His expression turned rueful. "I suppose you'll just go out and buy another one."

"I don't need to—I've got a spare in my suitcase."

He shrugged and released her. "Okay, wear it if you want. Just not around me."

In the instant he let her go, contrarily, she didn't want to be free. Taking the half step needed to bring her close again, she wound her arms around his neck in a loose hold.

She was aware that she was playing with fire, but she couldn't resist. Something had changed with Damon, and she couldn't put her finger on quite what it was, except that he seemed suddenly extremely confident of her.

"I'm interested. What else am I not allowed to wear around you?"

"Clothing. Of any sort."

With a grin, Damon swept her into his arms and carried her to a sumptuous master bedroom. He tumbled her onto the very large bed, which looked like it had been made for an entire family.

A little breathlessly, Zara watched as Damon peeled out of his shirt and pants. Lit by the golden glow of a single lamp, she decided that with his broad shoulders and olive-toned skin, the black hair and tough jaw, he looked remarkably like one of the Templar knights depicted in a Medinian oil painting she had once seen.

He came down on the bed beside her and propped himself on one elbow. He ran one finger down her throat to the first button of her shirt, popping it open. "Now you."

Her breath dammed in her throat at his playful streak, which was new and unexpectedly precious because it seemed to signal the kind of intimacy she hadn't dared hope for. She climbed from the bed and began to undress, but when she got down to her bra and panties her nerve gave out, and she clambered back onto the vast bed, making up for her sudden shyness by straddling him.

Damon pulled her so that she sprawled across his chest. "That's it?"

She cupped his jaw, the clean scent of his skin making her clench her stomach. "Uh-huh. I'm not *that* experienced at this."

Damon went oddly still. "What, exactly, are you saying?"

She frowned because when they had first made love she had expected him to *know*. When he hadn't mentioned anything, she had kept the knowledge to herself because the relationship was so new and she hadn't wanted him to think she was trying to tie him to her.

Before she could actually say it, he muttered something short and flat beneath his breath. "You were a virgin."

She traced the line of his mouth with the pad of her thumb and tried to make light of it She hadn't consciously set out to stay a virgin; she had just never met anyone she actually wanted to make love with until Damon. Petra's death and the problems with the media hadn't helped. Zara had basically retreated into her shell and stayed there.

She shrugged. "It doesn't matter now. But I'm glad that you know." Then, even if the worst happened and he hated her for being Petra's daughter, he would at least know that the tabloids had lied about her.

He caught her fingers in his and pulled them to his lips. "I'm sorry I missed that moment, babe. But I'm glad you've only ever been mine."

Babe. Happiness seemed to expand inside her as he rolled so that she was beneath him. But despite the heat that shimmered through her, despite the coiling tension that was already making it hard to breathe, let alone think, a tiny thought niggled. "What about you?"

Damon had dispensed with her bra, now he cupped her breasts, his palms faintly abrasive against her tender skin. His thumbs swept across her nipples, making it difficult to concentrate on what was, suddenly, a very important question.

His gaze captured hers. "What do you mean, what about me?"

She drew in a sharp breath as he took the nipple of one breast into his mouth. "I mean, Caroline."

Damon moved and she lifted her hips to assist him as he peeled down her panties. "Remember that reporter who came to your office?"

Zara drew in a sharp breath as Damon parted her legs with his thigh. She tried to think, but with his muscular weight now pressing her down into the mattress, her normally excellent memory had deserted her. "Um… Red Glasses."

Damon grinned and rewarded her with a kiss, which sent a ridiculously happy glow through her.

"Vanessa Gardiner. She was a friend of Caroline's. Why do you think Caroline put a reporter on my tail?"

Zara tried to gather her thoughts, but with the enticing pressure between her legs and the heated ache low in her belly, it was difficult to think of anything but how long it was going to take Damon to actually start making love to her. "I give up."

Damon's darkened gaze pinned her. "Caroline wanted to know who I was sleeping with."

Understanding finally dawned. "Because you weren't

sleeping with her." She swallowed, feeling suddenly, unexpectedly teary. "That means—"

"I haven't slept with anyone else."

Feeling just the tiniest bit fierce and possessive, she coiled her arms around his neck and pulled him close, relieved when he finally began entering her. When he was fully sheathed, she wrapped her legs around his hips, trying to pull him closer still.

She thought she had already felt everything she was going to feel with Damon, that nothing could be more intense and more meaningful than the lovemaking they had already shared. But as they began making slow, exquisite love to each other she discovered she had been wrong.

The knowledge that he had been celibate for the last thirteen months changed things. It made the deep, lasting love she craved with Damon seem possible. As she kissed him back, touched him back, with every breath, suddenly the night was alive with emotions that shimmered and burned, melded and entwined...

Zara awoke to sun streaming through the French doors and Rosie patting her cheek. A little startled that she had slept so late and that Damon had taken charge of Rosie, Zara shifted up in the bed, pulling the linen sheets around her breasts as she cuddled her daughter.

Damon looked gorgeous in light jeans and a white T-shirt, his phone to one ear. He terminated the call, bent down and kissed her on the mouth.

"Stay in bed and rest. I'm driving out to the house to talk to Ben. Rosie's had her breakfast, so if you like, I can take her with me. I'll only be a couple of hours at most, and Mark ordered a car with tinted windows and a car seat, so she'll be safe *and* incognito."

Zara watched, a faint lump in her throat, as Damon strapped on the front pack and neatly fitted a gurgling Rosie into the cushioned frame. He seemed to be an expert at the fatherhood thing already. But she was all too aware after Damon's revelation and the fact that they seemed poised on the brink of a real relationship that the bubble of happiness she was presently living in could burst at any moment.

She needed to tell Damon the truth today.

Zara showered and dressed in an ice-blue dress that made the most of her tan. Humming beneath her breath, she sat at the exquisite antique dressing table to do her hair. As she coiled the heavy, glossy strands into a knot on top of her head and began sliding in pins, she couldn't help noticing that she looked *different*. She had heard women speak of glowing when they were in love. She was glowing. Her eyes were alight, her skin radiant, her mouth softly curved.

She applied minimal makeup, fitted earrings and did a final check of her appearance. She had a floppy-brimmed hat to wear, but at the last minute decided she was over the hat idea. She dragged a pair of large sunglasses out of her handbag instead. *Good!* With the sunglasses hiding her eyes and her cheekbones, she barely recognized herself.

She checked her watch. Damon wouldn't be long. If she was going to visit Petra's grave, see her mother's lawyer, then go to the bank to see what, exactly, Petra had stashed in the safe-deposit box—if anything—she needed to hurry.

She bought an armful of pretty flowers from a street vendor, then took a taxi to the local cemetery, which was situated on the windblown side of a hill overlooking the sea. Finding Petra's grave was easy, because she was buried near the ancient stone chapel, right beside Zara's father. Chest tight, her throat locked, Zara gently laid the flowers down. She hadn't quite known how she was going to feel, but there was a wild beauty about the hillside and the stone cross of the chapel etched against blue sky, a curious sense of peace and closure.

A few minutes later, the taxi delivered her to the address on the last letter she had received from her mother's legal firm. The white limestone building was situated on one of the steep, narrow streets that were a feature of Medinos.

She stepped out of the glaring heat of the sun into the inky well of shade offered by the foyer. She stopped by the front desk, and the receptionist, who was on a call, put the phone down. Before she could show Zara to Takis's office, a plump, balding man with a rumpled suit stepped out of a door.

The receptionist spoke in rapid Medinian. Zara heard her own name and realized she was looking at her mother's lawyer.

Takis stared at her for a long moment. "You do not look like your mother."

Tell me about it. "Nevertheless, I am Petra Hunt's daughter."

He held his door open with discernible reluctance. Jaw set, Zara walked into the small, rather messy office.

"Please, take a seat. What can I do for you?"

"I would like to view my mother's file."

"You know she signed the prenuptial—"

"I'm not worried about that." She attempted a smooth smile. "It's the offer by the McCall estate that I'm really interested in."

Takis frowned. "I don't understand. I sent you a copy—"

"I burned it."

There was a moment of taut silence. Takis walked to a wall of files, searched for what seemed an age before pulling out a folder. The chair behind his desk squeaked as he sat down. He flipped open the file, turned it around and pushed it across the desk toward her.

Zara skimmed the document, turned a page and froze. Damon's signature seemed to leap off the page. When she had originally received the offer, she hadn't paid much attention to the signature. Since then, a part of her had hoped it hadn't been Damon who had signed it, that it actually had been some faceless lawyer.

"May I have a copy of this?"

Minutes later, still feeling numb because Damon had been the architect of that horrible offer after all, Zara strolled down the steep street and into the bustling center of Medinos. The midday heat poured down as she crossed at a busy intersection, thronged with holiday-makers, but she barely noticed the swarms of brightly colored tourists.

Feeling suddenly thirsty, she stopped at a small café and bought one of Medinos's signature drinks, an enticing cordial of plum and lemon poured over shaved ice that quickly dissolved in the heat.

The bank her mother had used was easy enough to find. An entirely new tension hummed through her as she took in the high-vaulted ceilings, plaster frescoes and elegant marble floor. A pretty bank clerk directed her to an office that opened off the reception area. A trim, darkly suited clerk checked Zara's ID and the copy of Petra's will she had brought with her before escorting her down an echoing corridor. He entered a code into a thoroughly modern keypad and waited for her to precede him into another room.

A guard seated at a desk asked to see her key. He took note of the number and disappeared into an adjacent room. Seconds later, he appeared with a key, then opened a steel door into the vault and indicated she follow him. Zara watched as he unlocked a steel compartment and pulled out a long, narrow steel box, which he laid on a small table. Nodding politely, he withdrew, leaving her in privacy to unlock the box.

Out of nowhere, her heart began to pound.

When her mother had died, Zara had been thousands of miles away and had not had the funds to get back for the funeral. A model friend of her mother's had packed up Petra's things and freighted them to Zara. Opening those boxes and sorting through her mother's clothes and personal effects had been the only ritual left to her. That was possibly why she was now unbearably aware that the last time this safe-deposit box had been opened, it had been by her mother.

Petra had stood in this same sterile room while she placed whatever it was that she had held most precious in the narrow steel box. Emotion swelled in Zara's chest—a sudden, powerful sense of connection with the mother she had lost, emotions she had avoided because losing Petra had cut the ground from under her. Despite their differences they had always been a pair—two against the world.

Taking a deep breath, she inserted the key, turned it and opened the box. She instantly recognized the faded leather cases that held Atrides family jewelry; she had seen them often enough as a child. After lifting them out, she opened them, emotion swelling as she looked at the pretty collection of French brooches and pendants, the huge old-fashioned cameo her great-grandmother had worn with a black bombazine dress.

Her fingers brushed against a small black velvet bag. She loosened the cord and emptied the contents into the palm of her hand. Not jewelry as she had expected, but a glittering cascade of diamonds; single stones of varying sizes, all of them glowing with an expensive fire.

Once, over a glass of wine, Petra had alluded to her *life savings*. She hadn't said what the savings were exactly. Zara had thought she was talking about money, but the amount in Petra's bank accounts had been too small to qualify as savings of any sort. Now she knew that her mother had been referring to this cache of diamonds, her hedge against the hard times that would come when her looks faded.

Heart thumping, she poured the diamonds into the pouch like so much liquid fire and carefully retied the cord. Her mother hadn't lived long enough to need the money the diamonds would bring. But Zara was certain Petra would love it that her *savings* would be put to good use, and not just for a deposit on a house—she would buy the whole thing.

The final items in the box were a plain white envelope, a solitaire engagement ring, a gold wedding ring worn thin over the years and a silver cross that she recognized as once belonging to her father.

Zara's throat closed up as she extracted the jewelry that had been the intimate, personal belongings of her parents. She had wondered what had happened to her mother's rings, which Petra was usually never without. She had assumed they had been lost in the accident somehow, or maybe misplaced by the people who had sorted through Petra's things.

Frowning, Zara opened the last item, the envelope, and extracted a sheaf of what looked like certificates. Her heart seemed to stop in her chest as the name *Mc-*

Call Electrical jumped out at her. Stunned, Zara flipped through a sheaf of numbered shares in McCall Electrical. Voting shares, the shares Damon had been chasing for the past year or so and which had blocked his takeover bid of the company. Shares that Tyler must have gifted to Petra and which now, technically, belonged to Zara.

With careful precision, because her fingers were shaking, she placed the certificates on the table. From her work on the McCall deal, Zara knew they represented a 10 percent chunk of McCall Electrical, which meant they were worth tens of millions of dollars.

Suddenly, her aunt Phoebe's motives in placing Zara at Damon's business made an even more horrible kind of sense. Her aunt must have known about the existence of the shares and their value. She had obviously hoped that if Zara got to know Damon before she found out about the shares, that she wouldn't reject them as she'd rejected the cash offer by Damon.

"Sorry, Phoebe," Zara muttered beneath her breath. "You should have known you were wasting your time. I wouldn't touch these with a barge pole."

As far as she was concerned, they belonged to Damon and Ben; she wanted no part of them. She stared at the shares, feeling suddenly utterly panicked. It was bad enough that she had to explain her true identity to Damon; having to explain the shares was too much.

First off, if she gave the shares back to Damon, he would know that her mother had had them, which would confirm his opinion of Petra and make him doubly suspicious of Zara. Second, she was almost certain that Damon would view her gesture as calculated. He was a billionaire and had already proposed marriage, so financially she would not need the shares. Whichever way she looked at it, giving the shares back to Damon herself could mean he would no longer want marriage with her, and she could not risk that.

She would have to find a way to get them back to Damon so that he would never know she'd had them all along.

Last night she had seen a glimmer of what the future could hold for them. She couldn't bear it if he rejected her outright. She loved him, and she wanted him to love her. With the shares in her possession, more than ever, she needed to pick the right time to tell him. Although, she was beginning to wonder if such a moment existed.

Hating even to touch shares that she would rather die than accept, Zara shoved them back into the envelope. As she did so, she noticed a slip of paper. It was a note written from Tyler to Petra in a clean, slanting hand. In essence it said that because Petra had insisted on a prenuptial agreement and refused to share in his wealth and assets, he insisted she accept the shares, which were an engagement present.

Knees feeling wobbly, Zara sat down. Her spine and scalp were tingling, all the fine hairs at her nape raised, her chest tight. The words Tyler had written were straightforward and businesslike, but Tyler giving Petra stock in his firm could mean only one thing, just as Petra taking off the wedding rings Zara's father had given her could mean only one thing.

They had been deeply in love.

Zara's fingers closed automatically over the thin wedding band and the pretty solitaire diamond. Petra had loved Zara's father to the point that no man had ever lived up to him. Even after his death, she had worn his rings and had never consented to wearing anyone else's jewelry. Zara had known that, because as a child, worrying about who might replace her father, she had come to realize that as long as Petra wore her wedding ring, there would be no replacement. Every time Petra had visited her at school, or taken her away on holiday, the first thing Zara had done was check her mother's left hand. Despite all the speculative media reports about who Petra was dating, if she was still wearing her wedding rings, that meant their small family of two was still intact.

Zara reread the note Tyler had written, and this time she noticed the date. Two days before Petra and Tyler had died.

Petra had been engaged. Her relationship had been real and valid. The shares proved that.

The shares.

Zara felt like flinging them somewhere, *burning them*, but she couldn't do either thing. She was caught between a rock and a hard place, because Damon needed the shares to gain control of McCall Electrical.

Feverishly, she tossed Tyler's note onto the table while she examined the envelope itself. It was plain and white, with no writing on it. Good. She would find a way to have the shares delivered to Damon, maybe pay someone to drop them off at the concierge desk. It had to be someone she trusted, yet who couldn't be connected to her.

Feeling like a cat on hot bricks—elated because the diamonds represented the financial security she and Rosie desperately needed, and utterly stressed at finding the missing McCall shares—she gathered everything from the table and shoved it all into her bag.

She had hoped she would recover some family jewelry today, and she had; what she hadn't expected was for the past to rush back at her like a freight train. A past she had to explain to Damon so he wouldn't end up hating her.

Above all, she didn't want him to think the reason she was so attracted to him had anything to do with his money. It wasn't true and it would never be true. What she wanted was what she had always wanted, to be loved and cherished for herself.

Pushing to her feet, she hooked the strap of her bag over her shoulder and checked her watch. Anxiety made her stomach hollow when she saw how much time had passed. Almost an hour, although it had felt like a lot less.

After handing in her key because she wouldn't be needing the box again, she made a beeline back to the main foyer of the bank. As she stepped out onto the pavement, the glare of the afternoon sun had her rummaging for her sunglasses. Sliding them onto the bridge of her nose, she hailed a cab. Relieved when the cab veered toward her, she slid into the back seat and gave the cabbie the hotel's address, suddenly anxious to get back to Rosie.

Five minutes later, the cab stopped at the hotel entrance. After paying the fare, Zara stepped into the foyer. She stopped dead when she saw Emily, who was sitting in one of the leather chairs, watching the entrance and clearly waiting for her.

"What's wrong?"

Emily dragged Zara toward the most secluded couch, positioned beneath a lush indoor palm right next to the elevators. "Damon's talking to Ben." Her face crumpled. "At first I thought Damon was okay with Ben and I being together, then Walter called, and everything changed. We had to come here because the cell phone coverage is practically nonexistent out on the coast and Walter had emailed some kind of report—"

"An investigative report."

Emily's face went white. "I think so, because Ben knows about Daniel now."

Zara took the seat next to Emily. "Daniel? I thought his name was Jason."

Emily flushed. "I guessed by now you would know too. Daniel was before Jason. He was a business partner of my father's. My father wanted me to marry him. I liked him quite a lot—I even thought I might be in love with him—so I agreed, but then I met Jason."

"So you pulled out of the marriage."

She shrugged. "I fell for Jason. He could have been a pauper for all I cared."

"But he wasn't. He was even richer, so it made you look like you were chasing a bigger catch."

Emily looked miserable. "I thought I'd made the right choice until Jason dumped me. Unfortunately, when it happened some columnist wrote a snarky piece about it, accusing me of bed-hopping and chasing a rich husband. I felt so humiliated, I left my job in my father's business—"

"Changed your name and came to work for me."

Emily flushed. "You seem so calm about this. I thought you'd be steaming mad. I thought you'd hate me." She grimaced. "Just like Ben will. I'm pretty sure Walter will have dug up that horrible article."

Abruptly, the fear that had been sawing at Zara ever since she'd discovered the shares died and was replaced by an odd sense of calm. If Walter had investigated Emily, then he would be investigating her, which meant she was out of time. She grimly wondered if Damon had also received a security report about her.

The last few days, her life had been tipped upside down and spun around and, quite frankly, she was over the stress of it. She was a good person. She loved her daughter and she loved Damon and she wanted to share her life with him. But if he preferred security reports and the rubbish the media invented over her word, then she was out of options.

A painful flush suffused Emily's face. "Damon's very protective of Ben. I can understand why he would want to warn him off—"

"Ben's an adult," she said crisply. "He doesn't need his older brother interfering in something that is none of his business."

Emily looked startled. "I thought you'd be furious, which is why I wanted to catch you before you spoke to Damon. It was bad enough that I walked out on my job—" She fumbled in her handbag, found a tissue and blew her nose. "I've made a real mess of things. I don't even know if Ben will ever let me explain—"

The elevator doors opened. Ben strode out, his face pale, his expression taut. His gaze zeroed in on Emily.

"You're still here," he muttered. "Thank goodness. I thought you would have run a mile."

Emily jumped to her feet. "Why would I run?"

"Because my family's so messed up. Why would you want to be a part of us? I've just heard it all. My father was a crazy, violent drunk and a womanizer who squandered the family fortune on mistresses. I was born after he died, so I never knew him, but Damon did, and he's literally got the scars to prove it. That's why he's so…overprotective. He doesn't want me falling into the same pit of snakes." Ben grinned lopsidedly.

Emily looked devastated. "He thinks I'm a pit of snakes?"

Ben instantly clasped her upper arms and pulled her close, his expression anxious. "Baby, that came out all wrong. The pit of snakes is the out-of-control, addictive behavior Damon thinks runs in the family line, not you."

"Phew," Emily said, with the glimmer of a watery smile. "For a moment there I thought Damon must hate me."

"Damon doesn't hate anyone. He just doesn't want me to get hurt."

Emily stiffened. "And do *you* think I'll hurt you?"

"Only if you leave me."

"I wasn't intending to leave. Why would I? I love you."

Relief washed over Ben's face. "Ditto. I don't care about your past relationships, and the truth is I've hardly been an altar boy myself, if you know what I mean. If you're happy with me, that's all I want to know."

Emily threw Zara a radiant glance as Ben hurried her out of the hotel. "Sorry about the job, Zara, but it looks like I'm definitely not coming back!"

Zara watched as Ben settled Emily into a low-slung sports car, which was parked just across the road. Feeling a little stunned by what Ben had revealed about Damon's past, Zara made a beeline toward the elevators.

Damon having a father who had driven the family broke with his spending on mistresses neatly explained his attitude toward Petra, and to Angel Atrides. It also made sense of his attempt to pay her off and get her to sign that insulting "go away" agreement. Ben had also mentioned scars, and that their father had been violent. She had always thought Damon's scars had been earned in battle, but some of them must have been inflicted by his father.

Slowly, quietly, the pieces of the puzzle fell into place and her heart squeezed tight at what Damon must have endured as a child. She was beginning to understand why he had such an issue with trust.

As the elevator whizzed upward, her stomach tensed. Emily's expression had glowed; she had gotten her happy ending. An ending Zara now very much doubted would be hers.

When she stepped into the suite, Rosie, who was lying on a rug on the floor playing with a rattle, crowed, flung the toy aside and held her arms out to Zara. A rush of pure maternal love brought tears to Zara's eyes. It might not be possible that she could ever have the true, adult love she needed from Damon, but she had her daughter.

Zara carried her handbag, with all of its incriminating evidence, into Rosie's room and stashed it in a dark corner. She walked back out to the sitting room and scooped Rosie up, needing the comfort of her child in her arms.

Damon strolled out of the adjoining study, a cell in his hand. Zara decided to take the bull by the horns. "I saw Emily and Ben in the lobby. Luckily, Ben had the maturity to see beyond Emily's past to what a nice person she is."

Damon dropped the phone into his back pocket. "I agree that Emily is nice," he said mildly. "But if she had been up-front about her past to begin with, there wouldn't have been a problem."

"Maybe Emily had some very good reasons for keeping her life, and her name, private."

"Most people don't deal with it by changing their name."

Zara stared at Damon for a long moment, wondering if there was a double meaning to his words because he knew she had changed her name. Rosie, who had slumped into a contented doze almost as soon as Zara had picked her up, stirred, as if even in sleep she could sense the uncomfortable currents. "You say that as if she did it to deliberately deceive Ben, when all she wanted was to escape the press and keep her privacy."

Damon frowned. "The press were not exactly hounding Emily. As I recall, it was one gossip columnist."

"Just one? Then Emily can't have been that notorious." Afraid that she would lose her temper and reveal too much, Zara walked through to Rosie's room, placed her in her crib and covered her with a light cotton blanket. She drew a deep breath and discovered that her hands were shaking. The one ray of hope was that, given that they were still talking about Emily, maybe Damon hadn't yet received a report about her.

When she walked out to the sitting room, Damon's gaze was wary. "What have I done now?"

He was standing at a set of French doors that opened out onto a sun-drenched patio. With his arms crossed over his chest, making his shoulders seem even broader, he looked brooding, utterly masculine and more than a little dangerous.

Zara got straight to the point. "Emily said you got Walter to dig into her past."

"Ben's my brother. He's in love with a woman who, at some point, changed her name." He shrugged. "Of course, I got Walter to do a little digging—"

"I suppose you think Emily's not good enough for Ben?"

Damon's brows jerked together. "These days what I think doesn't really impact Ben."

But it impacted Zara! "Okay, then, *you* don't think Emily's good enough."

Damon reached her in two strides. Linking his fingers with hers, he pulled her close, which was disorienting when she was still bracing herself for the fact that he had received some kind of damning report on her.

"Forget Emily," he muttered. "I had hoped we might be doing something else right about now."

The bell to the suite buzzed. Damon swore softly. "Talk about bad timing."

He opened the door to a waiter, who wheeled in a cart with a bottle of champagne on ice and two glasses. Damon tipped the waiter and closed the door behind him before wheeling the cart off to one side.

His expression was rueful. "I was supposed to give you something before that happened."

He fished a velvet box out of his pocket and flipped the lid. For a split second she thought he had an engagement ring, then she saw a pair of gorgeous diamond earrings.

For a moment she battled disappointment, then the sheer relief that Damon still wanted to give her a gift, and the sheer beauty of the earrings, took over.

Despite his contention that he wanted to keep things on a businesslike footing, he had obviously been thinking about her and wanting to please her, even down to doing something romantic like ordering champagne. A lump formed in her throat as it occurred to her that, even though everything seemed to be happening in reverse—as in having sex and a baby!—Damon was now courting her.

"You don't have to give me jewelry—"

"After last night, I wanted you to have something."

Understanding dawned. Last night she had told him that she had only ever been his.

Fingers shaking slightly, she picked up the gorgeous earrings, walked over to the mirror and inserted them in her lobes. She had been about to say that she couldn't accept them, but now she didn't want to let them go because she was certain they were a genuine gift of love, even if Damon didn't realize it.

"They're…beautiful."

Damon came up behind her and pulled her back against the warmth of his chest. "You're beautiful."

He turned her around in his arms and kissed her. Zara wound her arms around his neck and kissed him back, happiness shimmering through her as she wallowed in the sheer warmth and comfort of being back in Damon's arms, but the moment was bittersweet. As wonderful as it was to just be with Damon, to let her imagination run riot and pretend that they were both in love, it was a fact that they were on borrowed time.

And she had the sudden premonition that if she didn't make love to Damon now, she never would again.

A little feverishly, she began undoing the buttons of his shirt.

Damon lifted his head, his gaze heated. "Now?"

For an answer, she kissed him again and dragged at more buttons. Damon's shirt dropped to the floor. This time he pulled her close and kissed her. Long drugging seconds later her dress followed suit and she found herself propelled in the direction of the bedroom.

Damon kicked the bedroom door closed behind them as they stepped through. By the time they reached the bed, Damon had stepped out of his pants and her bra was gone. There was a momentary pause while Damon sheathed himself with a condom then they were lying tangled together on the sun-drenched bed.

She felt the glide of Damon's fingers as he peeled her panties down her legs. Desire shivered and burned as he came down between her thighs. With one smooth thrust he was inside her and they were deeply, perfectly linked.

Damon's gaze locked with hers and his fierce tenderness struck her to the heart. For a split second, she felt the utter rightness of being together, that he truly belonged to her and she to him.

She clasped his shoulders as they began to move, tears blinding her at the sheer intimacy of what they were doing. She felt as if she was finally, truly getting to know Damon and at the same time saying goodbye.

Eleven

Damon woke to small noises signaling that Rosie was awake. Carefully, so as not to disturb Zara, he disentangled himself, slid from the bed and pulled on his jeans. Walking into Rosie's room, he found her cuddle rug, which was lying on the floor, then looked around for her favorite toy, a rattle, which had also ended up on the floor. As he picked up the rattle, he noticed Zara's white leather handbag, which was lying at a drunken angle between an armchair and the wall with her phone precariously balanced on top. Probably in a rush to put Rosie in the crib, she had simply dumped the lot.

He handed the rattle to Rosie, who instantly started to chew on it, then retrieved Zara's phone. As he did so, the bag, which seemed stuffed full, slumped to one side. A number of items spilled out on the floor, among them a black velvet bag that scattered brilliant crystals.

Jaw tight, Damon stooped to gather up gems that burned with the fiery, unmistakable glitter of diamonds.

He was no expert, but given the size, number and weight of the stones, he was looking at a small fortune. He tipped the stones back into the velvet bag and placed it in Zara's handbag. As he did so, he noticed a thick envelope, which had also fallen out of the bag. The envelope was plain, but the contents, which had partly slid out of the envelope, looked gut-wrenchingly familiar. He picked up the envelope, already knowing what he was going to find. Even so, his stomach contracted when he pulled out the sheaf of old-fashioned and utterly familiar share certificates.

The missing McCall shares.

Why would Zara have the shares in her possession? How had she gotten hold of them?

The only answer that made sense was that Zara was somehow connected with Tyler. Because the voting shares were supposed to be held only by family members, he had considered the possibility that Tyler had given them to Petra, then on Petra's death they had ended up in Angel's hands. But the shares had never appeared on the market, so he had scrapped that idea.

It suddenly occurred to him that Zara was the same age as Petra's daughter, Angel Atrides. It was a leap—a big one. She looked nothing like Petra, but the more he thought about it, the more the facts fitted. It explained why Zara was so sensitive about any contact with the press, and why she had been so protective of Emily changing her name.

He had a sudden flash of Zara's bedroom, which had been decorated in a distinctly Medinian way and suddenly he was sure.

Zara Westlake was Angel Atrides.

It was there in the mystery about Zara's *nondisclosure*, the fact that she had gotten passports for her and Rosie, and had been surprisingly willing to come to Medinos. If he didn't miss his guess, Petra had stored the diamonds and the share certificates at some bank, and Zara had needed to come to Medinos personally to retrieve them.

Keeping hold of the envelope, Damon rose to his feet. He felt as if the scales had fallen from his eyes. He had been bedazzled, incapable of operating with his usual methodical precision.

A little grimly, he wondered if this was how Tyler had felt when he had fallen for Petra and handed over the shares of a business that had been his life's work. A company he had built up with clever innovation and long hours of hard work. A company he had always maintained would remain in the family.

A soft buzzing distracted Damon. He retrieved his phone from the back pocket of his jeans. Walter's text advised Damon that the report on Zara was in his inbox and he needed to read it before he did something stupid.

Too late. Damon walked to the study and used his laptop to read the confirmation that Zara Westlake was Angel Atrides.

Picking up the envelope that contained the shares, he walked back to the bedroom as Zara's eyes flickered open.

The words Ben had spoken over the phone just before he had flown away with Emily came back to haunt Damon. He lacked *emotional intelligence*.

He had no argument with that summation. He had ignored his usual caution and allowed himself to be conned by Petra's daughter.

It had all been a sham from the first moment.

He dropped the envelope on the pillow. Some of the shares slipped out, fanning across the tangled sheet. He saw the comprehension in Zara's gaze and the cold in his stomach seemed to settle a little deeper.

"How did you get hold of the shares?"

Zara jackknifed, clutching the sheet around her breasts. "You searched my bag?"

"I didn't search anything. I went in to check on Rosie. I noticed you'd left your phone on top of your bag. When I picked it up your bag fell over and a few things you obviously didn't want me to see fell out."

"It's not what you think." She averted her gaze from the certificates. "They were in a safe-deposit box at my mother's bank."

"Which was why you wanted to come to Medinos."

"I didn't know the stock certificates were there!"

"What about the diamonds?"

"Not those, either! I came because I wanted to find out what was in the box. I had hoped my Atrides family jewelry would be there, and it was."

"Atrides, as in Angel Atrides."

Her gaze turned fierce. "That's right. I changed my name for practical reasons—"

"Like Emily."

"I did it to escape the media. Not that I would expect you to understand that!"

"And the small fortune in diamonds didn't really matter?"

"Actually, *yes*, it does, because right now Rosie and I need the money. To be honest, I was *glad* there were diamonds."

"Not that you need the diamonds, with the shares being worth a small fortune."

Her face went white. "I told you I didn't know the

certificates were there. I didn't know any of it was there!"

Damon's jaw tightened. "Just like you didn't know when you slept with me that I was Tyler's nephew?"

"You think I slept with you and got pregnant, *deliberately*?" Zara clambered from the bed and dragged on one of the hotel robes, belting it tight. "You're wrong about my mother, and you're wrong about me! My aunt Phoebe pulled some strings to help get me the job. And, yes, *she* had an agenda, but she didn't let me in on it! If I had known which Smith you were, I wouldn't have taken the job—I wouldn't have touched you with a barge pole—"

"I can't believe you didn't know who I was."

"Your name is Smith. Do you know how many people have that surname? The firm is Magnum Security, which I had never heard of before. It wasn't until I started working on the McCall takeover that it finally clicked that you were *that* Smith."

Damon dragged lean fingers through his hair. He couldn't believe how much he wanted to believe her. "Maybe if the shares weren't involved—"

"Tyler gave those shares to my mother because he *loved* her."

"And you have proof of this?" Damon couldn't keep the sardonic twist from his mouth. Although there was no humor in a situation that took him straight back to his childhood and his father's penchant for lavishing expensive gifts on his mistresses.

Zara shot him a fiery glance. "You think you have all the facts, but you don't. My mother wouldn't agree to marry Tyler without a prenup, because she didn't want his money. Tyler agreed, but in return, he insisted she take shares in his company. I can prove it. There was a note from Tyler in the safe-deposit box."

Damon's expression was utterly neutral. "Sounds like true love."

"It was. My mother took off her wedding rings. If you had known her at all, you would have known what that meant, because she adored my father and grieved him for years. Until she met Tyler she never took off her rings. But you didn't know Petra, just like you don't know me."

Damon followed Zara as she marched into Rosie's room, found her bag, carried it out to the sitting room and feverishly searched through it. When she couldn't find what she was looking for she began emptying items onto the coffee table. After a few minutes, she quietly repacked her bag.

"No note?"

Frustration brimmed in her gaze. "I must have left it in the vault. Although you won't believe that because you think I'm lying."

He frowned. "I didn't say that."

"I've told you what happened," she said flatly, "but I don't think you want the truth. You'd rather see me as flawed and dishonorable, because if you were convinced that I was genuine, then that might demand some kind of genuine response from you, and that's something you don't want to give. What happened a year ago is a case in point. I left and you didn't come after me."

"I did," he said quietly. "And I found you, but I left before you saw me."

Her expression was oddly stricken. "That's even worse."

Zara marched back to the bedroom, gathered up the shares and shoved them back into their envelope. She

remembered the earrings Damon had given her and
which she was still wearing! Fingers shaking, she fumbled the earrings out of her lobes, located the box they
had come in, then placed the jewelry box on the coffee
table with the shares.

"The shares are yours—I don't want them. You
can have the earrings back, as well. Consider yourself freed."

Silence seemed to stretch between them, hollow and
unbridgeable.

Damon's phone buzzed. Turning on his heel, he
walked back into the study and closed the door.

Moving on automatic pilot, Zara made it to the bathroom and locked the door behind her. Feeling sick to
her stomach, she stared blankly at her reflection in the
lavish mirror, which occupied most of one wall. Taking a deep, slow breath that hurt because her chest was
tight with misery, she noted that, with her hair a wild
tangle around her face and the robe gaping slightly over
her breasts, she looked lush and wanton. The complete
opposite of the woman she knew herself to be.

Although, Damon could not seem to see *her*.

Suddenly unable to bear looking at herself, she
dropped the robe on the floor and stepped beneath
the shower. She winced as cool water struck her skin.
As the water gradually warmed, her numbness faded
and the decision she knew she had to make settled into
place.

She had to leave. Now.

She could not afford to argue with Damon anymore.
If she did, she would end up begging, and she absolutely
did not want to beg.

She loved him, but it was clear that Damon did not
love her. Not even close. The death knell had been when

he admitted that a year ago he had found her and *then walked away.*

If he had truly wanted her, he would have pursued her back then, and he would be fighting for her now, just like Ben had fought for Emily. But Damon was clearly more interested in pushing her out of his life than holding on to her.

She didn't blame him for being angry or distrustful, because she had hardly engendered his trust. She should have told Damon who she was a long time ago. She had been guilty of cowardice, guilty of running away, but it was also a fact that some things had just happened.

Their relationship had been fatally flawed from the beginning, but it had resulted in Rosie, who was gorgeous and lovable and who Zara could never regret having. To Zara's mind there was nothing that was not forgivable between her and Damon. The problem was that Damon did not trust in love. And the very strength she had found so attractive in him had ended up finishing them.

Minutes later, dried and with the robe once more belted around her middle, she opened the door and listened. Reassured by the silence that pervaded the suite that Damon had left, she walked quickly to the bedroom. A quick peek at Rosie told her that she had fallen back to sleep.

Zara dressed quickly in cotton jeans, a camisole and an airy white shirt. Leaving her hair loose, she used minimal makeup and slipped on comfortable sandals.

Her stomach churned as she quickly packed, but she knew it was the right thing to do. She could not stay with a man who felt contempt for her, no matter how wrong she knew his attitude to be.

She checked the bedside clock. Barely fifteen minutes had passed since she had stepped out of the shower. She didn't know how much time she had before Damon came back to the suite. All she knew was that after their horrible confrontation, she couldn't bear to see him again.

In her haste, she emptied an entire drawer into her suitcase, not bothering to fold or be neat. She remembered to grab her toiletries from the bathroom, shoving them into a plastic bag so nothing would leak.

She collected Rosie's bag and stuffed in clothes, bottles, baby formula and diapers. After making up a bottle, she zipped the bag closed with difficulty and deposited it, along with the folded front pack, in the tray below the baby stroller. After letting the backrest of the stroller down so that it formed a bed, Zara gingerly deposited Rosie in the stroller and tucked her cotton blanket around her. Rosie blinked sleepily.

Relieved, Zara checked the bedroom and the sitting room. She would not be able to take all of Rosie's equipment with her; the portable crib and the bedding that went with it would have to stay behind.

Zara wheeled her suitcase to the door and collected her handbag. She stopped dead when she checked inside to make sure she had her sunglasses and noticed the bag of diamonds jumbled in among the Atrides jewelry cases. No doubt Damon had thought all the wrong things about her when he had seen them, along with the share certificates.

Tucking the jewelry cases and the diamonds in the bottom of her suitcase, she looped the strap of her handbag over one shoulder, wheeled her suitcase out into the hall, then wheeled the stroller out. She tensed as she walked toward the elevator, pushing the stroller with one hand and wheeling the suitcase along behind her with the other. She didn't know where Damon had gone, but she was aware that he could return at any time. She punched the call button for the elevator. When the doors slid open to reveal an empty car, she breathed a sigh of relief.

She pushed the stroller in and turned it around and managed to drag the suitcase in beside her just before the doors closed. She pushed the ground floor button, then slid sunglasses onto the bridge of her nose.

As she struggled out of the elevator, she automatically scanned the foyer. There was a group of tourists checking out, their luggage attended by two bellhops. A couple sat in the sleek lounge area and, across an expanse of marble floor, the café and bar was filled with tourists enjoying the thick aromatic local coffee. Heart still beating too rapidly, Zara made a beeline for the door.

When the concierge started toward her, a frown on his face, she fell back into the training she had received at her finishing school and politely smiled as she shook her head. Dismissed, the concierge retreated and, with a weakening sense of relief, she made it through the doors to the first taxi.

She tipped the driver double what she expected to pay for the fare after he folded up the stroller and stowed it in the trunk, and asked him to drive her to the law firm. The driver waited for her while she took Rosie into the office. Fifteen minutes later, Zara exited the building with a baby who was now distinctly unhappy, but she had the document she needed, signed and witnessed by the receptionist.

Sliding into the back seat of the taxi, she rummaged in the baby bag and found the bottle of formula she had prepared. Popping it into Rosie's mouth, she asked the taxi driver to take her back to the hotel, but to park down a side street where she could walk through the hotel café to the foyer. That way she could get into the hotel without the exposure of parking at the front entrance.

With no alternative but to take Rosie with her, she asked the driver to wait once more, tipping him to make sure he didn't drive off with her luggage. Jamming the almost empty bottle back into the baby bag, she exited the taxi and walked into the hotel through the busy café, pausing before the open expanse of the foyer, just in case by some chance Damon might be walking through.

When the coast seemed clear, she walked briskly to the concierge's desk and asked that the document be delivered to Damon's suite.

Damon walked into the vault of the third and final bank on Medinos. He'd had to call in some favors, but he'd managed to get access to the vaults, long enough to check if there was anything that resembled the handwritten note Zara had claimed his uncle had written. Maybe it was a wild-goose chase, but despite the odds against finding a note, he couldn't forget the stark expression on Zara's face when he had tossed the shares on the bed or the raw hurt when he'd accused her. The report Walter had sent him had been just as conflicting, confirming her identity, and also confirming that— aside from the change of name—Zara was everything she claimed to be.

The first two banks had been dead ends, and he had literally turned those rooms over; this was his last chance to find the note, if it existed.

The clerk accompanied him into the vault and waited

while he did a quick search of the room. The small trash can was empty. He was just about to leave when a corner of white caught his eye. A piece of paper had slipped down between the wall and the stainless steel desk used for opening safe-deposit boxes.

He fished out the piece of notepaper and went still inside, all the hairs at his nape lifting. He would recognize Tyler's firm, slanted writing anywhere.

He read the brief note, then read it again. He tried to breathe, but his chest had closed up. Zara had been telling the truth.

And he had made a mistake, the biggest mistake of his life.

He suddenly became aware of how much time had passed. He checked his watch, thanked the clerk, then left the bank.

It took him ten minutes to reach the hotel, but he had the odd feeling that it was ten minutes too long. As he stepped into the lobby, the concierge stopped him and handed him an envelope.

Impatient to reach the suite, Damon opened the envelope as he stepped out of the elevator. He instantly recognized a copy of the letter he had instructed his lawyers to send to Zara's lawyer years before, which, if she had signed it, would have meant she relinquished any claim to the estate.

The fact that Zara had not gotten her lawyer to draft a new letter, but had obtained a copy of the old one he had originally sent to her, conveyed a message he couldn't ignore. Years ago, he had assumed Zara had refused to sign because she had wanted to keep him dangling and her options open, so she could sue for more money later on. Now he knew that her reasoning had been the exact opposite. She hadn't signed or corresponded with him because she quite simply hadn't wanted *anything* from him.

Her signature and the date seemed to jump out at him. It had been signed that afternoon, less than an hour ago, with an initialed condition that Zara would not accept the payment offered on signing or any family share certificates or payment of any kind, ever.

He unlocked the door to the suite and stepped inside and the sense of cold seemed to grow more acute, because he instantly knew that the suite was empty. He quickly searched the rooms, but Zara and Rosie were gone, and he only had himself to blame.

He had accused Zara of being deceitful and manipulative, had seen her as a pretty gold digger looking for the good life, just like her mother. Now he knew how wrong he'd been.

Raw with grief over Tyler's death, he now realized he had jumped to conclusions and bought into the media hype, but it was a fact that Tyler had been no fool when it came to judging character. He'd had zero tolerance for superficial relationships or fortune hunters, and yet he had fallen for Petra, to the point of asking her to marry him.

The fact that Petra had insisted on the prenup, then Tyler had countered by gifting Petra a 10 percent stake in the company he had loved said it all. Damon had been wrong about Petra. And at a gut level he knew he had been utterly wrong about Zara.

Too late to remember that one of the things that had attracted him to Zara had been her fierce independence, her desire to forge her own way and not lean on anyone, least of all him.

Damon found the number for the airport while he took the elevator to the underground garage. After a short conversation, during which he managed to establish that there were flights leaving for London and Dubai in the next hour, Damon terminated the call. He found his car and accelerated out into the street.

Zara's taxi was stalled in traffic.

She spoke in rapid Medinian to the driver, but he simply gesticulated. A truck had overturned on the road; they were going nowhere. Maybe in a few minutes.

Craning around, she checked the traffic lined up behind, trying to see if she could spot Damon's glossy black car. She was almost certain she had glimpsed it as she and Rosie had slipped out of the hotel, which meant he would have received the document she'd left for him and knew they had gone.

A car honked; they inched forward. Long minutes later, they idled past the overturned vegetable truck, moving at a snail's pace. She asked the driver to go faster. He gave her a blank look in the rearview mirror.

A wad of Medinian notes solved the problem. Minutes later, the taxi was zooming toward the airport at breakneck speed. The cluttered streets of Medinos finally gave way to hilly countryside dotted with goats and ancient olive groves. Lush vineyards lined with vines that were festooned with leaves and dripping with ripe black grapes signaled that the airport, situated on a plateau in the midst of the most fertile land on Medinos, was near.

Zara's phone chimed and her heart almost stopped in her chest. She checked who was calling—Damon.

She turned the phone off and held on for dear life as the taxi careened into a space outside the departures gate. After muttering her thanks and shoving more money at the driver, she scrambled out and put Rosie in the stroller. Looping her handbag over one shoulder, she grabbed her suitcase with her spare hand and headed for the desk.

She checked the overhead computer. There was a flight leaving for London in forty minutes. She pressured the attendant behind the counter to let her get on the flight, but was flatly refused. Zara checked the screen; the next flight out was an hour and twenty minutes away.

Just when she was about to give up, she saw Jorge. She called out to him, and he turned, his expression comical.

He grinned and shook his head. "So you're not too famous to talk to me today."

He held up a tabloid paper and she almost died on the spot. There was a blurry picture of her and Damon kissing in the underground garage. The janitor hadn't just overheard them, he had snapped them as well, then sold the story.

She stared at the grainy photo, her mind working quickly. She hated the notoriety of it, but for once she was going to use it. She stared at Jorge. "Now you see why I have to get off Medinos. Can you help me?"

Twenty minutes later, and after paying an exorbitant amount for tickets, she and Rosie were personally escorted to their seats. Zara had had to buy first-class seats, but for once the money hadn't mattered, and first class had fitted with her celebrity-on-the-run-from-the-paparazzi plea.

A few minutes after that, the flight taxied out, but instead of taking off, it wheeled to a halt. Apparently, there were birds on the runway. Zara's stomach hollowed out. She was beginning to wonder if they would ever get off the ground.

Twelve

Damon terminated his latest attempt to call Zara when he arrived at the airport terminal. Like every other call had, it would go straight to voice mail. He had already left a message and Zara hadn't replied, so there was no sense leaving another.

He parked and headed for departures. The flight to London was already on the tarmac waiting to depart, but the Dubai flight had yet to board. He skimmed the passengers massed in the lounge. Zara wasn't there, so she must have boarded the first flight out, which was London bound.

He called Walter. He needed confirmation of which flight Zara had taken. Walter had connections in the aviation world. If anyone could get the information, quickly, he could.

Walter called him back a few minutes later and confirmed that Zara and Rosie were on the London flight.

Jaw tight, Damon watched as the jet began moving down the runway, picking up speed. A few seconds later it was in the air. Taking out his phone again, he called Mac. He had already asked her to fuel the jet and get ready to fly, but he was aware that they would have to queue.

It took an hour to file the flight plan, another hour to get a takeoff slot. When they were finally in the air, Damon opened up the file on his laptop and read through Walter's report in detail.

Zara was Petra's daughter and, yes, there were a few wild media stories about her, but on close inspection, there wasn't a lot of substance to any of them. He studied the few photos that were included and shook his head. There was a photo of a child who was recognizably Zara, cute in plaits, and a blurred snapshot of a teenager with dark hair who could be anyone. Finally, he stared incredulously at an article entitled Angel Parties Hard. It was an article supposedly about Angel Atrides, but the photograph depicted a long-haired bottle blonde who was a complete stranger.

Grimly, Damon read on. The claims that she slept around were outright lies. He knew that for a fact because Zara had only ever slept with him. Claims that she was a fortune hunter looking for a rich husband were similarly flawed, because she had clearly never been a party girl, or dated anyone who actually had a fortune, except himself, and she'd had no compunction about ditching him.

Walter hadn't just dug for information, he had mined.

After Petra's death, Zara had been saddled with Petra's funeral expenses. Damon knew she could have taken the easy way out and accepted his money, but instead, as a student, she had paid off her mother's funeral expenses in tiny increments until the debt was cleared.

Those were not the actions of a woman who was looking for some man to bankroll her lifestyle. She hadn't *had* a lifestyle. What she'd had were debts and worry, then a child to care for—his child—and a determination to make her own way. *Without him.*

Zara had no credit cards and almost no debt, just the mortgage on her business. Somehow, in this modern day and age, she managed to make all of her purchases with cash. From what Damon could glean, despite the Swiss finishing school and the jet-setting mother, Zara only bought what she could afford, and that was mostly necessities. No designer clothing or shoes, and definitely no jewelry. That meant the diamonds were exactly what she had claimed.

Security and stability.

The final nail in the coffin was the information he already knew, but which he had stubbornly ignored. When Zara had become pregnant and could have demanded money from him, she had determinedly made her own way.

Her business was a case in point. Zara had gotten her business degree, worked and saved, gotten a loan, then opened her own business. She had accepted him as a client only because she had needed the cash flow. Then she had insisted on dealing only with Howard, making it clear that she didn't want Damon to step any further into her life.

Closing the file, Damon checked the time. They wouldn't land for several hours. He needed to sleep, but first he needed to figure out how he was going to win back Zara when he had done his level best to drive her away.

When they landed at Heathrow, it was only to find that Zara and Rosie had caught a last-minute connection to Los Angeles.

Mac yawned. "What do we do now?"

Damon noted Zara's arrival time in LA. He didn't know if she would take a connecting flight from there, or choose to stop over. What mattered was that she appeared to be heading home.

"We get some dinner, get some sleep and then go home."

Zara paid the taxi driver, who obligingly wheeled her luggage through her front gate while Zara carried Rosie.

Rosie was not happy. She had been fractious on the red-eye flight from LA to Auckland, which had taken thirteen long, horrible hours. Her lashes were spiky from crying and her cheeks were red. Zara suspected that she was cutting another tooth, which was, literally, the last straw.

Blinking against the brilliance of the morning sun, when her body clock wanted it to be night, she unlocked the front door and carried Rosie through to her room and settled her in her crib.

Feeling dizzy with exhaustion, she trudged back out to the porch to claim her luggage, only to be buttonholed by Edna Cross, who was waiting on the step with a woman's magazine. "It says in here that you're the daughter of that famous supermodel—"

"Petra Hunt. She was my mother."

Edna blinked. "That explains why that blonde reporter was hanging around. I called the police on her."

The sun seemed to shine a little brighter. "Vanessa Gardiner. Way to go, Mrs. Cross."

"If she comes back, I can slap a harassment charge on her if you like."

"Will that work?"

"Probably not, but it'll make her life difficult."

Zara's chest suddenly felt a little tight. "Thank you, Mrs. Cross."

"You can call me Edna. Just being neighborly. If there's anything else you need, let me know."

Zara watched as Edna ambled back to her house. Across the road another neighbor—old Mr. Harris, who was out washing his car—paused and lifted a hand. It was a strange moment to feel that, finally, she belonged somewhere.

After depositing her bags in the sitting room and opening up a few windows to air out the house, she called Molly to see how she was coping. Apparently, owing to the media attention, they'd had an influx of new clients and there was a long list of new job applicants to screen. The magazine article, and a number of tabloid follow-ups, all of which Molly assured her she had hated, had done wonders for business. She'd had to take on one of their temps to cope with the increased workload and Harriet was proving to be a real gem.

Molly paused. "Are you really Angel Atrides and a *contessa*?"

Zara smothered a yawn. Now that she was home, tiredness was closing in. All she wanted to do was sleep. "Yes and yes. But the *contessa* thing is a bit like the sheikh taxi driver who just dropped me off. Without an estate and a huge bank account, it doesn't actually mean anything."

"Hmm. Harriet thinks it's an asset. She's had a lot of experience with public relations and thinks it could provide an important point of difference for the agency.

Not to mention an opportunity to harness the media attention in a good way."

After a brief discussion, Zara decided that with Harriet in the mix, she could take a few days off and disappear from sight until the media furor died down. Molly instantly offered Zara the use of a family beach house on Auckland's west coast.

Even though she was exhausted, Zara decided to leave straightaway. They were already packed and even though Rosie was still out of sorts, at least if they went for a drive in the car, she might fall asleep.

Two hours later, with Rosie bathed, changed and fed, all of her luggage transferred to the car and enough groceries to last a few days, Zara drove until she found the small cottage, which was situated on a windswept cliff overlooking a wild stretch of coastline. She found the key, which was sitting beneath a flowerpot, unlocked the door and began ferrying bags inside.

Rosie, thankfully, had fallen into a deep slumber, so Zara gently transferred her from her car seat to a portable crib she had managed to borrow from a friend.

The sun was sliding into the sea by the time she made herself a sandwich and a cup of tea for dinner and collapsed into a faded armchair. She woke hours later to find that she had fallen dead asleep in the chair and was now freezing cold. She blinked at the noise that had woken her and realized it was her phone.

Retrieving the cell from the kitchen table, she checked the screen. Her heart slammed hard against her chest. Damon had tried to call her for about the twentieth time.

She stared at her voice mail, which also registered a message from Damon. What she really needed to do was throw the whole phone, which belonged to Magnum Security, away.

Switching on a light, she checked on Rosie who was warmly cuddled up beneath thick blankets and searched out a sweater and a warm pair of socks for herself. She checked her watch as she filled a kettle with water so she could make a hot drink and was shocked to see it was only ten o'clock. She was about to turn the kettle on when she thought she heard a noise. Frowning, she listened hard. There was a road not far from the cottage, which led to a popular beach suburb, so there was traffic, but this didn't sound like a car.

Another sound, this one more distinct, made her stiffen. Suddenly wondering if a reporter had tracked her here and was even now sneaking up to the window to snap a photo of her, she grabbed the kettle, which was full of cold water. Instead of walking out the front door and being an instant target for anyone with a camera, she padded out the back door and walked quietly around the small cottage.

A low sound behind her spun her around. Damon's gaze locked with hers, but it was too late to stop the flight of the kettle which, out of sheer fright, she'd flung in the direction of the sound.

He caught the kettle, but water sprayed, drenching his dark jersey and jeans. "Remind me to put you on one of my security teams." He wiped water from his face. "No, cancel that. Walter said you should be running a war. I'm in complete agreement. You can run the teams."

Zara rubbed her arms against the biting cold and tried to ignore the fact that even dripping wet and probably just as tired as she, Damon looked certifiably gorgeous. "What are you doing here?"

"Looking for you."

"Why?"

"I found the note from Tyler. It was in the bank, like you said."

Her heart pounded at that, but she refused to let herself hope. "So you believed *Tyler*."

Turning on her heel, she walked back into the house, but despite every effort to be indifferent to Damon her pulse was hammering and she was hopelessly aware of him. A little desperately she wondered what it took to get rid of the zing of attraction, or the crazy, heady feeling of hope springing to life again.

If she let herself hope, she thought ruthlessly, she would only set herself up to be hurt again and she was over being hurt.

She flicked on lights, illuminating the tiny rooms with their jumble of mismatched furniture, the miniature kitchen that fitted two or three people at the most. When Damon stepped into the kitchen, the room seemed to shrink even more.

He put the kettle on the bench. "I'm sorry I frightened you. I thought I heard someone around the back."

"That would be me!"

"As it turned out."

Okay, so he had been protecting her. She tried not to feel happy about that as she filled the kettle with water again and put it on to boil. Feeling crazily nervous to have Damon so close, in her personal space when she never thought he would be again, she busied herself finding a towel.

In the meantime, Damon had peeled out of his jersey, which was soaked, and hung it over the back of a chair. Zara tried not to notice his bronzed biceps, or the way the T-shirt clung across his chest. She concentrated, instead, on making tea. After he had blotted the worst of the moisture from his T-shirt, Damon tossed the damp towel over the back of another chair.

She poured tea and handed him a mug. His gaze caught hers. "You were right. I didn't believe you, and for the reason you said. I have difficulty with…trust."

Leaning against the bench, he began to talk about his childhood, the words at first hard and slow, then flowing more smoothly. Ben had given Zara a brief outline of how Damon's life had gone, but he had barely scratched the surface. By the time Damon had finished, the tea had gone cold.

Zara set her mug down. "But growing up, you must have realized your parents' marriage was…dysfunctional."

He set his mug down, the drink untasted. "Maybe, but I wasn't exactly brought up under normal circumstances even after they died. Tyler was the closest thing Ben and I had to a real father—"

"And he was a confirmed bachelor until he met my mother."

"Then there was my stint in the army. I'm not making excuses. I'm just trying to explain why I've been so resistant to a real relationship."

Her head came up. For a long, vibrating moment she thought she'd heard wrong. "What do you mean by a real relationship?"

He caught the fingers of one hand and drew her close. "I mean you and me and a second chance."

"Why? Because of Rosie?"

He pulled her closer still. "You know it's not about Rosie. I love her, she's my daughter and finding her jolted me. But it was falling for you and losing you that made me realize how empty my life was. I've been trying to control my relationships but that approach never worked. Lily hit it right on the button. If I refused to risk myself and go out on a limb for someone else, I couldn't expect to be in a relationship."

"Which explains why you walked away from me when you found me in Dunedin over a year ago!"

His gaze locked with hers. "I didn't say I wasn't stubborn. But, when you came back to town, it didn't take me long to track you down. And once I did, I tried to stay close. Why do you think I kept employing your temps?"

She tried not to drown in the molten heat of his gaze. "I did wonder." She suddenly remembered the question that had gnawed at her earlier. "By the way, how *did* you find me this time?"

"GPS. You've got a company phone."

She tried to breathe, but it seemed to be getting awfully hot and close in the tiny kitchen. "I was thinking of throwing the SIM card away."

He grinned. "Why do you think I got here so fast?"

He reached into his pocket and she caught the glint of something shiny. Her heart slammed hard in her chest. At first she thought he was returning the earrings to her, but she was wrong. It was an engagement ring.

Suddenly all the vulnerabilities that had gone with loving Damon surged back. If they were going to do this, she couldn't bear it if it all fell apart again.

Damon went down on one knee, with difficulty, because the space between the kitchen counter and the small table was so cramped. One shoulder bumped against a shelf of pots, sending a lid spinning onto the tiled floor. When Zara stepped back to allow him more room, a chair crashed to the floor. The noise woke Rosie, who began to make cute sounds in her room. It was bedlam and it was the most romantic thing that had ever happened.

Damon gripped her hand. "I don't want to lose you again. I've loved you from the first moment you stepped into that interview room. The problem was, you made me feel too much and I had gotten used to closing down and looking for reasons not to trust. I'm sorry, babe— I didn't mean to hurt you. I just didn't have the courage to admit that I needed you. When you walked out on me this time, I knew that I loved you. It was too late, but I finally understood exactly what I wanted. You, Rosie and the home we can make together, if only you'll trust *me*."

Damon grasped her left hand. "Will you marry me, for better or worse, for richer or poorer?"

The vows of the marriage service made Zara's throat close up so that when she spoke her voice was husky. "That's all I ever wanted. I just hadn't thought it was possible."

But as Damon slid the engagement ring onto the third finger of her left hand, and rose up to kiss her—knocking his mug of tea into the sink—she suddenly realized that it was more than possible.

Two people truly, honestly in love, and their baby.

It was real and just a little chaotic, and she knew it was going to be *perfect*.

* * * * *

RUNAWAY
TEMPTATION

MAUREEN CHILD

To Carter and Cade.
For the hugs. For the laughs.
For the love. For the future.

One

"I hate weddings." Caleb Mackenzie ran his index finger around the inside of his collar. But that didn't do a thing to loosen the tie he wore, or to rid himself of the "wish I were anywhere but here" thoughts racing through his mind. "I feel like I'm overdressed for my own hanging."

Caleb wasn't real fond of suits. Sure, he had a wide selection of them since he needed them for meetings and business deals. But he was much more comfortable in jeans, a work shirt and his favorite boots, running his ranch, the Double M. Still, as the ranch grew, he found himself in the dreaded suits more and more often because expansion called for meeting bankers and investors on their turf.

Right now, though, he'd give plenty to be on a horse riding out across the open range. Caleb knew his ranch hands were getting the work done, but there were stock ponds to check on, a pregnant mare he was keeping an eye on and a hay field still to harvest and store.

Yet instead, here he stood, in the hot Texas sun, in an elegant suit and shining black boots. He tugged the brim of his gray Stetson down lower over his eyes and slanted a look at the mob of people slowly streaming into the Texas Cattleman's Club for the ceremony and reception.

If he could, he'd slip out of town. But it was too late now.

"You're preaching to the choir, man."

Caleb nodded at his friend Nathan Battle. If he had to be there, at least he had company.

Nathan settled his cowboy hat more firmly on his head and sent a frown toward his pretty, very pregnant wife standing with a group of her friends. "I swear, I think Amanda really enjoys it when I have to wear a suit."

"Women'll kill you." Caleb sighed and leaned back against his truck. As hot as he was, he was in no hurry to go inside and take a seat for the ceremony. Given a choice, he'd always choose to be outside under the sky. Even a hot and humid August day was preferable to being trapped inside.

"Maybe, but it's not a bad way to go—" Nathan broke off and asked, "Why're you here, anyway? Not like you've got a wife to make you do what you don't want to do." As soon as the words left his mouth, Nathan winced and said, "Sorry, man. Wasn't thinking."

"No problem." Caleb gritted his teeth and swallowed the knot of humiliation that could still rise up and choke him from time to time. The thing about small towns was, not only did everyone know what everybody else was doing—nobody ever forgot a damn thing. Four years since the day his wedding hadn't happened and everyone in Royal remembered.

But then, it wasn't like he'd forgotten, either.

Amazing, really. In the last few years, this town had seen tornadoes, killer storms, blackmailers and even a man coming back from the dead. But somehow, the memory of Caleb's botched wedding day hadn't been lost in the tidal wave of events.

Nathan shifted position, his discomfort apparent. Caleb couldn't help him with that. Hell, he was uncomfortable, too. But to dispel the tension, Caleb said lightly, "You should have worn your uniform."

As town sheriff, Nathan was rarely dressed in civilian clothes. The man was most comfortable in his khaki uniform, complete with badge, walking the town, talking to everyone and keeping an eye on things. He snorted. "Yeah, that wouldn't fly with Amanda."

A soft smile curved his friend's mouth and just for a second or two, Caleb envied the other man. "When's the new baby due again?"

"Next month."

And, though he knew the answer already, Caleb asked, "How many will that make now?"

Nathan grinned and shot him a wink. "This one makes four."

A set of four-year-old twin boys, a two-year-old girl and now another one. "How many are you planning, anyway?"

Nathan shrugged. "Who says there's a plan? Mandy loves babies, and I have to say I do enjoy making them."

Marriage. Family. All of that slipped by him four

years ago. And now that Nathan had reminded him, Caleb idly wondered how many kids he and Meg might have had by now if things had gone the way he'd expected. But the night before their wedding, Meg had run off with Caleb's brother, Mitch. Now the two of them lived on the family ranch with their set of twins. Three years old, the boy and girl ran wild around the ranch and Caleb put whatever he might have felt for kids of his own into those two.

There might still be tension between him and his brother, Mitch, not to mention Meg. But he loved those kids more than he would have thought possible.

"Mitch and Meg still out of town?" Nathan asked, glancing around as if half expecting to see them walking up.

"Yeah. Visiting Meg's family." And Caleb had been enjoying the respite.

"That's one way to get out of going to a summer wedding."

"Amen." Caleb loosened his tie a little. Felt like he was beginning to melt out here in the sun. He spared a glance at the sky and watched a few lazy white clouds drifting along. "Who plans a wedding in August, anyway? Hotter than the halls of hell out here."

"You know how the Goodmans are," Nathan answered. "The old man figures he knows everything and the rest of them—except Brooke—just fall in line. Probably his idea to hold it in high summer. No doubt he was aiming for it to be the talk of the town."

That sounded like Simon Goodman. Though the man was Caleb's lawyer, that was more from inertia than anything else. Goodman had been Caleb's father's lawyer and when the elder Mackenzie died, Caleb just never bothered to change the situation. So his own inaction had brought him here. Truth be told, Caleb usually avoided attending *any* weddings since it inevitably brought up old memories that he'd just as soon bury.

"Anyway," Nathan said, pushing past the uncomfortable pause in the conversation, "I'm the town sheriff. I'm sort of *forced* to be at these society things. Why the hell did you come?"

Caleb snorted. "Normally, I wouldn't have. But Simon Goodman's still the ranch attorney. So it's business to be at his son Jared's wedding." And he made a mental note to do something about that real soon. He shrugged. "If Mitch and Meg had been in town I'd have forced my brother to go instead of me. But since they're gone, I'm stuck."

Served him right, Caleb told himself, for letting things slide. He never should have kept Simon on. He and Caleb's father had been great friends so that didn't speak well of the man.

He'd let the lawyer relationship stand mainly because it was easier than taking time away from work to find someone new. Between running the ranch and expanding the oil-rich field discovered only twenty years before, Caleb had been too damn busy to worry about a lawyer he only had to deal with a few times a year.

Looking for a change of subject, Caleb said, "Since you're here, that means the new deputy's in charge, right?"

Nathan winced. "Yeah. Jeff's doing fine."

Caleb laughed. "Sure, I can hear the confidence in your voice."

Sighing, Nathan pushed one hand through his hair and shook his head. "With Jack retired, I needed a deputy and Jeff Baker's working out. But he's from Houston so it's taking him some time to get used to small town living."

Caleb had heard about it. Jeff was about thirty and a little too strict on the law and order thing for Royal. The new deputy had handed out more speeding tickets in the last six months than Nathan had in years. Folks in Royal hit an empty road and they just naturally picked up speed. Jeff Baker wasn't making many friends.

"Hell," Caleb said, "I've lived here my whole life and I'm still not used to it."

"I hear that," Nathan replied, shifting his gaze to where his wife stood with a group of friends. "But I've been getting a lot of complaints about the tickets Jeff's handing out."

Caleb laughed. "He's not going to slow anybody down."

"Maybe not," Nathan agreed with a nod. "But he's going to keep trying."

"I expect so," Caleb mused, then glanced over at Nathan's wife who was smiling and waving one hand. "I think Amanda wants you."

Straightening up, Nathan gave a heartfelt sigh. "That's it, then. I'll see you after. At the reception?"

"I don't think so. Soon as I'm clear, I'm headed back to the ranch."

Another sigh. "Lucky bastard."

Caleb grinned and watched his friend head toward the Texas Cattleman's Club building. The place was a one-story, rambling sort, made of dark wood and stone, boasting a tall slate roof. It was a part of Royal and had been for generations. Celebrations of all kinds had been held there and today, it was a wedding. One he'd have to attend in just a few minutes.

Shelby Arthur stared at her own reflection and hardly recognized herself. She supposed all brides felt like that on their wedding day, but for her, the effect was terrifying.

Her long, dark auburn curls were pulled back from her face to hang down to the center of her back. Her veil poofed out around her head and her green eyes narrowed at the gown she hated. A ridiculous number of yards of white tulle made Shelby look like a giant marshmallow caught in netting. The dress was her about-to-be-mother-in-law's doing. She'd insisted that the Goodmans had a reputation to maintain in Royal and the simple off-the-shoulder gown Shelby had chosen wouldn't do the trick.

So instead, she was looking at a stranger wearing an old-fashioned gown with long, lacy sleeves, a cinched waist and full skirt, and a neckline that was so high she felt as if she were choking.

"Thank God for air-conditioning," she muttered, otherwise in the sweltering Texas heat, she'd be little more than a tulle-covered puddle on the floor. She half turned to get a look at the back of the dress and finally sighed. She looked like one of those crocheted dolls her grandmother used to make to cover up spare toilet paper rolls.

Shelby was about to get married in a dress she hated, a veil she didn't want, to a man she wasn't sure she *liked*, much less loved. How did she get to this point?

"Oh, God. What am I doing?" The whisper was strained but heartfelt.

She'd left her home in Chicago to marry Jared Goodman. But now that he was home in Texas, under his awful father's thumb, Jared was someone she didn't even know. Her whirlwind romance had morphed into a nightmare and now she was trapped.

She took a breath, blew it out and asked her reflection, "What are you doing?"

"Good question."

Shelby jumped, startled by the sudden appearance of Jared's mother. The woman was there, behind her in the mirror, bustling into the room. Margaret Goodman was tall and painfully thin. Her face was all sharp angles and her blue eyes were small and judgmental. Her graying blond hair was scraped back from her face into a bun that incongruously sported a circlet of yellow rosebuds. The beige suit she wore was elegant if boring and was so close to the color of her hair and skin the woman simply disappeared into her clothes.

If only, Shelby thought.

"Your veil should be down over your face," Margaret chastised, hurrying over to do just that.

As the veil fell across her vision, Shelby had a momentary panic attack and felt as though she couldn't breathe through that all-encompassing tulle curtain, so she whipped it back again. Taking a deep breath, she said, "I'm sorry, I can't—"

"You will." Margaret stepped back, took a look, then moved to tug at the skirt of the wedding gown. "We're going for a very traditional, chaste look here. It's unseemly that this wedding is happening so quickly. The town will be gossiping for months, watching for a swollen belly."

Shelby sucked in a gulp of air. "I've told you already, I'm not pregnant."

"We'll soon see, won't we?" One blond eyebrow lifted over pale blue eyes. "The Goodman family has a reputation in this town and I expect you to do nothing to besmirch it."

"Besmirch?" Who even talked like that, Shelby thought wildly. It was as if she'd dropped into a completely different universe. Suddenly, she missed Chicago—her friends, her *life*, so much she ached with it.

Moving to Texas with a handsome, well-connected cowboy who had swept her off her feet had seemed like an adventure at the time. Now she was caught up in a web that seemed inescapable. Her fiancé was a stranger, his mother a blatant enemy and his brother had a way of looking at Shelby that had her wishing she'd paid more attention in self-defense class.

Jared's father, Simon, was no better, making innuendoes that he probably thought were clever but gave Shelby the outright creeps. The only bright spot in the Goodman family was Jared's sister, Brooke, and she couldn't help Shelby with what was about to happen.

Somehow, she had completely lost control of her own life and now she stood there in a mountain of tulle trying to find enough scraps of who she was to cling to.

"Once the ceremony is finished, we'll all go straightaway to the reception," Margaret was saying.

Oh, God.

"You and Jared will, of course, be in the receiving line until every guest has been welcomed personally. The photographer can then indulge in the necessary photos for precisely fifteen minutes, after which you and Jared will reenter the reception for the ceremonial first toast." Margaret paused long enough to glance into the mirror herself and smooth hair that wouldn't dare fall out of place. "Mr. Goodman is an important man and as his family *we* will do all we can to support him. Is that understood?" Her gaze, hard and cold, shot to Shelby's. "When you've returned from your honeymoon…"

Her stomach sank even further. She wouldn't have been surprised to see it simply drop out of her body and fall *splat* onto the floor. Her day was scheduled. Her honeymoon was scheduled and she had no doubt at all that her *life* would be carefully laid out for her, complete with bullet points.

How had it all come to this?

For their honeymoon, Shelby had wanted to see Paris. Instead, Jared's mother had insisted they go to Philadelphia so Shelby could be introduced to the eastern branch of the Goodman family. And much to her dismay, Jared was simply doing as he was told with no regard at all for Shelby. He'd changed so much since coming back to Texas that she hardly recognized the man anymore.

Margaret was still talking. Fixing a steely gaze on the mirror, she met Shelby's eyes. "When you return to Texas, you will of course give up your ridiculous business and be the kind of wife to Jared that will enable him to further his own law career."

"Oh, I don't think—"

"You'll be a Goodman," Margaret snapped, brooking no argument.

Shelby swallowed hard. When they'd met in Chicago, Jared had talked about his ranch in Texas. He'd let her believe that he was a cowboy who happened to also have a law degree. And yes, she could admit that the fantasy of being with a cowboy had really appealed to her. But mostly, he'd talked about their having a family and that had sealed the deal for Shelby.

She'd told herself then that she could move her professional organizer business anywhere. But from the moment Jared had introduced her to his family, Margaret had made it clear that her "little business" was hardly appropriate.

Shelby met her own eyes in the mirror and read the desperation there. Maybe all of this would be easier to take if she was madly in love with Jared. But the truth was, she'd fooled herself from the beginning. This wasn't love. It couldn't be. The romance, the excitement, had all worn off, like the luster of sterling silver as soon as it was tarnished. Rather than standing up for himself, Jared was completely cowed by his family and that really didn't bode well for Shelby's future.

Margaret checked the slim gold watch on her wrist, clucked her tongue and headed for the door. "The music will begin in exactly five minutes." She stopped, glanced over her shoulder and added, "My husband will be here to escort you down the aisle since you don't have a father of your own."

Shelby's mouth dropped open as the other woman left the room. Stunned, she realized Margaret had tossed that last bit with venom, as if Shelby had arranged for her father to die ten years ago just so he could disrupt Margaret Goodman's wedding scenario.

She shivered at the thought of Simon Goodman. She didn't want him anywhere near her, let alone escorting her, touching her. And even worse, she was about to promise to be in Simon's family for the rest of her life.

"Nope, can't do it." She glanced at her own reflection and in a burst of fury ripped her veil off her face.

Then, blowing a stray auburn lock from her forehead, she gathered up the skirt of the voluminous gown in both arms.

"Have to hurry," she muttered, giving herself the impetus she needed to make a break for it before it was too late. If she didn't leave now, she'd be *married* into the most awful family she'd ever known.

"Not going to happen," she reassured herself as she tentatively opened the door and peered out.

Thankfully, there was no one in this section of the TCC. They were all in the main room, waiting for the ceremony to start. In the distance, she heard the soft thrum of harp music playing as an underscore to the rise and fall of conversations. She could only guess what they'd all be talking about soon.

That wasn't her problem, though. Clutching her wedding gown high enough to keep it out of her way, she hurried down the hall and toward the nearest exit.

She thought she heard someone calling her name, but Shelby didn't let that stop her. She hit the front door and started running. It was blind panic that kept her moving. After all, she had nowhere to go. She didn't know hardly anyone in Royal besides the Goodman family. But she kept moving because the unknown was wildly better than the alternative.

Her veil caught on one of the porch posts and yanked her back briefly. But Shelby ripped the stupid thing off her head, tiara and all, and tossed it to the ground. Then she was off again, tearing around a corner and running smack into a brick wall.

Well, that's what it felt like.

A tall, gorgeous brick wall who grabbed her upper arms to steady her, then smiled down at her with humor in his eyes. He had enough sex appeal to light up the city of Houston and the heat from his hands, sliding down her body, made everything inside her jolt into life.

"Aren't you headed the wrong way?" he asked, and the soft drawl in his deep voice awakened a single thought in her mind.

Oh, boy.

Two

A *real* cowboy.

Shelby tipped her head back to look up at him and caught the flash of surprise in his gaze as he reached out to steady her. Ridiculously enough, considering the situation—running away from her own wedding—she felt a hot blast of something…*amazing*.

The cowboy had shaggy light brown hair, icy-blue eyes, a strong jaw and a gray cowboy hat tipped down low on his forehead. He wore a black suit, crisp white shirt with a dove-gray tie and oh, sweet mama Lou, shining black cowboy boots. His hands were strong and warm on her upper arms and a slow smile curved his mouth as he took in what she was wearing.

And the soft drawl in his deep voice really worked for her. He was everything Jared wasn't. Although, even as she thought it, Shelby reminded herself that her judgment had been so crappy about Jared that she could be just as wrong about Mr. Tall, Dark and Yummy.

"Hey now," he said, that deep voice rolling along her spine again. "Are you all right?"

"Absolutely not," she said firmly. The humor in his eyes was gone, replaced by concern and she responded to it. "I have to get out of here. Now. Can you help me?"

His eyes narrowed on her and his delectable mouth moved into a grim slash. "You're running out on your wedding?"

Disapproval practically radiated from him and Shelby's spine went stiff as a board in reaction. "Just as fast as I can," she said. "Can you help me?"

Before he could say yes or no, another voice erupted behind her.

"Shelby! What the devil do you think you're doing?"

Spinning around until the cowboy was at her back, Shelby watched as Margaret Goodman stalked toward her, fire in her eyes. "Your guests are waiting."

"They're not my guests," Shelby said. Heck, the only people she knew in Royal was the family she was supposed to marry into and frankly, if they were the best this town had to offer, she was ready to *run* back to Chicago.

"Of course they are." Margaret waved her hand impatiently, dismissing Shelby's argument. "Don't be foolish."

Shelby moved back until she felt the cowboy's tall, strong body press up against hers. Cowardly? Maybe, but she'd live with it. Right now, this tall, exceptionally well-built man was the safest spot she could find.

Margaret's gaze snapped to the cowboy. "Caleb, bring her along inside right this minute."

Caleb. His name was Caleb. For a second, Shelby worried that he might do just that. After all, he didn't know her and the Goodman family, as they kept telling her, were a big deal here in Royal. Maybe he wasn't the safe harbor she'd thought he was.

Then the cowboy stepped out from behind her and moved to partially block Shelby from the woman glaring at her. While Shelby watched, he tipped his hat and said, "I don't take orders from you, Mrs. Goodman."

Margaret inhaled through her nose and if she could have set the cowboy on fire, she clearly would have. "Fine. *Please* bring her along inside. The wedding is about to start."

"Well now," Caleb said slowly, that deep drawl caressing every word, "I don't believe the lady wants to go back inside."

"No," Shelby said, exhaling in a rush. "I do not."

"There you go. She sounds pretty sure," Caleb said, shrugging as if he couldn't have cared less which way this confrontation turned out.

"Well, I'm sure, too." Margaret took a menacing step forward. "This woman is engaged to my son, God help me."

Insulted, Shelby frowned, but the older woman kept going.

"We have a club full of people waiting for the ceremony to begin and the Goodman family has a reputation to uphold in Royal. I refuse to allow some city tramp to ruin it."

"Tramp?" Okay, now she was more sure than ever that running had been the right thing to do. The very idea of having to deal with this woman as a *relative* for the rest of her life gave her cold chills.

Shelby took a step toward the woman with the plan to tell Margaret exactly what she thought of her. But the cowboy alongside her grabbed her arm to hold her in place.

"That's enough, Margaret," he said quietly.

"It's not nearly enough." Margaret fired a hard look at the cowboy before shifting her gaze back to Shelby. "You stay out of this, Caleb Mackenzie. This has nothing to do with you."

Though the urge to stand here and have it out with this appalling woman was so strong Shelby was almost quivering, she knew it would be a waste of time. And, since the most important thing was to escape before any more Goodmans showed up, she turned her head to stare up at the man beside her.

"Can you get me out of here?" Shelby asked, staring up into those cool, blue eyes.

"What?" Ignoring Margaret, the man looked at her as if he hadn't heard her right.

"Take me somewhere," she blurted, and didn't even think about the fact that she didn't know this man. Right now it was enough that Margaret clearly couldn't stand him. The enemy of my enemy, and all that.

"You want me to help you run out on the man waiting for you at the altar?"

"Well, when you put it like that, it sounds terrible," Shelby admitted, shifting uneasily from foot to foot.

"What other way is there to put it?"

"Okay fine. I'm a terrible human being," she whispered frantically as Margaret heaped curses on her head. "And I'll apologize to Jared later. But right now..."

Caleb stared down at her as if trying to see inside her. And Shelby was grateful that he couldn't. Because right now, her insides were tangled up into so many knots she'd probably look like a crazy person. Heck, she *felt* like a crazy person. One that had just made a break from the asylum and was now looking for a ride back to sanity.

Hitching the yards of tulle higher in her arms, Shelby murmured, "Margaret said your name's Caleb, right?"

"That's right."

God, his voice was so deep it seemed to echo out around her. His blue eyes were focused on her and Shelby felt a flutter of something she'd never felt for the man she'd almost married. Probably not a good thing. "Look, I don't have much time. If you can't help me, I need to find someone else. Fast." She took a breath and blew it out again. "So. Are you going to help me, Caleb?"

One corner of his mouth lifted briefly. "What's your name?"

"Shelby," she said, mesmerized by the motion of that mouth. "Shelby Arthur."

"I'm Caleb Mackenzie," he said. "My truck's over there."

He jerked his head toward a big, top-of-the-line black pickup that shone like midnight, its chrome bumpers glittering in the sun. At that moment, the huge black truck looked like a magical carriage there to transport her away from a nightmare. Shelby sighed in relief and practically sprinted for it.

"Where are you going?" Margaret's voice, loud, desperate, followed her. "You can't leave! What will people think?"

"Whatever the hell they want to," Caleb tossed over his shoulder. "Just like always."

He opened the passenger door and helped Shelby to

climb in. "We have to hurry," she said, throwing frantic looks at the building behind them.

"It'd be easier if you didn't have so damn much dress," he muttered, grabbing a fistful of the material and stuffing it into the truck.

"Never mind the dress," she said, staring down at him. She was doing it. Getting away. But she wasn't gone yet. Grabbing at the dress, she shoved it between her knees and then ignored the rest of the hot mess gown still hanging down the side of the truck. "Just get in and *drive*."

He looked up at her and again, Shelby felt that rush of something hot and unexpected. That was just too weird. A few minutes ago, she'd been set to marry another man and now she was getting all warm and shivery for a cowboy in shining armor? What was *wrong* with her?

"Yes, ma'am," he said. "You're the boss." Then he slammed the truck door, leaving a couple of feet of dress hanging out beneath the bottom.

Shelby didn't care. All she wanted was to get away. To feel free. She pushed her hair out of her face as it slipped from the intricate knots it had been wound into. While Caleb walked around the front of the truck, she stared out the window at the woman still cursing her. Shelby had the oddest desire to wave goodbye and smile. But she didn't. Instead, she looked away from her would-be mother-in-law and when Caleb climbed into the truck and fired it up, she took her first easy breath. When he threw it into gear and drove from the parking lot, Shelby laughed at the wild release pumping through her.

He glanced at her. "Are you crazy?"

She shook her head and grinned. "Not anymore. I think I'm cured."

* * *

Caleb told himself that if she wasn't crazy herself, she was probably a carrier. How else did he explain why he was driving down the long, nearly empty road toward his ranch with a runaway bride sitting beside him?

Two words repeated in his brain. *Runaway bride.* Hell, he was helping do to Jared what Mitch and Meg had done to *him* four years ago. Was this some kind of backward Karma?

Caleb shot a sideways look at his passenger. The dress was god-awful, but it was fitted to her body like a damn glove. Her high, full breasts were outlined behind yet another layer of lace. The high neck only made a man wonder what was being hidden. Long sleeves caressed her arms and a damn mountain of white net poofed out around her body even while she fought it down.

Her face was pale, making the handful of freckles across her nose stand out like firelight in a snowstorm. While he watched, she rolled down the window and her hair was suddenly a wild tangle of dark red curls flying in the wind.

She closed her eyes, smiled into the wind, then turned to look at him and smiled even wider. "Thanks for the rescue."

Yeah. He'd rescued her and helped to humiliate Jared, just as he himself had once been. Caleb didn't much care for Jared Goodman, but that didn't make what he'd done any easier to take.

"Why'd you wait to run?" he asked.

"What?"

"Why wait until the last damn minute to change your mind?"

"Good question." She sighed, pushed her hair back, then propped her elbow on the door. "I kept thinking it would get better, I guess. Instead, it just got worse."

He could understand that. It was the Goodmans, after all.

"And you couldn't leave before today?"

She looked at him and frowned. "I could have. But I gave my word. I said I'd marry Jared—"

"But you didn't."

"Couldn't," she corrected, shaking her head. "Staring at myself in the mirror, wearing this hideous dress, listening to Margaret tell me about the honeymoon plans *she* made…" Her voice died off and it was a few seconds before she spoke again. "It finally hit me that I just couldn't go through with it. So I ran. I suppose you think that's cowardly."

"Well…"

She shifted in her seat, hiking all of that white fabric higher until it was above her knees, displaying a pair of long, tanned legs. When she stopped just past her knees, Caleb was more than a little disappointed.

He looked back at the road. Way safer than looking at her.

"You're wrong," she said. "It took more strength to run than it would have to stay."

Frowning to himself, Caleb thought about that for a minute. Was it possible she had a point?

She threw both hands up, the fabric spilled off her lap to the floor and she muttered a curse as she gathered it all up again to hold on her lap. Caleb spared another quick look at her long, tanned legs, then told himself to keep his eyes on the road.

"Honestly," she said, "I could have gone through with

it and not been called a 'tramp.' I could have stayed, knowing that I didn't really love Jared after all, but going through with the wedding to avoid the embarrassment. But it wasn't right for me or fair to Jared for me to marry him knowing I didn't want to be married, especially to him, you know what I mean?"

Before he could say anything, she rolled right on.

Waving one hand, then grabbing up fabric again with another curse, she said, "I know he'll be angry and probably hurt today but sooner or later, he's going to see that I did the right thing and who knows, maybe he'll even *thank* me for it at some point."

"Don't hold your breath," Caleb muttered.

"What? Never mind." Shaking her head, she took a deep breath, looked out over the open road and said, "Even if he doesn't thank me out loud, he'll be glad. Eventually. This is better. I mean, I don't know what to do *now*, but this is definitely better. For both of us."

"You sound sure."

She looked at him again until he felt compelled to meet those forest green eyes of hers however briefly. "I am," she said. "So thank you. Again."

"You're welcome." Caleb didn't know what the hell he was supposed to do with her, so he was headed home. Back at the ranch, she could call her own family. Or a cab. And then she could be on her way and he could get out of this damn suit.

With that thought firmly in mind, Caleb focused on the familiar road stretching out ahead of him and did his best to ignore the beautiful woman sitting way too close to him.

There were wide sweeps of open land dotted with the scrub oaks that grew like weeds in East Texas. Here and there were homes and barns, with horses in paddocks and cattle grazing in the fields. The sky was the kind of clear, deep blue he'd only ever seen in Texas and those few gusting clouds he'd glimpsed earlier had gathered up a few friends.

Everything was absolutely normal. Except for the bride in his truck.

"Weird day," he muttered.

"It is, isn't it?" She whipped her hair out of her eyes to look at him. "I never thought I'd be a fugitive from my own wedding. And I know I've said this already, but thank you. I kind of threw myself at you and didn't give you much room to back off, so I really appreciate you riding to the rescue."

"I could have said no," he reminded her.

She tilted her head to one side and studied him. "No, I don't think you could have."

He snorted. "Is that right?"

"Yeah. I think so." She shook her head. "You've got the whole 'responsible' vibe going on. Anyway, I didn't know how I was going to get away. Didn't even think about it. I just ran."

"Right into me." And he had gotten a real good feel of the body beneath that ugly-ass gown. High, firm breasts, narrow waist, nicely rounded hips. He frowned and shifted as his own body suddenly went tight and uncomfortable. Hell. Just what he needed.

"Yeah, I'm sorry you got dragged into this."

He glanced at her. "No, you're not."

She grinned. "No, I guess I'm really not. Hard to be sorry about finding a white knight."

He let that one go because he was nobody's hero.

"So now what?" he asked. "What are you going to do from here?"

She sat back and stared at him. "I have no idea."

"Well, what was the plan?"

"Like I said, there wasn't a plan. I just had to get away." Shaking her head, she stared out the windshield. "I didn't even know I was going to run until just before I did."

She'd torn down her hair and now it was a tangled mess of dark red curls that flew around her face in the wind whipping through the opened windows. He'd had the AC on, but she'd shut it off and rolled down her window, insisting she needed to feel the wind on her face. Caleb didn't know what it said about him that he preferred that hair of hers wild and free to the carefully pinned-up style she'd had when she ran from the club.

She still had the skirt of her wedding dress hiked up to her knees and Caleb took another admiring look at her long slim legs. Then he fixed his gaze on the road again. "Look, I'll take you out to my ranch—"

"Your ranch."

"That's right."

"Jared said he had a ranch."

Caleb snorted. "The Goodmans used to run a ranch, generations ago. Now they rent the land out to other ranchers so they can live in town."

"So I discovered." She held her hair back, narrowed her eyes on him and asked, "Anyway, we know I'm not crazy."

"Do we?"

She ignored that. "Now I have to ask. Are you a crazy person?"

Both eyebrows lifted and he snorted a laugh. "What kind of question is that?"

"One I probably should have asked *before* I hopped into your truck."

"Good point." A reluctant smile tugged at his mouth.

"Well, I thought I should ask before we go much further down this pretty empty road."

Amused in spite of everything, he asked, "What happened to me being a damn hero rescuing you?"

"Oh, you're still a hero," she assured him, "but you could be crazy, too. You aren't, though, are you?"

"Would I admit it if I was?"

"You might." She shrugged. "There's no telling with crazy people."

"Know a lot of nut jobs, do you?" Caleb shook his head, he couldn't believe he was having this conversation.

"A few, but you don't seem like you're one of them." A wide swath of lace lifted into the wind and she snatched it and held it down on her lap. "Have you ever seen so much tulle?"

"What's tulle?"

"This." She lifted the swath of netting again. "It's awful."

"If you don't like it, Why'd you buy it?"

"I didn't." She sighed. "Jared's mother picked it out."

Caleb laughed. "Sounds like her."

"Okay, you're not crazy." She nodded and gave a sigh of satisfaction. "If you don't like my almost mother-in-law you're obviously stable."

"Thanks." Still shaking his head, he said, "Like I was saying, I'll take you to the ranch. You can figure out where to go from there."

"I don't know where I can go," she said quietly turning her head to stare out the window at the scenery flying past. "I don't have my purse, my wallet. God, I don't even have clothes."

Caleb didn't like the sound of the rising hysteria in her voice.

"I don't know what I was thinking," she said, and her words tumbled over each other in their rush to get out. "My God, I don't have anything with me."

"I can take you to an ATM—"

"No purse," she interrupted. "No wallet, remember? No clothes except for this giant marshmallow of a dress." She slapped one hand to her chest as if trying to hold her heart inside her body.

"You're starting to panic," he pointed out.

"Of course I am." Her eyes were wild. "Now that I got away, I can think about other things and what I'm thinking is that I'm alone. In a strange place. Don't know anyone but the people I'm escaping from."

He watched from the corner of his eye as she shook her head frantically.

"I can't exactly go over to the Goodmans' house and say please can I have my things? My clothes. My purse. My ID. My *phone*." She dropped her head into her hands and now her face was covered by what looked like an acre of tulle. "This is a nightmare," she muttered.

"Remember, you wake up from nightmares."

She lifted her head to glare at him. "Easy for you to say since I'm assuming you actually *have* a change of clothing."

"Good point." He nodded. "Yeah, you're about the same size as my sister-in-law. You can wear some of her stuff."

"Great. And what if she doesn't feel like being generous?"

"She's out of town."

A short laugh shot from Shelby's throat. "So I've been on my own about fifteen minutes and already I'm stealing clothes."

"Not stealing. Borrowing." He paused. "Are you always this dramatic?"

"Only when my world implodes," she said and looked at him again. "So basically, I'm homeless and destitute. Well, hasn't this day turned out all sparkly?"

He laughed.

She narrowed her eyes on him, then reluctantly, laughed herself. "This is not how I pictured my life going."

"Yeah, not how I saw my day going, either," he replied, grateful that she seemed to be coming down from that momentary panic.

"Honestly," she said with another shake of her head, "I didn't think beyond moving to Texas to marry Prince Charming who turned out to be a frog."

"And you didn't notice that right off?"

"No." She huffed out a breath and turned her face into the wind. "Usually I'm a terrific judge of character."

When he didn't agree, she reminded him, "I picked *you* to rescue me, didn't I?"

Amused again, Caleb laughed. "Yeah, but your choices were limited."

"I could have just run screaming down the street," she pointed out. "Which was first on my to-do list until I saw you." She paused for breath. "Did you ever notice how appropriate the name Grimm was for an author of fairy tales?"

"Can't say I ever thought about it."

"Well, I've had the time lately. And the motivation. I mean, seriously. Look at this mess. It's got it all. The feckless fiancé who'd gone from hero to wimp. His vicious mother and creepy father, not to mention his grabby brother."

"Grabby?" Caleb scowled at the road ahead and admitted silently that he was really starting to sympathize with his runaway passenger. The Goodman family wasn't exactly the best Royal had to offer and Shelby Arthur had discovered that the hard way.

She shuddered. "Justin is not someone a woman should be alone with. The only bright spot in that family was Jared's sister, Brooke. She must be adopted," Shelby added under her breath, then continued, "but by now, even *she's* probably furious with me."

"Do you need me to respond or are you good to talk all on your own?"

"God this is a mess."

"Seems to be."

She turned to look at him. "Not going to try to console me?"

"Would it do any good?"

"No."

"Then it'd be a waste of time, wouldn't it?"

"Are you always so chatty?" she asked.

"Yep."

Shelby laughed, and the sound was soft and rich and touched something in Caleb he didn't want to acknowledge. Still, her laughter was better than the anxiety he'd just been listening to.

"Look," he said. "You come out to the house and

you can stay there a day or two. Figure out what you want to do."

"Stay there. With you."

He shot her a look. "Don't look so damn suspicious. I'm not offering you a spot in my bed." Damn shame about that, he admitted to himself, since just looking at her made him want to reach out and cover her mouth with his. And a few other things besides. But not the point.

"You can stay on the other side of the house," he said. "My mother died a couple years ago. You can have her wing. We won't even see each other."

"Her *wing*?" Shelby frowned. "How big is this house?"

"Big enough."

At the Texas Cattleman's Club, the reception for the wedding that didn't happen was in full swing. A band played dance music as a Goodman wedding would never have accepted something so pedestrian as a DJ. The tables were decorated with snowy white cloths and a bud vase on each table held a single pink rose. The soft clink of china and crystal was an undercurrent to the music and, while the crowd gathered in knots to exchange gossip about the runaway bride, Rose Clayton sat alone at a table watching it all.

At sixty-seven, Rose was an attractive woman with a figure she took care of, stylishly cut dark brown hair with just a hint of gray—thanks to a talented stylist— that swung in a loose fall at her jawline, and her sharp, smoke-colored eyes never missed a thing.

Conversations rose and fell around her like a continuous wave. She was only half listening, and even at that, she caught plenty of people talking about the upcoming TCC board elections. There had been a time when she wouldn't have given them a thought. But, now that women were also full-fledged members in the Texas Cattleman's Club, she was more than a little interested.

As far as Rose was concerned, their current president, James Harris, was doing a wonderful job and she saw no reason to make a change. It was nice to eavesdrop and hear that most of the other members felt the same way.

As people passed her table, they nodded or smiled, but kept moving. Rose's reputation as the uncrowned queen of Royal society kept people at bay even as they treated her with the respect she'd earned through years of a stubborn refusal to surrender to the unhappiness in her own life.

Rose knew everyone at the reception. She'd watched many of them grow up. Including Margaret Fraser Goodman. The woman, Rose thought, had been *born* an old stick. She had always been more concerned with appearances than with what really mattered. But even as she mentally chastised Margaret, Rose had to admit that she had done the same. The difference was, she assured herself, that Rose found enjoyment within the parameters that had been forced on her so long ago.

Her gaze fixed on Margaret Goodman briefly and noted the crazed look in her eyes and the grim slash of a mouth she kept forcing into a hard smile. Rose had already heard bits and pieces of chatter, no doubt started by Margaret, that had turned the situation around. Now, the story went, it was *Jared* who had changed his mind at the last moment. Told his unfortunate bride to leave.

And a part of Margaret might even believe it. Rose

had never met the now missing bride, but damn if she didn't admire the woman. She'd taken charge of her own life and done what she'd had to do. Who knew how Rose's life might have turned out if she'd had the same gumption?

But times had been different fifty years ago and Rose's father, Jed, had been a man no one crossed. Her gaze swept the room until she spotted her grandson Daniel. Daniel Clayton was her reward for all of the misery she'd managed to survive over the decades.

A grown man now, he was handsome, intelligent and damned funny when he wanted to be. He was the light of her life and there wasn't a thing she wouldn't do to see him happy. Within reason.

"Oh, that is simply unacceptable," Rose murmured to herself as she saw Daniel bend down and gently kiss a pretty woman who looked dazzled by his attention.

Alexis Slade.

The granddaughter of Gus Slade.

Just thinking the man's name gave Rose's heart a jolt. Once upon a time, she'd been crazy in love with that old goat and risked her father's wrath to be with him. Until the night her father made the threat that had ended everything between her and Gus forever.

She squared her shoulders and lifted her chin. Nodding to people who addressed her, she was a part of the crowd and yet separate from it as her mind raced back through the years.

For decades now, the Claytons and the Slades had been if not enemies, then at least at odds. They didn't socialize. Didn't trust each other. And they surely didn't look at each other as Daniel and Alexis were right that minute. She wouldn't have it. And what's more, Rose was quite sure that on this subject at least, Gus would agree with her.

Their grandchildren had been sweet on each other years ago, but Rose and Gus had put a stop to it. Gus sent Alexis off to an out-of-state college, while Rose kept Daniel so busy with ranch work, he didn't have time to miss the girl he couldn't have.

"Unacceptable," she whispered again, tapping her manicured nails against the tablecloth in a muffled staccato. Again, she scanned the room, but this time, she was looking for someone in particular.

When she found him, Rose stood, crossed the room and stopped at his table. "Gus. We have to talk."

Three

Gus Slade wore a steel-gray suit with a white shirt and a bold red tie. His black cowboy hat rested on the table alongside his arm. His thick hair, once black as midnight, was silver now, and his skin was tanned and leathered from years of working out in the Texas sun. He was leaning back in his chair, one booted foot resting on a knee. At sixty-nine, he was still a powerful, magnetic man.

Damn it.

His piercing blue eyes fixed on Rose with neither welcome nor warning. "Talk about what?"

Ignoring his rudeness, she took a seat near him, glanced over her shoulder toward their grandchildren and said pointedly, *"That."*

He took a look, then frowned. "Nothing to talk about. Keep your boy away from my girl and we have no problem."

"Take another look, you old goat," Rose said in a whispered hush. "It's Alexis doing the flirting. And she's got the look of a woman who's been thoroughly—recently—kissed."

Gus's frown deepened and his gaze shifted to Rose. "A woman flirting doesn't mean a damn thing. And kisses are fleeting, aren't they, Rose?"

She took a gulp of air at the implied insult. Rose had been sixteen years old when she fell head over heels in love with Gus. And if she had to be honest—the man could still give her insides a jump start. But damned if she'd sit there and be insulted.

"I didn't come over here to talk about the past."

"Then why are you sitting at my table?" he snapped.

Rose swallowed back her annoyance. Since the death of his wife, Sarah, from cancer a few years before, Gus had become even more unsociable than usual. And another piece of her heart ached. Sarah Slade had once been Rose's best friend, but Rose had lost them both when she'd rejected Gus. He had turned to Sarah for comfort and soon the two of them had been together, shutting Rose out completely.

But old hurts couldn't matter at the moment. It was the present they had to worry about, not the past. "Gus, unless we're prepared to have the two of them getting together—*again*—we have to come up with something."

He scrubbed one hand across his jaw in a gesture Rose remembered. Deliberately, she shut down a surge of memories and waited impatiently for the man to speak. Gus always had taken his time choosing just the right words. And even back when she had loved him, that particular trait had driven Rose crazy.

"Fine," he said at long last, keeping his voice low as he glanced around to make sure no one could listen in. "But not here. Don't need a damn audience of gossips trying to figure out why we're suddenly being friendly."

Rose winced. She hadn't really considered that. Her one thought had been to enlist Gus's help in breaking up any attachment between her grandson and his grand-daughter. "You're right."

He flashed a grin. "Well, this is a banner day. Rose Clayton admitting Gus Slade is right about something."

She was unamused. "Write it on your calendar in big red letters. Meanwhile—"

"Fine, then. We'll meet tomorrow. Two o'clock at the oak."

Rose inhaled sharply at the jab. *The oak* could have been anywhere in the state of Texas. But Rose knew exactly what meeting spot Gus was talking about. She was almost surprised that he remembered. Then, as his gaze focused on her, she realized that he was testing her. Seeing if *she* remembered.

How could she not?

"Agreed. Two o'clock." She turned to walk away, un-willing to give him the satisfaction of seeing that he'd gotten to her. Then she stopped, looked back and said, "Try not to be late this time."

Smiling to herself at the accuracy of her own little barb, Rose walked back to her table.

Shelby stared up at the main house and gave a sigh.

She'd been impressed when Caleb drove through the gates with the scrolled ironwork *M*. Then the oak-lined drive had taken her breath away. But the house itself was amazing.

It was big, sprawling across the ground, like a lazy dog claiming its territory. The house jutted out at different angles that told Shelby people had been adding on to the house for generations. There was a long, wide front porch running the length of the house, with stone pillars holding up the overhang roof.

There were chairs and swings along the length of the porch, crowded with pillows and huge pots filled with flowers spilling down in rivers of bright colors. The effect was a silent welcome to sit and enjoy the view for a while. And the view was pretty spectacular. It was exactly the kind of ranch you would find in a *House Beautiful* article called "The Lifestyles of Rich Ranchers."

She turned in a slow circle, still holding her wedding dress up around her knees. There was a barn, a stable, a corral where three horses were gathered in a knot as if whispering to each other. There was another house, a two-story cottage style just across the yard and in the distance, there were other long, low buildings.

"Wow." She half turned to look up at Caleb. "This is all yours?"

"Mine and my brother's, yeah." He frowned. "Part of your dress is in the dirt."

She looked over her shoulder and muttered a curse. Then she huffed out a breath. "I don't care. Not like I'm going to wear it again. Ever."

He shrugged. "Your call." He pointed to the two-story house. "My brother and his family live there. I'll go get you some of Meg's things."

"I don't know…" It felt weird. She was already so much in his debt, how much deeper could she go? He'd rescued her, offered her a place to stay and now he was going to give her clothes.

"Hey, okay with me if you want to stay in that dress."

Biting her lip, she looked down at the white nightmare she was wearing. "Okay, yes. I'd like to borrow some clothes." *Please don't let him be crazy.*

"Be right back. Oh," he added, "when you go inside, just…watch yourself."

What kind of warning was that? She turned to glance at the wide oak front door and wondered what she was going to find behind it. A torture chamber? Rat-infested rooms? A collection of wedding dresses from the brides he'd rescued before her?

Shelby groaned at that last ridiculous thought. How many brides could one man run across, anyway? After what she'd already been through that day, what in that house could possibly affect her?

So, bracing herself for everything from explosives to bears, Shelby walked across the porch and opened the door.

A blast of icy, air-conditioned air greeted her and she nearly whimpered. She'd thought Chicago summers were killer. But Texas was a brand-new ball game. The humidity here was high enough to fill a swimming pool. Eager to get into the cool, she pushed the door wider but it hit something and stopped.

Curious, Shelby peeked inside and gasped.

Stuff.

Wall-to-wall *stuff.*

The door wouldn't open all the way because there was an antique dresser right in front of it. She didn't need to ask why, either. One step into the main room told Shelby everything she needed to know about Caleb's late mother.

The furniture was lovely, but jammed into what

should have been a large, generous room. And on every table, every dresser, every curio cabinet, was stuff. Not old newspapers or magazines, but statues and crystals and rings and bracelets and candlesticks and crystal bowls and baskets and trays.

If Caleb had thought this room would send her screaming, he couldn't have been more wrong. Shelby's organized soul was instantly energized. Her business, Simple Solutions, depended on people like Caleb's mother. Back in Chicago, she'd built her reputation on being able to go into a mess, straighten it out and teach the homeowner how to keep it tidy. Her client list had been built on word of mouth and she was thinking of expanding, hiring more employees, when she'd met Jared Goodman.

Frowning a little, Shelby realized it was hard to believe that she'd given up everything she knew for a man who had ended up being nothing but a facade. She'd trusted him. Believed him. Thought she was in love.

But as it turned out, she'd been in love with the idea of being in love and the reality of actually *marrying* Jared had been enough to jolt her out of the illusion.

Shelby walked farther into the room, lifting one of the crystal bud vases for a closer look, then carefully setting it down again. In her business, she'd learned early about maker's marks on crystal and glass. She knew antiques when she saw them and had a pretty good idea of the value of different pieces.

She did a slow turn, admiring the bones of the room and she wondered why Caleb's mother had felt that emotional need to surround herself with things. The ranch itself was elegant and even in its current state, Shelby could see that the home would be, once cleared out, amazing.

"Yeah, it's pretty bad," Caleb said from behind her.

She turned to look at him. "I've seen worse."

He laughed shortly. "Hard to believe."

"Oh, this is nothing, really." She lifted a porcelain tray and ran her fingertips across the library table it rested on. "No dust. I've been in places where the dust was so thick the furniture looked like ghost pieces. The wood was white with neglect."

"My foreman's wife, Camilla, takes care of things around here."

"Well, she does a good job of it." Shelby looked around again. "It can't be easy to keep all of this dusted."

He sighed and gave a look around. "I keep telling her that we'll get people in here to haul all of this stuff away, but—"

"But you get busy," Shelby said.

"Yeah."

"And that's where I come in."

He turned a wary look on her. "What's that mean?"

"I'm a professional organizer," Shelby said, smiling up at him. "This is what I do. I go into people's homes and help bring order to chaos. I had my own business in Chicago. A successful one."

"And you gave it up to marry Jared," he mused.

"Yes, well." She stopped, frowned. "Bad judgment aside, I'm excellent at what I do." She turned to look at the room again before staring up at him. "I can take care of this for you."

"Is that right?" He was holding a pair of jeans and a T-shirt.

She supposed shoes were too much to hope for.

"Sure. It's great, really." Shelby's mind was racing, figuring, planning and when she had most of it all set, she started talking again. "I need a place to stay for a while."

"Now, wait a second…"

"Just hear me out." She took a breath and released it in a rush. "You've been fabulous. Really. So thanks again for the whole rescue and bringing me here and not being a serial killer."

One corner of his delectable mouth quirked briefly. "You're welcome."

She grinned at him. Really, he was ridiculously good-looking, but when his mouth hinted at a smile, his looks went off-the-chart hot. Still, not the point at the moment.

"But the truth is," she said, "until I can get all of my stuff from Jared's parents' house—not to mention get into my money, I'm stuck."

"What about family?" he asked. "Isn't there someone you could call?"

"No." Sorrow briefly landed on her, gave her a fleeting kiss, then moved on again. "My mother died last year, so I'm all that's left."

"Sorry." He looked uncomfortable.

Shelby understood that, since she'd seen it often back home. So she spoke up quickly to even things out between them again. "Like I said, I'm a professional organizer.

"The plan was to open a business here in Texas…" She frowned, unsure now just what she would do about that. "Back in Chicago, I had hundreds of satisfied clients."

"Uh-huh."

He didn't sound interested, but he hadn't walked away, either. Which meant she hadn't lost him completely. And seeing this house had given her the first shot of good news she'd experienced in days. Before, she'd felt like a beggar, asking for help, borrowing clothes. But if he let her do this, she could feel as though she were paying her way. And that, more than anything, was important to her. She liked being her own boss. In charge of her own life. And right now, she could use a jolt of that in her system.

"My point is," she said eagerly, "I can straighten all of this out for you. I can organize everything of your mother's. All you'll have to do is decide what you want to do with everything."

He glanced around the room again and looked back to Shelby. "It's a big job."

"I'm up to it."

He studied her for a long minute, long enough that she shifted position uncomfortably. What was he seeing when he looked at her? He was seriously gorgeous, so Shelby had to wonder if he was feeling the slightest bit of attraction that was humming through her blood. And the minute she thought it, she pushed it away. *Really? Run away from your wedding and have some completely indecent thoughts about your rescuer? God, Shelby, get a grip.*

"My brother and his wife have already taken what they want, and as for me, keep what works in the room and we could donate the rest of it, I guess," he said.

Concession, her mind shouted and she jumped on it. "Absolutely, and that would be very generous. The crystal alone is probably very valuable. I could contact an antiques store and see about selling some of it if you want me to. I can check all of it for you. Make lists of what you have and where it is and—"

"Do you *ever* stop talking?"

She frowned at him. "Not often. And this is important. I really need to get you to agree with this or I'll be sleeping in a park or something. So I'll do all the work here in exchange for room and board until I can get my life back on track."

"And how long do you figure that will take?"

She winced. "Depends on how cooperative the Goodmans are."

"So forever," he said.

She sighed and felt a momentary dip in her enthusiasm. "I know it's an intrusion on you and I'll try not to bug you much…"

He was watching her and she wished she could read whatever thoughts were digging furrows between his eyebrows. The man was unreadable, though. He was the embodiment of the iconic cowboy. Tall, rugged, gorgeous, stoic. So she was forced to wait. Thankfully, it didn't take long.

"I suppose we could try it."

She sighed, grinned and slapped one hand to her chest. "Thanks. Wow. I feel better already. This is great. You won't be sorry. I'll have this taken care of so fast you won't even recognize the place."

"Uh-huh." He started walking toward the wide hall. "Anyway. You can stay over here in the east wing."

Shelby was looking around the house as she followed him. From what she could see in the hallway, there were plenty of places for her to organize there, too.

"I've never lived in a house with wings."

He glanced down at her as she hurried up to walk

at his side. "Yeah, this one's got all kinds of wings spreading out from here, the center. Every generation has added to it for nearly a hundred and fifty years."

"Wow." Shelby was impressed. She and her mother had been constantly on the move, from apartment to condo, to rental house. They'd never stayed anywhere longer than three years. So hearing about a family who had been in the same spot for more than a century filled her with a kind of envy she hadn't expected. That was roots, she told herself. Digging in, planting yourself and building your own world. One for your children and your children's children.

And that hunger for family, for roots, was what had prompted her to allow herself to be swept off her feet by Jared. Lesson to be learned there, Shelby told herself.

The walls in the house changed from log to stone and back again as they walked. The hardwood floor was shining, letting her know that the house was well cared for in spite of the clutter in the main room that had dribbled into the hallway. She imagined that Camilla had to work like a Trojan to keep everything as clean and beautiful as it was.

Caleb opened a door on the right and stepped inside. Shelby was right behind him, but she stopped on the threshold to simply stare. She gasped because she couldn't help herself. The room was beautiful. Big, with a four-poster cherrywood bed covered by a dark blue-and-white star quilt. There were two end tables, a chest at the foot of the bed and a dresser on the far wall. Two bay windows offered a view of the front yard and the oaks lining the drive.

"This was my mom's room."

Shelby looked at him. "She didn't clutter this one."

"No," he said with a slow shake of his head. "She only did that in the main room and the kitchen. Anyway—" he pointed to a door "—there's a bathroom through there."

"Okay, thanks." Shelby walked farther into the room, laid one hand on the footboard and looked back at Caleb again.

How quickly things turned around, she thought. Only that morning, she'd been in the Goodman family home, dressing for her wedding. She'd felt trapped. Dreading the future she'd set for herself. Boxed into a corner and hadn't been able to see a way out.

Now, hours later, she was in a *real* ranch house with a gorgeous cowboy who'd rescued her from Jared's dragon of a mother. Yeah. Life could turn on you in an instant, so you'd better keep your seat belt on at all times.

"I've got work," he said, dragging her up and out of her thoughts. He tossed his sister-in-law's clothes onto the foot of the bed. "I'll be at the stable or in the first barn."

"Okay." He was so close she could smell the aftershave still clinging to his skin. It was like the woods, she thought. At night. With a full moon. Maybe skinny-dipping in a lake— Okay. She shut her brain off, then blurted, "Just where do *you* sleep?"

"In the west wing," he said. "On the other side of the great room we were in before."

"Oh. Okay." Probably not far enough for her peace of mind, but there wasn't much she could do about it.

One eyebrow lifted. "Problem?"

"No," she said, and then went on because she couldn't tell him that the problem was she was really attracted to him and wanted to see what it would be like to kiss him. Especially since just a couple hours ago, she was supposed to be marrying somebody else. For heaven's sake. It was like she was two people—and one of them was in serious trouble. "You already said you're not crazy and I don't suppose you'll be sneaking over here during the night."

His gaze swept her up and down, then locked on her eyes. "I'll try to control myself."

Frowning, she said, "Well that's flattering, thank you again."

"Do you really need me to tell you that you're beautiful?"

A flush of pleasure snaked through her even as she said, "Of course not."

"Good, because I won't be."

"Is that an insult?"

"Nope. It's a promise." Caleb nodded. "I try not to seduce women wearing wedding gowns. Sends the wrong message." He turned around and headed down the hall. He stopped halfway, looked back over his shoulder and said, "My housekeeper, Camilla, and my foreman, Mike, live in a house behind this one. Out the kitchen door and across the yard. To find the kitchen, just take the main hall straight back."

"Right." She wasn't hungry. Her stomach was still in knots of desperation mingled with relief. But she might go in search of a coffeepot later. And if she was staying—at least temporarily—she would have to meet Camilla and enlist her help. "And, um, thanks. Really."

He nodded and his gaze moved over her again. This time, his inspection was so slow, so thorough, Shelby felt heat flicker to life in her bloodstream.

Seriously, what was wrong with her? She had just

run from one man and now she was getting all fizzy over another one? Maybe this was a breakdown. Some emotional outburst to relieve the tension she'd been living with for weeks.

He shrugged out of his suit jacket and slung it over one broad shoulder, hanging it from the tip of one finger. He tipped his hat back farther on his head and gave her one last, long look. Then he turned and walked away.

His long legs moved slow and easy and Shelby's gaze dropped to his butt. A world-class behind, she thought and swallowed hard. Whatever was happening to her, it hadn't hurt her eyesight any. Dragging in a deep breath, she fought to steady herself and hadn't quite succeeded by the time he disappeared around a corner.

Leaning back against the wall, Shelby sighed a little. *What was it about a cowboy?*

Rose was waiting at the oak the next day when Gus arrived. True to his nature, he was a good fifteen minutes late. Back in another life, when she was young and in love, his tardiness had always irked the hell out of her. But then he'd smile and kiss her and every thought in her head would just melt away.

But that was then.

"You're late."

"And you still like to point out the obvious," Gus said, taking a seat beside her on the bench he had built for the two of them nearly fifty years ago. He slapped one work-worn hand onto the wood, rough from surviving years of wind and rain and sun. "Nice to see this held up."

"You were always good with your hands," Rose agreed.

He glanced at her and one graying black eyebrow lifted. "You used to think so."

She flushed and was surprised by it. Who would have guessed a woman her age was even capable of blushing? Taking a breath, she smoothed her hands across the knees of her khaki slacks and found herself wondering when her hands had aged. How was it the years flew past so quickly?

A lifetime ago, she and Gus would meet here beneath this oak tree. On summer nights, the wind whispered through the leaves, the stars shone down on them like points of flame and it had been as if the two of them were alone in the universe. The present had been exciting and the future looked bright and shiny.

Then it all ended.

Frowning to herself, she looked out over the land. This part of her family ranch hadn't changed much in the last fifty years. There were still cattle grazing in the distance beneath a steely blue sky and the thick canopy of leaves overhead muted the sun's power and lowered the temperature a good ten degrees. And here she was again. With Gus.

"Why did you pick here to meet?"

"Because I knew it would bother you," he admitted with a shrug.

That stung. "At least you're honest about it."

"I put a great value on honesty," Gus said, his voice deep and meaningful as he stared into her eyes. "Always did."

And Rose knew what he was talking about. Once

upon a time, she'd promised to love him forever. Then she'd later turned him away and told him she would never marry him. That she didn't love him and never had. And the lies had cost her, slicing at Rose's soul even as they tore Gus's heart apart while she was forced to watch.

"We're not here to talk about the past," she said, dragging air into tight lungs.

"No, we're damn sure not," he retorted. "So let's get to the point. You tell your grandson to keep his hands off my girl or there's going to be trouble."

Rose laughed shortly. "Don't use that 'lord of all you survey' voice on me. It won't work. And it won't work on Daniel, either." She lifted her chin and met her old lover glare for glare. "My grandson is made of tougher stuff than that. You won't scare him off, Gus, so don't bother trying."

"Well, what the hell do you want me to do, then?" He pushed up from the bench, walked a few feet through the dry brush, then spun about and came back to stand in front of her. "I assume you've got a plan. You always did have more ideas than you knew what to do with."

She sniffed a little, but stood up to meet him on her own two feet. He was still taller than her, but thanks to her Italian-made boots with a two-inch heel, she didn't have to crane her neck to meet his eyes.

"As it happens," she said, "I have been thinking about this."

"And?"

He was irritated and impatient, and she couldn't help but remember that he hadn't always been so anxious to get away from her.

"What we have to do is find each of them someone else."

"Oh," he said, laughing, "is that all?"

Rose scowled at him. "You might hear me out before you start mocking the whole idea."

"Fine." He folded his arms across his wide chest. "Tell me."

"I was thinking we could do something in Royal. An event. Something big. Something that would attract attention not just here, but in Houston, too."

"Uh-huh." Frowning, Gus said, "And what've you got in mind?"

"Well, nothing. Not yet. But you could throw out a few ideas you know." She tapped the toe of her boot against the ground. "This affects both of us, remember?"

"Wouldn't if you could just control your grandson," he muttered.

"Or if you could get your granddaughter to stop looking at Daniel with stars in her eyes," Rose countered.

His scowl deepened, but he gave her a grudging nod. "All right. So something that would involve the two of them, but throw them at other people."

"Exactly."

He scrubbed one hand across his jaw and Rose watched him, seeing not just the powerful man he was now, but the man he had once been. The man who'd stolen her heart when she was only sixteen years old. The man she had thought she'd be with forever.

The man her father had stolen from her.

The irony of this situation wasn't lost on her. Her own father had kept her from the man she loved and now she was scheming to do the same thing to her grandson. But she didn't have a choice. Claytons and Slades were just not meant to be together.

"All right," Gus said, his voice low and deep and somehow intimate. "I'll do some thinking on this, too. We can meet up again in a few days. See what we come up with."

"Fine." She nodded, refusing to acknowledge, even to herself, that she was glad she'd be seeing Gus again.

They stood only a few feet apart, separated by fifty years of mistrust and pain. A soft wind rattled the leaves overhead and pushed through Rose's hair like a touch.

"Well, I've got to be getting back," Gus said abruptly, and Rose jolted as if coming up out of a trance.

"Of course. Me, too."

Nodding, Gus said, "So we meet here again in three days? Same time?"

"That works," she agreed and watched as he turned to walk to his truck. Rose felt a sting of regret, of sorrow and spoke up before she could rethink it. "Gus."

He stopped, turned and asked, "What is it?"

Looking into those eyes that were at once so familiar and so foreign, Rose said something she should have told him two years ago. "I'm sorry about Sarah."

His features went tight, his eyes cool at the reminder of his wife's death. Sarah had once been Rose's best friend, closer than a sister, but Rose had lost her, too, when she had broken things off with Gus. Then lost any chance of reaching out to her at all when she died two years ago.

"Thank you."

Rose took a step closer because she couldn't stand that shut-down look in his gaze. "I should have said something before, but I thought you wouldn't want to hear it from me."

He studied her for several heartbeats before saying softly, "Then you were wrong, Rose."

When he walked away again, she let him go.

Four

For the next couple of days, Caleb did his best to avoid Shelby Arthur. It wasn't easy though because every time he turned around, there she was. She came out to the stables or the barn every so often with a question about one of his mother's "treasures."

He'd been ignoring the problem of his mom's collections since her death a couple of years ago. Hell, with the ranch to run, cattle to see to and the new oil leases to oversee, who had time to clear out furniture? Besides, Caleb didn't know anything about antiques and had no interest in learning.

But now, Shelby was determined to, as she put it, "earn her keep," so he was bombarded with questions daily. She had even enlisted the help of his housekeeper, Camilla, with the job of hauling furniture out to the front porch and covering everything with tarps.

Raina Patterson, the owner of Priceless, the antiques

store at the Courtyard shops in Royal, had already been out to the ranch once. She'd looked everything over and bought a few pieces right away. Soon, there'd be a truck rolling up to take most of it away. But Shelby wasn't half-finished. She was working with Raina to catalog the smaller things Caleb's mother had been hoarding for years.

Caleb already knew his brother, Mitch, wasn't interested in their mother's things, and Meg had taken the few pieces she wanted to remember her mother-in-law by. So the road was clear to clean out the house—and Shelby seemed determined to get it done fast.

Leaning on the rail fence surrounding the corral, Caleb watched the woman working on the front porch of the house. Even from across the yard, Caleb felt that hot zip of something tantalizing shoot through his blood and settle in his groin. Shelby was still wearing Meg's jeans, and they were a little tight on her, which worked fine for him. She'd also asked Caleb for a couple of his T-shirts, and she was wearing one of them now.

The shirt was way too big, but she'd fixed that by tying it off under her breasts so that her midriff was bare and he could admire that swath of tanned skin and daydream about seeing more of her. Her curly auburn hair was pulled up into a ponytail that danced across her shoulders, and the wedding sandals she wore looked both out of place and enticing on her long, narrow feet.

Caleb gritted his teeth as Shelby bent in half to tug a table out the front door. Her butt looked good in those faded jeans and he'd give a lot to see it naked. To touch it. To stroke down the curves of her body and then to—

"She's a hard worker, you gotta give her that."

Squeezing his eyes shut briefly, Caleb willed away

the tightness in his jeans and turned his head to watch his foreman, Mike Taylor, walk up to join him.

"Yeah, she's busy enough. Driving me nuts with all the questions, though."

"I can see that," Mike allowed, bracing both arms on the top fence rail. "But gotta tell you, Cam's happy as hell that Shelby's getting all that extra furniture out of the house. She's been grumbling about keeping it all dusted and clean."

Caleb nodded and turned his eyes back to Shelby. She'd moved on from tugging the furniture outside and now she was stretching to cover it all with yet another tarp. Of course, stretching like she was bared more of her midriff and had her extending one leg out like a ballet dancer.

Clearing his mind of every wicked thought currently gleefully tormenting him, he said only, "Will be nice to be able to walk through that room again."

"Uh-huh." Mike glanced at him, then grinned when he followed Caleb's gaze. "She's a good-looking woman."

"And you're a married man."

"Don't make me blind," Mike said, grinning. "Couldn't help but notice you noticing her."

"Is that right?" Caleb pushed off the fence and stuffed both hands into his jeans pockets. "If you've got so much extra time to spend 'noticing' things, maybe we should find you more work."

"You could do that," Mike said, teasing tone still in his voice, letting Caleb know he wasn't the least bit intimidated. "Or you could admit that woman's got you thinking."

"What I'm thinking is, we need to call the vet back out to check on the mare again."

"Yeah. You know, Cam tells me Shelby's not only beautiful, but she's smart, too. Hell, she has to be. Got herself out of marrying Jared Goodman."

"Got herself *into* it, too," Caleb reminded him. And in spite of the attraction he felt for her, that was the one thing that kept nibbling at his mind. Yeah, she was gorgeous and had a body that haunted him day and night. God knew she could talk the ears off a statue. And she wasn't afraid of work, so that was another point for her.

But bottom line was, she'd run out on her own wedding and left her groom—even if it was Jared Goodman— standing at the altar looking like a fool.

And that hit way too close to home for Caleb. He'd been in Jared's position and he knew firsthand just how hard it was. Yes, Meg had run off the night before their wedding, so Caleb hadn't actually been caught standing in front of a roomful of people looking like a jackass. But close enough. How in the hell could he be with a woman who had done to a man what had been done to *him*?

Caleb had been keeping his finger on what was going on in Royal over the failed wedding. The Goodmans were handling all of this a lot differently than he had, of course. They'd spun the story around until Jared was a damn hero who'd cut a gold digger loose before she could marry him.

Shelby hadn't heard any of that yet and he had a feeling she'd be furious when she inevitably did. Most people in Royal weren't buying the story, but enough folks were that he'd heard all kinds of ugly rumors about Shelby when he'd gone into town the day before.

And though a part of him wanted to defend her, he'd kept quiet because hell, he didn't even *know* the woman who'd taken up residence in his house. All he knew for sure was that he wanted her more than he'd ever wanted anyone and he couldn't have her.

"True enough," Mike concurred. "She did agree to marry him. But the important part is, she was smart enough to see the mistake before she made it permanent."

Caleb turned his head to look at his friend. "And that makes it okay?"

Mike frowned, squinted into the afternoon sun and shook his head. "Didn't say that, Boss. But you've got to admit this situation isn't like yours was."

He hated it. Hated that everyone knew what had happened and could drag it up and toss it at him when he least expected it. But memories were long in Royal.

"This isn't about me."

"Isn't it?" Mike smiled now. "I've seen the way you watch her." He laughed a little. "Hell, like you were watching her a minute ago—until she went back in the house."

Caleb shot his friend a hard look. "Since when is looking at a pretty woman a crime?"

"Since never. Yet, anyway," he added. "I'm just saying, she's single, you're single—what the hell, Boss?"

"It's complicated and you know it."

"I know you can untangle any knot if you want to bad enough."

Caleb ground his teeth together, took a long, deep breath and said, "Don't you have somewhere to be? Something to do?"

"Sure do. Just came over to tell you Scarlett's coming over later to give the mare another checkup."

Scarlett McKittrick was the town vet and there was

nobody better with every animal—from puppies to cows to stallions. "Fine. Let me know when she gets here."

"You got it. Hey…" Mike jerked his head toward the long, oak-lined drive. "What's the sheriff doing here?"

Caleb turned his head and watched Nathan Battle's black Suburban approach the house. "Guess I'd better find out."

Rather than walk around and go through the gate, Caleb hopped the fence and was waiting when Nate brought his car to a stop and parked opposite the ranch house front door. The sun was hot, the air was still and dripping with humidity. And the look on Nate's face promised trouble.

"Hey, Caleb," he said as he climbed out of the car. "Shelby around?"

"Yeah. She's in the house. What's this about, Nate?"

Nathan tugged his hat off, swept one hand through his hair and grimaced. "The Goodman family's making some noise about suing Shelby."

"What?" Behind him, the front door opened, slammed shut and Shelby's quick footsteps sounded out in the stillness.

She moved up to stand beside Caleb and he could have sworn he felt heat pumping from her body into his. Probably just the Texas sun—or at least that's what he was going to tell himself.

"They're going to sue me?" she asked, dumbfounded.

"Didn't say that, miss," Nate told her, turning his hat in his hands. "Said they're making noises about it."

"Sue me for what?"

Caleb was interested in hearing that, too.

"Well, miss," Nate winced and looked as though he

wished he were anywhere but there. "They say defamation of character. That you've made Jared look bad in his hometown."

Caleb snorted. "Jared's looked bad since he was in grade school."

Giving Caleb a wry smile, Nathan nodded. "I know that, but his mother sure doesn't seem to."

"They can't sue me," Shelby whispered and turned her gaze up to Caleb. "Can they?"

Why in the hell he would feel like protecting her, he couldn't say. But there it was. In the couple of days he'd known her, he'd seen fight and spirit and joy and relief in her eyes. He didn't much care for the worry he saw there now.

"They can," he said firmly, "but they won't."

"I wish I could believe that," she said softly.

Nate and Caleb exchanged a long look that Shelby saw. "What? What is it you two know that I don't?"

Giving a sigh, Caleb turned to her. "To Margaret Goodman, the only thing that matters is how something *looks* to someone else. It's all about appearances with her. Margaret's not going to drag Jared into a court battle where every woman in town would testify on your behalf that he's a weasel and you were smart to back out."

"Oh, God. I'm sort of relieved and a little horrified." Taking a step backward, Shelby kept moving until the backs of her knees hit a rocking chair, then she dropped into it. "How could I have been so stupid?"

Caleb almost answered, then he realized she was talking to herself, complete with wild hand gestures and shakes of her head that sent her ponytail swinging like a pendulum in a tornado. All he could do was stand there and listen.

"I never saw it," she muttered. "But truthfully, I didn't want to see it, either. I wanted the fantasy. He said he was a cowboy. Who could turn down a cowboy?"

"Is she all right?" Nate asked, a worried frown etched into his forehead.

"Damned if I know," Caleb admitted, watching the woman as she continued her private rant. He thought maybe he should say something, but then she might not even hear him. She wasn't really paying any attention to him and Nate at all. It was as if she were all alone and she was having a good argument. With herself.

"He said he had a ranch, but he doesn't have a ranch. He's a *lawyer*. And he's afraid of his *mother*. But then, everyone's afraid of her. I was, wasn't I?"

"Shelby…" Caleb wasn't sure she could hear him.

She shook her head even harder and that dark red ponytail went swinging again. "Was I really that stupid? Or just lonely? He was cute, sure, but I think I just wanted to be in love so badly that I purposely didn't see what I should have seen if I'd been really looking, you know?"

"Uh…" Nate was still watching her as if she might explode. "Is she actually talking to us?"

"I don't think so," Caleb mused.

"Texas is so different from home, but I thought that would be a good thing, but is it? Oh, no. So now I don't even have any extra *underwear* and they want to sue me? How is that fair?"

Talking to Caleb, even while he kept a wary eye on Shelby, Nate said, "I did manage to get her purse back from Mrs. Goodman—"

"My *purse*?" Shelby shot from the chair and snatched it from Nate's hand as soon as he pulled it out of his truck. She clutched the big, brown leather bag to her chest like a beloved child. Then she glanced inside. "Oh, my wallet. And my phone and lip gloss and my knife…"

"You have a knife?" Caleb asked.

"Doesn't everyone?" Shelby retorted, pulling a small Swiss Army knife out to hold up and show them. Then she looked past Nate toward his car as if she could find what she was looking for. "But what about the rest of my stuff? My suitcases? My clothes? Shoes?"

Nate grimaced. "Margaret says she's holding on to them for now."

"What?" She looked up at him. "Why?"

"Pure cussedness, I'd guess," Caleb muttered. Nate caught his comment and nodded.

"That's what it looks like to me, too."

"I have *one* pair of underwear," she snapped. "I can't live like that. Nobody could."

Nate's expression went from concerned to embarrassed and back again. But Caleb wasn't thinking about Nate. It was Shelby who had his full attention.

The disappointment on her face tore at Caleb. In the last couple of days, she'd been hanging on, doing what she had to, to cling to whatever part of her world was left. She'd been working hard the last few days, making sense of his late mother's collections and trying to bring some order to the house. It hadn't been easy.

And hell, Caleb could admit, at least to himself, that he hadn't helped any. He'd avoided her, ignored her presence as best he could, since the mere thought of her was enough to tighten his body to painful levels.

Hell, he was no fan of Jared Goodman, but he felt for the man. Caleb had been in Jared's position and it was hard to let go of that. But at the same time, he had to admit that Shelby had done what she thought was right. Had made a decision that couldn't have been an easy one and now she was still paying for it.

"Give Margaret a couple days to cool off some. I'll get your things back for you," Nate said in a soothing tone that seemed to ease some of the tightness from Shelby's features.

She smiled at Nate, then looked up at Caleb. He saw the shine in her eyes and hoped to God she wasn't going to cry. He hated it when women cried. Always left him feeling helpless, something he wasn't accustomed to.

She blinked the tears back, forced a smile he knew she wasn't feeling and said, "Well, at least I have my purse. I can go shopping for clothes and—"

"Yeah." Nate sighed and said, "About that. You'll have to use a credit card. Apparently Jared took you off the joint bank account, so your ATM card won't work."

"He can't do that," she argued, and all hints of tears evaporated in a rush of fury. "All of the money I got from the sale of my house is in that account. It's *my* money."

Caleb dropped one hand onto her shoulder and he felt her tremble. But he had the distinct impression that tremor was caused by pure rage. He couldn't blame her for it.

"Nate," Caleb said, "they can't do that. It's the same as stealing."

"You think I don't know that?" Shaking his head, the sheriff looked at Shelby. "I've already spoken to the judge and she says if you have proof of the deposit you made, she'll release the money to you."

"Do you?" Caleb asked. "Have proof, I mean."

"I do, but the problem is, it's in my suitcase." Her

shoulders slumped in defeat. "And the suitcase is at the Goodmans' house."

"I'll go over there," Caleb said. "Get her things."

"You'll stay out of it," Nate warned, aiming a steely look at Caleb. "Margaret's already half-convinced that *you're* the reason Shelby ran out on Jared."

"Me?" He was honestly stunned.

"Him?" Shelby echoed.

Caleb scowled at Nathan. "How the hell did Margaret come to that?"

"Shelby ran from the wedding straight to you." Nate shrugged helplessly. "You drove off with her. Now she's living here in your house."

Caleb bit back a curse. Damn it, he'd spent the last four years trying to live down a rich gossip vein and now he'd opened himself up to a brand-new one. Royal would be buzzing and though it was irritating as hell, it didn't really bother him as much as he would have expected it to.

Maybe it was because Shelby was standing there beside him looking outraged. Her eyes were flashing and there were twin spots of color in her cheeks. A hot Texas wind kicked up out of nowhere and sent those dark red curls of hers flying and all in all she made a picture designed to bring a man to his knees.

"But that's ridiculous," Shelby argued. "All he did was *help* me."

"Doesn't matter to Margaret," Nate said, then turned his attention back to Caleb.

"Yeah, I don't care what Margaret Goodman has to say and most people in Royal feel the same." Not completely true. He did hate the thought of being the subject of speculation and more gossip. But he didn't give a good damn what Margaret Goodman thought of him. Caleb looked at Shelby. "Whatever gossip springs up around this won't last long." He hoped. "The town's wagging tongues will move on to something more interesting."

"Just keep your distance from the Goodmans," Nathan said. "I'll go talk to Simon. See what I can do about getting your things, Shelby. If I have trouble with it, we can always email your bank and have them send you a copy of everything."

"Right. Okay. Yes. Good idea. Thanks I can do that. I'll do it tomorrow. Just in case." She kept nodding and Caleb figured it was just reaction. A hell of a lot of information dumped on her in just a couple of minutes. And not much of it was good.

He couldn't help but wonder what she was thinking. Her eyes gave nothing away, but thankfully they weren't filled with unshed tears anymore, either. And he had to admit it was worrying how quiet she'd gotten all of a sudden. He'd become used to her just talking his ears off.

He glanced at his friend. "Thanks, Nate."

"Sure. I'll be in touch. Shelby," he added, "we'll get this all straightened out."

She only nodded at him, making Caleb wonder again. He never would have believed he'd actually *miss* her rambling conversations and monologues.

The sheriff got back in his car and drove away, leaving the two of them alone on the porch.

Shelby was still petting that brown leather bag lovingly and holding it as if it were a life vest keeping her afloat in a churning sea. She didn't say anything, but Caleb could guess what she was thinking. Her world

was a damn mess and for a woman with an organized
soul like Shelby, that had to be hard to take.

"Well," she finally said with a shrug, "I guess I
should get back to work."

No complaints. No cussing. No kicking the porch
railing in sheer frustration. Just acceptance and moving on. Damned if Caleb didn't admire her. Shelby Arthur was an impressive woman. She'd had the world
tipped on her again and she wasn't letting it drag her
down. He'd never known anyone who bounced back
from bad news as quickly and completely as she did.
Maybe that was why he heard himself make an offer
he hadn't planned on. "The work can wait."

"What? Why?" She looked up at him, so he was staring into her eyes when he spoke again.

"How about I take you shopping?"

The flash of pleasure in those green eyes of hers
stirred simmering embers inside him into blistering
hot coals that threatened to immolate him.

It would be a hell of a burn.

Five

Caleb didn't take her to Royal and Shelby was grateful. She knew the small town was still gossiping about her and that catastrophe of a wedding. If they'd been in Royal, everyone would have been staring. Whispering. There was already talk and if people had seen the two of them together, that would have only fueled the fire. Not to mention there would have been a chance of running into some of the Goodman family.

But in Houston, no one knew her. No one cared that she and Caleb were walking together down a busy street. The only people looking at them were women, taking quick, approving glances at Caleb. He didn't seem to notice, but Shelby did. And if truth be told, she'd been sending him quite a few of those glances herself.

He was wearing black jeans and boots, a white shirt with a black blazer tossed over it. That gray hat he always wore was pulled down low on his forehead, shadowing his eyes and making him look…fantastic. The man was so sexy, her imagination was constantly fueled just by the thought of him.

There. She'd admitted it to herself. Caleb Mackenzie was like a walking sex dream. That slow drawl of his rumbled along a woman's skin like a touch and when his eyes fixed and held on her, Shelby felt as though he was looking right down into her soul. It was a little unsettling and at the same time thrilling in a way she'd never known before. Then there were the boots. And his long legs and the way jeans clung to them. His chest was broad and his hands were big and calloused from years of hard work and she really wanted to know what those hands felt like on her skin.

Then, as if he wasn't already droolworthy, there was the shopping. He could have gone to a bar or something to wait for her, but he'd walked with her. Kept her company and offered opinions—whether she wanted them or not—on the clothes she'd purchased. The only time he'd left her alone was in the lingerie department and she wished he had stayed. Having him watch while she picked out bras and underwear would have been…exciting. Which was just ridiculous, she lectured herself. She had no business fantasizing about *another* cowboy so soon after turning her whole world inside out for a would-be cowboy.

Shelby slapped her forehead. She must be losing her mind. Had to be the strength of the Texas sun broiling down and baking her brain.

"Is there a reason you're hitting yourself in the head?"

She glanced up at him and instantly, her stomach did

a flip-flop and her heartbeat skittered a little. Not that she could tell him that. Heatstroke. That had to be it.

"Um, no," she said. "Just wishing I'd picked up a pair of sandals at the last store."

Oh, good one.

He shook his head. "The ones you bought aren't enough?"

"Right. Right." Idiot. Really. She *had* bought a pair of sandals. God, she was a terrible liar.

The sidewalk was bustling. Businessmen, teenagers, women out with friends to do some window-shopping or just hurrying to work. The city was loud and crowded and the sizzling sun ricocheted off the cement and slammed back into you just for the hell of it. And Shelby was loving every minute.

In the month or so she'd been in Texas, she'd gotten used to the small town feel of Royal, and she loved it, really. But there was an excitement and a buzz about being in a big city and a part of her had missed it. Especially right this minute.

She was wearing a brand-new dress that was sky blue, summer weight with spaghetti straps and a full skirt that fell to just above her knees. The three-inch taupe heels she wore with it were perfect and it was good to feel…pretty, again. She was so tired of borrowed jeans and T-shirts.

"Most big cities are pretty much alike you know," she said, pitching her voice to be heard over a blasting car horn.

"That right?"

"Well, that's what I've heard people say. And I actually believed it until today. I thought, how different can

Houston be from Chicago?" She grinned. "Turns out, *very* different."

"The hats?" he asked, showing off the half smile that turned her insides into jelly all too briefly.

"Oh, absolutely," she said, "but it's more than that, too. Houston's busy and loud and people are racing around to get somewhere else. But even with all that, it's more...relaxed. More, casual somehow."

Caleb stepped out of the way of a businessman in a hurry and steered Shelby to one side with his hand at the small of her back.

She took a breath and held it. It didn't mean anything, she knew. It had been just a simple, polite gesture. Yet, the touch of his hand sent arrows of heat dipping and diving through her body. Her physical reactions to him were getting stronger, harder to ignore.

Every time they were anywhere near each other, it felt like a fuse had been lit and sparks were flying. She couldn't be sure if he felt it, too, but she was guessing he did because he was actively ignoring her. And she'd let him, figuring it was best all the way around.

After all, she was just out of one relationship and she wasn't looking for another. But no matter how much she ignored Caleb during the day, her dreams were full of him. Every time she closed her eyes, there he was. It seemed her subconscious was all too eager to explore possibilities.

"I want to say thank you again, for everything, but it feels like I'm always thanking you," she said abruptly in an attempt to drag her mind out of the bedroom.

"Yeah, you don't have to." He took her arm and steered her around yet another businessman—this one in an ill-fitting suit yelling into his cell phone, oblivious to any-one else on the sidewalk.

"Thanks," she said, then added, "oops."

His mouth quirked and Shelby silently congratulated herself. Honestly, when she coaxed that half smile out of the man she felt as if she'd been awarded a prize.

"This is great," she said, clutching two bags from local shops. "And oh, boy, am I looking forward to wearing fresh underwear. It's really a pain washing my one pair out every night and hanging them on a towel bar to dry. I was afraid I was going to wear out the fabric."

Okay, probably shouldn't be talking about her un-derwear.

"And shoes. I love my shoes. Especially those boots we found. I feel very Texan," she said, rattling the bag containing the boots.

"I don't think you can call hot-pink cowboy boots *Texan*."

"I bought them here, so… Texas."

"You bought *everything* here," he mused, holding up the three bags he was carrying.

She thought about everything in the shopping bags and smiled to herself, though she knew that when her credit card showed up, she'd probably have a heart at-tack. But that was a worry for another day. At least she didn't feel homeless *and* clothesless anymore. Her world was still up in the air. Her ex-about-to-be-mother-in-law was still making trouble for her. She couldn't touch any of her own money, but damn it, she had new underwear.

"I really love this," she said, looking around the busy street and the high-rises surrounding them. "It's nice, getting away from Royal for a while."

"The city's all right, once in a while," he agreed, frowning when a bus stopped at the sidewalk and belched out a cloud of dark smoke. "But Royal's better, even if small towns are hard to take sometimes."

"Oh, I like the town and most of the people I've met but I hate knowing they're talking about me. I mean, back in Chicago, I was just a face in the crowd." She looked around at the city and the thousands of people. "Like I am here. I wanted the small town life, you know? Roots. Home. Family. That's mostly why I agreed to marry Jared, I think. I wanted it so badly, I didn't notice that the man offering it to me wasn't real. Wasn't worth it."

A woman pushed past them, shoving Shelby into Caleb and he took her arm to steady her before letting her go again. "Was it really so important to you?"

"Spoken like a man who's always had a home. A place." They stopped at the corner and she laid one hand on his forearm. "My mother raised me on her own after my father died. We were happy, but we never stayed. Anywhere."

Caleb's eyes met hers and she kept talking, wanting him to understand why she'd done what she had. "I always wanted a real home, you know? A place where people would know me, where I'd belong." Her hand dropped away and she looked past him, at the busy street. "When Jared came along, I think I convinced myself I loved him because I *did* love what he represented."

A sea of people walked past them, and neither of them moved—or even noticed.

"Why'd you wait till the last minute to walk out?" Caleb watched her, waiting for her reply. "You were in Royal a month before the wedding."

"I know." She sighed and started walking again. In her heels, they were nearly eye to eye when she glanced at him. Caleb moved up alongside her. The sun was hot on her back and she was squinting against the glare. In the bustle and noise of the city, she kept talking. "I felt… trapped. I'd said yes already and so I let Jared's mother steamroll me. It was easier to go along than to try to stop what I had put into motion, you know?"

"Not really," he said.

She gave him a wry smile. "Yeah, I don't really understand it now, either. But the day of the wedding, I just suddenly *knew* I couldn't go through with it. Couldn't let one lie become a lifetime lie. So I ran."

She glanced at him and was relieved to see him nod as if he got it, though his mouth was a grim line. Shelby didn't know why she cared what Caleb Mackenzie thought of her, but she did. Talking about the wedding, the Goodman family, all brought back what the sheriff had said to her earlier and as his words replayed in her mind, she worriedly chewed at her bottom lip. Shelby hadn't wanted to make a big deal about it at the time, but the more she thought about it, the more nervous she felt. "What if the Goodmans do sue me?"

"They won't."

She wished she felt as sure as he sounded. "We don't know that."

"Yes, we do." He stopped at an intersection along with what seemed like half the city as they waited for the light to change. Caleb glanced down at her and though his eyes were shadowed by the brim of his hat, she could read the reassurance there. "Simon Goodman's a lawyer—and honestly, not all that good a one.

He's not going to start up a court case he's not sure he can win."

Sounded reasonable. And yet… "But like you said. Small town, people know him and don't know me, why wouldn't he win?" Shelby smiled at a baby in a stroller.

"Mainly because people *do* know him," Caleb told her as the light changed and they moved with the herd. "Know him and don't much like him."

"Isn't he *your* lawyer?" Shelby hurried her steps to keep up with his much longer stride. Even on a crowded sidewalk, Caleb walked like a man with a purpose. Determined. Unstoppable. Was there anything sexier? *Back on track, Shelby.* "I mean, Cam told me that's why you were at the wedding in the first place."

"Yeah," he admitted. "He is and that's my fault. He was my father's lawyer. I just never changed. Should have. Just got busy."

"Wow. Five sentences in a row."

"What?"

"The stoic cowboy spoke—almost at length," she said, tipping her head up to look into his eyes. It was weird, but now that she'd told him why she'd come to marry Jared and why she hadn't, she felt…free. Shelby had never been good with secrets. They always came back to bite her in the butt. So having the truth out there and Caleb's seeming understanding, lifted a weight off her shoulders.

He looked down at her and his mouth quirked again. Score.

"I must be a good influence on you," she said, giving him a wide smile. "I bet until I came around, nobody at the ranch talked much."

"Nobody comes close to you, that's for damn sure," he muttered.

"Isn't that nice?" He didn't mean it as a compliment but she was taking it as one. When he smiled again, as if they were sharing the joke, Shelby's heart gave a quick flutter.

"Caleb!" A feminine voice called his name and beside her, Shelby sensed him flinch in reaction.

They stopped, let the pedestrian crowd flow past, and then Shelby watched what was left of the crowd part, like a scene from a movie, to allow a drop-dead-gorgeous woman rush forward.

Her hair was long and blond, her eyes were blue and she wore a sleek, black dress that hugged every voluptuous curve. Black heels completed the outfit and Shelby, despite her pretty new dress and shoes, suddenly felt like a country bumpkin. Whatever that was.

"Caleb, you look fantastic!" The blonde hurled herself into Caleb's arms and even Shelby caught the cloud of floral scent that clung to her.

"Marta," Caleb said, extricating himself as gently as possible. "Good to see you."

To Shelby, it looked as though he was trying to get away from an octopus and he didn't look very happy about it. Which really made her feel better. Although why this little scene should bother her at all was beyond her. She and Caleb weren't a thing. She'd only known him a short time. And yet…logic didn't seem to have a lot to do with what she was feeling at the moment.

"God, it's been forever," Marta exclaimed, stepping back, but keeping a tight grip on one of Caleb's hands as if afraid he might try to escape.

"Yeah," he said, "I've been busy."

She playfully slapped at his chest. "You and those cows of yours."

"Cattle," he corrected, but Marta obviously didn't care.

"How long are you in the city for?" She gave her hair a playful toss and pouted prettily. All the while continuing to ignore Shelby's presence completely. "We've got to have dinner, Caleb, do some catching up. You can come to my place and—"

"Sorry can't do it," Caleb said, interrupting the flow of words and startling Marta into temporary silence.

Caleb looked down at Shelby. "We've got to be getting back, isn't that right, darlin'?"

Stunned, Shelby could only stare into those icy-blue eyes of his. His gaze was fixed on hers and she could see that he wanted her to play along with him. For his own reasons, he wanted to get rid of Marta and that worked for Shelby. She smiled, letting him know that she was on board, ready for whatever he had in mind. Briefly, he let his forehead rest against hers as if in solidarity.

"That's right, honey," she said softly.

Smiling then, Caleb draped his free arm around her shoulders, pulled her in tight to his side and dropped a kiss on top of her head. "Shelby, honey, this is Marta. An old friend."

"Really. How old?" she asked innocently, and watched Marta's eyes flash and narrow.

"Marta, this is Shelby and we're together now, so…"

The blonde gave Shelby a quick inspection and judging by the look in her eyes, wasn't impressed. Then Shelby wrapped her arm around Caleb's waist and rested her head against his chest in a clearly proprietary gesture. A few seconds later, the blonde surrendered.

"Well, all right, then, if that's how it is."

"Good to see you, though," Caleb said.

"And I just love meeting my honey's old friends," Shelby added, snuggling in even closer to Caleb.

"Yes, I can see that," Marta said, amused now. "Well, you two enjoy your day in the city. Caleb, you've got my number if things change."

"They won't be changing," Shelby assured her. A part of her really wished that were true.

"Right. Well, I'll be getting along to my lunch appointment. Still, it was good to see you, Caleb."

"Yeah. You, too."

Marta walked away and they watched her go. Caleb's arm was still around Shelby's shoulders as she tipped her face up to look into his eyes. "You know those boobs are fake, right?"

He laughed and gave her a hard squeeze before letting her go. "You can trust me on this. They're real."

"Hmm." People streamed past them like a creek rushing past rocks in its way. "You know what? After all this shopping, the least I can do is buy you a late lunch. Or an early dinner." She glanced around. "Is there a diner or a burger place around here?"

Caleb shook his head. "I think we can do better than that."

"Mr. Mackenzie," the hostess at the Houston Grille said, giving him a wide smile. She had jet-black hair cut into a wedge that hugged her cheekbones. "Good to see you again."

"Thanks, Stella," Caleb replied, looking into the main dining room. Windows fronting on the busy street boasted dark red awnings over them, giving the diners a nice view without being blinded by the sun. The atmosphere was muted, with weeping violins at a whispered volume pumped through speakers mounted discreetly on the walls. Tables were covered with white linen and the waitstaff moved across the floor like ballet dancers, with grace and efficiency. "Is my regular booth available?"

"It sure is." She picked up two menus, smiled at Shelby and then stopped when Caleb asked her to keep their shopping bags for them. Once they were stowed, Stella preceded them to a booth with a wide view of downtown Houston.

Shelby slid across the maroon leather bench seat and Caleb followed right after. "Can we get a couple of iced teas as soon as possible?"

Stella said, "Right away," and moved off.

Shelby's eyes were wide as she took in the restaurant before turning to him. "This place is beautiful."

"Why are you whispering?"

She laughed and he wondered why the sound of it should affect him as much as it did.

"It feels like I should. Everything is so dignified and well, quiet."

"You'll have to come back on a Saturday night. It's a lot louder then." He nodded to the waiter who brought them their drinks, then looked at Shelby again. She really was beautiful. That new dress of hers hugged her figure and highlighted everything he wanted to touch.

"This has been a really terrific day, Caleb. Thanks for bringing me."

"Stop saying thank you."

She shrugged, took a sip of her tea and set it back down again. "If you want me to stop saying it, then you need to stop doing nice things for me."

A waiter came to the table then. "Are you ready, Mr. Mackenzie?"

Turning to Shelby, he asked, "How hungry are you?"

"Very."

"Okay. Trust me with the order?"

She looked at him and those grass-green eyes fascinated him as they always did. "Sure."

Nodding, he looked at the waiter. "We'll each have the strip steak, rare. Cheese potatoes and the bacon asparagus."

"Right away." The waiter hurried off and Caleb looked back to Shelby.

"Is there anything else you want to buy while we're in the city?"

"No," she said, her fingers delicately tracing the prongs of the sterling silver fork in front of her. "This will do me until I get my own clothes back from the Goodmans." She looked at him. "How much longer do you think?"

Irritation spiked. Caleb had been raised to do the right thing. Always. To have the Goodmans treating Shelby this way, holding back her property from her, just for spite, annoyed the hell out of him. Especially since Nate was convinced that if Caleb did anything, he'd only make the situation worse.

Caleb didn't much care for *waiting*.

"No telling, really," he finally answered. "But Nate's a good man and an even better sheriff. He'll take care of this and get it all sorted out as soon as he can."

"That's good," she said.

"I hear a *but* in there," Caleb pointed out, his gaze fixed on her. The woman held his attention no matter what she was doing. And now her eyes looked anxious and the way she was chewing at her bottom lip sent tugs of heat to his groin even while he wondered what the hell she was worried about.

She smiled. "*But*, I can't just stay at your ranch forever. That's not right. I'm nearly finished clearing out your mother's collection and when that's done..."

He didn't want her to leave. What the hell? Caleb told himself it was because he was used to having her around. But the truth was more unsettling. He simply *wanted* her. There. In his house. In his bed. Under him. Over him.

He wanted Shelby Arthur like nothing else ever in his life.

But he could hardly admit to that. "Don't worry about it," he said dismissively. "Stay as long as you need to. There's plenty more in the house that could use organizing. Talk to Cam about it. In fact, have her show you the attic when you're finished with the kitchen and great room."

"The attic?"

"There are things up there dating back more than a hundred years." This was, at least, the truth. "It'd be good to get it sorted out, with the family papers and such filed properly."

Her eyes gleamed and he smiled to himself. The woman was hell on wheels when it came to straightening things out. Heck, if it kept her in his house, he'd create new chaos somewhere.

"Hey, Caleb."

He turned and smiled, holding out one hand to the man greeting him. Reese Curran, best horse trainer Caleb had ever seen and now married to Lucy Navarro Bradshaw. Just a few months ago, Reese had come home to Royal and it hadn't taken long for he and Lucy to find each other again. It was good to see Lucy happy again. "Reese. Nice to see you. Lucy," he added, with a nod to the woman standing beside the tall, lanky cowboy.

"I'm so glad to see you," Lucy said, then turned her gaze to Shelby and held out one hand. "You must be Shelby. Good to finally meet you."

"Thanks."

"Shelby, this is Reese and Lucy Curran. They run a horse rescue operation at Paradise Farms, on the McKittrick ranch. Not far outside of town." Caleb looked at his friend. "So what're you two doing in the city?"

"Shopping," Lucy crowed, with a grin as she wrapped an arm around her husband's waist to give him a squeeze.

"Lot of that going around," Caleb mused with a sly smile at Shelby. She grinned back at him and a fork of heat sliced right through him.

"Yes, but we're shopping for maternity clothes," Lucy said with a delighted smile.

"Well, congratulations." Caleb shook Reese's hand again, then pushed out of the booth to give Lucy a quick hug. He'd known Lucy's family his whole life, so Lucy was like a little sister to him. He'd watched her suffer when she'd lost her first husband, the father of her boy, Brody. He'd seen her worry over her brother Jesse and her step-brother Will when they'd recently tackled some hard family issues. And he'd celebrated with her when she and Reese had found each other not too long after Jesse and Will had both found loves of their own.

"That's wonderful," Shelby said as Caleb settled back into the booth.

"It really is," Lucy agreed. "And it's one more reason

I'm glad to meet you. Cam told me what a whiz you are at organizing things. I'd really like you to come out to the ranch and take a look at our plans for the new house Reese is building. Brody needs a big-boy space all his own and I'd love to get your opinions on what to do for the baby's room."

Eyes sparkling at the idea of a new challenge, Shelby said, "I'd love to."

"Great." Lucy grinned at her husband again. "As soon as you get some time, come on over to the ranch. I'm always there."

"Because she doesn't trust anyone but herself to take care of the horses," Reese said wryly.

"Wrong, I trust you." When he quirked an eyebrow at her, she added, *"Now."*

Their food arrived, and Reese and Lucy said their goodbyes. Once the waiter was gone, too, Caleb looked at Shelby. "See? No reason for you to think about leaving. Reese and Lucy's place is close to mine. So looks like you'll be busy for a while, yet."

"It does, doesn't it?" Satisfied, she turned to her meal and was unaware that Caleb watched her silently for a long minute, lost in his own thoughts.

Later that night, Caleb was restless. Maybe it was seeing Marta again. He hadn't seen her in more than six months and truth be told he hadn't given her another thought since the last time he'd walked out of her apartment. All they'd shared was sex. Great sex, but nothing more than that. So if he hadn't thought about her in all this time, why would seeing her today make him feel like he was about to jump out of his skin?

"Because it's not Marta," he muttered. "And it's not

seeing Reese and Lucy so damn happy and now pregnant on top of it."

No, it was the memory of holding Shelby. The feel of her. The smell of her. The touch of her hand at his waist and the feel of her head against his chest. They'd left Houston soon after a late lunch and the minute they got back to the ranch, Caleb had dived into work to keep his body so busy his mind wouldn't have time to dredge up images to torture him with.

That hadn't worked.

Hell, nothing had. He hadn't been able to stop thinking about Shelby all evening. Caleb had even skipped dinner because he hadn't trusted himself to sit across a table from her and not make a move. So now he was restless *and* hungry.

He walked through the silent house without making a sound. Caleb didn't bother to hit the light switches. He could have found his way around blindfolded. The kitchen was dark, as always, once Cam had cleared up and gone home. There was just moonlight sliding through the windows, casting a pale glow over everything. He noticed as he walked into the huge room that Shelby had made some headway in the kitchen, too.

His mother had collected kitchen appliances. Antiques, new, didn't matter. She had teapots, kettles, coffeepots, mixers and so many bowls she could have opened her own pottery shop. His mom had been like a magpie—if something shiny caught her eye, she had wanted it.

But Caleb didn't want to think about his mother—or Shelby. He just wanted to grab some cold fried chicken and then try to get some sleep before morning.

He was halfway to the fridge when he heard a voice

from the eating nook by the bay window. "I think I should tell you, you are not alone."

"Shelby." Caleb stopped dead, glanced over his shoulder and spotted her in a slant of moonlight.

"Good guess," she said. Her head tipped to one side, spilling that beautiful hair of hers across one shoulder. "Got it in one."

"Why are you sitting here in the dark?" *Why are you in the kitchen*, he asked silently.

"The moonlight's pretty and light enough." She shrugged. "What're you doing sneaking around in the dark?"

"I don't sneak," he corrected and suddenly felt like an idiot for having done just that. What had it come to when he slipped through a quiet house in the dark to avoid seeing the woman driving him crazy? "Besides, this is my house and—" He sniffed the air. "Do you have the chicken?"

"Yes and it's great." She pushed a plate of chicken into the middle of the table. "Cam is a fantastic cook. Did you know she went to a culinary school in Park City, Utah, when she was a teenager? She told me stories about some of the chefs she met there and you wouldn't believe—"

"Stop." He held up one hand. "Just stop talking. I beg you. I came down here for some damn chicken before I sleep."

"No problem. Get a plate."

"Don't need a plate."

"Yeah, you do." She scooted off the bright blue bench seat and hurried past him to a cupboard.

He watched her go and swallowed the groan that rose up to choke him. She was wearing a tiny tank top and a pair of low-slung cotton shorts that just barely managed to cover her crotch. He couldn't tell what color they were. The moonlight disguised that. Could have been white or gray or yellow. And it didn't matter.

Her long legs looked silky and all too tempting. Her curly red hair fell loose around her shoulders, sliding back and forth with her every movement and he couldn't seem to look away.

"Here. Now sit down." She passed him again and he caught her scent. Unlike Marta's heavy floral perfume, Shelby smelled like summer. Fresh and clean and cool. She set the plate and a fork and napkin down opposite where she was seated. "I've got Cam's potato salad out, too. I wasn't hungry at dinner but a little while ago, I realized I could probably eat one of your cows, hooves and all, so…here we are."

"Yeah." He sat down and tried not to think of just how lovely she looked in moonlight. How close she was. All he had to do was stretch one arm across the table and he could take her hand, smooth his thumb across her palm, feel her pulse race.

She leaned forward and her thin tank top dipped slightly, allowing him an all too brief glimpse of her breasts. Somewhere there was a god of lust with a nasty sense of humor. He'd spent most of the afternoon and evening avoiding her and now she was here and he was more than tempted.

"Thanks again for taking me to Houston today."

Burying another groan, Caleb took a bite of chicken and scooped up some of Cam's famous potato salad. "Stop thanking me."

"I tried, but I can't seem to," Shelby said, taking a

sip from the water bottle in front of her. "So you'll just have to get used to it."

Caleb sighed, filled his plate and then stood to open the fridge and grab a bottle of water. In the slash of bright light that lit up the room, Shelby looked far more delicious than the chicken he'd come in here for. Her nipples were outlined against the thin fabric of her tank top and that wonderful hair of hers fell in tumbled curls across her shoulders. Her green eyes were clear and bright and locked on him.

He let the door swing shut, cutting off the light, slamming the room into darkness again.

"I was avoiding you tonight." His eyes adjusted quickly to the dim glow of the moonlight sliding through the window she sat beside.

"Yeah," she said softly. "I picked up on that when you didn't come in until after dark. Why do you think I'm here now?"

"You set a trap?"

"Oh, *trap* is a hard word."

Maybe, but he had the distinct impression it was accurate, too. "What was the plan?"

"Do I need one?"

No. All she had to do was sit there, staring at him, looking like a promise. Something stirred inside him, and Caleb did his best to smother it. Hell, he was the one who needed a damn plan.

She was talking again. Of course.

"I knew you had to get hungry at some point. We ate a long time ago."

"Oh, I am." He stared directly into her eyes so she could see he wasn't talking about the damn chicken now.

"Me, too," she whispered.

Everything in Caleb twisted into painful knots. "This is a bad idea."

"Oh, no doubt," she agreed, but she didn't look away.

Caleb had the opening there. The chance to back the hell off. This was the Godzilla of bad ideas. And that still wasn't enough to sway him from taking what he wanted.

"Damn it, Shelby," he ground out.

"Oh," she said softly, "you're talking too much."

He choked out a harsh laugh, took two long steps, pulled her to her feet and kissed her like he'd wanted to for days.

Since the moment she'd run into his arms while escaping her wedding.

Six

She felt even better against him *now*, Caleb thought.

Her arms snaked around his neck, she leaned into him and opened her mouth under his. Their tongues twisted and tangled together. Breath came fast and hard. Hearts pounded, blood boiled and need rose up, quickening with each passing second.

Caleb's hands moved up and down her back, tracing her spine with his fingertips. Then he swooped down again, his hands settled on her butt and squeezed, pressing her to his aching groin in a futile effort to ease the throbbing within. She sighed in response and that soft sound of surrender crashed down on him.

Caleb groaned, lifted her off her feet and spun her around until her back was against the wall. Breaking their kiss, he looked into her eyes and saw passion glittering in the moonlight.

"Don't stop," she said, her voice a whispered plea.

"Won't," he promised and slid one hand down the front of her shorts.

She gasped and tipped her head back against the wall as he touched her. Damp heat welcomed him and she hooked her legs around his hips, and arched into him. He stroked her center, driving them both a little crazy. She rocked her hips into his hand and let her breath pant from her lungs. When he pushed one finger, then two, deep inside her, she gasped and shuddered in his grasp.

"Caleb!" Her body trembled and her eyes closed briefly as she savored what he was doing to her.

He caressed her, inside and out, his thumb brushing over the heart of her, and as he watched her react, his body tightened to the point of agony. He hadn't wanted this to happen. Hadn't wanted to start something between them that would lead them both exactly nowhere. And now he couldn't imagine *not* touching her. She was driving him wild with desire. Had been from the moment he first saw her.

Caleb wanted her so much he could hardly breathe. He wanted—*needed*—to slide his body into hers, to feel her surround him and take him in. Darkness filled the room but between them there was light and heat and a bone-searing desire.

Touching her was filling him up and tearing a hole in him at the same time. It was good, but it wasn't enough. He needed more. Wanted more. She was a craving like nothing he'd ever known before and he poured his own desire into touching her more deeply, thoroughly, until her breath came short, fast. Until her body coiled in expectation. Until release slammed into her and she shook with the force of it. Until he held her in the darkness and felt her heart race against his.

At last, she took a long, deep breath, looked up into his eyes and grinned. "Wow."

Caleb stared at her for a second or two, then choked out a laugh. "You surprise me."

Tipping her head to one side, she asked, "Why? Did you expect regret? No. How could I be sorry *that* happened?"

He eased her onto her feet, letting her body slide against his, just because he was apparently a masochist and needed a bit more torture. Now that the initial frenzy of hunger had faded and he didn't have his hands full of her, Caleb could think clearly again. Beyond what he wanted to what he knew, so he took a long step backward and shook his head.

"This isn't going to happen."

"It already did," she said. "And at least from my point of view, it was really good."

He smiled briefly and wondered what it was about this woman that she could drive him nuts one second and make him laugh the next. She was honest and strong and funny and so damn hot, she was keeping him twisted into knots. Knots that couldn't be undone because there was nothing here for him. Nothing more than giving her a place to stay until she got her life back. Then it was done. He didn't need another woman in his life. Especially one who, like Meg, had made the choice to run from a situation rather than face it.

"Yeah, well," he muttered thickly, because each word cost him, "good time's over."

"What's going on, Caleb?" she asked, reaching out to him.

He grabbed her hand, squeezed it, then let her go. "Nothing, Shelby. That's the point."

Because he didn't trust himself to leave if he stayed even one more second, Caleb grabbed the damn plate of chicken and left her there in the dark.

Rose took extra care with her hair and makeup before her next meeting with Gus. Not for his benefit, of course. It was a small vanity to know that she'd kept her looks but for a few stubborn wrinkles she tried to ignore and the subtle gray streaks in her hair.

Her cream-colored slacks were matched with a butter-yellow shirt and a pair of light brown boots. The summer heat was at a blistering level, which made her grateful for the shade of the old oak she sat beneath. While she waited for Gus—who was late again—she checked her email. When she saw one from her grandson, Daniel, she frowned.

Gran,
Meeting a friend for dinner. Will be out late.
See you tomorrow,
Daniel

"A friend," she mused and tapped her well-manicured finger against the now darkened screen. She knew very well whom he was meeting. Alexis Slade. Did he think she was blind? Or too old to recognize the signs a man gave off when he'd found a woman he was interested in? She remembered all too well how Gus had once looked at *her*.

Her husband, Ed, never had, but then why would he? He'd been handpicked by her father to be her husband because Ed had been willing to take the Clayton surname and keep the family line going. Romance had had nothing to do with it.

Sliding her phone back into her purse, Rose looked up when she heard Gus approaching. He was still tall, built tough and strong, and just watching him walk stirred things inside her better left unstirred. Standing, she said, "You're late. Again."

"Good to see you, too, Rosie."

The familiar name took her breath away for a second. No one but Gus had ever called her *Rosie* and he hadn't done it in close to fifty years. His expression let her know that he was as surprised as she was that he'd said it now.

He scrubbed one hand across his jaw, cleared his throat and said, "This thing with Alexis and Daniel is getting serious. You've got to keep your boy away from my girl. Alex is telling me she's meeting her girlfriend for dinner tonight, but she's never bought a new dress to go out with her friends. It's *him* she's meeting."

"I know it," she said, "and I think I've come up with a solution."

"Glad to hear it." He braced his feet wide apart, crossed his arms over his chest and waited.

"A charity bachelor auction," Rose said. The idea had come to her while she was watching some silly TV reality show. "It's perfect. Daniel will enter and meet other women—hopefully finding one more suitable than your Alexis."

"Suitable? There's nothing wrong with my girl," he said in a near growl.

Rose waved one hand at him. "You know very well

what I mean. Alexis is a perfectly nice woman, but neither of us wants those two together. Do we?"

His jaw worked as if he were chewing on words he didn't like the taste of. "No. We don't."

"Well, then." Rose picked up her purse again and rummaged inside. Pulling out a piece of paper, she handed it to him. "I've jotted down a few ideas. I thought Alexis could be a part of this, as well. Meet some new eligible bachelors to distract her from Daniel. She wouldn't bid on him so publicly."

He scanned her list, nodding as he read. "It's not bad. If we make it a fund-raiser—say for pancreatic cancer—Alexis will jump on board."

Rose's heart sank a little. Gus's wife, Sarah, had died of the disease two years ago and she knew how hard her passing had hit both Gus and Alexis. Royal was a small town and people were always willing to talk about other people's business. So even though Rose and Gus hadn't spoken in decades, she had been able to keep up with what was happening in his life.

"That's a wonderful idea, Gus."

He looked at her and seemed to study her forever before he spoke again. "Sarah missed having you in her life, Rose."

"I missed her, too." They'd been inseparable once, when they were girls. But then life happened and things had gotten so twisted around.

His voice was gruff, accusatory when he said, "You didn't have to cut her off just because you didn't want me."

Old pain echoed inside Rose. She'd never told anyone why she'd acted as she had so long ago and it was too late now to dredge it all up again.

"You don't know what happened, Gus."

"Then tell me."

"What purpose would it serve now?" she asked, "After all these years?"

"Purpose? Truth is its own purpose."

"Truth isn't always kind."

"What the hell does *kind* have to do with anything?" Gus scowled at her and his tanned features twisted with it. "Damn it, Rose, you owe me the explanation I never got."

"We're here to talk about the kids."

"We're finally talking after too many damn years. So while we're at it, let's get to the bottom of all this." He tucked the paper into his shirt pocket, balled his fists on his hips and gave her a cool stare. "What the hell changed while I was off making enough money for us to get married? Why'd you cut me loose?"

It seemed they were going to do this, after all. And maybe he was right. Maybe he was owed that long-held explanation. "My father wanted me to marry Ed. To make sure that happened, he threatened me. Told me that he'd take away my mother's doctor. Her medicine, if I didn't break it off with you."

Gus snorted. "He wouldn't have done it."

"Yes, he would." Rose thought back to her life under Jedediah Clayton's thumb. Her father had ruled his slice of Texas through fear and intimidation and no one had been spared. Rose's mother had always been delicate and Jedediah used that to keep Rose in line.

"Papa didn't like you. Didn't like me wanting something of my own, so he stopped it." She swallowed hard as she met Gus's eyes. "He *made me* stop it."

"That's it?" Gus was astonished. And furious. "You sent me away because you were afraid of your father?"

"Not for myself," she argued. "If it was just me, I'd have defied him. But I couldn't risk my mother. I was a kid, Gus," she reminded him. "I had no power. I couldn't stand up to him."

Gus turned away, then spun back around to face her. "*We* could have, Rose."

"You weren't there," she said. "I had no way of contacting you. Finding you. I had to do what I did to save my mother."

"You didn't give me a chance. Didn't give *us* a chance."

She shook her head, unwilling to even consider the possibility now that she could have done something different all those years ago. "You didn't know him."

"Damn it, Rosie, you should have trusted *me*!"

His shout thundered in the air.

"It wasn't about *you*, Gus. It was about my mother. When you went away to make enough money for us to get married, I was alone with him. He was in charge and he never let me forget it." Damned if she'd apologize for doing what she had to, to protect her mother. "I kept hoping you'd come back, but you didn't. You were gone four years, Gus."

"For us, Rose."

"But in those years, my father ate away at my mother, at me, until there was nothing left. I was alone," she repeated for both their sakes. "I did what I had to."

Shaking his head, he looked at her. "You cut me off, fine. But you cut Sarah off, too."

Heart twisting, Rose said, "Sarah was my best friend.

Do you think I didn't miss her? Didn't *need* her, especially with you gone?"

"Then why?" he asked, voice tight and low.

"My father. He wouldn't allow it. Wouldn't allow me to have anything he didn't give me."

"I hope that old bastard's burning in hell," Gus muttered.

"You are not alone," she assured him.

Shaking his head, Gus asked, "Were you happy at least?"

She gave him a wry smile. For more than forty years, Rose had kept the secret of her hellish marriage. To outsiders, the Claytons were town royalty. Happy. Successful. But in reality, "Ed drank too much. When he did, he—"

"Did he hit you?"

Rose met his gaze and saw flashes of fire there. "Just once."

"Just *once*?" Gus's eyes nearly popped out of his head. "Damn it, Rose. Why the hell would you stay with him?"

"Where was I supposed to go?" she demanded. "He was drunk when he hit me and I hit him back. Let him know I wouldn't stand for that. You were already married. To Sarah. I'd lost my love and my best friend. I had no one else. I had my children. So I stayed. And I kept out of Ed's way."

"I can't believe what I'm hearing," Gus muttered and shot her another hard look.

"Oh, stop it, Gus. I'm not a battered woman. I'm not a victim."

"He hit you."

"Once."

"And that's okay?" His voice was thunderous again.

"Of course not." God, how had this gone so wrong? She hadn't meant to paint herself as a pitiable figure. "I survived my marriage. I kept my children safe. And now I've got Daniel and he is the light in my eye."

Gus's jaw worked furiously and Rose knew that he wanted to curse a blue streak. But she also knew he would never swear like he wanted to in front of a woman, so he was stuck.

"I'm not looking for sympathy," she said. "The past is past. Ed's gone now and I live my life the way I like it."

"You always did have spine," Gus mused. "It's why I always wondered why you didn't stand up to your daddy."

"For myself, I would have," Rose reiterated. "I couldn't risk my mother."

"Guess I understand that." He took off his hat and scrubbed his hand across his shaggy, silver hair. "But you should have told me. Told Sarah. You didn't have to cut yourself off from everydamnbody."

"Yes, I did." Rose smiled and shook her head sadly. "How could I watch you and Sarah being happy together when I—" She stopped, held up one hand and fought for control. Blast it, she hadn't meant to open up any of this mess and now that she had, she needed a way out.

Rose strove for dignity. Lifting her chin, she said simply, "I'm happy you and Sarah had so many good years together."

As if he understood that she had said all she was going to say about the past, Gus nodded. "We did. And now you and I are going to make sure our grandchildren have the futures they should have. Right?"

"Right." Grateful to be back on solid ground, Rose

took a seat on the bench and patted it. "Have a seat, Gus, and let's talk about the bachelor auction."

"A man auction," Gus said with a shake of his head. "Who would have thought it?"

"Earth to Shelby," Camilla said with a laugh.

"Huh? What?" Shelby gave herself a mental shake and looked at the other woman. "I'm sorry. Zoned out there for a second."

"Again," Cam pointed out.

Shelby sighed as she gave Caleb's housekeeper her full attention. Cam was short, curvy and had a long, blond braid that hung across one shoulder, and her blue eyes were shining with amusement.

"You're right." Returning to the task at hand, Shelby looked into the trunk of Caleb's big Suburban and let her gaze slide across all of the crystal packed in there carefully. "Now I'm back, though. This is everything?"

Cam nodded. "Everything we set aside for the first trip, anyway. Mrs. Mackenzie really did hold on to a lot of stuff."

"She did, but I've seen worse," Shelby told her.

"I'm glad I haven't." Cam shook her head. "And I can't even tell you how happy I am that you're clearing this stuff out. I know Caleb is, too."

"He hasn't said much one way or the other," Shelby said. Her gaze slid across the yard to the stable, then to the barn. There was no sign of Caleb, but that was hardly surprising. Since their little interlude in the kitchen two nights ago, he'd been darn near invisible.

"Well, take it from me, he's happy," Cam said. "Before you showed up the man couldn't even sit down in the great room. Now it's more like a home than a warehouse."

A home that Caleb was avoiding. Because of *her*. A spurt of irritation spiked inside her and Shelby let it fester and grow. She'd tried to be understanding. But honestly, the man was acting like she'd laid out an ambush for him and then thrown herself at him.

Well, okay, she had set him up, sitting in the dark, waiting for him. But what happened after that was on both of them. For heaven's sake, why was he acting as if they'd done something *wrong*? And why was he making her feel as though it was all her fault?

"Shelby?"

"I'm sorry, Cam." Shelby glanced at all of the crystal she was supposed to be taking into the Priceless antiques store, then looked at the woman beside her. "Can you do me a huge favor? Could you drive this stuff into town? I have to find Caleb."

Cam frowned a little, but nodded. "Sure. No problem. But you know Caleb's out on the range somewhere. You'll have to get a horse."

"I can ride," she said, with more certainty than she felt. Shelby hadn't ridden a horse in years. But it had to be like riding a bike, right? Some things you didn't forget.

"Okay, then. Ask my husband where Caleb went. He'll point you in the right direction."

An hour later, Shelby spotted Caleb in the distance. It shouldn't have taken so long, but since she hadn't ridden a horse in forever, Mike had insisted on giving her a mare with all the energy of a snail. But the sky was a blue so pure and deep, it almost hurt to look at it. The sun shone down like fire from heaven and the surrounding pastureland was varying shades of dusty green and brown. There were cattle grazing and she was glad to note they were on the other side of a fence that seemed to stretch on forever.

As Shelby rode closer, she enjoyed the look of pure surprise etched into Caleb's handsome features. She'd enjoy it a lot more if she wasn't already starting to ache all over.

"What the hell are you doing out here?"

"Well, that was charming."

"I'm not trying to be charming," he ground out, "I'm trying to *work*."

"Good to see you, too," Shelby said and took a good, long look at him. Caleb was tightening a strand of barbed wire around a fence post. He'd taken his shirt off and the sight of that tanned, muscular chest made Shelby's mouth go dry. If he weren't scowling at her, she'd have melted a little.

"How'd you find me? And since when do you ride horses?"

"Mike told me where you'd be and I took lessons for years as a kid." She looked down at him while her horse nuzzled his.

Still scowling, he bent his head to his work. "Fine. You found me. Go away."

Both eyebrows arched high on her forehead. "This must be that Southern hospitality I've heard so much about."

"Damn it, Shelby, I'm busy."

"Me, too. I'm supposed to be taking a load of your mother's crystal into town right now."

"Why aren't you, then?"

"Cam's taking it for me because I told her I had to talk to *you*. Who knew it would be this difficult?" She swung her leg over the horse's back and jumped down from the stirrups. Taking a step toward him, she stopped, said, "Ow," and rubbed her behind.

"Serves you right," he muttered. "Haven't ridden in years, then hop on a horse and ride for miles? Be lucky if you can walk tomorrow."

"If you'd quit avoiding me," she said, "I wouldn't have had to resort to this."

"I'm not avoiding you." He turned his back on her and her gaze instinctively dropped to his butt. Yeah, the view from this angle was pretty spectacular, too.

"Me being out here has nothing to do with you. I'm working," he reminded her.

"Right." She didn't believe it for a minute and was surprised that he thought she might. "And you don't go to the kitchen for food anymore, so what? You're dieting?"

He sent her a glare, tied off the wire and clipped the excess. Tucking that bit of wire into a worn, cowhide belt he wore draped around his hips, he yanked off his gloves, tipped his hat back and fired a long, hard look at her. "What do you want? An apology? Fine. I'm sorry."

"You never listen, do you? I already told you I don't regret what happened."

He snorted. "You should."

"Why?"

He ignored her, tucking his work gloves into the saddlebags. Shelby laid one hand on his forearm and demanded again, "Why?"

Caleb looked from her hand to her eyes. "Because,

damn it," he ground out, "there's nothing here for you, Shelby. Not with me."

Her hand dropped away. "I never asked you for anything."

"Not yet."

She swayed back a little, almost as if his words had delivered a physical shot. "Are you under the impression I'm trying to trick you into a relationship or something?"

"You said yourself you waited in the dark for me the other night."

"Yes, because I was attracted to you," she snapped. "Though right now I don't remember why."

He took off the belt, hooked it on his saddle horn, then turned back around to face her. His jaw was tight, mouth grim and those icy eyes of his looked steely and dangerous. "I gave you a place to stay..."

"And I'm grateful—"

"Not the point." He held up one hand for quiet. "I don't go around using women just because they're handy."

Shelby just stared at him. "I don't let myself be used, either, so we're on the same page there."

"All I'm saying is that you're not the one-night kind of woman and that's all I've got to offer you—" He broke off, turned to snatch his shirt out of a saddlebag and then shrugged into it, leaving it unbuttoned. "So I'm staying clear of you."

"I don't know what to feel here," Shelby admitted, watching him, sorry to see him cover most of that really great chest. "Should I be flattered you think I'm worth more than one night? Or offended that you think I'm waiting for you to get down on one knee and promise me forever?"

"I didn't say—"

"No, you already said what you had to," Shelby said, and this time held up *her* hand for quiet. His mouth quirked at the gesture. "Now it's my turn. I'm grateful that you gave me a place to stay—but I don't need you to take care of me. To protect me. I'm a big girl—"

"I noticed."

Her mouth twitched briefly. "We're two adults, Caleb. If we want to be together, why shouldn't we? I don't expect anything from you—no wait. That's wrong. I do have one expectation."

"Yeah?" Wary now, he watched her.

Irritated, she said, "Oh, for heaven's sake. You really don't listen at all, do you? Stop getting that trapped look in your eyes."

He frowned at her, folded his arms across his chest and huffed out a breath. "Fine. What's your expectation?"

"That you'll stop avoiding me." She moved in on him, closing the distance between them. A soft, hot wind blew across the land, lifting her hair and blowing the edges of Caleb's shirt back. "That you'll kiss me again. Often."

As if thinking about what she'd said, he took a deep breath and released it slowly as he shifted his gaze to the wide pasture stretching out behind her. Several long seconds passed before he met her gaze again and when he did, Shelby saw storm clouds in his eyes.

"Damn it, woman." He set his hands at her hips and Shelby sighed as the accompanying rush of heat swept through her. "You should be careful what you wish for."

"I'm not wishing, Caleb. I'm *saying.*" She reached

up and tugged the brim of his hat lower over his eyes. Smiling at him, she said, "Stop pretending there's nothing between us."

"And if I do?" His voice was a low growl that hummed across her skin. His hands at her hips tightened, and Shelby sighed a little.

"If you do, then we're good." She stepped out of his grasp, took a step toward her horse and said, "And now that we both know where we stand, I'll go back to the house."

In a blink, he grabbed her hand, tugged her to him and then fisted one hand in her hair. Pulling her head back, he kissed her like a dying man looking for salvation. His tongue demanded, his breath pumped into her and when he finally let her go, Shelby's knees wobbled.

Looking deeply into her eyes, he said softly, "*Now* we're good."

Seven

When Caleb rode back into the ranch yard a couple hours later, his mind was on Shelby. As it had been since she'd left him and ridden back to the house. He'd thought it through and come to the conclusion that she was right. They were adults. They clearly wanted each other. So what the hell was he waiting for? Kissing her had fed the fires inside until it felt as if the Texas summer sun couldn't even compete with what was happening within.

The yard was busy. A couple of the men working with horses in the corral, two more putting a fresh coat of white paint on the stable fence. It was hot and miserable and Caleb wasn't thinking about work. All he wanted now was to find Shelby and ease the ache that had been torturing him for days.

Then he noticed the shining silver Porsche parked near the front door. Scowling at the thought of unexpected company, Caleb swung down from his horse, tossed the reins to Mike and jerked his head at the car. "Who's here?"

Mike frowned. "Jared Goodman."

"Hell." Caleb swiped one hand across his face and gritted his teeth. He supposed it made sense that Jared would show up eventually. But why *now*? "What did Shelby say?"

Mike shrugged. "When I saw him drive up, I went to the house, offered to stay with her while Jared was here but she insisted she was okay."

That sounded like her. Stubborn and strong and independent as hell. "Is Cam in there?"

"Nope." Mike shook his head and stared at the house as if he could see through the walls to what was happening inside. "She went into town a couple hours ago. Not back yet."

So Shelby was alone. With a man who had to be furious at the humiliation she'd served him. Caleb remembered all too well how he'd felt when Meg had dumped him in favor of his brother. It hadn't been pretty. The thought of Shelby facing Jared down alone was something he didn't care for. Though why it bothered him, he wasn't willing to explore. "I'll see about it."

Caleb trotted across the ranch yard, opened the front door and the first thing he heard was Shelby's voice. She was talking fast. Not a surprise.

"I'm really sorry, Jared, but I did the right thing. You'll see that, eventually."

"Right." Jared's voice came across in a sneer. "I'm sure I'll be real happy that my bride ran out on me in front of the whole damn town."

They were in the great room and Caleb moved quietly across the hall, so he could see what was going on. If she was handling things all right, he could always slip out again. She wouldn't even have to know that he'd checked in on her.

But he was distracted almost instantly. His first impression was, he hardly recognized the damn place. Since Shelby had been at the house, he'd been coming and going through the doors in his wing. Hell, he'd been using those doors since his mother started her "collection." Caleb hadn't seen the great room since Shelby went to work on it.

And in a matter of just a few days, she'd cleared the place of all the extra cabinets and dressers and the mountain of crystal and glassware. This was a room people could sit in. There were couches and chairs he barely remembered and a couple of tables that belonged there, but the room was once again a huge space with a wide, unobstructed view of the ranch yard. Of course, at the moment, the custom wooden shutters were closed over the glass, keeping this little scene private.

But his interest in the room faded as he focused on the man standing way too close to Shelby. Jared Goodman, like his father, stood a few inches shorter than Caleb. His black hair was slicked back and his gray suit looked out of place on a ranch. His features were twisted with anger and his eyes flashed sparks of heat as he loomed over Shelby.

Beyond the slash of fury that surprised the hell out of him, Caleb felt a quick jolt of admiration to see Shelby holding her own. She faced the man down and didn't look the least bit worried.

"I've heard the stories your mother's put out," Shelby

said calmly. "The word is that you're the one who called things off."

"But *we* know the truth, don't we, Shelby?" His voice was low and hard.

Impatient, she huffed out a breath. "Jared, it's over. We never should have tried this and you know that, too. I let myself believe that I was in love, but the truth is, I wasn't. I was just really flattered at how you swept me off my feet and that's not enough to build anything on, Jared—and you know it, too." She sighed a little, then added, "Honestly, you wouldn't be happy with me anyway. I talk too much and I'm a little bossy and I like to organize things all the time and you hate that. I mean, look at your office, it's just a mess, with files everywhere. We would never work out."

Jared tried to get a word in and failed. Caleb almost felt sorry for him.

"It's just that I'm sure you'll find the right person for you, but that's not me and it won't change, so we should just shake hands and part friends. I can do that, Jared," she said, "can you?"

"Friends?"

She gave him a sympathetic smile that was completely wasted on him. "Oh, Jared. This was never going to work. Really, it never should have *started*. So I'm sorry for that. But I'm not sorry for leaving."

"We're not friends," Jared snapped when Shelby finally wound down. He moved in closer and Caleb didn't like the look on the man's face. "You don't get to just walk away from me."

Okay, that was enough.

"She already did." Both people turned to look at him

as Caleb walked across the room to stand beside Shelby. "You should go, Jared."

Shelby was clearly startled to see him, but Jared's features went tight and even harder.

"What the hell do you have to say about any of this, Mackenzie?"

"Caleb—" Shelby started talking, but Caleb cut her off.

He kept his gaze fixed on Goodman. "For one thing, this is my house. My land. You've got no business here, Goodman, and no right to stand here trying to intimidate Shelby. You're not welcome and it's time for you to go."

"I'll go when I'm ready," Jared said. "You don't worry me, Mackenzie."

"I should, though." Caleb wrapped one arm around Shelby's shoulders and pulled her in to his side. "I work hard for a living, Goodman. You push papers. So don't try to throw your weight around in my place."

Jared's gaze fixed on the way Caleb was holding her.

"That's right. Shelby's with me, now, Jared." She stiffened against him and Caleb hoped to hell that she for once, didn't start talking. "She ended your relationship when she ran out on the wedding. So I don't want to see you back here again. You had some things to say and you said them. So now you can go."

"That's why you walked out?" Jared demanded hotly, ignoring Caleb to focus on Shelby. "You expect me to believe you left me for *him*?"

"You can believe whatever you want," Caleb said before Shelby could speak.

"This is ridiculous."

Caleb dismissed him, bent to Shelby and gave her

a fast, hard kiss to prove to Jared that he was telling the truth. And with the taste of her in his mouth, he turned to glare at the other man. "Now get out before I toss you out."

Jared looked at Shelby. "You bitch."

Caleb took a step forward and was pleased to see Jared skitter backward. "That's it. Go."

He did, storming across the room and out the door, slamming it behind him just to continue the child-having-a-tantrum attitude. Before the echo of that loud slam had faded, Shelby pushed away from Caleb and stared up at him.

"Why did you do that?" She lifted both hands to her temples and squeezed. "It just makes everything harder. I was handling him. I didn't need help."

Caleb remembered the look on Jared's face as he towered over Shelby and he wasn't so sure about that. Even the most timid dog finally bit if it was pushed too far.

"Not how it looked to me," Caleb said, gazing down into worried green eyes. "Jared was just getting madder by the second and with a man like him, you can't trust his reactions."

"He wouldn't have hurt me!" She seemed astonished at the thought.

"He won't now, anyway," Caleb agreed.

Frowning, Shelby seemed to think about that for a second or two. Then something else occurred to her. "The Goodmans still have my clothes. My money. Do you think he's going to be helpful now?" Letting her hands drop, she sighed. "Now he thinks we're a couple and that's just going to make this an even bigger mess."

"Maybe." Caleb pulled his hat off and tossed it onto the nearest table. He hadn't really been thinking about what Jared might believe or what he might do down the road. Hadn't been thinking much at all. It was pure instinct that had driven him across the room to stand between Shelby and potential danger.

He'd acted on impulse and Caleb couldn't even say he was sorry about it. He dropped both hands on her shoulders and held on tight. "I don't give a damn what he thinks. No one comes into my house and bullies you. Nobody."

She slumped a little and gave him a smile that was part pleased and part impatience. "That's really sweet, but didn't I tell you I don't need you to protect me?"

"Yeah, but turns out, *I* needed to protect you."

"Oh, Caleb. You realize this is only going to make the Goodmans even more furious with me." She chewed at her bottom lip. "Jared will tell his parents what you said and his mother will be spreading even more gossip. And now, you've told her she was right all along and that I'm with you."

"She already thought it. Remember?"

"Now she has your word on it. And then you just had to kiss me in front of Jared."

"He's not real bright," Caleb mused. "Thought he could use a visual aid."

"It's not funny, Caleb," she said, though her mouth curved briefly. Shaking her head, she said, "They'll never give me back my things now. And Jared's still got my money. I can't find a place to live or start a business or even move back to Chicago without that money."

Caleb frowned when she mentioned moving away. He hadn't really thought about it, but there was nothing holding her in Royal—or Texas, for that matter. She'd come to get married and now that she wasn't…well, hell.

"That what you're planning?" he asked. "To move back to Chicago?"

She looked up at him. "Honestly, I haven't thought that far ahead yet. What's the point? I can't plan anything until I have access to my money."

Not an answer, but it wasn't important, was it? Hadn't he been trying to avoid her for days? So why should he care if she moved out of state? Wouldn't that be the perfect ending to this situation? Shaking his head, he shoved those thoughts aside and got back to the matter at hand.

"The bank emailed you the receipt for the sale of your house, for the deposit," Caleb reminded her. "If Nate doesn't get the money for you, the judge will have the Goodmans turn it over."

She blew out a breath and nodded. "That's true. I have proof that the money is mine. They can't keep it. And I know I shouldn't get so worked up over Jared, but this is all my fault. I never should have said yes when he proposed but it seemed right at the time, you know?"

She wasn't looking for a conversation, Caleb knew. This was another rant and damned if he wasn't starting to enjoy them.

"I never meant to pull you into the middle of all this, Caleb," she said, pushing one hand through her hair. "You were just being nice and I told you I didn't need to be defended, but it was really sexy when you came in and kissed me and told Jared to get out, and it shouldn't have been, but I can't help how I feel about it, can I?

"I mean, it's so old-world cowboy movie for you to come striding in with your hat and your stoic expression and be all—" she scrunched up her face and deepened her voice "—'That's my woman, so back off,' and for some reason, it made my stomach do a dip and spin that took my breath away—"

That's my woman. He hadn't meant it like that. Not really. He was pretty sure. But Caleb could admit that seeing Jared looming over Shelby, bullying her just by being bigger and taller than her had really pissed him off, so that all he could think to do was stand in front of her. To get rid of Jared so her face wouldn't look so damn pale.

And now, all he wanted was for her to quiet down and the best way to do that, he'd already discovered, was...

He kissed her.

Like he had out on the range, one hand in her dark auburn curls, holding her head still so he could take his time and indulge in the taste of her. And in less than a second, she was kissing him back, hooking one leg around his, snaking her arms around his waist and holding on. His tongue caressed hers. He took her breath as his and gave her back his own. Then held her so tightly, he could feel the soft, full mounds of her breasts against his chest. Her hips ground into his, spiking the ache in his groin to epic proportions. He'd never known the kind of want she inspired in him. Never experienced the kind of desperation pushing at him.

He lifted his head, looked down into those grass-green eyes of hers and saw them shining with the same kind of pulsing desire hammering at him. "I want you, Shelby. Right the hell now."

"What took you so long?" She grinned, then kissed him, opening her mouth to him, tasting him as he had her. Her hands went to his belt. He felt her unhook the damn thing and undo the top button of his jeans. Then she tugged the hem of his shirt free and slid her hands up beneath the fabric to stroke her palms across his chest.

He sucked in a gulp of air, lifted his head and smiled. "Glad you cleared out this room so nicely. Because that couch is a hell of a lot handier than a bedroom."

"Yes," she said on a breathy sigh and flicked her thumbs across his flat nipples.

He gritted his teeth and felt every drop of blood in his body rush to his groin. He was hard and aching and if he didn't have her in the next few minutes, Caleb was sure he'd die.

In two steps they were at the couch and he tipped her back onto it in one smooth motion. She landed with a thump and laughed up at him.

Her eyes were shining, her delectable mouth curved in a smile that promised all sorts of wicked things. When she tore off her tank top to reveal a skimpy piece of sky blue lace covering her breasts, he couldn't look away. Then she unhooked the front of the bra and let the delicate cups slide away, baring her breasts to him. In the cool, air-conditioned room, her dark pink nipples peaked instantly and Caleb didn't waste a second. He came down on top of her and took first one of those nipples, then the other, into his mouth. His lips, tongue and teeth tormented her while she writhed and panted beneath him.

She tugged at his shirt so furiously that he finally paused long enough in his enjoyment of her body to rise up and let her pull the shirt off. Then her hands were on him. Small, smooth, strong. She stroked, caressed and scored his skin with her short nails while he again suckled at her breasts.

"God you smell good," he whispered, lingering to give one nipple another licking kiss.

She shivered. "So do you."

Caleb laughed. "No I don't." He half pushed up from her. "Just wait. Give me five minutes in a shower and I'll be back—"

"No, you're not going anywhere," she said, shaking her head against the brown leather couch. She licked her lips, let her fingers trail down his chest, across his flat abdomen to the button fly of his jeans.

Caleb went perfectly still. He felt every skimming touch of her hands as she worked the buttons free, one by one. And with each inch of freedom gathered, his dick hardened further. Finally, she reached down and curled her small, strong hand around him and squeezed, while stroking up and down his length.

Caleb dropped his forehead to hers and took deep, deliberate breaths. If he didn't maintain control, he'd explode before he'd done what he'd been dreaming of doing to her. Reaching down, he grabbed her hand and held it pinned to the couch above her head.

"Don't. You'll push me over the edge and I want to stay there for a while."

His free hand dropped to the waistband of the knee-length white shorts she wore and quickly undid the snap and zipper. One glance told him her skimpy panties matched the blue lace bra and everything inside him twisted in response. One time, he wanted to see her dressed only in those wisps of lace. But now, he wanted her in *nothing*.

He slid down the length of her body, trailing kisses and long, slow licks as he went. She shivered again and he loved it. His hands tugged her shorts and panties free and when she was naked, he took a long moment to simply enjoy the view.

"Slide that bra all the way off," he ordered.

She ran her tongue slowly across her bottom lip, then lifted off the couch high enough to pull the bra off and drop it to the floor. When she stretched out on the couch again, she crooked a finger.

"You're wearing too many clothes."

"Yeah, I am." He kept his gaze fixed with hers while he quickly stripped, so he saw the flash of pleasure dart across her eyes when she saw him, long and hard and ready.

Her hips rose off the couch in eager anticipation. She planted her feet, parted her legs more widely and whispered, "Be inside me, Caleb."

Four little words that tore him to pieces. There was simply nothing he wanted more. But first… He took hold of her thighs, held them wide and looked at the core of her, hot and pink and wet. She was as ready as he was and that pushed him over that dangerous edge he'd been clinging to.

He bent his head to her, covering her center with his mouth, tasting her, licking at her, nibbling until she was whimpering, rocking her hips and softly begging him for what he wouldn't give her. Not yet.

Again and again, he teased her, tormented her, relishing every sigh and groan she made. She reached down and threaded her fingers through his hair as she cried his name brokenly.

He rode the power of her passion until he was nearly blind with the need choking him and only then did Caleb rise up, cover her body with his and slide into her heat.

He pushed deep and she wrapped her legs around his hips, giving him a better angle, allowing her to take all of him in. Locked together, they stared into each other's eyes as he moved inside her. He watched her eyes flash. Watched her lips part on a sigh that welled up from deep within her.

Caleb pushed deeper, higher, groaning as he filled her, as she surrounded him with a kind of heat that burst into an inferno within. Friction bristled between them as he set a rhythm that she raced to match. She was with him, every step of the way and he'd never known anything like this before. There was a connection here, linking them in ways that were more than physical. Everything she felt was stamped on her features. Every touch she bestowed on him left streaks of flame burning down into his bones. His blood.

Again and again, he moved, claiming her, taking them both well past that slippery edge until they were left, staggering wildly, fighting for balance, for release.

"Come now," he ordered, voice thick, strained with the effort to hold himself back when all he wanted to do was empty himself inside her.

She shook her head, gasping, panting. "We go together. Both of us."

Reaching down, she cupped him and rubbed, stroked him until he was beyond pleasure, beyond the boundaries of everything that had come before. And so he slid one hand between their bodies and stroked her core as he continued to pump into her.

And finally, together, they jumped off the edge and fell crashing into lights brighter than he'd ever seen before.

* * *

When her heart stopped racing, Shelby took a deep breath and closed her eyes in complete satisfaction. Her body was still buzzing, the echoes of a world-class orgasm still shuddering inside her. Sex had never been like that before. Until this moment, she'd always thought of it as a pleasant enough time that ended with a delicious little pop of release.

Caleb Mackenzie had changed all of that.

He knew things that all men should know. His hands were magic and his mouth should be bronzed. In fact, Shelby felt a bit sorry for every woman who had never been with him. While at the same time, she wanted to keep him all for herself and never let another woman near him.

A frown settled between her brows. Where had that thought come from? Caleb wasn't hers. There was nothing between them but convenience and blistering sex.

Well. That was nearly enough to take the shine off her feelings.

With his big, strong body pressing into hers, Shelby felt a stirring of a warmth that was slower and steadier than the heat she had just survived. That realization should have worried her. Instead, she took a second to revel in it. To enjoy this one perfect moment.

Then Caleb lifted his head, looked down at her and solemnly said, "This is a really bad time to be asking, but—are you on the Pill?"

There went the rest of the shine.

"Yes," she said and saw relief flicker in his eyes. "I've been on the Pill for a few years now so—" She broke off and thought about that for a second.

"What?" Caleb watched her warily. "What is it?"

"Probably nothing," Shelby assured him, though she wasn't as confident in that as she was trying to sound. Forcing a smile, she added, "I'm sure it's fine…"

"But?" he asked.

"*But*, remember I didn't have my purse for three days…"

"Yeah?" One word drawn out into five or six syllables.

"Well, my pills were in my purse, so…"

"So you didn't take any for a couple of days."

"No." He was literally right on top of her and she still felt him take a mental step backward. "I'm sure it's fine, though. I took the Pill yesterday and today and I'm sure I've got all kinds of those wonderful little hormones all stored up in my system."

"Uh-huh." Caleb pulled away, sat up and grabbed his jeans off the floor. "Damn it."

"No reason to panic," she said.

"Is that right?" He snorted a laugh and shook his head as he stood up to yank his jeans on.

It was a shame, she thought idly, to cover up that really amazing body.

"I don't know what I was thinking," Caleb said tightly, more to himself than to her. Then he looked at her. "I have *never* failed to use a damn condom."

"Until today." She shrugged, reached down for her blue bra and pulled it on.

"Yeah." He pushed one hand through his hair in sheer frustration. "Until today. Until *you*."

Shelby smiled. "The words sound like a compliment. The tone really doesn't."

"I should apologize, I guess, and if I can find a way to say it and sound like I mean it, I will."

Well, clearly their postcoital conversation was coming to an end with a whimper. Reaching down for her shirt, Shelby tugged it on, then grabbed her panties. Standing up, she wriggled into them and enjoyed the flash of interest in Caleb's eyes.

"No apology necessary," she said and stepped into her white shorts. Once they were snapped and zipped, she tossed her hair out of her eyes and said, "I didn't think of it, either. All I could think about was you. Having you inside me."

His eyes burned like a fire in ice. "Hell, that's all I can think of right now."

She gave him a slow smile and felt her body stirring. "Me, too. And I'm not going to regret that, no matter what else happens. Honestly, Caleb, I'm sure it's fine."

"Yeah." He sent her another long look. "You be sure and tell me if it's not."

"I will. But I'm not worried." Not quite true, so she added, "Well, maybe a little."

Grabbing his shirt off the floor, he tugged it on. "Not much slows you down, does it?"

"Well, what would be the point of being all…" She mocked tearing her hair out, throwing her head back to shriek, then looked at him and grinned. "Would it help to gnash my teeth and howl at the moon?"

His lips twitched and her heart gave a hard jolt.

Moving in closer to him, Shelby laid both hands on his chest and relished the heat when his hands cupped her shoulders. "My grandmother was Irish," she said softly, staring up into those beautiful eyes of his. "She always told me, 'If you worry, you die. If you don't worry, you die. So why worry?'"

Caleb just stared at her and, slowly, another smile

curved his mouth. "You always throw me for a loop, Shelby. Never sure just what you're going to say next."

"Well, then," she said, sliding her arms around his waist, "brace yourself. What do you say we both go and take a shower?"

He cupped her face between his palms, bent his head and kissed her softly, gently. Everything inside Shelby fluttered back into life again and now that she knew just what he was capable of, she trembled with it.

"I think," he said, "that's a great idea. Plus, there're condoms in the bathroom."

She looked up at him and grinned. "How many?"

"Let's find out." Caleb picked her up and tossed her over his shoulder. Shelby's laughter trailed behind them.

Eight

Mitch and Meg returned home the following morning and everything between Shelby and Caleb changed in a blink of time.

In the rush and noise of the family arriving, and the kids shrieking with joy to be home again, Shelby felt Caleb pull away from her. He distanced himself so easily it was almost scary to watch. It was as if, for him, the night they'd just shared had never happened.

Only that morning, she and Caleb had been wrapped together in his bed, after a long night of incredible sex and putting quite a dent in Caleb's condom supply. They'd laughed and kissed and had a picnic in that bed in the middle of the night and yet, the minute Mitch and Meg had arrived, Caleb had shut down. He'd become cold. Distant.

With his family around, he was a different man.

Except with the twins, she reminded herself. The two children had thrown themselves at Caleb and he'd held nothing back with them, smiling, laughing, swinging them around.

It was when he faced Mitch and Meg and Shelby that his features turned to stone. He'd introduced her to them and briefly explained why she was there, but beyond that, he'd hardly spoken to her since his family arrived. She had to wonder why. Was it her? Was he pulling back to remind her that there was nothing but sex between them? Was he making sure his family understood that Shelby was only there temporarily?

And if he was trying to shut her out, why was he being so cold to his brother and sister-in-law, too?

To be fair, though, she had to admit that Meg and Mitch weren't exactly being warm and friendly toward Caleb, either. Families were complicated, she knew that, but there was more here than simple sibling issues. And she really wished she knew what exactly it was bubbling beneath the surface of the Mackenzie family. Maybe then she could find a way to reach Caleb.

She probably should have gone into the house and busied herself with the organizational job that wasn't finished yet. But for two hours, she sat on the porch instead, watching the family she didn't belong to. It was fascinating to watch the play of relationships and as she studied them all from the shade of the front porch, she tried to spot signs that might explain what was going on.

Mitch Mackenzie was a younger, shorter version of Caleb, but to her mind, Caleb was much better looking and she couldn't help but notice that the brothers were *cautious* around each other. They kept a safe distance between them as they stood at the corral watching a few of the men work the horses. If body language could actually speak, theirs would be shouting. The two men couldn't have been more ill at ease with each other.

Meg Mackenzie was tiny, just five feet or so, with short blond hair and big blue eyes. Her husband appeared to adore her, but Caleb barely acknowledged her existence. Caleb treated her with a cool detachment, hardly glancing her way. And Shelby wondered again just what was happening here. The Mackenzie family was simmering with tension.

Except when it came to the twins. At three years old, they looked like miniature Mackenzies. Jack and Julie were loud, adorable and seemed to have an infinite amount of energy. For a couple of hours, it was crazy while the kids ran around and Caleb and Mitch talked business. Meg was in and out of their house across the yard, settling in.

Shelby tried to stay out of the way because she could see there was friction between Caleb and his brother—not to mention Meg. She didn't want to add to the problems, so she kept to herself in a rocking chair on the porch.

She'd brought out a pitcher of iced tea, four glasses and a plate of homemade cookies. But so far, she was snacking all by herself. Still, she was in the shade and had a bird's-eye view of the Mackenzie family. But for the first time since coming to the ranch, she felt exactly what she was—an outsider.

With her gaze locked on Caleb, Shelby wished she could see what he was thinking. Feeling.

"Sometimes," she murmured, "stoic is just annoying."

Still, she couldn't look away from him. He and his

brother both stood, one booted foot on the bottom rung of the corral fence, their arms resting on the top rung. Did they even realize how alike they were? Or was that lost in whatever it was that was keeping them divided? She'd like to talk to Caleb, see what was driving the coolness that had dropped onto him like a shroud. But that wouldn't happen until he stopped shutting her out.

She took a sip of her tea then set her glass down on the table beside her. A hot wind bustled across the ranch, lifting her hair from the back of her neck and stirring the dust in the yard into a mini cyclone that dissipated as quickly as it rose up. The steady, pounding clop from the horses running in circles around the corral was like the heartbeat of the ranch. Shelby took a deep breath and let it slide from her lungs again.

Strange how much she'd come to love this place. The wide sky, the openness of the land, the horses... Caleb. And now she was forced to acknowledge that as much as she liked being there, she didn't *belong*. That admission hurt more than she would have expected and she wondered when this place, and this man, had become more than a port in the storm.

Then the twins spotted her and bulleted across the yard, headed right for her. Shelby smiled, watching their shining faces and those eyes, as bright a blue as the sky.

The little girl beat her brother by a couple of steps, climbed up onto Shelby's lap and grinned. Her soft brown hair was pulled into two impossibly short pigtails and she had a dimple in her right cheek. "Daddy says you live here. You do? Can I have a cookie?"

Hmm. Problem. How did she give them cookies without asking their mother first? Then Jack scrambled over, shouted "I like cookies!" and grabbed one, stuffing half of it into his mouth.

Not to be outdone, Julie squirmed on Shelby's lap until she could grab one, too. With crumbs on her cheek, Julie said, "Uncle Caleb lives here."

"Yes, he does."

"You like Uncle Caleb?" Jack demanded.

Danger zone, she thought and then dismissed it. The children were too young to read anything into her answers, so she kept it simple. "Yes, I do. Do you?"

"Uh-huh," Jack said. "He's funny."

"Uncle Caleb is crabby sometimes," Julie told her thoughtfully. "Can you make him not crabby?"

Out of the mouths of babes. Laughing, Shelby dusted the crumbs off the girl's face. "Well, I don't know, but I can try."

"I ride horsies," Jack announced.

"Ponies," Julie corrected, with a sisterly sneer.

"He's a *big* pony," her brother argued back.

"Okay, you two, take a hike."

Shelby hadn't even seen their mother arriving; she'd been too busy fielding questions and being entertained. Now Meg climbed the steps, sat down in the chair beside Shelby and sent both kids off with a cheerful, "Go bug your daddy for a while."

Both of them took off at a dead run toward the spot where Mitch and Caleb still stood side by side, yet separate, at the corral fence. Little Jack's small cowboy hat flew off and he circled back to snatch it out of the dirt. When Julie came up on her father, he swung her up to his shoulders. Then Caleb did the same for Jack when the boy tugged at his jeans.

The summer sun was blazing out of a bright blue sky

with only a few meager white clouds to mar the perfection of it. Shelby watched Caleb with the kids and everything inside her melted.

"Sorry," Meg said, "the kids are so glad to be out of the car, they're a little more excitable than usual."

"Oh, they're wonderful. And adorable, too."

"Well, you do know how to make points with mothers," Meg said with a grin.

"I wasn't—" Shelby stopped herself and smiled. "Sorry about the cookies. I should have asked you, but they just—"

"Swarmed you?" Meg nodded in understanding. "They double-team you and you don't stand a chance. Trust me. I know."

"They're so cute."

"And busy." She patted her flat belly. "Hopefully this next one will be a single."

"You're pregnant?" Her voice sounded a little wistful even to herself. "Congratulations."

"Thanks." Meg tipped her head to one side and studied Shelby for a couple of seconds. "You're staring."

Shelby jumped, startled away from looking at Caleb. "Yeah. I guess I was."

Meg mused, "Handsome, aren't they?"

"Hard to argue with that."

"Of course," Meg said, "I'm partial to Mitch, but Caleb's not bad…" She slid a glance at Shelby and seemed to like what she saw because her smile widened. Then she poured a glass of tea, took a long drink and went on to say, "Bless you for this. Honestly, visiting my folks in Oregon, I forgot just how hot it was going to be when we got home."

"It really is awful, isn't it?"

"Summer in Texas," Meg said on a sigh, "the devil's vacation spot. And, now that we've talked about the weather, why don't you tell me how you're doing after escaping your wedding and all?"

She blinked and swallowed hard. Just how much did Meg know? "What?"

"I heard about what happened."

"Caleb told you?"

"Oh, no." Meg shrugged and waved one hand at her. "You must have heard about the gossip chain in Royal."

"Yes, but you weren't here."

"Doesn't seem to matter," the other woman said and grabbed a cookie. "I love chocolate chip. Anyway, I called my friend Amanda—the sheriff's wife—to tell her she wasn't the only one pregnant, and she told me what happened at the wedding."

"Oh, God." Shelby covered her eyes with one hand as if she could simply hide from everyone with that one gesture. "This is so embarrassing."

Meg reached out and patted her hand. "Believe me when I say you don't have to be embarrassed."

"Well, I am," Shelby muttered, smoothing her palms across her khaki shorts.

"Why? Because you were strong enough to walk out of a marriage you knew would be a disaster?" Meg shook her head firmly. "As hard as it was, it was the right thing to do. Jared Goodman? No."

"That's embarrassing, too." Shelby looked at the woman next to her. It seemed weird to be talking about such private things with someone she'd only just met, but Meg had an open, friendly air that was hard to re-sist. "Why I didn't see what clearly everyone in Royal already knew."

Meg sighed and turned her gaze back to her husband and his brother. "I don't know. Sometimes I think we're deliberately blind to things we'd rather not admit."

Shelby wondered what Meg was thinking, but then, all of the Mackenzies seemed to have secrets and no outsider would breach the walls containing them.

Several hours later, Caleb told himself that this was the first time in memory he'd been glad to have a TCC meeting to attend. But he'd never needed to get away from the ranch more than he had today. With Mitch and Meg and Shelby all there, he felt like he had one foot caught in a damn bear trap.

He was glad his brother was back home, if only to share the burden of running the ranch. But things had been strained between them since Meg had walked out on Caleb to marry Mitch. He'd tried to get past it, but damn it, he was faced with the reality of what had happened every day.

It wasn't that he was still in love with Meg. Hell, that had faded faster than he'd thought possible and maybe every now and then he'd admitted to himself that it was possible his ex-fiancée had done the right thing—though she'd gone about it the wrong way.

Then there was Shelby. He'd gotten too close to her last night. Sex was one thing, but laughing and talking during and after that sex was another. Sure, being with her had been spectacular, better than anything he'd ever known before. But it wasn't the great sex that worried him.

It was sleeping with her in his bed. Waking up with her legs tangled with his. Staring down at her, waiting for her to open those beautiful green eyes and smile up at him.

Came too damn close to caring and he wasn't going to risk that again. Especially with a woman who'd done to another man exactly what Meg had done to him.

Well, hell, he told himself as his thoughts circled crazily, he hadn't gotten away from a damn thing. He'd dragged them all here to town with him. He forced thoughts of his family and the woman to the back of his mind and concentrated on the meeting.

Caleb sat in the back of the room, listening to everyone talking about the upcoming elections. Hell, he didn't have time to serve on the board, so he had to admire those who were willing to not only put in the time, but put *up* with the constant stream of complaints from the members.

The meeting was in the main dining room, mostly because it was big enough for everyone to be comfortable. And, you could get something to eat or drink if you felt like it. The TCC was a legend in Royal. The building itself had taken a beating over the years, but the club had been undergoing some renovations recently.

The dining room was big, with dozens of tables covered in white linen. There was a fireplace, empty now, since even a summer night in Texas was hotter than hell. The walls were dotted with framed photos of members through the years. There were historical documents—including a signed letter from Sam Houston himself and even the original plans for the club, drawn up more than a hundred years ago.

Tradition ruled the TCC and every member there had a long history with the place, through family or marriage. Caleb's father had been a member, and so were the Goodmans. Simon was at the meeting tonight, too, shooting glares at Caleb from across the room. He really had to fire that man.

"So, thinking about running for president?"

Laughing, Caleb slid a look at Nathan Battle sitting beside him. They both had a beer in front of them but they'd been nursing the drinks all night since they both had to drive home.

"Yeah," Caleb said, "right after I run naked down Main Street."

Nathan grinned, leaned back in his chair and shook his head. "Feel the same. Man, you couldn't pay me to be on the board and put up with all the politics and the fights."

Caleb shook his head and watched James Harris break up a heated argument that probably would have become a fight in a few more minutes. A rancher and horse breeder, James was tall, African American and gravitated toward calm, which served him well as president of the TCC. Caleb was pretty sure the man actually *enjoyed* being in charge of the club.

"Look at that, how he can calm folks down without breaking a sweat. I swear, if James wasn't glued to his ranch, I'd hire him as a deputy." Nathan sighed. "My new deputy could learn a few things."

"Well," Caleb said, "now that James has got his nephew to raise, I think he's stepped up his patience game."

True. James had been named guardian of his eighteen-month-old nephew and Caleb admired how he'd stepped up to the new challenge. Couldn't be easy, ranching and being a single father to a baby.

"Simon Goodman's giving you looks that could kill," Nathan pointed out.

"Yeah, I know," Caleb said. "I'm ignoring him."

"Good luck with that." Nathan leaned closer to whisper, "Tell Shelby I'll be going to see Simon tomorrow about getting her money back. I wanted to give him some time to cool off."

"Yeah, I don't think that's happening." Caleb told his friend about Jared's visit to the ranch the day before.

"Damn it, Caleb." Nathan took a swig of his beer and winced as if it tasted bad. "You realize you just made this worse by lying about you and Shelby…"

Caleb thought about yesterday with Shelby. And last night. And this morning. He scrubbed one hand across his face, but it didn't do much to wipe away the mental images that were burned into his brain. Shelby naked in his bed. Shelby crying his name as an orgasm rocked her. Shelby rising up over him as she took him into her body, bowing her back, her long, thick hair falling across pale, smooth skin.

"You *were* lying, right?"

"What?" He looked at his friend and saw suspicion on Nate's features. "Sure. Of course."

His eyebrows lifted.

"All right, I don't know," Caleb said. He took a sip of his own beer. "There's something there. I just don't know what it is."

"I hate complications," Nate muttered.

"You're telling me," Caleb agreed.

Then James called the meeting to order. "All right everybody," he said, "if you'll settle down, we've got a few things to discuss tonight, but first, Gus Slade wants the floor. He's come up with a fund-raising idea that I

think is interesting. I hope you all agree to take part—
I sure as hell am."

Gus stepped up and laid out his plans for a bachelor
auction to benefit pancreatic cancer research. And while
he talked, Caleb glanced around the room. A few of the
men his age looked intrigued by the idea, which Caleb
did *not* understand. Damned if he'd put himself on the
auction block for a night out on the town.

James's expression didn't give away what he was
thinking—but of course as president, he'd be in the
auction, too. Just another reason to not be on the board.
Daniel Clayton appeared to hate the idea, yet in the
next second, he was announcing that his grandmother
was insisting he take part and so should everyone else.

Caleb couldn't be persuaded to enter, but after a
back-and-forth discussion, it was decided to go ahead
with the auction. Gus looked happy about it, James
looked resigned and most of the younger members were
downright eager. Took all kinds, Caleb thought.

A few hours later, Shelby was wide-awake. Her bedroom was dark and outside the night was quiet and still.
She saw headlights spear through the blackness and
knew that Caleb had gotten home from his meeting.
She was tempted to go and find him, tell him to talk
to her. Find out what exactly was going on with him.

But the truth was, she didn't want to know. How
could he have gone from the world's greatest lover to a
distant, cool stranger in the blink of an eye? Was it possible that the fire between them had already burned out?

Or was he deliberately pouring water on it?

"You're being ridiculous," she told herself, her whisper lost in the empty room. There was no relationship

here. She'd only known the man for a *week*. But a voice in her head argued, *Yes, but what a week it's been.* True, they'd been through a lot in just a short amount of time. But the moment his family showed up, he tossed her aside. He couldn't have made himself any more clear.

She heard the click of the doorknob turning and her breath caught as her bedroom door swung slowly open. Shelby's heart gave a hard thump in her chest as Caleb walked into the room.

Moonlight drifted through the window, illuminating everything in a soft glow. He was wearing black slacks, a white shirt, open at the neck, and his hair looked as though he'd been shoving his fingers through it.

"Sorry," she said wryly. "I didn't hear you knock."

He walked to the foot of her bed and stared down at her. "Yeah. That's because I didn't."

He stared at her for a long minute—long enough for Shelby to shift position uneasily. It seemed he was finally ready to talk. Whether she wanted to or not.

"How was your meeting?" She didn't care about the meeting, but she couldn't stand the strained silence another moment.

"What?" He shook his head. "Oh, that. Fine. How was your night?"

"Aren't we polite?" she murmured and had the satisfaction of seeing one of his eyebrows wing up. "My night was fine. Quiet. I organized the pantry in your kitchen."

"The pantry?" He frowned.

"Where the food is?" The longer this went on, the more impatient Shelby became. "Did you really come in here to talk about nothing?"

"No," he said abruptly and shoved both hands into his pockets.

"Then why are you here, Caleb?" Shelby threw the duvet off and climbed off the bed. Foolish or not, she felt better, more sure of herself, standing on her own two feet. "You ignored me all day. Left tonight without a word and then walk into my bedroom unannounced. What's going on with you?"

The moonlight accentuated the grim slash of his mouth and the frown etching itself between his brows. Ridiculous that what Shelby most wanted to do was *soothe* him. She should want to kick him.

"It's you," he said abruptly. "Damn it, this is all about you, Shelby."

There went the softer instincts.

"No," she said, firmly shaking her head. "You don't get to blame this on me." She walked around the side of the bed to stand right in front of him. "You're the one who changed, Caleb. The minute your family showed up, you turned into the Iceman."

His scowl deepened and she wouldn't have thought that possible.

"So you just don't want them to know that we—"

"We what, exactly?" he interrupted. "Slept together? Nobody's business but ours."

"Then *what* is it?"

He looked down at her, staring into her eyes with such concentration, it felt as if he were looking all the way into her soul. "I can't get my mind off of you," he admitted finally.

"And that's a bad thing?" she asked.

"It is," he said flatly, and his eyes flashed with temper she knew was directed internally. "I don't want to want you, Shelby."

She huffed out a breath to disguise the hard lump that had settled in her throat. Honesty might be the best policy but it was a bitch to hear it.

"That's very flattering, thanks." She folded her arms across her chest in a defensive posture. After the night they'd spent together, to hear him dismiss her like that was more than hurtful. It was devastating. And it shouldn't have been.

She never should have let herself care. Let herself be pulled into a situation that she had *known* wouldn't last. But it had happened anyway. Shelby couldn't even pinpoint exactly when she had fallen for him. Maybe it had all started that first day, when she'd raced into his arms and he'd helped her when he hadn't had to. Maybe it was when he'd trusted her with his late mother's treasures. Or when he'd kissed her out on the range. Or when he stood between her and Jared even when she hadn't wanted him to be some shining knight in armor.

Whenever it had happened, Shelby now had to deal with the fallout. She'd come to Texas to marry a man she hadn't really loved. Now she was in love with a man who didn't want her. She was really batting a thousand in the romance department.

What she felt for Caleb dwarfed what she'd thought was love for Jared. Shelby hadn't wanted to admit even to herself that she was falling in love with Caleb, because that would only make it more real. But now, staring into icy-blue eyes, she knew it was true.

"I'm not trying to flatter you," he snapped. Pulling his hands from his pockets, he grabbed her shoulders and held on, pulling her close while still, somehow, keeping her at a distance. "I'm trying to be honest, here. There can't be anything between us, Shelby."

"Oh, you're making that clear," she said tightly and squirmed to get out of his grasp.

He held on more tightly. "I don't want to want you, but I have to have you."

She went absolutely still. His eyes were fire now, ice melted away in a passion she recognized and shared. It was so stupid, she told herself, even as her body hummed into life. Why should she sleep with him when he'd made it plain he didn't want to care? But how could she love him and *not*?

"You're making me crazy, Shelby," he ground out, his gaze moving over her, his hands sliding from her shoulders to cup her face in his palms. "Can't stop thinking about you."

She covered his hands with hers and took a deep breath. "Why do you want to?"

He bent his head, kissed her, then stared into her eyes again. "Because it's better for both of us."

"You're wrong," she said. "And I can prove it to you." Shelby went up on her toes, wrapped her arms around his neck and kissed him as she'd been wanting to all day. Her lips parted over his and her tongue swept in to claim his. He reacted instantly, jerking her close, holding her so tightly to him she could feel his heartbeat pounding against her. Breathing was fast and hard.

His mouth devoured hers and she took everything he offered and returned it to him. His hands snaked up under her tank top and cupped her breasts, his thumbs and fingers tweaking and tugging at her nipples until everything in her melted into a puddle of need. Her fingers stabbed through his hair, holding his head to hers, his mouth to hers.

Shelby's entire body was throbbing, her heart was racing and her blood felt thick and hot as it pumped through her veins. When he stripped her top off and bent his head to take one nipple then the other into his mouth, she swayed unsteadily and kept a tight grip on his shoulders to balance herself.

Caleb tipped her back onto the bed and she went willingly, eagerly. Shelby tore at his shirt, sending tiny white buttons skittering across the floor. She didn't care. She wanted to hold him, feel him.

"I missed you today," she admitted, kissing his shoulder, trailing her lips and tongue along his heated skin until she found the spot at the base of his throat that she knew drove him wild.

He groaned, tipped his head to one side and gave her free access. Shelby lavished attention on him, licking, nibbling until he stabbed his fingers through her hair and pulled her head back. "I missed you, too."

His mouth covered hers as she shoved his shirt off his shoulders and down his arms. Her fingers went to his belt and undid it, then unhooked the waistband of his slacks and slid the zipper down. She reached for him and sighed when her hand closed around the hard, solid length of him.

His hips rocked into her hand and he threw his head back and hissed in a breath. She half expected him to howl and everything in her fisted into tight knots of expectation. Anticipation. She stroked him, rubbed him, caressed the tip of him with the base of her thumb until he trembled and Shelby thought there was nothing so sexy as a strong man being vulnerable.

"Wait, wait," he ground out and pulled away from her.

"Come back," she said, coming up onto her knees to crook one finger at him.

He sighed. "Oh, yeah." Then he stripped, pausing only long enough to grab a condom from the pocket of his slacks. "Stopped at my room before I came here."

"I like a man who thinks ahead," she said and slowly shimmied out of her tank top. Moonlight pearled on her skin and she loved the flash in his eyes as he stared at her.

Then he was back on the bed with her and he was pulling her sleep shorts down and off, running his hands over her behind, stroking the hot, damp core of her. Shelby was writhing, twisting in his grasp and as the promise of another earth-shattering climax hovered closer, she reached for him. "Inside me, Caleb. Be inside me again. I need to feel you."

"What you do to me," he said, shaking his head as he watched her. "All I can think about is being with you. In you."

"Then *do it*," she demanded.

Nodding, he flipped her over onto her stomach and before Shelby could even manage a response, he was lifting her hips until she was kneeling. She looked over her shoulder at him and felt fresh need grab her by the throat. He looked dark, dangerous and deadly sexy. His skin was tanned, his body rock hard and as he smoothed on the condom, her heart leaped into a gallop.

Then he was behind her, sliding into her and Shelby cried out his name. He held her hips in his big, strong hands and rocked in and out of her in a fast, breath-stealing rhythm. She had no choice but to follow his lead. She curled her fingers into the sheet beneath her and held on.

She pushed back against him, moving with him, taking him higher and deeper than she would have thought possible. He became a part of her. Shelby didn't know where she ended and he began and she didn't care. All that mattered was what he was doing to her, making her feel. Her body erupted and she turned her face into the mattress to muffle the scream torn from her throat.

Shelby was still trembling, still shaken when Caleb shouted out her name and his body slammed into hers, giving her everything he was and promising nothing.

Nine

The Courtyard shops were a few miles west of downtown Royal. It used to be a ranch, but when the owners sold off, the property became an eclectic mix of shops. The latest was a bridal shop and Shelby had taken a moment to look through the window. In just ten seconds she'd seen five prettier gowns than the one she'd been forced to wear to her disastrous almost wedding.

A large, freshly painted red barn housed Priceless, the antiques shop, plus a crafts studio where people could come in and try their hands at everything from painting to ceramics and more.

Several other buildings on the property showcased local craftsmen such as artists, glassblowers and soap and candle makers. Local farmers rented booths to sell their fresh produce and canned goods and there was even a local cheese maker who always had a long line of customers.

Shelby loved it all. Actually she pretty much loved everything about Royal. Small town life really agreed with her. She wasn't looking forward to moving back to Chicago once she got her money from the Goodman family.

Which should be soon, since the sheriff had told Caleb that he was going out there today to take care of things.

And that left her exactly where?

Shelby sat at a small, round table outside the tiny coffee shop and sipped at a tall glass of iced tea. August hadn't cooled off any and she couldn't help but wonder what winter in Texas would be like.

But she didn't think she'd be finding out.

Watching people stroll past her, some hand in hand, Shelby sighed a little. Last night, she and Caleb had come to a détente of sorts. He didn't want to care for her and she couldn't care for him. It didn't matter how she felt because he wouldn't want to hear it.

"What a mess."

"Excuse me. You're Shelby Arthur, right?"

The woman was blonde, with big blue eyes and a wide smile. She wore a pale green summer dress that showed off tanned, toned arms and legs.

"Hi, yes."

"Do you mind if I sit down and talk to you for a second?" Without waiting for consent, she pulled out a chair and sighed as she sat. "I'm Alexis Slade and thanks for sharing the shade under your umbrella."

"No problem." Shelby smiled at her. "Didn't I just see you at Priceless?" She had been at the antiques store, to talk to Raina Patterson about the last load of crystal and glass they'd taken in. Raina already had buyers for most of the items and the others she would sell in her shop and pay Caleb when they sold.

She should have felt a lot of satisfaction for how Caleb's house was turning out with a little organization. Instead, she was sad because it seemed that her time in Royal was quickly coming to an end. But she shook off those feelings and concentrated on Alexis.

"Yes. I was there to talk to Raina about a fund-raiser the TCC is going to be putting on."

"Oh." Shelby nodded. "Sure, the bachelor auction. Everyone here is talking about it."

Alexis rolled her eyes, set her cream-colored bag on the table and dug out a notebook. When she flipped it open to an empty page she sent Shelby a wince of embarrassment. "I know. Paper and pen. I'm practically a cave person. But it's so much easier for me to just write things down."

"I do the same thing," Shelby assured her as a hot wind blew through the courtyard, tossing her hair across her eyes. She plucked it free, then asked, "But what did you want to talk to me about?"

"I'm not ashamed to admit that I need help," Alexis said, smiling. "You know, I run our family ranch, the Lone Wolf, with no problems at all. But running this auction and getting things like invitations and sponsors for prizes and the bachelors all lined up is giving me a headache."

"I can imagine." She tried to sound sympathetic, but Shelby couldn't help but feel a quick zip of excitement. There was nothing she liked better than taking over a confused mess and bringing order to it.

"Raina was telling me what a great job you did out at Caleb's ranch, organizing his mother's collection…"

"It's been challenging," she admitted, "but yes, it's all coming together."

"Well," Alexis said with another smile, "I figured if that didn't scare you off, then maybe I could find a way to coerce you into helping me get this auction off the ground?"

A little boy careened past the table, trailing a helium balloon in his wake. His giggles floated like soap bubbles on the air. A waitress came out with a fresh glass of tea for Shelby and one for Alexis, though it hadn't been ordered.

"Thanks, Ella," Alexis said on a sigh. "You're a lifesaver."

The young woman grinned. "You want your usual salad, too? Or something else?"

Alexis looked at the brownie on the table in front of Shelby and winced. "I'll have one of those, please, and screw the calories."

Shelby laughed and Ella said, "In this heat, you'll burn them right off as soon as you eat them."

Once they were alone again, Shelby said, "I'm happy to help, but I don't know how long I'll be in town."

Alexis sipped at her tea. "So you've decided to move back to Chicago when you get your money back from Jared?"

Shelby's jaw dropped and her eyes went wide. "Wow. Small town grapevines are really impressive."

"Yeah, sorry." She smiled and shrugged. "But I was at the wedding that didn't happen."

"Oh, God."

"Hey, don't worry about it," Alexis said and reached out to give Shelby's hand a reassuring pat. "I totally understand. I mean, I know you and Caleb are together and how could you marry Jared when you loved someone else?"

"Oh, Alexis, we're not—" God, she had to clear this up. People were talking and that wasn't fair to Caleb, even though he was the one who'd said it, feeding Margaret's gossip until it had become a huge blob of innuendo with a life all its own.

"I felt the same way, you know?" The friendly woman leaned back in her chair, crossed her legs and said, "Back in high school, Jared asked me out constantly, but I didn't go out with him because I was crazy about someone else..." Her words trailed off and a thoughtful frown etched itself briefly on her features.

She knew how Alexis had felt. Shelby was crazy about Caleb. And crazy for letting her emotions get so deeply involved. It was one thing to make a mistake unknowingly. But when you walked right into one with your eyes wide-open, that had to be nuts.

"Anyway," Alexis said and thanked Ella when her brownie arrived, "will you help me get this started? I'd be so grateful."

Shelby thought about it and realized that even if her time in Royal was short, she had to keep busy. Otherwise, she would torture herself with wishing things could be different with Caleb.

"I'd be happy to."

"Great!" Alexis pulled a pen out of her purse and looked at Shelby in expectation. "So. Where do we start?"

Shelby laughed and proceeded to do what she did best.

"Time we talked."

Caleb glanced over his shoulder and watched his

younger brother walk into the shadowy barn. "Not now."

"Yeah," Mitch countered, still walking toward him in a determined stride. "You've been saying that for four years now."

"Then I probably mean it." Caleb turned back to the stall door and stroked the nose of the mare poking her pretty head out for some attention. Just last night, she'd had her foal and done it all on her own, with no supervision from the local vet.

He had a million things to do and not one of them included talking to his brother about ancient history. Caleb took a deep breath, letting the familiar scents—straw, horses, leather and wood—soothe him. But that didn't last because it seemed his brother was determined to finally have his say.

"Damn it, Caleb," Mitch said, stopping right beside him. "What the hell did you expect Meg and me to do?"

"You don't want to do this, Mitch. Just let it lie."

"You mean let's just go on like we have been?" Mitch asked, throwing his hands high then letting them slap back down against his thighs. "With you acting like you've still got a knife in your back?"

Caleb shot him a hard look and turned away, headed for the wide double doors. Mitch stayed with him, finally reaching out and grabbing his brother's arm to stop him in his tracks.

"Nobody wanted to hurt you," Mitch said quietly.

"Didn't stop you, though, did it?"

Mitch yanked his hat off and rubbed his hand back and forth over his nearly shaved head. "No. It didn't. Nothing would have stopped me from having Meg."

Caleb winced. That's how he'd felt about having

Shelby. Instantly, images from the night before filled his mind and his body went tight and hard. The woman had touched something inside him that he hadn't even known was there. But as much as he wanted her, as much as being inside her burned him to a cinder, how could he trust her? How could he trust any woman enough again to risk the kind of humiliation he'd already lived through once?

Mitch drew his head back and stared at him. "You're not still in love with Meg, are you?"

"What?" Caleb exclaimed. "No."

Just the thought of it shocked him. He hadn't been bothered by Mitch and Meg being happy together on the ranch. Not jealous or even bitter about what they'd found together. It was the betrayal that had hit him harder than anything else. And wasn't that enlightening? If he'd really loved Meg in the first place, it would have driven him crazy watching his brother with her.

What did that say? Hell, looking back now, he wasn't even sure he'd loved her *then*. He'd wanted to be married. To have a family. And Meg was the one he'd chosen to fulfill the role of wife and mother. God, had he been that big an ass?

"That's good to know. I always admired you, Caleb. You know that. But Meg." Mitch shook his head and gave a wistful smile. "Hell, we'd all known each other for years and then that summer it was like I was seeing Meg for the first time. Love just slammed into us both. Neither of us was expecting it or looking for it. It was just *there*. And when you find something like that, you can't just turn from it."

He could see that now, with four years of clarity behind him. And, maybe, Shelby dropping into his life gave Caleb a little more insight into how it must have been for his brother. Still… "Running away the night before the wedding wasn't the way to handle it."

"Yeah, I know that. And you should know, Meg didn't want to do it. I talked her into making a run for it. Cowardly? Okay, yeah it was." Mitch nodded thoughtfully. "But damn it, Caleb, you were always so damn self-righteous. So sure of yourself and how the world ought to run. If we had come to you, would you have listened?"

He hated to admit it, but the answer was most likely *no*. He'd had his plan and he wouldn't have listened to anything that would disrupt that plan.

"Maybe not," he allowed.

Mitch blew out a breath. "Thanks for that. And you should know we're both damn sorry for what we put you through. Hell, Caleb. I'm sorry."

Caleb nodded and looked at his brother. It had been four years since they'd really had a conversation that didn't revolve around the ranch. And it felt *good* to get this out in the open. To hopefully get past it.

"You and Meg are good together," he said finally and watched his younger brother's smile broaden.

"I love her like crazy," Mitch said. "More even than when I married her."

"Yeah. I can see that." Caleb slapped one hand against Mitch's shoulder and took a step that would end the enmity between them. "I guess things worked out just how they should in the end."

"You mean that?"

"Yeah," Caleb said, a little surprised himself, "I do."

"Good. That's good." Mitch nodded and blew out a breath again. "You know, you're gonna be an uncle again."

"Is that right?" Caleb grinned at the thought and realized that the hurt of four years ago was well and truly gone now. He could enjoy his brother. And his sister-in-law. He could put the past where it belonged and reclaim his family.

So, a voice in his mind whispered, *does that mean you can put what Shelby did aside and take a leap of faith?*

He shook his head to dislodge that thought, because he just didn't have an answer for it. Caleb could understand what Meg and Mitch had done, but the bottom line was, Shelby was a different matter altogether. How could he trust her to stay when she'd run out on Jared? She hadn't done it for love. She'd simply bolted when she couldn't handle the thought of going through with the wedding. If he took a chance with her, would she run again when things didn't go her way?

Shaking his head, he pushed those thoughts aside for now. He had no answers anyway. So he looked at his brother and said, "Let's go up to the big house and have a beer. We should talk about the new ranch land we're buying and the oil leases are coming due again in six months. We need to decide if we want to renew or start drilling ourselves."

Mitch settled his hat on his head and grinned. "Sounds good to me."

As they walked, Caleb was glad to finally be more at ease with his brother. But thoughts of Shelby made sure he wasn't at ease with anything else.

Cam had left a big bowl of pasta salad in the fridge and roast beef sandwiches on a covered plate for their dinner. After a long hot day, it sounded perfect. But for right now, Shelby sat at the kitchen table, making a list of things for Alexis to look into for the auction.

First, of course, had to be advertising. If they really wanted to make the most of this auction, then they needed as many single women as possible to take part.

"Houston papers as well as Royal," she murmured, making notes as she talked. "A website would be good, too. Maybe they could have a link on Royal's town site, but one of its own would be even better."

"Talking to yourself?" Caleb asked as he came into the room.

She looked up and smiled. Memories flooded her mind, how he'd been last night, how *they'd* been, together. Maybe she should have been embarrassed but instead all she could think was that she wanted to do it all again. And again.

Squirming a little on the bench seat as her body warmed, she forced cheer into her voice. "No, I actually told Alexis Slade I'd help her with the bachelor auction."

Caleb went to the fridge for a bottle of beer. Once he had it open, he took a long drink and shook his head. "Can't believe they're going to do it."

"Are you going to be one of the bachelors?"

"Oh, that's a big hell no," Caleb said, firmly shaking his head for emphasis.

Foolishly, relief washed over Shelby. Heck, she might not even be in Royal when the auction happened, but she was glad to hear he wouldn't be bought by some woman who wasn't *her*.

"I think it sounds fun," she said, deliberately making herself smile. "We're thinking of a Christmas theme."

"Christmas? It's *August*," Caleb pointed out.

"Well, it's not going to be held tomorrow. The auction is set for November, so a Christmas theme will really work. There's a lot to be done in not very much time." She looked back to her list and started a new column for decorations. "Plenty of mistletoe, and wreaths and ribbon. Probably a hundred yards or so of ribbon, since Alexis says they're holding the auction at the TCC in the gazebo. To make it look like a winter wonderland it will take a few miles of pine garland and red ribbon—"

"Ribbon."

"And snow." She looked up at him. "Does it snow in Texas? Heck, does it ever cool off in Texas?"

He grinned. "It doesn't usually get cold enough to snow."

"Fake snow, then. It could be mounded in corners with little signs pointing the way to the dessert tables and the bar and the auction itself... Ooh, write that down. We should have lots of different desserts. I bet Jillian at Miss Mac's Pie Shack would do the desserts for us and—" She paused and narrowed her eyes on him. "What're you smiling at?"

He shook his head. "Just that I'm sort of getting used to your monologues."

"Well," she said, "I talk to myself because I always understand me."

"Uh-huh." He walked to the kitchen island, hitched one hip against it and asked, "How do you know Jillian Navarro at Miss Mac's Pie Shack?"

"I was in town and hello. *Pie.* I stopped in to try some and got to talking with her, and her daughter is just adorable and her desserts are amazing."

"Right. So you're helping Alexis with the auction. Making friends all over town. Does that mean you've decided to stay in Royal after you get your money back?"

Shelby sighed. She'd been thinking a lot about just that. Stay or go. The truth was, she had nothing in Chicago to go back to. A few friends, some loyal clients, but nothing else. Here in Royal, she could start over. Build a new business. Make new friends. But even she didn't believe those reasons were the only ones she was considering staying for.

She'd like a chance with Caleb. But there was no guarantee that would happen and if she stayed and couldn't have him, would she be able to live with it?

"Honestly, I don't know," she said, looking up at him. "Until I get the money, I don't have to make that decision so I guess I'm putting it off."

He simply stared at her for a long minute or two and once again, Shelby was left wishing she could read what he was thinking. The whole quiet cowboy thing was irritating in the extreme when you wanted answers and got nothing but more questions.

Then his manner shifted. He straightened up, set his beer down on the counter and pointed at the window behind her. "Looks like we've got company."

Shelby turned in her seat in time to see Brooke Goodman get out of her car. Darkness was lowering over the ranch, but the porch light was bright enough to see that Brooke's light blond hair was lifting in the ever-present wind. She wore skinny black jeans, a dark red shirt with long sleeves and a pair of black sandals. She took a long look at the house, then turned back to her flashy red convertible and reached into the backseat.

When she lifted out one of Shelby's suitcases, Shelby gave a *whoop* of excitement. "She's brought my stuff!"

Jared's sister was the only one of the Goodman family that Shelby had actually *liked*. Brooke had been her one and only bridesmaid at the wedding that hadn't happened. And if she was here now, with her suitcase, maybe she was also going to deliver the money that was Shelby's.

She scooted out of the bench seat and headed for the door. "I'll go talk to her."

"Yeah," Caleb said, walking right behind her. "*We* should."

Shelby rolled her eyes. Whether he wanted her or not, the man couldn't seem to stop trying to protect her. But with Brooke, no protection was necessary.

She opened the door just as Jared's sister was lifting one hand to knock. Instead, she slapped that hand to her chest and gave a short laugh.

"Wow. You scared me."

"Sorry," Shelby said and reached out to hug her. "I'm so glad to see you, Brooke."

"I'm sorry it took me so long to get your things back to you," she said, as Caleb took the suitcase from her and pulled it inside. "There's another one in the backseat."

"I'll get it."

Meanwhile, Shelby steered Brooke into the great room and took just a second for a little self-congratulatory smile. She really had made a huge difference in this house. The room was open, welcoming. The ranch was now looking exactly like what it was, a luxury ranch house with eclectic details. She waved Brooke onto the couch and sat down beside her.

Brooke was petite and pretty and so nice it made up for the fact that she seemed nearly perfect. She was also a talented artist, though neither of her parents were supportive of her goals.

"Thank you for bringing my things," Shelby said.

"Don't thank me." Brooke took a breath and let it out in a rush. "I couldn't get your money. The family is still furious and it was all I could do to sneak your suitcases out."

Shelby felt a wave of disappointment rise up, then dissipate. She would get her money, it was just a matter of *when*. "It's okay. Really." She forced a smile. "This is all my fault, anyway. I should have called the whole thing off long before the wedding day."

Brooke shook her head. "Don't ruin it for me. You're actually my hero in all of this. You stood up to the Goodman family and that's something I've never been able to do."

Shelby knew that Brooke's dream was to go to Europe to study painting, view the old masters in person. But her parents had control over Brooke's inheritance and they refused to give her what her grandmother had left her.

"Brooke," Shelby said, reaching out to give her hand a squeeze, "just *do* it. Don't wait for your parents to agree. Just go."

The other woman sighed a little. "I can't touch my money unless my parents give permission or I'm married."

"Wow." Shelby sat back. "Couldn't you go anyway? Work to support yourself while you're there?"

"It sounds wonderful, but I'm not trained to do anything," Brooke said. "Unless someone wants me to arrange a sit-down dinner for thirty. I can do that."

"You're being too hard on yourself," Shelby said.

"You're so talented. You have to do something with your art."

Brooke instantly brightened. "Actually, Alexis Slade asked me to do some painting at the TCC. I'm doing a mural at the day care and more in the public garden areas. It's not Europe, but it's exciting."

Shelby grinned. "What did your parents say?"

Brooke laughed. "They don't know."

Caleb walked back into the room and took a seat near the two women. "I put your things in your room, Shelby."

"Thanks. Brooke was just telling me—"

"What the hell?" Caleb cut her off, looking through the wide front windows at a long, black sedan hurtling down the drive and coming to a hard stop behind Brooke's car.

Both women turned to look and Brooke groaned. "Oh, God. That's my father. What's he doing here?"

"He probably knows you brought my things over," Shelby said, standing up. "I'm so sorry. You shouldn't have to get in trouble over me."

"Doesn't matter," Brooke said. She stood up, too, and all three of them watched as Simon Goodman stomped toward the front door.

He didn't bother to knock, just came inside and slammed the door behind him. "Brooke! Where the hell are you?"

She gave Shelby a sad smile. "Right here, Father."

Caleb took a step forward, automatically putting himself between Simon and the rest of the room. He stood there, Shelby told herself, like a soldier. Back straight, legs braced wide apart, arms crossed over his chest. He was a solid wall of protection and she felt a rush of warmth for him. He would always stand for someone he felt needed defending.

Simon Goodman marched into the room like a man on a mission. His features were thunderous, his dark eyes burning as he swept the room before landing on his daughter. "The minute I saw that woman's suitcases gone from the hall, I knew you were behind it."

"Father," Brooke said with calm, "these are Shelby's things. She deserves to have them."

"She deserves *nothing* from us," he countered and shifted his gaze to Shelby. "You've dragged my son's name through the dirt. And for what?"

Caleb speared him with a hot look. "You're going to want to watch what you say, Simon."

"It's all right, Caleb. I can handle this," she said, then looked at the older man vibrating with fury. "Mr. Goodman, I didn't mean to—"

"You didn't mean," Simon said with a harsh sneer. "Is that supposed to make this all go away? People are gossiping about my son and here you are, living with a rancher, no better than you should be."

Caleb took a step closer to him. "That's enough, Simon."

The older man glared at him. He wore a suit and tie, but his hair was disheveled as if he'd been electrocuted recently and his eyes fired with indignation.

"It's not enough. You were a guest at my son's wedding and left with the bride." Simon looked him up and down with one quick, dismissive glance. "What does that make you? Or *her*?"

"Now, just a minute," Shelby said.

"Father, you're making this worse."

"You keep your mouth shut," Simon snapped. "You're a damn traitor to your family."

"Hey, there's no need to punish Brooke," Shelby protested.

"Simon," Caleb warned, ice dripping from his words. "You should leave. Now. You don't need to be here."

"I'm here to deliver this tramp's money." He reached into his inner suit pocket and pulled out a check. Then he tossed it at her and watched as it fluttered to the floor.

"Pick it up." Caleb's voice was cold. Tight.

"Damned if I will," Simon said.

Brooke bent to pick up the check and instantly handed it to Shelby. "I'm sorry for all of this," she whispered.

"Sorry? You're sorry?" Her father's eyes wheeled. "This woman smeared your family, your *brother* and you would apologize to her?"

He looked back at Shelby, a sneer on his face. "There's your damn money." He shifted his gaze to Caleb. "I brought it because I had to see this tramp myself. To tell her that she should leave Royal because a life here will be a misery for her." He looked at her. "I'll see to it myself."

"You'll do *nothing*." Caleb moved in on the man and Shelby noticed how quickly Simon backpedaled.

Still, she didn't want to cause even more chaos in this house. This town. "Caleb, I told you I don't need to be defended."

"There is no defense for you, young woman," Simon blustered.

Caleb ignored him and focused on Shelby. "You think I don't know you can handle this? I do. But I'm damned if I'm going to stand in my own house and listen to insults."

"It doesn't matter," Shelby insisted. "Not to me. Not anymore."

Brooke put one hand on her arm and shook her head slightly, as if silently telling Shelby to let Caleb handle it.

"It matters to me," Caleb said. "I've seen more of the Goodmans in the last week than I have in the last year and I can truly well say that but for Brooke, I've had more than enough."

"You would insult me? Your father wouldn't stand for this," Simon said.

"Well then, that convinces me I'm doing the right thing." Caleb took another step closer to the other man. "You're fired."

"What?" He genuinely looked surprised.

"Should have done it years ago, but it's done now."

"Caleb," Shelby said.

"You're going to let this woman ruin a good working relationship?" Simon was clearly stunned at the idea. "Are you blind, boy? She's just a city girl come looking for a rich cowboy. She turned my boy loose and she's aiming at you, now."

"Oh, for…" Shelby muttered.

Caleb never glanced at her. "You should leave, Simon. Your business is done here."

"You'll regret this, boy."

"Not a boy," Caleb reminded him. "And the only thing I regret is waiting so long to fire your ass."

"Brooke," Simon ordered, "you go get in your car. We'll not stay and be insulted."

"Brooke," Shelby said quietly, "you don't have to go."

"Now," Simon roared.

"It's better if I go," Brooke said. "Don't worry. He's all thunder, no lightning. I'll talk to you soon."

Simon stomped from the room and Brooke was just a step or two behind him. She turned at the threshold and gave them one small smile before following her father out to the yard.

Caleb and Shelby stood side by side, watching as the Goodmans drove off. Shelby was more than a little rattled by the encounter, but her suitcases were in her room and she held a check in her hand. She glanced down at it, making sure the total was right. It was.

Caleb looked at it, too, then caught her gaze with his. "So, guess there's nothing holding you here now, right?"

She lifted her gaze to his and wanted to wail when she saw the blank look in those icy-blue eyes. Just a moment ago, he'd stood in front of her, defending her. Now it was as if he'd erected a wall between them, closing her off, turning her back into the outsider she had been when she'd first come here.

"I don't know," she said simply. "I don't know what I'm going to do."

"Come on, Shelby." He shook his head, his gaze locked with hers. "We both know what you're going to do."

"No—" She didn't. How could she know when everything inside her was in turmoil?

"You'll go back to Chicago, now that you've got the means to do it," he said in a clipped tone that carried a sheen of ice. "Your reason for staying's gone. Probably best all the way around. No point dragging this out, is there?"

God, it was as if he'd already said goodbye and

watched her leave the ranch. Was it so easy for him, then? To let her go? Would he not miss her? Even a little? "Caleb…"

He spoke up quickly as if he simply didn't want to hear whatever she might have said. "I don't blame you for leaving. Royal's not your home. Nothing holding you here anymore. Sorry you had to go through all of that, but at least it's finished now." He took a step back from her.

"I've got things to check on," he muttered. "Don't wait on me for dinner. Don't know when I'll be back."

Shelby watched him go and knew he was doing more than walking out of the room.

He was walking out of her life.

Ten

Two days later, Shelby was still in limbo, and it was a cold, lonely spot.

Caleb had cut her out of his life with the smooth efficiency of a surgeon. Yes, she was still living at the ranch, but she might as well have been on the moon. Caleb didn't come to her in the middle of the night. They didn't share dinner in a quiet kitchen, telling each other stories of the day. She hadn't been back in *his* room since their first night together.

In the mornings, he left at first light, so she didn't even see him over the coffeepot. And Shelby tried to avoid the kitchen altogether now, since the sympathy in Cam's eyes simply tore at her.

"If you had any sense, you'd just leave," she told herself firmly.

She'd taken her check and opened a bank account in

town. But that didn't necessarily mean she was going to stay, she reminded herself. She could always have the money wired to another account. In Chicago. Or maybe New York. Or even Florida. Somewhere far away from Texas so she didn't have to be reminded of what a nightmare the month of August had become.

"Sorry," Meg said as she hurried back into the twins' bedroom. "Sometimes I hate that phone."

"It's okay," Shelby said, putting on a smile and a lighthearted tone that she didn't feel. No reason to depress Meg. Especially since the woman was giving Shelby something to *do*. Something to focus on besides her own broken heart. "Gave me a chance to look around, get some ideas."

"Thank God," Meg said, doing a slow circle to take the room in.

Just like the main ranch house, Meg and Mitch's place quietly spoke of money. There was nothing overt, but the furnishings were all high quality and the house itself had obviously been built with care. Hardwood floors gleamed in slashes of sunlight that speared through wide windows. Heavy rugs dotted the floors, giving warmth to the space and the twins' beds were side by side, divided only by a child-sized table holding a grinning, cow-shaped lamp.

The space was huge and Shelby's imagination raced with ideas for making the space more like a child's dream room.

"You know, with the new baby coming, I really want to get Jack and Julie's room redone. And with the miracle you worked at the big house, who better to help me?" Meg walked over, picked up a pair of Julie's pink sneakers and stowed them neatly beneath the bed.

Shelby nodded thoughtfully as her mind whirled with idea after idea. "I love how it is right now. It's decorated beautifully."

"It is, but it's more adult pretty than kid pretty, you know?"

Shelby knew just what she meant. The furnishings were lovely, but there was nothing about the room that sparked a child's imagination.

Meg looked around again. "We had a designer come in originally, but—" she winced "—the woman didn't actually *have* children, so she set the room up as if kids never move or do anything. I mean, it's pretty and I do like it, but the toys and clothes and just the general flotsam created by two tiny humans is staggering. Even the housekeeper is ready to throw up her hands."

Shelby grinned. "Well, I don't have kids, either, but I know what I'd like. I think there are a few simple things we can do to make it all easier on you and them."

"I'm all ears," Meg assured her.

"Organization first, and then we can spruce it all up and make it more…fanciful."

"I like it already," Meg assured her.

Shelby walked to the wide walk-in closet and threw the doors open. "This for example. There's a lot of wasted space. On hangers, kids' clothes don't hang down very low. We can put a shelving system here and add wicker baskets on the bottom. That way the kids can put their own toys away in the baskets while you'll have the top shelf for shoes, sweaters, whatever else you need, but don't hang."

"I like it," Meg said, nodding as if she could see it.

"And, we can have beds made that come with storage beneath, so the twins can have their own treasure chests, keep things that are important to them stored away."

"Oh, they'd love that," Meg agreed.

Shelby gave an inner sigh. Those children were adorable and pulled on every one of her heartstrings. Along with giving her own biological clock a good, hard kick.

She shook the feeling off and concentrated on bringing her imagination to life. "And in the corner, we can put in a table and chairs, kid-sized, where Julie can practice her drawing. With a series of smaller shelves and small baskets there, we'd have a space for her paper and crayons and markers."

Meg grinned. "Oh, my God, this is great. Keep going!"

Laughing now, Shelby turned and pointed to the far corner. "This room is so big, we could build a playhouse there for both of the kids and make it like a tree house." She was thinking as she spoke and smiled when another idea hit her. "You know, Brooke Goodman is an excellent artist. I bet she'd love to paint a tree mural on the wall and we could build the house to look as though it's hung on the tree branches. With little steps and ladders and secret passages... Oh, and maybe a place inside where they could nap."

"I love it. I love all of it," Meg said, wrapping her arms around her middle. "I can't even tell you. It's perfect. Honestly, Shelby, you're brilliant."

"Thank you, but sometimes, it just takes an outsider to look at a space and see it differently."

Meg frowned a little. "You're not an outsider, Shelby."

Shaking her head, she ignored that because the truth was that Caleb had cut her out. Pushed her out.

"I just love to bring a room together and make it functional, you know?" She looked around and could almost see what it would be like when it was finished. A sharp pang settled around Shelby's heart when she realized she most likely wouldn't see the completed project. How could she stay when Caleb was making it clear he didn't want her there?

"This is more than functional," Meg said. "You're talking about building a kid's dream room."

Shelby smiled. "For now. Then, when they want their own rooms, you could make this one a shared play space and decorate other bedrooms for them."

"God knows the house is big enough for it," Meg said, nodding. "And Mitch is already talking about adding on another wing. The Mackenzies are big on *wings*," she added with a laugh. "He wants a *lot* of kids, but then, so do I."

"It sounds wonderful," Shelby said and, though she thought she was being stiff-upper-lippy, Meg must have caught something in her tone.

"What's going on, Shelby?"

"Nothing. Really." Even she heard the lie and Shelby wished she were better at it.

"Is it you and Caleb?"

Shelby shook her head. There really was no point in pretending, when she'd have to leave the ranch soon. Everyone would know the truth then. "There is no me and Caleb."

"What? Why? Since when?" Meg walked closer. "I can see the way you look at each other. Your eyes practically devour him when he walks into a room. And he's clearly crazy about you, Shelby."

"No, he's not," Shelby said and looked down into the

yard. From the kids' bedroom, she had a good view of the corral where Caleb was working with one of the horses. He held the reins as the huge, black animal trotted around the perimeter. Mitch and the three-year-old twins stood at the fence, watching, but Shelby couldn't tear her eyes away from Caleb.

Everything about that man called to her. Sadly, he obviously didn't feel the same about her. Otherwise, he never would have been able to simply ignore her existence as he had the last couple of days.

"What happened, Shelby?" Meg asked, her voice soft. "Did you guys have a fight?"

Shelby laughed, but it hurt her throat. "No, we didn't. That's the hardest part to accept. Nothing happened. Nothing at all. No fight. No huge, defining moment that tore us apart. It might be easier to take if there had been a big blowup." She sighed a little and kept her gaze locked on Caleb. "He just…shut down. Shut me out. The Goodmans gave me my money and Caleb assumed I'd be going back to Chicago. He actually told me it was probably for the best."

"Idiot," Meg muttered.

Shelby smiled sadly at the camaraderie. "After that, he simply closed himself off. For the last two days, he's ignored me completely. Avoided me. He won't even talk to me, Meg. I don't even know why I'm still here."

She turned to look at the other woman. "At this point, I think maybe Caleb was right and it would be for the best if I just left. For both our sakes."

"Oh, God, I was afraid of this." Meg sighed and moved up to stand beside her at the window. "This isn't about you, Shelby. This is about me."

Confused, she turned to look at her friend. "What do you mean?"

"God, it's like a Karmic circle."

"What are you talking about?" Shelby asked. Misery was stamped on Meg's features but her eyes simmered with a low burn.

"This is about me. And Mitch and what happened four years ago." Meg turned around to look at Shelby. "Once upon a time, I was engaged to Caleb."

Stunned, Shelby stared at her. She hadn't known what to expect, but this was still a shocker. Caleb was always so cool with Meg, it was hard to imagine the two of them engaged. "Really?"

"I know. Weird to think about now. It's funny, but Caleb never even really proposed." Meg sighed, reached up and tucked her hair behind her ears. "It seemed like a natural progression, you know? We'd known each other forever. He wanted family and so did I and…" She sighed. "That sounds so lame, but—"

"It's okay," Shelby assured her. Hadn't she done the same thing with Jared? Given in to her need for family, for home and then come to regret the decision? "Believe me, I understand."

Meg gave her a weak smile. "Thanks. Anyway, long story short—a few weeks before the wedding, Mitch and I discovered we loved each other. But what could we do? I was engaged to his brother for heaven's sake. Neither of us wanted to hurt Caleb, but that's what we did."

This explained so much, Shelby thought. Why Caleb would pull back every time a connection began to grow between them. And knowing this, she didn't have a clue how to fight it. How to get through to him and expect him to trust her.

"At the time, I tried to find a way to talk to Caleb, but he's so damn single-minded he wouldn't listen." She held up one hand. "Don't misunderstand, I'm not saying that any of this was his fault. Mitch and I were in love and it seemed like there was only one way to be together. So, the night before the wedding, Mitch and I eloped."

"Oh, God." Shelby shifted her gaze to the man in the middle of the corral.

"Yeah." Meg stood beside her. "I left Caleb a letter, trying to explain it all, but of course it wasn't enough. Apologies weren't enough. And for the last four years, Mitch and I have tried to make it up to him, but that's hard to do when the man won't acknowledge your presence."

"I know that, too," Shelby murmured.

"Caleb and Mitch kept working together, but they used to be close and that ended when we eloped. I still feel guilty about that. I know that it hurts Mitch daily. And I think Caleb misses his brother, too." Meg took a breath and sighed it out. "Just the other day, though, Caleb and Mitch talked and it might be getting better between them. But he'll never forgive me."

She turned, and her gaze locked with Shelby's. "So when you ran out on your wedding, it really hit home with him."

"Of course it did." Shelby's heart actually *sank*. She felt it drop to the pit of her stomach where it sat like an icy stone. This was why she couldn't get past the wall he'd built around himself. This was at the heart of the darkness she'd glimpsed in his eyes a few times.

No wonder he couldn't trust her. She understood how it had to seem to him. Shelby had done to Jared exactly what Meg had done to him. He'd already experienced betrayal and didn't want to risk it again.

"I'm so sorry, Shelby. He's being an ass because of something I did."

She wanted to agree. A part of Shelby wanted to give Caleb that out. Let him off the hook. But by doing that, she heaped guilt on Meg's head and she wasn't willing to do that.

"You know what?" Shelby said with a slow shake of her head. "No. It's not your fault. You did the right thing four years ago just like I did the right thing. Caleb should know that."

"Yes, but—"

"No. If he doesn't want to trust me, then he has to do it for real reasons. For things I've done—well, okay I did run out on my wedding, so yeah. But I didn't do it to Caleb. Why should he expect that I'd be untrustworthy? I'm practically a golden retriever I'm so loyal."

"A dog?"

"And he should know that," Shelby said, getting angrier the longer she thought about it. "We've been together nonstop for nearly two weeks. And in dating time, that's like two years or something—"

"Well, two years is—"

"He should know me better," Shelby continued, talking to herself more than Meg. She stared out the window at Caleb's broad back and half expected him to turn around and look at her just from the power of her stare. "And if he doesn't know me better than this, then he should have *told* me what he was thinking. Heck, he's still mad at you and Mitch for not talking to him.

"Told me himself that I should have talked to Jared, but *he* doesn't have to talk. No, not the great Caleb

Mackenzie. He gets to keep his secrets," Shelby muttered, warming now to her rant and letting it all out as she stared down at the man she loved. The man she was suddenly furious with.

"He just walks out and then ignores me. Does he tell me why? *No.* Did he hope I'd just go away? Slink out of town to make his life easier? Well, why would I do that? He should have talked to me, damn it. He's acting like a child and I don't like it one bit."

"Shelby—"

"Why should I go back to Chicago?"

"Who said you should?" Meg was watching her warily.

"Caleb tried, but why does he get a say in what I do when he won't even talk to me? No, I don't want to go back. I was going to anyway, because it was too hard to be here and not be with Caleb. But that would make it easy on him, wouldn't it? And why should I do him any favors? Why does he get it easy when *he's* the reason this is all happening?"

"Um," Meg said, "I don't know."

"If Caleb Mackenzie wants to ignore me, then I'm going to make him work for it." Shelby turned around and headed for the door, riding a wave of anger. "I'm staying in Texas. I'm staying in Royal. And I'm going to start up my business and I'm going to be so successful he'll hear my name everywhere he goes."

"That's great, but—"

Shelby stopped at the threshold and looked back at her friend. "The good news is, I'll be here to help you make this room fabulous. And I'm going to help Lucy Curran, too. And help Alexis run the auction. And we'll design your new baby's room together, too, and when you're ready to add on the new wing, we can plan it all out together."

"Yay?" Meg said, clearly a little shocked at how quickly Shelby had moved from misery, to sympathy to fury. "Um, where are you going now?"

"To tell that stoic cowboy that he loves me. And to let him know that if he can't trust me, then it's his loss." She didn't wait to see if Meg had a response.

Shelby took the wide staircase at a fast clip, crossed the elegantly appointed hall and went out the front door. She walked straight to the corral and paused only when the kids rushed up to her.

"Sheby!" Jack looked up and shouted, "I get a puppy!"

Shelby's heart melted a little at the way Jack mutilated her name.

Julie was there, too. "*We* get a puppy! He's mine, too."

"Is not."

"Is, too."

Mitch came over, scooped up both kids into his arms and grinned at Shelby before telling his kids, "It's my puppy! Let's go find Mom so we can go get that poor dog that's going to be killed with love."

"Yay!" The twins shouted in excitement as their father carried them off to the house. Then she turned back to Caleb, still in the corral, busily ignoring her.

Now that she knew what was behind his behavior in the last few days, she was torn. She loved him. And she was furious with him. She wanted to kiss him and kick him. Shelby wondered if most women felt that way.

"Caleb!"

He glanced over his shoulder at her. "I'm busy."

"That's too bad," she said and kept walking. She was wearing her pale green camp shirt, white capris and completely inappropriate sandals to be walking through the dirt, but that couldn't be helped. She wasn't going to stop now.

Opening the corral gate, she started inside when Caleb shouted, "Stay outside! I don't want you near this horse, he's still a little wild."

Well, that stopped her cold. She was angry and ready for a come-to-Jesus meeting, but she didn't want to be killed by a horse, either. "Fine. Then you come out. We have to talk."

He glared at her for a long minute and she wondered how she could be both angry and attracted at the same time. The look on his face was fierce and it didn't bother her a bit. If anything, it made her insides churn with the kind of longing that had been eating at her for the last few days.

She watched as he released the lead from the horse's bridle, then turned him loose to race crazily around the corral. Caleb walked to the gate and opened it, closing it again securely behind him. Then he didn't glance at her before heading for the barn.

Shelby was just a step or two behind him. "Will you stop so we can talk?"

"Whatever we have to say to each other is going to be private," he growled out, "not said out in the yard where every cowhand nearby can listen in."

"Oh. All right."

In the shadowy barn, Caleb finally stopped, turned around to look at her and said, "What is it?"

Huh. Now that she had his complete attention, she hardly knew where to start. But that irritated gleam in his eyes prompted her to just jump in, feetfirst. "Meg told me what happened four years ago."

"I'm not talking about that," he said and turned away.

She grabbed his arm and he stopped. "Fine. We don't have to. But we do have to talk about the fact that it's the reason you're shutting me out."

"Don't be ridiculous."

"I'm not. You don't trust me, Caleb." It broke her heart to say it, to read the truth of it in his eyes as he looked down at her. "Because I did to Jared what Meg did to you. So you're thinking that I'm completely untrustworthy. But I'm not. I did the right thing in walking away. It wasn't easy, but I did it."

"I didn't say I don't trust you."

"Oh, please, you didn't have to," she countered, waving him into silence. Horses in their stalls moved restlessly. The scent of straw and wood and leather surrounded them and she knew it was a scent she would always associate with Caleb.

"I understand why you feel that way, but you're wrong."

"Well, thanks. Now I'm going back to work."

"I'll just follow you until I say what I have to say," she warned.

He believed her and sighed irritably as he crossed his arms over his chest. "Fine. Talk."

"You love me, Caleb."

He blinked at her. "What?"

"You love me and you don't want to and that's sad for both of us because we're really good together. I mean, I know we've only known each other a little while but like I told Meg, we've been together nearly every second, so that's like two years' worth of dates and really, does it matter how long you know a person before you love them?"

She answered her own question. "It really doesn't. The love is either there or it's not and it is. For you. And for me. And you don't want to admit it because you're scared."

"Scared?" He laughed, dismissing the very idea.

But Shelby knew him well enough to see the truth in his eyes. "Terrified. You know, I was going to leave Royal. Because I knew you didn't want me here anymore so I thought it would be best if I just left. Make it easier on you—"

He opened his mouth to speak but she cut him off.

"—but I don't want to make it easy on you. You *should* suffer because I'm here in town but not with you. Because it'll be your own fault because you're too stubborn to see that what Meg did four years ago was right. And what I did was right, too. Doing the right thing isn't always easy, Caleb. But it's necessary. I still believe that. And did you ever think that maybe fate brought me here to Texas so that I could realize a mistake and find *you*?"

"Fate?"

She kept going. "Just so you know, I'm opening my business in Royal and I'm going to work for Lucy Curran. And Alexis. And I've got a job working with Meg, too, so I'll be here at the ranch. A lot. So get used to seeing me. And not having me."

Her heart was breaking, but she also felt good, telling him exactly what she was thinking, feeling. How could she have fallen for a man so stubborn? So resistant to the very idea of taking a chance again?

"You should know that I love you, but I'm going to

try to get over it." She turned around and headed for the door, determined to get out before she cried. After that wonderful speech, she didn't want to ruin it all by looking pitiful. Which is just how she felt, beneath the simmering boil of anger.

"Where the hell are you going?" Caleb shouted.

"To Royal," she called back. "I'm going to buy a house."

An hour later, Caleb was still thinking about what she'd said. And how she'd looked, facing him down, challenging him, calling him a damn coward.

Was she right?

She was staying in Royal. She'd be right there. In town. Every day. And she wouldn't be with *him*. Is that what he really wanted? Caleb had spent the last two days ignoring her, avoiding her, because he thought it best to get used to being without her. So it wouldn't hit him so damn hard when she left for Chicago.

But she wasn't leaving.

And he missed her already, damn it.

"Uncle Caleb!" Julie's voice and the clatter of tiny feet stomping into the barn.

"Look! A puppy!"

Grateful for the distraction from his own thoughts, Caleb looked up to see the twins rush inside, a black Lab puppy in Jack's arms. A local rancher's dog had had another litter and Mitch had been determined to get one of the pups for the twins. Looks like that, at least, had gone well.

Meg was right behind the kids, though, so his smile didn't last long.

"He's a girl," Jack said proudly.

"She don't have a name," Julie announced.

"Doesn't," Meg corrected. "You kids set the puppy down, but keep an eye on her while I talk to your uncle, okay?"

As the kids settled in to play with the puppy who was busy peeing on the straw floor, Caleb drew a sharp breath and narrowed his eyes on her. Setting things right with Mitch had been one thing. But he didn't know that he was ready to talk to Meg about any of this. Hell, he'd had too much already of strong-willed women. "I'm busy, Meg."

"You're always busy, Caleb. But this little chat is long past due." Meg reached out and stroked the long nose of a mare who'd stuck her head through the stall door hoping for attention. "I told Shelby she could use my car, so she's in Royal right now, looking for a place to buy. Or rent."

"She told me."

"Uh-huh, and you're still standing here, so I'm guessing you didn't listen to anything she said any more than you've ever listened to me." She gave him a look he'd seen her pin the twins with and he didn't much care for it.

Then he glanced at the kids shrieking and laughing with their pup. "Now's not the time for this."

"Now's the perfect time," Meg corrected. "I knew you wouldn't be rude to me in front of the twins."

"So you used them."

"You bet," she agreed. Laying one hand on his forearm, Meg leaned into him and said, "You're a good man, Caleb. But you're being deliberately deaf and blind."

"Butt out, Meg," he warned quietly.

"No, I've done that for too long." Smiling sadly, she

said, "We were friends once, Caleb. Good friends who made the mistake of thinking that meant a marriage would be good for us, too.

"We were wrong. I'm sorry I hurt you when I ran out on the wedding, but can't you see now that I did the right thing? For all of us? You and I are too much alike, Caleb. We're both so damn quiet usually that we never would have spoken to each other."

He thought about that for a second and had to agree. Mitch was the louder brother and he kept Meg laughing. Just as Shelby did for Caleb. Already, he wasn't looking forward to the silence that would greet him in the house every day once Shelby left for good. Hell, the last two days had been bad enough, even knowing she was there.

"Damn it, Caleb, everyone can see that you feel for Shelby what I feel for Mitch." Meg looked up at him, serious and determined. "You and I would have made each other miserable. But you're happy with Shelby. The two of you just *work*."

He sighed, looked over her head at the slash of sunlight outside the barn. In his mind's eye, he could see Shelby in those foolish sandals, marching through the dirt and straw, her chin held high, riding the mad she had for him. He saw her in Houston, wearing that blue dress, laughing up at him.

And he saw her in bed, hair a wild tumble, her eyes shining and a soft smile on the lips he couldn't taste enough.

"Don't hold what I did to you against Shelby, Caleb," Meg was saying. "Don't cheat yourself out of something spectacular because you're holding on to old hurts. Oh, and by the way, I'm glad you and Mitch worked things out. He's missed you, you big jerk. I've missed you."

He blinked at her and laughed. She was standing up for Mitch as he stood up for Shelby and Caleb realized that she was right. Had been all along. Yeah, he wished they had handled it better, but Mitch and Meg were good together. As he and Shelby were.

For the first time in four years, he could look at his sister-in-law and not be reminded of betrayal. Which told him that he was the only one who had been preventing his family from healing. Maybe Shelby had a point. He'd never thought of himself as a coward, but what else could you call a man who refused to forgive? Refused to trust? Refused to grab his future because of his past?

He'd hated the thought of Shelby moving away from Royal, going back to Chicago or wherever. But he hated even more the idea that she would be living in town without him. He couldn't stand the thought of being without her damn it and she was right. He did love her. He just hadn't wanted to admit it, even to himself.

Idiot.

"I hate lectures, Meg. You know that."

"Yes, but—"

"Especially," Caleb added, "when you're right."

"I am?" A slow, self-satisfied smile curved her mouth.

"Don't gloat," he said, giving her a one-armed hug that eased away the last of the pain, the last of the aloofness he'd treated her with for too long.

When she hugged him back, Caleb relaxed. "Hell, I have been blind. I see how good you and Mitch are together, Meg. And I'm glad of it."

She tipped her head back and smiled, her eyes shining. "Don't cry."

"Absolutely not," she said, shaking her head as a single tear dripped down her cheek. "Pregnant hormones. I'm good. So what're you going to do now?"

Only one thing he could do. "I'm going to Royal and I'm going to bring Shelby back home. Where she belongs."

Shelby liked the condos well enough, she thought as she walked down Main Street. But after living at Caleb's ranch, they all felt small, confined. There was no view of ranch land or ancient oaks. There were no kids playing in the yard and mostly? There was no Caleb.

"You're going to have to get used to that, though," she muttered. She walked past Miss Mac's Pie Shack and waved to Jillian through the glass.

Across the street, she saw Lucy Curran and waved to her, as the woman hurried to her truck. Alexis Slade was heading into the TCC and Shelby realized that Royal had become home to her. She had friends here. Work here. She would be fine. She'd get over Caleb. Eventually.

"Shouldn't take more than ten or twenty years," she told herself.

Stepping up her pace, she hurried along to the TCC. If nothing else, she could go inside and tell Alexis that she was going to be staying in Royal, so she'd be available to help with the bachelor auction. "Keep busy, Shelby. That's the key. Just keep busy."

She heard the roar of the engine before she looked up to see it. Caleb's huge black truck came hurtling down Main Street and careened into the TCC parking lot.

Shelby's heart was pounding hard in her chest even before Caleb shut off the engine and leaped out of the truck, slamming the door behind him. Her mouth went dry and her stomach started spinning. He stalked toward her and his features were tight and grim.

"Caleb, what're you doing here?"

He moved in close, grabbed her upper arms and lifted her up onto her toes, pulling her face within a kiss of his. "Damn it, Shelby, what the hell do you mean you love me but you'll get over it?"

Surprised, she could only stare up at him as he loomed over her. The brim of his hat shadowed his face, but his eyes, those icy-blue eyes, were on fire. "Just what I said. I'm not going to be in love all by myself, how stupid would that be? So I'll just work on getting over you and—"

"Stop," he ground out. "Just stop and let me talk for once. There's a lot to say. A lot I should have said before now." He eased his grip on her arms, but he didn't let her go. "First things first, though. You're not in love alone. I love you, Shelby."

Her breath caught and she felt tears sting her eyes.

"You sneaked up on me," he said, his gaze moving over her face as if etching her features into his mind. "Before I knew it, I was loving you and trying not to."

"Great," she murmured.

He grinned, then sobered. "You're right you know, the time we've spent together is as good as two years of dating. I know you, Shelby," he said, his fingers gentling his hold on her but not letting go. "I know I can trust you. I know that. I was just…"

"A big stoic cowboy?" she finished for him.

"Yeah, I guess," he admitted wryly. His hands slid

up her arms to cup her face as his voice deepened and the fire in his eyes became a low, simmering burn. "The point is, I didn't want another woman in my life. I was so mad at Meg and Mitch and never took the time to notice that she was right to do what she did. Just like you were."

"Oh, Caleb…" He couldn't have said anything that would have touched her more.

"Not finished," he warned and gave her that half smile that never failed to tug at her heart. "I don't want you to ever get over loving me, Shelby. I need you too badly."

"I didn't want to get over you," she said softly, as she sensed that all of her dreams were coming true. "I love you, Caleb. I always will."

"I'm counting on that darlin'." He gave her another half smile. "I was an idiot. I didn't want to risk love again. Thought it was just too dangerous to even try. Since you, though, I realized that losing you would be the real risk— to my heart and my sanity. How the hell could I live in a quiet house? I'd miss those rants of yours."

"I'm going to choose to be flattered," she said, smiling up at him because her heart was racing and her hopes and dreams were about to come true, right there on the busy Main Street of Royal, Texas.

"Good. That's how I meant it." Caleb shifted one hand to cup her face and he said, "I love you, Shelby. Don't think I'll ever get tired of saying it. I know I'm not easy to live with—I tend to go all quiet and pensive—but I think you're tough enough to pull it off."

"I really am," she promised. "When you get too quiet, I'll just follow you around, or ride a horse out to find you and I'll stick to you until you talk to me again."

"You won't have to follow me, Shelby," he said, his gaze locked with hers. "We're going to be side by side. And we're going to have a hell of a good marriage and we'll make a lot of babies, fill up all those empty rooms with laughter and love. Because that's what you deserve. It's what we *both* deserve."

"It sounds perfect," Shelby said. "And I think we might have already started on those babies. Skipping a few days of pills probably wasn't a good idea."

His eyes went wide and bright and his smile was one that lit up every corner of her heart. "Yeah? That's great, because you know Meg's pregnant again, so they're three ahead of us."

"We'll catch up," Shelby said.

"Damn straight we will." Caleb leaned down and kissed her, hard and long. When he lifted his head, he said, "Let's go."

"Where?" she asked, a laugh tickling her throat.

"Down to the jewelers," Caleb said firmly. "We're picking out a ring. Biggest one he's got, because I want everyone who sees it to know you're mine and I'm yours."

"You don't talk a lot," Shelby said with a sigh, "but when you do, you say just the right thing."

"There's just one more thing I have to say," Caleb whispered.

"What's that?" What more was there? He'd already given her the dream. Home. Roots. Family. *Love.*

"Shelby Arthur," he said softly, "will you marry me tomorrow?"

She sighed, filled with the love she'd always longed

for and looked up into icy-blue eyes that would never look cold again. Then she grinned and asked, "Why not tonight?"

Caleb picked her up, swung her around, then planted another kiss on her mouth. "That's my girl."

* * * * *

COMING SOON!

We really hope you enjoyed reading this book. If you're looking for more romance, be sure to head to the shops when new books are available on

Thursday
6th September

To see which titles are coming soon, please visit
millsandboon.co.uk

LET'S TALK
Romance

For exclusive extracts, competitions
and special offers, find us online:

f facebook.com/millsandboon

⬚ @millsandboonuk

𝕏 @millsandboon

Or get in touch on 0844 844 1351*

For all the latest titles coming soon, visit
millsandboon.co.uk/nextmonth